00 1625

DATE DUE

SEP 0 5 2000	
SEP 1 6 2000 SEP 2 7 2000	
NOV 2 5 2000	
DEC 0 6 2000	
DEC 2 8 2000	
JAN 1 2 2001	
FEB 0 3 2001	
APR 2 8 2001	
MAY 1 9 2001	

GAYLORD   PRINTED IN U.S.A.

LOOT

Aaron Elkins

LOOT

WHEELER
PUBLISHING, INC.
ROCKLAND, MA

★ AN AMERICAN COMPANY ★

Published in Large Print by arrangement with William Morrow and Company, Inc., in the United States and Canada.

Wheeler Large Print Book Series.

Set in 16 pt Plantin.

Library of Congress Cataloging-in-Publication Data

Elkins, Aaron J.
    Loot / Aaron Elkins.
        p. (large print) cm.(Wheeler large print book series)
    ISBN 1-56895-750-5 (hardcover)
    1. Art thefts—Germany—History—20th century—Fiction. 2. World War, 1939-1945—Art and the war—Fiction. 3. Art dealers—Massachu-setts—Fiction. 4. Art treasures in war—Fiction. 5. Large type books. I. Title. II. Series
[PS3555.L48L66   1999b]
813'.54—dc21
                                                                    99-31996
                                                                        CIP

ACKNOWLEDGMENTS

In May of 1945, days after the Germans' surrender in World War II, Lane Faison, a young lieutenant in the three-man OSS Art Looting Investigation Unit, was among the first outsiders to set eyes on the hoard of plundered art stored in the caverns of the Altaussee salt mine, and one of the first to grasp the enormity and thoroughness of the vast German looting operation.

Half a century later, seated on his deck overlooking Mt. Greylock on a sunny October afternoon, Lane Faison, distinguished professor of art, *emeritus*, Williams College, graciously answered question after question about those momentous times, for which I am glad to have the chance to acknowledge my appreciation.

Constance Lowenthal, director of the Commission for Art Recovery of the World Jewish Congress and formerly executive director of the International Foundation for Art Research, was most kind in sharing her immense knowledge of the art world (and the stolen-art world).

Sergeant Detective Margo Hill of the Boston Police Department was very helpful on police procedures in Boston, and Professor Walter von Reinhart of the University of Rhode Island cheerfully set me straight on matters of German language and Austrian culture.

In fifteen previous novels I've always gotten my share of support from my agent, my wife, and my editors, yet I've never expressed my appreciation in print. (If you can't expect help as a matter of course from your wife, your editor, and your agent, then from whom?) But this time out I took even more than my usual share of wrong turns, so that I required—and received—some serious straightening out. So for once I would like formally to say thank you to my wife, Charlotte, to my agent, Barney Karpfinger, and to my editor, Zach Schisgal, for their terrific suggestions and ideas. I hate to think of what *Loot* would have been like without them.

PROLOGUE

Altaussee Salt Mine, Altaussee, Austria, April 19, 1945, 11:35 a.m.

Madness.

For two days and nights the mud-spattered trucks with their bone-tired drivers and their canvas-covered payloads had flowed without pause up the mountain road, four convoys in twenty-four hours, until the mine compound overflowed with filthy vehicles jammed willy-nilly against each other, all pretense of organization long ago swept away. Drivers who had managed, against all odds, to successfully unload their cargoes tried futilely to get back down the mountain to the control point, cursing and blaring their horns and even ramming trucks that blocked their way. Men at the ends of their tethers yelled and fought, gouging and rolling in the rutted mud like animals. The guards shouted and threatened, but few paid attention. Not at this point in the war.

For Dr. Professor Erhard Haftmann, the chief registrar, it was a nightmare beyond comprehension. For forty hours he had gone without sleep, without changing his clothes, remaining on the receiving dock and growing more desperate with every hectic minute, every new, improperly recorded shipment. He had screamed himself hoarse and bitten his lips raw with frustration. His ulcer stabbed at him like a knife, his hemorrhoids tormented him, and the fiery rash encircling his waist and running down the backs of his legs had erupted again, in long, spiraling streaks that no lotion, no cream, could soothe.

Confusion piled on confusion, irregularity on irregularity. There were drivers with consignment orders that were not complete, that were for the wrong shipments, that weren't there at all; there were partial inventories, and missing inventories, and illegible inventories. And even if everything had been in order, there was no time to process it properly, not with the unending, impossible crush. Ever since the Allies had mounted their round-the-clock bombing of the cities, there had been a tidal wave of art rolling up the mountain to the safety of the mine chambers, but never until now had it reached such insane proportions.

The system, he thought, with tears stinging his eyes, the system was in shambles, a tattered ruin. When would there ever be time to record and catalogue the new material? What would he do tomorrow, and the next day, when still more convoys streamed out of the repositories at Neuschwanstein, at Hohenfurth, at Wiener-Neustadt?

Where was it going to end?

For three years, since the day of his appointment, Professor Haftmann had proudly, gratefully dedicated his life to the system. First to its creation and then to its maintenance. Long before the first shipment had arrived, while

2

the technicians were still laboring underground to put into place the immense network of shelving, electric wiring, and protective sheathing that would physically protect the treasure that was to come, Haftmann was constructing the even more vast and elaborate structure of forms, procedures, checks and cross-checks that would take chaos and make from it order. No museum—not the Louvre, not the Metropolitan, not the National Gallery—had ever devised so meticulous and efficient a record-keeping system under such demanding conditions.

And he had been successful. Every last one of the vast forest of art objects in their underground chambers could be classified, identified, and instantly found. Never—not once in all this time—had anything been miscatalogued or lost once it had been admitted through the great iron doors. Reichsleiter Bormann himself had sent him a letter of appreciation in which the Führer's personal gratitude was handsomely expressed. Haftmann had it still, mounted in a silver frame.

But now...now the Führer was no longer expressing personal gratitude from his rambling chalet in Berchtesgaden. He was said to be raving mad, said to be in hiding under the rubble of Berlin, whence poured—always through Bormann—a wild sequence of contradictory and impossible orders supposedly to be imposed by a demoralized SS and a shattered, incoherent Wehrmacht, most of which was on the run from the Russians in the east or from the Anglo-Americans in the south.

For weeks the mountain passes had been lousy with defeated, straggling remnants of the once-mighty German Sixth Army. The Americans, so they said, were already on the outskirts of Munich, the Russians even now raping and plundering their way through Dresden.

Yet through it all Dr. Professor Haftmann had kept an iron grip on his matchless system of ledgers, registers, and precisely cross-indexed card catalogues. Whatever was happening aboveground, whatever the eventual outcome of the war, the Vermeers, Rembrandts, Dürers, Michelangelos—thousands of priceless masterpieces, the greatest art collection that the world had ever known— would continue to repose in orderly, minutely documented security in the quiet, dark chambers of the ancient salt mine beneath his feet.

But now, with this impossible—

"You wanted to see me?"

He started. How had he failed to notice the man come up? Soon, somehow, he would have to lie down somewhere, to close his eyes for a few minutes, but how, when?

"Yes, I wanted to see you," he said curtly. "You are the commander of the convoy from Neuschwanstein?"

The man barely dipped his chin, not bothering to take the thin, ill-rolled cigarette out of his mouth. The corners of his lips curled down. "I have that great honor."

So, one of the surly ones. A sergeant he was, older than Haftmann, in his fifties, with a week-old beard, a greasy, misbuttoned uniform, and an insolent manner. Not a career soldier but a man with some education, too good for the job he was doing, or so he thought. A schoolmaster, Haftmann guessed. No, a civil-service bureaucrat; a petty functionary who had safely sat out the war behind a desk and resented being forced at last to do something useful for his country.

Haftmann spoke with asperity. "How many consignments are in your convoy?"

"Consignments?"

"Trucks."

"Ah, trucks," the man said with a smile, then shrugged. "About thirty."

Haftmann's eyes narrowed. "*About* thirty?"

"Thirty-five, I think."

"You think?" He drew himself erect, put out his hand, and snapped his fingers. "Your register, please."

The man opened a button in his tunic, pulled out a stained leather wallet, and handed it over.

Haftmann removed a grimy document and compared it, line by line, to a sheaf of papers of his own, making an irritable gesture with one hand. "Please blow your smoke elsewhere."

The sergeant shrugged and stepped back to lean against the stucco wall, picking away with a clasp knife at the whitish mud that caked his boots. Dried clumps pattered on the wooden floor. Haftmann checked his temper. His insides were in enough turmoil as it was. All morning the bile had been backing up into his throat, bitter and burning. After a minute he nodded and handed the papers back.

"You verified this register personally?"

The sergeant shrugged again. "What's all the fuss about, is there a problem?"

"Yes, there's a problem. Your register lists thirty-five consignments from Neuschwanstein, as does the preshipment inventory."

Through the haze of cigarette smoke the man gave him a careless nod. "As I said."

"But there are only thirty-four trucks here. Truck number N-thirty, containing lots four-oh-eight to four forty-four, is not present."

The sergeant regarded him indifferently. "Is that so?"

"Yes, that's so," said Haftmann, his temper beginning to get the better of him after all. "You're in trouble, Sergeant. This discrepancy should have been accounted for—by you, right here, on the cover sheet, before the convoy ever started. Do you have any idea how much work your slipshod attention has already cost my assistants?"

The sergeant's red-rimmed eyes half closed. He let smoke drift slowly from his mouth and sucked it back into his nostrils. "Fuck your assistants."

Haftmann's ulcer tweaked at him, exactly as if a pair of pincers had nipped his insides. In a burst of rage he flung the sheaf of papers at the man's chest. "You're not—you think—" But he was stopped by a rasping, choking cough that ground on and on. The sergeant picked up the papers and looked noncommittally on.

At last the coughing fit was over, leaving Haftmann sore and winded. He removed his spectacles—they'd been on so long they pulled away some skin—and squeezed the bridge of his nose between his fingers. This was what came of the terrible, unrelenting pressures of his work. He would make himself ill yet. But this sergeant, arrogant as he was, wasn't to blame; if not for the awful toll the war had taken on Germany's true soldiers, he would have been back in Berlin where he belonged, supervising letter carriers or railroad inspectors, not leading an important convoy at the front.

"Here is the situation, Sergeant," Haftmann said with frigid calm. "I do not intend to validate your voucher until the discrepancy is accounted for. You will please explain in this space, in your own writing—"

"And just how the hell am I supposed to do that? How do I know what happened to the damn truck?" He hunched his shoulders. "It was there when we started."

For a moment Haftmann couldn't speak. "How...do you mean to tell me you left with thirty-five trucks, with your full complement? That you...you *lost* one?"

For the first time the sergeant's tired eyes seemed to snap into focus, even to gleam.

He took a last drag on the cigarette and savagely flicked the stub into a corner.

"Do you have any idea what's going on out there? Do you ever go outside this compound? Have you seen the soldiers coming back from the front with their ears and noses frozen off? Without faces, without fingers? There's no food to be had in the villages, do you happen to be aware of that small fact? Crazy old grandmothers are on the roadsides trying to sell themselves for a potato, a candy bar, a cigarette." He gave a fierce little laugh. "You want me to worry about a few pictures going into a cave?"

"But, but it was your responsibility! Those pictures, those pictures are—"

"Yes, I know what those pictures are," the sergeant snapped. "A million years ago I was a professor of Western civilization, so I know, all right. I also know that in Lauffen we saw an old man, a veteran from the last war, wearing his raggedy old uniform; a genuine hero he was, with a tunic full of medals. And what was he doing, this genuine hero? He, too, was standing by the side of the road. He was trying to trade a beautiful little Correggio *St. John* he'd stolen from some church for a pair of boots. A pair of boots! That's what your precious pictures are worth."

He leaned back against the wall, the bright, brief light in his eyes extinguished, the heat gone. "Everything is over, the Fatherland is destroyed. Germany will never recover from this, never."

His knees watery, Haftmann stood as if

paralyzed. It had happened then, it had finally come to the worst, the unthinkable.

One of the consignments had been lost.

A Road in the Fischbacher Alps,
Southeastern Austria, April 19, 1945, 5:50 P.M.

ALL DAY LONG THE storm had held off while the veil of high, thin clouds gathered and thickened and the temperature dropped. But now, as the light yellowed, the first heavy, wet flakes came down. In ten minutes the air was gray with snow. The mountains disappeared behind layered curtains of flakes. The sky itself was visible only as a whitish glare.

Behind the wheel of the truck, Corporal Friedrich "Fritz" Krimml offered up a wordless little prayer of thanks and let himself fully relax against the seat back for the first time.

He had done it! Surely he was safe now. Dutifully he had helped to load and secure the trucks, as he had many times before, and he had maintained his place in the convoy all the way from Neuschwanstein. But always he had kept his eyes open for his chance, and finally, when he had almost given up, only ten kilometers from the mine, he had seen it and had not hesitated. In the village of Bad Aussee a bomb crater had forced them to turn off the main road and snake through the local streets for a few blocks before going on. Fritz had maneuvered his truck to the end of the line,

9

had gradually drifted back a hundred meters or so, and then had simply failed to make the last left turn with the rest, continuing straight ahead for three more blocks until he came to the *Hauptstrasse*. There he had turned right, in the opposite direction from Altaussee, and had pressed the pedal to the floor.

For the first couple of hours he'd been shaking with fright. What a chance he was taking! What if they came after him? What if the SS stopped him, a lone truck with a full payload of valuable artwork but without orders to explain what he was doing here in the mountains, going south, toward Italy? He would be shot. But no one came, and the SS, if they were still out there at all, weren't interested. And now, with the snow, how could anyone come after him? Even if they knew which way he had gone.

Of the regular Wehrmacht soldiers he had little fear. They were all coming in the opposite direction, exhaustedly working their way back toward what remained of Germany, with their tails between their legs and no wish to interfere with anyone crazy enough to be heading the other way, into the jaws of the enemy.

The British planes overhead had made him nervous at first— droning squadrons of Lancasters lumbering toward Munich or Stuttgart. While the big bombers would waste no time on small fry like him, you never knew when the pilots of the accompanying fighters, bored and edgy, might take it into their heads to get in a little strafing practice on a moving target—a nice slow-moving target unable to get off its all-too-visible ribbon of road. But with the snow coming down, that, too, had ceased to be a worry. If he couldn't see them, how could they see him?

Corporal Krimml was not a German but an Austrian from the province of Styria. Before joining the Wehrmacht's transportation corps (if you could call what happened to him "joining") at the unlikely age of fifty-two, he had been a printer in Liezen, not so very far from Altaussee, so he had some idea of the lay of the land. But precisely where he was at this moment, or for that matter where he was going, he didn't know. As long as he headed roughly south or southwest, however, he was bound eventually to run into the Americans. And that was his aim.

It was his cousin Dieter who had put the idea into his head. Dieter was a baker—a one-armed baker, no easy trick—and a few weeks earlier he had told Fritz of having heard from an Austrian sergeant that the Americans were hunting for the great quantities of looted art that the Third Reich was supposedly hoarding away in mysterious underground caverns. More than that, the conditions of surrender were reputed to be very generous indeed for anyone who could deliver such art or tell them where it could be found.

Whether there really was any great storehouse of looted art, or for that matter whether the Americans could be trusted...well, that Dieter couldn't say; the whole thing might be nothing but rumor, but he thought there just might be something to it.

Fritz, on the other hand, knew there was something to it. He wasn't blind or stupid; he could see what he had been loading with his own hands into the trucks for the last three weeks: great, glowing pictures in heavy gilt frames, old, old tapestries—worn so thin you could see through them in places—heavy boxes of ancient coins and medals, beautiful sculptures in wood and marble. And all of them had disappeared, one after another, down into the mine at Altaussee. Until now.

At the thought he even smiled a little. Dr. Haftmann, the despotic German registrar, would surely have realized by now that one of his precious trucks was missing and he would be crazier than ever, probably tearing out his hair in clumps, or hanging by his fingernails from the roof of the cavern, like one of the bats.

And as for trusting the Americans, Fritz was more than ready to do it. As a young man he had spent two months in Ohio with his Uncle Werner, and he had taken back with him an admiring vision of America and Americans that he'd never lost. Oh, yes, he would trust them.

This despite the steady barrage of German propaganda that had been on the radio for the last several weeks, in which, to put it mildly, the situation had been misrepresented. Some of the broadcasts he (and everyone else with access to a radio in Germany and Austria) had heard enough times to know by heart:

12

Like hyenas the Anglo-American barbarians in the occupied territories are falling upon German works of art in a systematic looting campaign. Under flimsy pretexts, private houses are searched by art experts, most of them Jews, who confiscate all works of art whose owners cannot prove beyond doubt their property rights. These works of art, stolen in true Jewish style, are dispatched to the United States, where...

Well, you had to give the Germans credit, they never ran short of gall, but Fritz knew better than that who the hyenas and barbarians were, and they weren't the Americans.

The wind had picked up as evening had come on. The cold was beginning to seep into the cab of the truck. The heater, needless to say, didn't work, and one of the headlights was out. The windshield wiper, managing only a halfhearted swipe every four or five seconds, seemed ready at any moment to give up the ghost. With the snow turning drier, so that it was beginning to stick to road and windshield, that would soon present a problem, but Fritz's spirits remained high. When he could drive no longer, he would stop for the night. He had a blanket on the seat beside him, a jug of ersatz coffee tucked into one of the crates, and thirty liters of reserve fuel over and above what was in the tank. He could wait out a night, or even two or three nights, with ease. He had no food, but in three days he wasn't going to starve, and for drinking there were plenty of streams and melted snow. If he got all the way to the Italian border without encountering the Americans, he might just sit and wait for them to find him, why not?

His one great worry was that he might accidentally be drifting eastward along these winding, confusing roads. There was no sun to guide him, and the few highway signs were meaningless. East was where the Russian advance troops were, and he dearly wanted to stay as far away from them as possible. They had not, and were not about to, issue any "generous" terms of surrender to the Nazi army that had pitilessly ravaged them in the early years of the war. And when it came to dealing with captured soldiers, he doubted very much that they were going to be making any fine distinctions between Germans and Austrians.

Driving was becoming difficult now, not only because of the straining wiper and the faltering light of the single headlamp, but because the snow had begun to hump and drift, blurring the edges of the road and making the tires slip. Still he crept on, almost blindly, the blanket pulled over his shoulders and head, always going to the right at forks and intersections when he was unsure.

By eight o'clock he was, according to his reckoning, nearing the Italian border, safely away from any scouting Russians, but driving farther was out of the question; he was progressing more by feel than by sight, and why

14

risk an accident at this point? The truck and what it contained were his passport out of the horrible disaster that the war had become; he could hardly afford to leave it stuck in some roadside ditch.

He was inching along, looking for what seemed a good place to pull over, when a light blazed on a few meters ahead of him. He jerked upright—had he been dozing at the wheel?—and with shaking fingers immediately turned off the engine. The glare of the beam and the spotlit, dazzling flakes had left him momentarily blinded, but he could hear boots—two pairs?—crunching through the snow toward him. A roadblock. God in heaven, he prayed with everything that was in him, let it not be the SS.

He rolled down the window, raised empty, trembling hands, and stared, sightless and grinning, into the light. He began to make them out now. There were six or eight of them, and, God be thanked, they weren't in the heavy gray winter greatcoats of the SS. The coats, almost down to their ankles, were a welcome reddish brown. Americans! Despite the cold, he was sweating with anxiety and relief, almost unable to find his voice. Careful now. Americans, too, could shoot first and ask questions later. "Good evening," he croaked in English—he had rehearsed it often enough in the truck. "I wish please to surrender. My name is Friedrich Krimml. I am an Austrian conscript, not a German. I have in my truck—"

"Get out," one of them said in coarse German.

"Of course," he said quickly, reaching for the door handle, "I am ready to—"

The one who had spoken jerked open the door and roughly, mutely, pulled him out into the freezing air, spun him around, and shoved him against the truck. The blanket slipped from his shoulders and fell into the snow. Flakes that burned like dry ice stung the back of his neck.

"Please...sir..." he began, but by then he'd had a good look at them and the words dried in up in his throat. They wore lamb's-wool astrakhans pulled low over their eyes, and each had the flat, blank, unmistakably Slavic face that, except in time of war, was not to be seen west of the Urals.

God help him, he had stumbled into a Russian patrol.

A Roadside Camp in the Fischbacher Alps, Eastern Austria,April 19, 1945, 9:20 P.M.

At least they hadn't shot him on the spot, that was something.

To his immense relief, Fritz had been believed when he tried to explain that he was an anti-Nazi Austrian conscript ("Stalin, da! Hitler, nyet!"). The Russians, drunk and gregarious, had clapped him on the back and called him *Kamerad,* and even given him a drink from a bottle of captured German brandy. They undid the canvas flap at the back of his truck, pried open two of the crates to look inside, and just laughed. When they climbed down, still grinning happily, they clapped his back some more and offered him the bottle again.

Then two of them had gotten back into the truck and set to work on the crates with axes and sledgehammers, swinging them like crazy men. Splinters flew, screws shrieked as heavy blows wrenched them from the wood.

Fritz, horrified, choked on his brandy. "What are you doing? Are you insane? Stop! Stop!"

When he reached into the back of the truck to grab the swaying skirts of one of the men's greatcoats, another swatted him carelessly back and motioned him, not threateningly, to stay out of the way.

Only minutes before, Fritz had been paralyzed with fear for his life, only his life. Now all he could think of was the precious cargo. "Stop, I tell you! *Herr Kommandant!*" he screamed at the top of his voice. Snowflakes fell into his mouth. "*Herr Kommandant!*"

At his cries the group's interpreter, a Chinese-looking private who had learned German God knows where, ran up to him, appalled. "What's the matter with you? Shut up!" He had been kind to Fritz during the initial, cursory interrogation, but now he was making frantic shushing motions. "Do you want to make them angry?"

Fritz grabbed him by the heavy collar of his coat. "What are they doing?"

The corporal looked at him as if he were crazy. "Making firewood, what do you think?"

"Firewood!" Fritz laughed wildly. "Tell them to stop!"

"And if I did, you think they'd listen to me?"

"Then, please, take me to the commander."

"The commander's dead."

"There must be someone in charge!" He was near-hysterical. From the truck, the terrible crashing sounds went on. The vehicle was swaying on its tires.

The corporal sighed. "All right, it's your funeral. Come, I'll take you to the closest thing we have to a leader. His name is Petrochenko, Sergeant Petrochenko."

"*Hurry,* then!" Pieces of wood and chunks of gilded picture frames were now being tossed out of the rear of the truck.

"All right." But the corporal held back for another moment. "Listen to me—he's not like the others; be careful how you act. If he's not in a good mood, he can make trouble."

PAVEL ILICH PETROCHENKO WAS not in a good mood, had not been in a good mood for a single second since they'd given him a ludicrous battlefield promotion to junior sergeant and put him in charge of this ragtag squad of thick-skulled Asiatic louts that was used for the most dangerous job of all—delivering ammunition from the supply dump to the front—because, and this Petrochenko knew to be a fact, nobody gave a damn about their life expectancy. And why should they? Uzbeks,

18

Tadzhiks, Kazakhs—not a real Russian among them. Brave as lions, but ignorant oafs and wildmen all, barely able make themselves understood with their barbarous grunts, interested in nothing but women and drink, understanding only force and threat. Already two of them he'd had to shoot for disobeying orders. You'd think one would be enough, they'd get the point, but no, two days after he'd sent that shirker Tursunzade to his reward, Baytursinuli (what names they had!) tried to get out of overhauling a truck and smart-mouthed him besides. So that was the end of Baytursinuli, too. If necessary he'd shoot them all before he was done. The law was on his side, there were always more, and who would miss them?

Unless, of course, they slit his throat first or he was blown to bits in one of the ammunition trucks. The damn things were like traveling gunpowder factories, liable to go up from a single stray machine-gun bullet or one of the lit cigarettes that his crew of simpletons was unable to learn to snuff out. Four months earlier, when he was on the maintenance detail, he'd lost his right thumb and forefinger when an idiot corporal had tossed a match near the gasoline pump. But if one of these creatures were to make a mistake like that with the ammunition (a not-unlikely possibility), he'd be lucky if there was so much as a finger left of him.

He turned over, trying to make himself comfortable for sleep, but there was no getting

19

comfortable on the frigid earth floor of an exposed, wooden mountain hut, with hat, boots, gloves, gun, map case and all, and wrapped in two greatcoats. From mild Odessa, as he was, he felt the cold in a way that none of these others did. And why was it snowing this time of year anyway? If not for the storm, they'd never have lost their way and he'd be back at the supply base in Hirschwang, on the valley floor, lying on his own cot in a cozy stone barn.

"Babayan," he said, "where's that damn firewood? Go out and see what's holding them up."

One of the other figures that was huddled on the floor stirred and grumbled but didn't rise.

"Babayan! Don't try to make me think you're asleep. You know I can see in the dark."

"It's cold out there," Babayan said.

"What do you think it is in here, warm? Now move, fuck you, or I'll shoot you where you lie."

"All right, I'm going," Babayan grumbled while his mates sniggered. He stood up, broke wind—that was the one thing these Uzbeks and Kazakhs were naturally gifted at—and stumbled to the door to laughter and cheers, pulling his coat around him.

But before he got there, the door opened and in peeped Ghulam, the little Tadzhik who spoke German. "I'm sorry, Comrade Sergeant—"

"Shut that door, damn you. Where the hell is that wood?"

Ghulam stepped quickly inside. A step behind him, looking frantic, was the Austrian corporal they'd stopped on the road. "This man—" Ghulam began.

Petrochenko sat up. "Babayan, light the candle."

Before the match was struck, the old Austrian started gabbling so fast that Ghulam could barely keep up. It took Petrochenko only seconds to understand. Paintings! Old Masters! That idiot guard had simply told him "some pictures," and Petrochenko had been too dull from weariness to—

He was on his feet and running toward the truck in an instant. When they didn't hear his cries to stop he fired his pistol in the air. The men in the truck, lit up by the handheld searchlight, peered curiously out the back. "What's wrong, Comrade Sergeant?"

Half an hour later he had seen enough. He returned to the hut, nearly frozen but filled with satisfaction and with plans. This was his ticket out of the ammunition detail. The candle was guttering now, but still alight, and some of the men, crouched on their haunches in their filthy greatcoats, had made tea. Ghulam and the Austrian were still waiting for him; the Austrian began at once to bargain and to wheedle. Petrochenko, brushing the snow from his shoulders, nodded. "*Ja, Kamerad, gut, gut,*" he said soothingly, at the same time making a small motion to Babayan with his chin.

Babayan, smiling, patted the old Austrian on the shoulder, tugged gently on his arm, and

21

took him outside. *"Komm', Kamerad."* Thirty steps from the hut, Babayan shot him between the eyes.

By the time the pistol's short, sharp report had clattered off the mountain walls, the candle was out and Petrochenko was curled up on the floor again.

No longer was he in a bad mood.

Hirschwang, Austria, Supply Base Camp, Second Armored Division, Army of the U.S.S.R., April 20, 1945, 11 A.M.

I DON'T HAVE TO tell you, Petrochenko, that it's your duty as an honest soldier to report to me immediately the whereabouts of this so-called treasure of yours—if, that is, it actually exists. You are entitled to no 'conditions.'"

Junior Sergeant Pavel Petrochenko, standing sullenly at attention, studied the speaker. The handsome, black-haired Captain Shaposhkin was a funny one to be talking about honesty. It was well known that in his position as aide to the colonel in charge of the divisional supply depot he had been robbing the army blind, that he was by now quite rich, and that he had devised some secret way of getting the black-market money he made safely out of the country; some said to Switzerland, some said England.

None of this Petrochenko begrudged him. The captain had a head on his shoulders, there was nothing wrong with that. What did bother him was that Dimitri Nikolayevich

Shaposhkin was only twenty-one, a mere two years older than Petrochenko himself, and look what he had already achieved. By comparison Petrochenko had accomplished nothing, and the war with all its opportunities wasn't going to go on forever.

Well, that was about to change. "I understand that, Comrade Captain," he said, looking at the floor. "I expressed myself badly. I didn't mean to set conditions. I only meant to say that, in my opinion, my abilities might better serve Russia if I were given a different assignment." He raised his eyes to the captain. "I would hope I could be of more service to you, too."

Shaposhkin, seated behind the painted kitchen table that served as his office desk in the front room of the farmhouse headquarters, scowled at him, then suddenly relaxed and smiled. He pointed to the samovar on the crude sideboard. "Help yourself, Petrochenko. Sit down."

"Thank you, Comrade Captain." He took no tea but sat on the kitchen chair beside the table.

"I like you, Pavel," Shaposhkin said. "I always have. It wasn't my doing that got you put in the ammunition detail."

"I know that, Comrade Captain."

"Tell me, then, where would you like to be assigned? Clothing and uniforms? I'm not making any promises now."

"Sundries," Petrochenko said without hesitation. Cigarettes, tobacco, candy, all small and easily hidden, all eminently salable in the army and infinitely more so out in the starved countryside.

"Ah." The captain brushed some nonexistent dust from one of the medals on his tunic. Like most of the officers, he had a chestful of them. "And what would I do with Yegorov?"

Petrochenko shrugged. "There's always the ammunition detail."

Shaposhkin was amused. "Yes, I suppose that's possible. All right, let's be frank, we're both sensible men. This is between us. There's a lot of money to be made in sundries, you know."

"I suppose there is. I never thought about it."

"What Yegorov does there, as long as the men don't squawk too much, I don't ask and I don't care. What I do care about is that I receive from him exactly twenty rubles a week or its equivalent— the form is negotiable, I am not a stickler—for the privilege of having such a desirable job. Now, you, being a smarter fellow than Yegorov, would surely make more of the opportunity than he does, and so I would think it would be worth...shall we say forty rubles a week?"

Petrochenko grinned. "Comrade Captain, I have my own sources. Yegorov gives you ten rubles a week. But you're right, I am smarter than he is, and I will make more of the opportunity. I will be able to pay you *twenty* rubles a week."

The captain looked at him for a long moment, and then came a fractional smile followed by the tiniest of nods, a minuscule jerk of the chin. It was done! Only with difficulty did Petrochenko manage to keep his face from showing his relief.

"Now then, Pavel, what about these paintings you've described?" Shaposhkin asked. "Where do you have them?"

But there had been a subtle rebalancing of authority, and Petrochenko was quick to take advantage of it. He leaned back in the chair and stretched out his booted legs, crossing them at the ankles, a posture that would have been impossible in Shaposhkin's presence yesterday. "Let me ask you, Comrade Captain, what is it that you'll do with them?"

"Exactly what regulations require, of course. See that the Trophy Brigades are informed, so that they can be seized as reparations."

"Of course. And this will be of advantage to you, I assume?"

"How could such a thing be of advantage to me?"

Petrochenko answered honestly. "I have no idea, but I also have no doubt that you will find a way. I think it only right that I should profit as well."

Shaposhkin gave him a noncommittal smile. "For example?"

Petrochenko uncrossed his legs and leaned confidently forward, his elbows on the table. "Comrade Captain, if you find these pictures to be as I say, I propose that the twenty rubles a week to which we previously agreed should be canceled."

Shaposhkin stared at him. "You would pay me *nothing*?"

"Precisely."

The captain's dark, handsome face stiffened, and Petrochenko thought for a queasy moment that he'd overplayed his hand. Shaposhkin could shoot him, and get away with it, too, every bit as easily as he himself had shot Baytursinuli.

But then the captain threw back his head and laughed. "I'll tell you what. I will accept ten rubles weekly. *If* the paintings are as you say."

"Done," said Petrochenko.

Shaposhkin's high, pleasant laugh rang out again as he reached across the table to shake hands. "Pavel, I'm going to enjoy doing business with you."

TWO DAYS LATER, A truckload of valuable paintings was sold for an unprecedented price to the Red Army's Trophy Brigade at Vienna by the commander of an Austrian anti-German partisan unit, who declined to say how it was that he had come by them.

Three days after that, Pavel Ilich Petrochenko, returning from a business transaction in the partially ruined town of Neunkirchen, was driving along a section of highway thought to be cleared of Germans when he encountered a retreating, rear-guard Wehrmacht unit that was as surprised to see him as he was to see them. Reaching for his pistol, but forgetting in his excitement that he no longer had a thumb and forefinger, he tried to hold them off, but the gun rolled out of his hand and fell to the ground. The laughing Germans commandeered the car in which he was riding, and Petrochenko and his driver were added to the wretched, shuffling gaggle of Russian and partisan prisoners that was being marched along in the general direction of Germany.

Exactly one week later, on May 2, 1945, in Lower Saxony, Hans von Friedeburg, First Admiral of the German Navy, had himself conveyed to the headquarters of Field-Marshal Bernard Montgomery, commander of British-Canadian forces in Northern Europe, there to surrender his forces and those of the German Army.

The war was over.

CHAPTER 1

Boston, Massachusetts, the Present

So far, so good. Boston two, Seattle one. But with the Mariners due up in the ninth with the meat of their order-Rodriguez, Griffey, and Martinez-I was beginning to feel that late-inning sense of impending doom so familiar to Red Sox true believers.

When the telephone chirped, it was almost a relief. The phone was in the kitchen, the TV was in the living room. If I got up to answer it, at least I wouldn't have to see the actual bloodshed. On the other hand, who was there that I wanted to talk to? It was a toss-up, your classic case of avoidance-avoidance conflict, but when Rodriguez promptly smashed a screaming double down the left-field line, it tipped the balance. I put down the carton of leftover, take-out lo mein I'd been making an early dinner of, hauled myself up from the sofa, and lumped off in my socks to get the phone.

"Hello?"

"Ben, is that you? Benjamin Revere?"

"Simeon?"

"Yes, that's right, Simeon." He sounded pleased at having his voice recognized. If he'd had any idea of the pathetic size of my social circle, he wouldn't have been so flattered. Besides, how many of them had Russian accents?

Simeon Pawlovsky and I had known each other almost two years. Now in his late seventies, he had left Russia in the sixties, and for the past three decades he had owned a pawnshop on Washington Street, in the grittiest part of Boston's South End. I had first run into him while working on a case for the police department—I'm an art historian by training, an honest-to-God, certifiable expert, and as such I do some consulting, not only for private individuals but once in a while for the police or for the Customs Department. In this particular case, the hunt for a stolen Courbet had led back after many a twist to Simeon's shop. Simeon had been extremely helpful; with his assistance the painting had gotten back to its rightful owner and some of the bad guys had been put away, even if not for very long. The old man had gotten a bang out of it, and since then, whenever a piece of "suspicious" art came into his shop, he had called me. The calls had rarely panned out into anything, but we had become friends of a sort, and occasionally, if I happened to be in the neighborhood-his shop was only a five-minute drive from the Museum of Fine Arts-I dropped in to sit on a stool behind the counter with him and pass the time. Sometimes, if it was a nice day, he'd lock up the store and put up one of those little clock signs showing when he'd be back, and we'd walk around the block. He'd have his face tilted up the whole time, as if he couldn't get enough sun.

"What am I hearing, baseball?" he asked now.

"On a day like this you're sitting in the dark watching a baseball game?"

"I'm not in the dark, Simeon."

"Baseball at four o'clock on a Monday afternoon," he said in quiet dismay.

If he only knew, I thought. I'd watched a ball game Sunday afternoon, too. And Saturday. No, that was wrong; on Saturday it had been golf, a thought that momentarily gave me pause. Baseball was one thing, but does a normal human being watch golf for three and a half hours straight? If I didn't get my act together, pretty soon I was going to wind up spending my afternoons in front of beach volleyball or ice dancing. It could happen.

"Well, you're in your store, aren't you?" I said lamely. "Is that so much better?"

"Yes, but I have to be here. I have a business to run. Tell me, what's your excuse?"

Well, yes, there was the rub.

I sighed. "Simeon, what can I do for you?"

"Ben, I took in a painting yesterday. You think you could have a look at it?"

"What is it?"

"I—Well, I wouldn't want to say. I think it's valuable. I'm ninety percent sure it's stolen."

"But what is it? I mean, Impressionist, Modern—"

"It could be seventeenth century, could be early eighteenth," he said. "Spanish would be my guess." Then, too excited to keep still, "Ben, it's a wonderful picture, it should be in a museum. I have it in front of me right now. I think-well, if you want to know, I think it could be by Velàzquez. That's my opinion, for what it's worth."

For what it was worth. The last time it had been a "Giorgione" that turned out to be a murky landscape grimy and shellac-encrusted enough to be centuries old, but wasn't.

"Uh-huh," I said. "And what makes you think that?"

"For one thing, there's a label on the back that says so."

"A label? There's no signature?"

"No, just a label on the back."

"Simeon, anyone can stick a label—"

"Benjamin, for God's sake, give me a little credit, I wasn't born yesterday. I'm telling you, it's a real work of art. In my opinion—"

"And someone walked into your shop and pawned it, just like that."

"Yes, just like that. What do you think, they make appointments ahead of time to come here? A Russian he was, not in this country very long—"

"How much did you give him for it?"

"He wanted a thousand dollars."

I laughed. "He took a thousand dollars for a genuine Velàzquez?"

"He took a hundred dollars. I'm a businessman. I don't run this place for the entertainment value. Besides, I didn't like his looks. The minute he came in, I knew something wasn't right."

"What's it a picture of, Simeon?"

He took his time. "A man," he said at last.

"A man. Well, that's helpful."

31

"Dressed in black."

"A man dressed in black. That certainly narrows it down—"

"Listen, Ben, instead of wisecracks, why not just look at it? How about tomorrow, can you come over?"

I hesitated, interested but doubtful. There were only a hundred or so authenticated Velàzquez paintings still around, mostly in the world's museums, but at least twice that many were known to have been painted by him and then lost at one point or another over the last 350 years. Every now and then one of them really did turn up, although a pawnshop was a pretty unlikely place for it, and Simeon wasn't the art connoisseur he liked to imagine he was. Still, I couldn't call myself much of an art historian if dreams of finding and authenticating one of them weren't already dancing in my head.

"Yes, okay, sure, I'll come over," I said. "I'll try to get there on the early side."

"Fine, I'll be here all day."

In the living room the announcer was recapping what I'd missed: "...so the Red Sox certainly have their work cut out for them in their half of the ninth. With explosive two-run homers by Griffey and Buhner and a five-run Mariner lead..."

In other words, the usual. I turned off the TV, picked up what was left of the lo mein, and went into the study to see what I had on Velàzquez.

CHAPTER 2

Where my mornings go is a continuing source of wonderment. Usually I let the sun wake me—one of the genuine pleasures of not having an honest job—then make myself coffee, read the *Globe* over cold cereal (or eggs over easy if I'm feeling unusually ambitious), take a shower, and then—well, that's the part I'm not sure about; turn on *Classics in the Morning* on WGBH, catch up on my reading, look at my mail—hell, I don't know what I do.

In any case, it wasn't until two-fifteen in the afternoon that I got out of my car in front of Simeon's shop on Washington Street. On one side of it was a warehouselike discount-furniture store, on the other a closed-down Thai take-out restaurant, its windows covered by graffiti-coated plywood boards. Between these two neighbors, Simeon's pawnshop was just what anyone would expect. CA$H IN A FLA$H!!! proclaimed the peeling metal sign above the entrance. FAST, FRIENDLY, CONFIDENTIAL!!! OPEN 8–5 MON–SAT. ESTAB. 1970. Additional encouragements, in red neon tubing, hung in the windows: BUY*SELL*TRADE*LAYAWAY*— MONEY TO LOAN— WE SELL FIRST QUALITY MERCHANDISE AT LOW, LOW PRICES!!!

The window bays were stuffed with every kind of junk imaginable, and then some: a row of ukuleles strung on a rod; electric drills; cameras seemingly from the dawn of photography; VCRs; fishing rods; a signed photograph of Ginger Rogers; a three-D movie projector; a set of strobe lights (A ONCE IN A LIFETIME BARGAIN—$39!!!); a pair of white, forlornly elegant women's ice skates, much used; chain saws; rings; pearl necklaces; even a folding electric wheelchair.

To get into the place I walked through the open metal accordion gate that folded across the front when the shop was closed, through a vestibule in which a rusting generator and a scuzzy old moped were chained to the foundation (as they'd been since the first time I was there), and through a second open folding gate that Simeon pulled across the front door and the rear of the bays when he closed down for the night. The store had been broken into several times in the eighties, and Simeon had learned to take precautions. In addition to the gates there were a cheesy-looking, red-eyed "video camera" that oscillated back and forth in one corner of the room, surely fooling not even the most gullible thief, and a convex mirror mounted up near the ceiling behind the counter, which gave Simeon a view of the shop when his back was turned. And on his skinny hip was the usual Colt revolver (empty) that looked as if it might have been pawned by Wyatt Earp himself.

When I came in, Simeon was methodically counting out five-dollar bills—an old-fashioned thumb-licker, he was—for an aged, birdlike woman in a track suit and Velcro-fastened jogging shoes.

Simeon wasn't much bigger than she was; maybe five-five and a hundred and twenty pounds, a neatly groomed, small-boned, gray-haired old man, not at all the sort that went with all those exclamation points out front; a bit stiff, even prim, in his movements, and dressed as always in a black suit, a white shirt, and a nondescript, tightly knotted tie; a businesslike outfit except for that six-gun, which he insisted on wearing on a gun belt strapped around his waist on the outside of his jacket. ("If I wear it underneath, no one will see, so what's the point?")

"Thirty-five...forty," he was saying, putting the bills into a used white envelope. His glasses, rimmed in thick black plastic, were hiked up onto his forehead.

"There you are, Mrs. Kapinsky."

"I thank you, Mr. Pawlovsky."

It was hard to keep from smiling. I might have been listening to the start of a vaudeville routine.

"Now, don't you forget to come back and redeem it," Simeon told her, dryly playful. "I'd hate to have to sell this beautiful piece of quality jewelry."

"You better not if you know what's good for you," she said with a waggle of her finger. This *was* a routine, I realized; they were old hands at it. She slipped the red cardboard pawn ticket into a zippered pocket. "I'll see you next week for sure, you can count on it." On the way out she gave me a brisk nod, one business client to another.

"You see this ring?" Simeon said. "Every month when her check runs out, she comes in and leaves it here for forty dollars, and every month, like clockwork, when she gets her check the next week, she comes back and gets it out for forty-five dollars. Better than borrowing from a bank."

"Pawlovsky's Loans, the poor people's ATM," I said.

"Absolutely," said Simeon earnestly. "You got it exactly right. Not everybody has a big bank account. Not everybody can make it from one check to the next."

He tied a tag to the ring and put it in a drawer behind the glass-topped counter. "You know, at first she used to show up lugging this big orbital sander—her husband was a roof-framer before he died. It must have weighed thirty pounds, and you saw how skinny she is? So I said to her, look, why not trade the sander for a ring? It weighs next to nothing. So she did, and now she carries it in on her little finger. A wonderful person; for twenty years she's been coming in here. Come, let me show you what I have."

He grabbed the cane that he kept hooked over the counter— Simeon's right foot was twisted inward, his knee stiff, so that he moved with a rocking, foot-dragging limp—and led the way up two wooden steps to the little foyer between the shop and his living quarters. Beyond were a kitchen, bathroom, and combination bedroom–sitting room, all facing through barred windows onto a shared central courtyard with tired brown grass, a bench, and a few rhodo-dendrons that hadn't been pruned or fed in a decade. Only once before had I been invited back here. We'd had tea at the kitchen table, and we'd both been awkward and constrained. To get to the kitchen it had been necessary to walk through the old man's shabby bedroom, with his worn felt slippers beside the bed. It had made me feel like an intruder, as if I were seeing a part of his life that I wasn't meant to. Simeon had been embarrassed, too; the invitation hadn't been repeated.

This time we stopped in the foyer itself, where an ancient monster of a safe sat on a reinforced section of the floor, filling half the cubicle. THE MACHINISTS' INSURANCE CO., it said in faded gilt lettering, barely readable against the black metal, 342 WYONA STREET, BROOKLYN, N.Y. Simeon knelt with difficulty, absent-mindedly shoving his rigid leg to one side with his hands, and worked the combination. When the heavy door swung smoothly open— apparently he kept it oiled—he slid out the only object inside, an unframed picture on a rec-tangular piece of Formica-coated wood, rev-erently carried it back to the counter, and stepped aside to let me have a look.

It was about two feet by three, a dark, sober portrait on a simple, brown background. Across the bottom was a line of spidery, ele-gant script: "*El Conde de Torrijos.*"

Simeon looked at me. "Well?"

I let out my breath. A man, yes. Dressed in black, yes. In the somber fashion of the seventeenth-century Spanish court, as Simeon had implied. But no wonder he'd been moved. The pensive, melancholy face of the balding, aging aristocrat with the white goatee—the Count of Torrijos—gazed at me with an immediacy—a living, real presence—that only a few painters had managed to capture more than once or twice in their lives. You knew at once that, despite the quaintness of costume, or trappings, or pose, this was a real person you were looking at—or rather, was looking at you—and you couldn't help feeling that if you could only look at him long enough, or in the right way, you might make a connection, an actual human connection, over all those years. Rembrandt, above all, had had that magical gift. Rubens. Van Dyck. Vermeer. Holbein. Copley. Hals.

And Velàzquez.

Now, don't jump to conclusions, I told myself, leaning over the picture. There are a lot of things this could be—a painting made by an apprentice in some seventeenth-century artist's workshop— possibly even Velàzquez's—or a copy by a talented student, or an outright forgery done in the nineteenth or even twentieth century, smoked, and baked, and crackled to look old.

No, not a modern forgery; too painstaking and too good for that. Besides, I could spot a few signs of antique restoration here and there; the right cuff and an area near the elbow had been touched up, as well as the region around a small, repaired gash in the background—all three of them exactly the sort of shoddy jobs that had been all too common in the nineteenth century. You just don't see forgers who go to that kind of trouble to make a painting look like the real thing. Not when it's so much easier and more effective to buy (or steal) a picture by some unknown but reasonably competent seventeenth-century journeyman and simply replace the signature with that of the artist of your choice. That way, assuming you'd picked your painter with a little care, the materials, the techniques, even the frame, would all be right for the time and place. The only fake part would be the signature.

This one didn't even have a signature, and in a way that was the most convincing element of all. One thing you could count on with a fake was a nice, legible signature. Without one, even the most beautifully forged Rubens or Rembrandt might wind up being relegated to a generic "School of Rubens" or "Studio of Rembrandt," and what self-respecting forger is going to settle for that when a discreet little "PP Rubens" or "RHL" (Rembrandt Harmenszoon Leidensis) in the lower-right corner would increase its selling price a hundred times, say from twenty thousand to two million dollars?

So whatever it was, Velàzquez or otherwise, it was almost certainly old. In good shape, though. Other than the holes and creases around the edges where it had been tacked to its stretcher, a little nearby flaking of the paint, and the repaired gash, the canvas had suffered nothing beyond the normal damage of time. I went over it inch by inch with the lighted magnifying lens I'd brought, gently touching it here and there with a finger, even rubbing a bit of saliva over it in one place to check the varnish, both of which were capital crimes if discovered (but perpetrated all the same by anyone evaluating a work of art—in private, at any rate).

The more I examined it, the more I leaned toward Velàzquez. The dark, dramatic colors, the ochers and earth tones of the deceptively plain background, the detached yet sympathetic way the subject was portrayed—all shouted Velàzquez...or possibly, to be fair, one of Velàzquez's better students. But the technique, the actual application of the paint, was another thing, and it would be an extraordinary student who could match that feathery brushwork, so different from that of his contemporaries and so far ahead of its time. Two hundred years later Manet, himself one of the founders of Impressionism, would credit Velàzquez as his own inspiration.

There was more: the characteristic use of a soft-hair blending brush to tone down outlines, and the expert, patient application of layer upon layer of glazes. Outside of the Venetian school—Bellini, Titian, Tintoretto, Giorgione—Velàzquez was the undisputed master of glazes, sometimes lathering on as many as thirty layers.

In addition, there were pale vertical streaks, visible through pigment that had become transparent with time, that showed where the artist's brush had been wiped clean on the as-yet-unpainted canvas, a habit for which Velàzquez had been criticized in his own time. He was also famous for his *pentimenti,* his changes of mind as he worked, and these, too, probably invisible for the first couple of hundred years, now showed as ghosts through the time-thinned overpainting. The old count's collar had been made smaller, his left hand had been repositioned, a book in the foreground, originally closed, had been opened.

"Well?" Simeon demanded. He was practically hopping with impatience. "So?"

I straightened up. "Simeon, this time I think you just might have something here."

"Ah," he said with deep satisfaction.

"But I'm not sure yet. Let's look at the back."

Gingerly, I lifted the stiff canvas by its edges and turned it over, holding it so that the painted surface didn't touch anything. There were the usual things you'd expect to find on the back of an old painting—flyspecks, smudges, cryptic scribbles, and randomly placed symbols of one kind or another: *R-B, GRA, Osuna 127/6, S2,* a star within a circle, and a monogram that said either *TC* or *CT,* all in faded ink or pencil, plus a couple of dull, black rubber-stamped markings in pointy, angular Gothic lettering: *ERR* and *ne-2.* In addition there were two pale fingerprints (Velàzquez's?) in ochre pigment, some scraps of glue where labels had once been pasted on, and two labels still attached, one large, one small.

The big one, in the center, was a dealer's sticker on expensive paper: *Pierre Severac, Paris. 13, Boulevard de la Madeleine. Peintures Françaises et étrangères.* Turn of the century, from the look of it. The smaller label was made of cheap, thin paper torn from a perforated roll and unevenly typed in faint red ink. *Velàzquez, Graf Torrijos,* it said. *Paris, Dez. 1942.*

Simeon gestured at the "Velàzquez." "See?"

"Mm," I said, and stared at the faded tag of paper for a long time. "You know, this painting's had a bit of history, Simeon."

"History, what do you mean, history?"

"The label's in German. You didn't mention that."

He leaned over it, bringing his glasses down from his brow. "Who cares what language? All I could see was that 'Velàzquez.' What difference—" He looked at me. "Ah, I see what you mean. The Nazis."

"Yes, the Nazis."

In December 1942 Paris had been an occupied city for two years, and for all of that time the Germans had been busy plundering, confiscating, or coercing works of art from Jewish families, from the homes of Frenchmen who had fled the city, and from other "enemies of the Reich." It was a subject I knew something about. The dissertation I'd written for my Ph.D. in art history not so many years before had been called *The Ethics of Plunder: Theft and Restitution of Cultural Property in Time of War.* Naturally enough, a big part of it had dealt with Germany's looting of art during World War II and the Allies' remarkable postwar program to restore it to its owners. It was a subject in which I continued to be interested, delivering an occasional paper and serving on panels from time to time.

And so I knew all too well that the tag on the back of the Velàzquez was part of their inventory-control system, and that the *ERR* stamped not far from it, also in the black Gothic letters still in use in Germany in the 1940s, was their proprietary imprint; it stood for *Einsatzstab-Reichsleiter Rosenberg,* Adolf Hitler's personal art-looting machine. Its director, Alfred Rosenberg, had operated with a simple mandate from the Führer: He was to see to "the transportation to Germany of cultural goods that are deemed by him to be valuable." In other words, the wholesale plunder of Europe's art. From museums, from individuals, from governments. Rosenberg's disciplined thugs had applied themselves mightily, amassing the greatest collection of art in the history of the world. In Eastern Europe the methods had been brutal and direct. With Poles and Czechs officially classified as *Untermenschlich,* a subhuman, their property was technically—and conveniently— "ownerless." The jackboots simply walked in and tore it off the walls.

France, being officially inhabited by fellow human beings (Jews, Communists, Gaullists, and others naturally excepted), was a more delicate matter, calling for methods that were less direct, but no less brutal. Here, "purchase" was the method of choice, which resulted in a mountain of legalisms but amounted in the end to the same thing: Victims had nothing to say in the matter. Those who protested were "persuaded." Those who refused to be "persuaded" died or disappeared. The ERR made off with what they wanted, and usually "paid" (when they paid at all) in Occupation francs, the funny money of the day.

And they had wanted *El Conde de Torrijos*.

"These things the Germans stole," Simeon said, frowning, "they had to give them back after the war, didn't they?"

"Most of them, yes. That is, the Americans and the British ran a huge program getting them back to the rightful owners. But... Simeon, you said this guy, the one who brought it in, was Russian, didn't you?"

"That's right, Russian. So?"

"Well, I was just thinking. You know, the Russians saw things differently, and almost all the Nazi loot they got their hands on disappeared behind the Iron Curtain after the war and never showed up again. Until lately, that is. Now, with an active mafia in Russia, and wide-open borders, pieces are starting to turn up on the black market. Could be this is one of them? Of course, there are a lot of other possibilities—"

But Simeon had seized on this one. He nodded, his dark eyes alight. "Ah, I knew he was a gangster, a desperado. A little runt he was, but a real tough guy, a brawler, you know?" He made a growling sound and put a hand up to his right cheek. "A big scar here, half an ear missing, a busted nose—"

"This was someone you never saw before?"

"Never," Simeon said, staring again at the painting. "You know, I get a lot of green-horns in here. They ask around and people tell them Pawlovsky is the one to go to. And it's true, I like to help people from the old country. But this one I didn't trust from the minute he walked in. In the first place, he tries to tell me he's a Jew—to get on my good side, you know—but, Benjamin, if that man was a Jew, then I'm a Seminole Indian. A Jew that gets into brawls? A Jew with hair like it came off a haystack? Brodsky, he said his name was, but he had no papers, no identification, nothing."

"An illegal, you think?"

Simeon shrugged. "He had a story, they all have stories. Technically I'm not sup-posed to accept anything from someone with no identification—you can understand why—but in this case, once I saw..." He gestured at the picture.

"Of course. You did the right thing."

"What now?" He hesitated. "Should I call the police?"

"Would you like me to do that for you?"

"Please," he said with visible relief. He was like most expatriate Russians in that regard. Dealing with the police didn't come naturally to him.

"Simeon, how did he get it here? Was it rolled up?"

"No, he had it in a valise."

I looked at the picture again. "Must have been a pretty big one."

"It was. One of those old canvas ones with flowers on it, all beat up, with leather straps around it, you know the kind? And he just walks right in with it and starts in with this long story about his uncle, and his sister-in-law, and how he needs the money to settle an accident claim—"

I was only half listening. "Look, I need to do a few more things before we contact the police. I want to make sure we know what we're talking about. Do you have a tape measure?"

"A yardstick."

"Good enough. And how about a camera? Do you have a camera?"

"Do I have a camera," he said, taking his cane and heading for a corner of the shop. "What a question." In a moment he brought back a Polaroid with a tag attached and handed it to me.

"Does it have film in it?"

Simeon made a face. "What, do I look that dumb?"

The bell on the front door jingled, and a man in a suit peeked in.

"Can I help you with something?" Simeon called.

"Hallo. Ey vwawn buy vwiolyin," he said in the slow, forceful, but barely understandable accent of a newcomer determined to show his command of his recently learned language even if no one can understand what he's talking about. Another of Simeon's green-horns, apparently. "For nyephew."

"Fine, come in," Simeon said. "I'll come out there and show you what I have. A looker, not a buyer," he murmured to me, unhooking his cane from the counter. "He won't buy anything, never in a million years."

I took half a dozen photographs of the painting, front and back, and then used the wooden yardstick to measure it while they developed: thirty-seven inches by twenty-five inches. On the small side for Velàzquez, but within his normal range. One of the photos came out fuzzy, and I retook it.

In the meantime the man had left without his violin, promising to return later with his nephew.

"What did I tell you?" Simeon said. He turned once more to the painting. "So what now?"

"Now I want to go on over to the staff library at the museum and check a few things. But first I need to make a phone call."

Simeon pointed to the cordless telephone on the counter. "Help yourself. You want something cold to drink?"

"Coke?"

"Iced tea?"

"Sounds good. Not too sweet, though."

"Too late, it's already made."

Simeon went back to his kitchen. I used my calling card to telephone CIAT, the Center for the Investigation of Art Theft in New York, with which I'd worked a few times.

CIAT maintained a database of all the current known stolen art in the world—at any one time a staggering eighty thousand items, give or take a couple of thousand.

I described the picture to Christine Valle de Leon, CIAT's director and an old friend, and promised to fax her the photos as soon as I could. Christie, brisk and businesslike, told me she'd get back to me within a day or two.

I hung up as Simeon came in with the iced tea. We stood looking silently at the painting and sipping the supersweetened liquid. When Simeon drank hot tea, which he always had from a glass, he sucked it through a sugar cube held between his teeth and replaced with another, and then another, as each one dissolved. When he had iced tea, he simply dumped in about half a pound of sugar to start, tempering it with squeezed lemon. Actually, as long as it didn't come as a complete surprise, I didn't find it all that bad.

"I guess I'll head over to the library now," I said, putting down my drained glass. "I'll swing by when I'm done and let you know what I find out."

"Good," he said absently. "Five o'clock is when I close up, so if you come back after that, rattle the gate and I'll let you in. Or maybe I should just leave it open for you."

"Close it," I said. "In fact, maybe you ought to lock things up right now."

"And my customers, what about them? Ah, Benjamin, you'll never be a businessman.

Listen, what about the police? I thought you were going to call them."

"I will, but I'd rather have just a little more information before we bring them in. Look, I really think this is a remarkable piece of art you have here, Simeon. Wouldn't it be better to put it someplace more secure? I could drop it off at the museum for you. I know the people there. They'll hold it for us."

"No, I don't think so. How long you going to be gone?"

"An hour. Two at most."

"For two hours, I think we can take a chance. Here's a painting that Hitler himself wanted and couldn't get, and now, all this time later, here it is right in front of me, in my own shop, for me to look at for my own pleasure. I want to take it in the kitchen, pour myself a glass of beer, and sit down with it at the table and think about what a funny world it is. I'm entitled to that much, don't you think so?"

I smiled. "I suppose you are at that, Simeon."

"Give me half an hour to enjoy the experience. Then I'll put it in the safe until you get here, I promise."

"But what if this Brodsky comes back in the meantime to take it out of hock? You'd have to give it to him."

"Him, he's not coming back."

I didn't think so either.

"Well, there's the conservation angle to think about. At the museum they regulate the temperature and humidity, they—"

"What are you telling me, that two hours here is going to hurt it? You think people have been regulating the temperature and humidity every day for the last three hundred years?"

I capitulated. "Okay, but tonight, later, it goes into the museum, right? You really can't keep something like this in the shop, Simeon. You can't treat it like—"

"I heard you, I heard you. Don't nag. That's a bad habit you're developing."

"If it is by Velàzquez, we're talking about millions of dollars here, Simeon."

"No, *you're* talking about millions of dollars. Me, I got exactly one hundred bucks out on it. What's the big deal?"

"I'll talk to you later," I said, laughing, "as soon as I have something to tell you."

"Sure, sure. Listen, Ben..." he said tentatively, hardly his usual manner. "I'm going for dinner with my niece tomorrow night. There's a new Russian restaurant in Brighton that's pretty good, they say. I think...I've been thinking for a while that you and Alex would get along. So I thought maybe, you know, if you weren't doing anything anyway..."

It surprised me on two counts. First, unless you counted that awkward tea in his kitchen, Simeon, despite his warmth whenever I was there, had never before made a social overture that went beyond "Drop in next time you're around." And second, not once had he ever referred to relatives. It was startling to suddenly think of him as not just an independent old man who lived in three rooms behind a pawnshop but as someone with a family. Did his niece call him Uncle Simeon? Did he have nephews, too? Brothers, sisters? Even children, perhaps, that he had once dandled on his knee?

It was almost like the feeling I'd had when I looked at *The Count of Torrijos:* Well, what do you know, the guy had an actual past, an actual life. For a moment it embarrassed me that I'd never once taken the trouble to learn anything about Simeon's world, but then what did he know about mine? Not much. Nothing.

"Gee, I'm sorry, Simeon, I'm afraid I'm tied up," I said, not knowing why I did, because of course I wasn't tied up. "Maybe another time."

"Sure," Simeon said good-humoredly. "Maybe."

CHAPTER 3

The William Morris Hunt Memorial Library is one of the handsomer rooms in the Boston Museum of Fine Arts, though seldom seen by visitors. There are gleaming chandeliers, tall ceilings, great paintings. From high on the two-story walls, rearing horses and enraged gods and goddesses look down from vast canvases by Luca Giordano and Benjamin West. Below, however, all is restful, even cozy: handsome, oak-paneled wainscoting, green-shaded bankers' lamps, musty volumes, and drowsy, occasionally snoring researchers.

The worn, broken-spined volume I had open on the table in front of me was suitably musty, but I was anything but drowsy. What I was reading was almost too good to be true, so exciting I could hardly sit still. The book was *Velàzquez: A Catalogue Raisonné of His Oeuvre*, José López-Rey's classic 1963 compendium of all known works by the great Spanish artist, and I had it opened to page 216, entry 245.

Don Juan Carlos de Mendoza, Sixth Conde de Torrijos
Half-length. 1630–31.
Height 0.941 m. Width 0.633 m.
Minor puncture damage in upper left quadrangle (repaired).
Unsigned. Inscribed at bottom: El Conde de Torrijos.
Almost certainly painted as one of a pair with No. 257, Dona Leonor María de Mendoza, Condesa de Torrijos.
Paris: Aguado Sale, No. 77.
Madrid: Osuna Sale, March 1843, No. 127/6.
Madrid: Marquis de Casa Torres.
London: Lord Rhys-Burton.
London: Gordon-Radcliffe-Attley Collection.
London: Private collection.
Paris: Christiane Lisle—Pierre Severac.
Paris: Vallon sale, 1902, No. 3.

So it was actually true; Simeon had been right. The size matched, the inscription matched, the absence of a signature, the damaged area, the art dealer's name—"Severac"—everything. And while the catalogue didn't mention the back of the painting, the entry paralleled much of what I'd seen on it: Osuna 127/6 was a clear reference to the Osuna sale of 1843, right down to the lot number; the CT monogram stood for Casa Torres; the R-B was Rhys-Burton, and so on. In the illustrated section of the catalogue there was a photograph of the painting, and that matched, too. It was the real thing, a fabulous once-in-a-decade happening. I had a wild urge to yell out the news, right there: *A stolen Velàzquez masterpiece, lost to the world for more than fifty years, was sitting right that minute in a tacky pawnshop not more than a mile from the museum, what did they think of that?*

I didn't, of course. I restrained myself to a gently jubilant rap on the table with my fingertips as I got up. And even that mild display earned poisonous stares and angry murmurs from fellow scholars who felt they had every right (and did) to the Hunt's long tradition of sound and healthful repose.

WHEN A MAN IS sitting in his kitchen with a glass of beer and a lost Velàzquez and contemplating what a funny world it is, you can hardly expect him to keep a religious eye on the clock.

53

So I thought with a smile when I saw that Simeon hadn't come back out front to pull the metal shutters closed, although five o'clock had come and gone. I walked through the empty shop and banged on the door to the back rooms.

"Simeon, it's Ben!"

No answer, but then hearing wasn't his long suit. I hesitated for a moment, because under ordinary circumstances I wouldn't have invaded the old man's sanctum. But what I had to tell him, I felt, was sufficiently exciting to allow for an exception. I climbed the two wooden steps, rapped on the door again, and turned the knob. "S—"

A shower of stars exploded behind my eyeballs. I went hurtling backward off the steps, struck my hip hard on the edge of the counter, and kept going, tumbling over the glass surface to sprawl heavily onto the floor on my side. That is, it seems reasonable to assume that that was the order of events. At the time it all seemed to be happening at once, but not so quickly or confusedly that I couldn't grasp, however dimly, what had occurred. Someone had been behind the door, waiting for me to turn the knob. The instant I did, he'd hurled himself against the door, flinging it wide open and smack into my face, and launching me on a parabola that took me over the counter and onto the floor of the shop.

Only hazily conscious of what I was doing, I rolled over onto my hands and knees, my head down. I was dizzy and nauseated, and blurry pinpoints of light were still shifting sickly in and out of focus at the edge of my vision. The top of my right hipbone hurt so much there were tears in my eyes, and when I touched my numbed left cheek, just below the eye, it felt like an overinflated basketball.

At first I thought I'd been knocked out for seconds or minutes, but when I realized that the rattling sound in my ears wasn't from inside my head but from the door, which was still shuddering on its hinges, I knew that couldn't be true. I managed to shove myself into a sitting position, but my motor skills weren't all there yet, and I fell clumsily back against an open case of kitchen implements. That dropped a lobster pot into my lap, startling the hell out of me and making me realize abruptly that my mind wasn't working right yet. Was hardly working at all, in fact.

Because if I'd never lost consciousness, then whoever had slammed the door open on me had yet to come out. With the bars on the windows of Simeon's apartment making it impossible to leave through the back, the only way out was through the front door of the shop, which meant stepping directly over my body. And even with my mental processes not at their keenest, I was pretty sure I would have noticed anyone doing that.

So where was he?

And the darker, less articulate thought: Where was Simeon?

I sat without moving, trying to will away the wooziness, to will the strength back into my legs. The shop was absolutely still. Aside from the traffic on Washington Street, the only sound was the slow, peaceful ticking-away of old clocks on the shelves. After a few seconds I pulled myself painfully to my feet. The queasiness welled up again. I closed my eyes and leaned on the counter.

"Hoo," I said softly.

And took another whack in the face.

Now, I may not be the fastest learner in the world, but given enough time the message generally gets through, and when I get clouted in the head twice inside of thirty seconds, I take that as a sign to start paying serious attention.

This time, with no door handy, he'd used his fist; a sloppy, mauling blow that caught me on the nose and upper lip, not cleanly enough to do any real damage, but bringing a spurt of blood from my nose and sending me reeling back off balance. The punch had come as a complete surprise, but what had happened was clear enough. The guy had thrust the door open with so much force that he'd pitched down the steps right behind me, but whereas I, traveling in a higher trajectory, had arched gracefully over the counter, he had landed in a heap behind it, at the base of the steps. Like me, he'd stayed on the floor, possibly stunned, possibly figuring out what to do next, possibly listening to see if I was moving around. Then, when I'd leaned on the counter directly above him, with my eyes conveniently closed, he'd seized the opportunity and reached up to slug me.

So now we were both standing up, mutely glaring at each other over the counter. *I know him,* I thought dazedly, *but from where?* He was my height but about a foot wider, all right angles and thick limbs, built roughly along the lines of a stand-alone freezer. He was wearing a 1960s skinny tie and a dark, poorly cut suit that hung slackly around his thighs and was overly tight in the chest (but then where would you go to buy a freezer-shaped suit?), making him look all the more massive. I had the definite impression that this kind of situation wasn't that unfamiliar, or even that unpleasant, to him. Speaking for myself, I was wildly out of my element. As far as I could remember, this was the first time in my adult life that I'd been involved in a physical altercation. I couldn't think of anything to say that wouldn't have sounded stupid, so I just watched him and waited.

He made a rough motion with one heavy forearm, warning me back and out of his way. The grimace that accompanied it showed me a mouthful of badly cared for teeth, brown and crooked, with one of the bottom ones in front missing. His dark hair was stiff and close-cropped; poorly cut, as if it had been done with the help of a soup bowl. Where had I seen him before?

I shook my head. "No," I said between clenched jaws. Not only that, but I moved forward, to block his path to the front door.

Don't ask me what I had in mind. I didn't feel brave, I can tell you that. My knees were shaking, my mouth so dry that I couldn't have swallowed if I'd wanted to. All I knew was that I couldn't simply step meekly out of his way and let him walk out. I mean, how could I?

He stared at me for a second with nothing much going on in his eyes, then took from the shelf beside him a flat, black, evil-looking pry bar, the two-foot-long kind that an enthusiastic carpenter can bring down a three-story house with. He held it in his right hand, slapping it heavily against the palm of his left, eyeing me all the while, giving me a chance to reconsider just how much I really wanted to try to keep him from leaving.

But whatever plane I was operating on, it didn't allow for reconsideration any more than it had for consideration in the first place. Without letting myself think, and without taking my eyes off him, I reached behind me, scrabbling for a weapon of my own. Unfortunately, whereas he seemed to be in the construction workers' section of the shop, I was still in housewares, and what I came away with was a medium-weight Teflon-coated skillet. Still, I brandished it at him to show I meant business.

For some reason he wasn't intimidated. He stepped carefully but confidently out from around the counter so that we faced each other from three or four feet apart, then made a prodding, grimacing feint with the pry bar. I flinched but stood my ground. I had my eye on the shelf of tools at his side, among which was a pipe wrench that looked a hell of a lot more formidable than my frying pan, which made me feel like an irate housewife in the Sunday comics.

Something changed in his eyes. The next time he used that thing, I knew, it wasn't going to be a feint. Still operating on automatic pilot, I gulped a breath, heaved the pan at his head, and dived for the wrench. The skillet clanged off the middle of his forehead with a sound like a mallet hitting a gong, but if it bothered him, he didn't let on. Almost casually, he swung the bar backhanded, catching me in the ribs with the hooked end. It doubled me over instantly, so that I lurched against the wall, paralyzed by the astounding pain. More pans clanged onto the floor. I'd gotten my fingers on the wrench, but hadn't been able to hang on. And if I had, it sure wouldn't have made any difference at this point.

"Enough?" he asked.

I couldn't speak. It took everything I had to try to get my breath going again. He lifted the bar as if to take another crack at me, but when I couldn't even wince, he uttered a grunt, tossed the pry bar contemptuously to the floor, and strode out past me.

I could no more move than fly. My eyes were streaming with tears, my left arm was clamped rigidly to my side. I leaned my head back against the wall, eyes closed, until I got my breathing under control again, or if not quite under control, then at least going alternately in and out. But anything beyond a shallow breath resulted in a sharp, wincing stab of pain to my side. I would have let myself slip to a sitting position on the floor, but I was worried about getting up again.

It took me a long time to realize that someone was standing in the doorway and had been for a while. "Hey, man?" he asked hesitantly. "Hey, man, you okay?"

I turned to look at him. If I hadn't already known it, his drop-jawed expression would have told me that I looked like something out of *Nightmare on Elm Street.*

"You want me to call the cops, man?" It was a Hispanic kid with a skateboard under one arm.

"Yes," I said, not too intelligibly, but the kid disappeared, and in a couple of seconds I heard the skateboard clatter to the sidewalk and go into action.

I went back to leaning my head against the wall with my eyes closed. My side was beginning to go numb now, so that the pain, which had shut out everything else in the world for a few agonized minutes, blessedly retreated, and it was possible to concentrate on something else.

Simeon.

It was unthinkable that he had gone away somewhere and left the place wide open. It was also unthinkable that he would have remained quietly in the back, had he been able to come out, while we made a noisy shambles of the shop. That left several other possibilities, all of them thinkable, all of them bad.

The back door, half ajar, was about fifteen

feet from me, a long way in my condition. I pushed myself off the wall and tried a tentative couple of steps. If I hugged my side, breathed cautiously, and slid my feet carefully over the floor, I found that I could walk, if not in comfort, then at least without coming apart. So, groaning and bent like a man of a hundred and ten, I slowly shuffled to the door at the back of the shop, using one hand to prop myself on anything that came to hand. The two wooden steps were a problem, but I managed to climb them by going up sideways—left leg first, then drag the right after it—and then, with a stopped-up throat and a sick, sinking sensation squeezing my heart, I pushed the door open.

"Oh, Simeon, no," I whispered.

He was crumpled on the floor, partly on his right side, partly on his back, sprawled across the threshold between the foyer and his bedroom with his eyes closed, his head against the base of the safe. There was a smear of blood at his mouth and another dark, thick blob of it in his left ear. His glasses lay a few feet away, unbroken. His face seemed to have collapsed in on itself; his entire body seemed caved in and shrunken, like a mummy's. So much so that a shock shot across my shoulder blades when his eyelids opened and his mild, dark eyes immediately took me in and watched me, moving as I moved.

"Simeon!"

I knelt quickly beside him, almost passing out when I forgot to allow for my own damaged ribs.

One of his hands lay open and jerking on the worn carpet. I took it gently in my own. "Don't try to move; I'll have an ambulance here in a few minutes. You're going to be all right...."

But as I spoke I could see that he wasn't really seeing me, or anything else either; that while his eyes continued to watch me, there was no awareness, no comprehension behind them. He began to tremble now, and I could hear his breath coming in quick, panting little hiccups—*ech...ech...ech*—as if he were breathing only in, not out. His eyes continued to observe me with calm, impartial, utterly empty interest.

I didn't know if he could understand anything, but I patted his hand one more time. "I'm calling an ambulance now. I'm not going away, I'll be right here. You're going to be okay, Simeon."

I struggled down the steps to the counter, dialed 911, and turned to smile reassuringly at Simeon, the receiver to my ear. "It's going to be all right," I said, practically choking on the words.

"Nine-one-one, emergency," came matter-of-factly over the telephone. "Is this fire, police, or medical?"

I cupped my hand over the speaker. "It's medical," I said, and gave her what details I could, although when it came time to tell her the address and the nearest cross street, I went blank. "It's a block or two east of Lenox," I said. "Pawlovsky's Loans. Please tell them to hurry."

When I turned around to look at Simeon again, his eyes were still open but no longer following me. That last false light in them had glazed over and gone out.

"Oh, God," I murmured, and leaned over the counter, resting my head on my forearms.

CHAPTER 4

We could tape your ribs up for you, if you like," the emergency room physician at Boston Medical Center Hospital offered. Dr. Kavrakos, his name tag said; a balding, abstracted, no-longer-young man with a bemused philosophical bent. Or else he'd been on duty too long and was maybe just the least little bit punch-drunk as a result.

I was pretty punch-drunk myself, having been given an injection of painkiller and sedative twenty minutes earlier.

"Will taping them up help?" I asked. I was slumped on the edge of an examining table dressed in nothing but a pair of blue socks and one of those paper tutus that tie at the back, and feeling appropriately ridiculous about it.

"Not really, no," said Dr. Kavrakos.

"Then why do it?"

He looked at me thoughtfully. "Good question."

"Let's skip it, then."

I was hoping for more in the way of medical advice, but he just stood there, lost in contemplation, blowing his thinning, longish hair out of his eyes by sticking out his lower lip and puffing upward. It made him look like a philosophical chimp.

"Uh, do you suppose I could get dressed and get out of here now?" I asked.

He considered the question. "Do you have somebody to keep an eye on you at home?"

"Sure." A lie, of course, but, like most people, I find that a little bit of hospital goes a long way. I just wanted to go home.

"I suppose I don't see why not, then. No driving, though. That's a pretty powerful shot you've had."

"If the cop I gave my statement to is still around, he said he'd get me home. If not, I'll take a taxi." The whereabouts of my car were a bit fuzzy anyway.

He scribbled out a prescription and tore it off the pad. "Every four hours as needed. It's codeine, so I'm afraid trapeze swinging and bungee jumping are out for a while."

"Gee, that's going to wreck my plans. Anything else I need to do—or not do?"

As usual, he took his time answering. "Don't do anything that hurts."

That, I thought, wincing as I got down from the table, wasn't going to leave a whole hell of a lot. "Is there anything else I need to worry about besides the broken ribs?"

He shrugged. "The rest of it's inconsequential."

"To you, maybe," I said.

Even after the painkiller I felt like one big ache. My cheek had swelled up so much that I couldn't see out of my left eye, my hip felt has if it had been shattered with a hammer, and my head was pounding so hard I could feel it shudder with every throb. Those— aside from my ribs— were the major sources of discomfort, but there were plenty of minor ones, too.

"I mean," he explained, "in the great scheme of things."

"Ah, the great scheme of things," I said, beginning to fall into his rhythm. "Doctor, you're sure right about that."

However, the stuff he'd pumped into me had me good and mellow by now, and I wasn't about to dwell on the great scheme of things. Time enough for that tomorrow. For the moment, all I could think about was going to bed.

BUT TWENTY MINUTES LATER, when the bored but solicitous young cop was helping me into the elevator in my building, another thought broke through the walking doze I had fallen into. I made some kind of noise and stopped in my tracks.

He gave me an anxious look. "Sorry, did I hurt you?"

"Ey vwawn buy vwiolyin," I said.

"Come again?"

I repeated it more distinctly. "Ey...vwawn... buy...vwiolyin. For nyephew."

"Yeah? No kidding. Come on, let's get you on up—"

"I'm telling you," I said, wondering crossly at his lack of comprehension, "that I just remembered why he looked familiar."

"'He' being...?"

"The guy in the shop," I said. "The son of a bitch that killed Simeon."

CHAPTER 5

The thing that gets you down about broken ribs, I was finding out, is not so much the pain, but the tortoiselike slowness with which you have to do everything in order to avoid the pain. When you forget and do something reckless—like turning over in bed without first devising a plan for the sequence of bodily realignments necessary—you are promptly zinged with a reminder of the need for prudence. As a result, you soon start moving like a deep-sea diver on the floor of the ocean. Everything—getting out of your chair, brushing your teeth, going to the bathroom—takes five times as long as it ought to and demands a meticulously drawn-up battle plan besides. But at least it can be done. You think you can't learn to hiccup or sneeze in nonjarring slow motion? I assure you, you can.

However, I hadn't yet gotten to that stage when the telephone beside my bed rang the next morning at a little after nine, dragging me out of a deep, drugged, eleven-hour sleep. Naturally enough, I reached for it without thinking. And naturally enough, under the circumstances, I promptly yelped at the teeth-grinding, spine-rattling jolt and fell rigidly back. After the fourth ring the answering machine in the study clicked on, but it was too far away for me to hear the message, and anyway, I had lost all interest in it. All I wanted to do was lie there, motionless and if possible mind-less, until my nerve endings stopped gasping and flopping around.

After four or five minutes I was able to (very, very slowly) reach for the plastic vial of codeine tablets that I had somehow thought to leave on the bedside table before falling into bed in my clothes. I was able to get the cap off in a mere ten seconds (no childproofing, thank God) and pop a couple of pills. There was no water to help them down, but I wasn't about to get up and go to the kitchen. In a few minutes the codeine kicked in and let me relax my muscles. For another minute or so I felt as if I were in heaven. And then, like a stifling, black cloud filling the room, came that awful first-thing-in-the-morning feeling that something was terribly, terribly wrong, and that in another moment I'd remember what it was.

And in another moment I did. I remembered the day before. I remembered why I needed the codeine in the first place. I remembered Simeon.

It's funny how the mind tries to get around facts it doesn't want to accept, and how it doesn't necessarily do it logically. He can't be dead, I told myself, how could he be dead? I'd been right there in the shop, chatting with him, listening to his gentle, ironic jokes at four o'clock yesterday afternoon. How could he have been so wholly alive then, so wonderfully excited about the painting, and then be dead an hour and a half later? Impossible. And yet, of course that's the way it was, how else? You didn't get dead gradually, over time. There wasn't any in-between; one minute you were living, the next minute you weren't. And for Simeon, that last, critical millisecond had come while I was calling 911. I'd practically seen the switch turn off and the light go out.

Remembering it now, I felt suddenly feeble and hollow, as if a spigot had been opened somewhere in my belly and my insides had drained out. He was dead because of me. It was the first time that particular thought had hit home. There was no way around it; I should have stood my ground, shouldn't have let him talk me into leaving the picture in his shop. I had known better, known it was a stupid thing to do. How much effort would it have taken to convince him to let me put it someplace secure? Not a whole hell of a lot. But I'd shrugged my shoulders and hadn't pursued it, and now that decent old man, my friend, was dead.

I must have dozed off, because the next time the telephone rang, it woke me up again. This time I was smarter; I let it finish chirping, then carefully felt my way for the first time through the elaborate process that was to be my getting-out-of-bed routine for the next several weeks: turn from lying on my back (the only position I could sleep in without pain) to my left side; worm my way to the edge of the bed by getting my fingers over the side of the mattress and tugging; hold on to the bedpost with my left hand while I slid both feet sideways to the floor; pause to regroup; slide my legs with infinite care down to the floor so that I was kneeling on the bedside rug, still hanging on to the bedpost; pull myself up, section by section—right leg, left leg, knees, hips, head—and *voilà*—an upright (more or less), bipedal human being!

In a mere two minutes.

There was no way the telephone messages could be anything I was eager to deal with, so I slowly got out of my clothes (believe me, space doesn't permit the procedural details), took a hot shower followed by a hot bath, shaved, put on a bathrobe, and toasted up my last two chocolate fudge Pop-Tarts for breakfast. By the time I slithered through the living room to the answering machine with a cup of coffee, it was 11:00 A.M.

There were two messages. The first was Christie Valle de Leon's return of my call of the previous day, letting me know that CIAT had drawn a blank. They had run a search in the files of London's Art Loss Register and of Interpol as well, and the only currently missing Velàzquez that anyone knew about was a study for *The Forge of Vulcan*, stolen many years before from a private collection in Leeds,

England, and of doubtful attribution. No *Count of Torrijos* or anything remotely resembling one.

The other message was from Sergeant Detective Ron Cox of the Boston Police Homicide Unit, asking me to call him.

I lowered myself as comfortably as I could into the old swivel chair at my desk, made sure the coffee was within arm's reach, and dialed. He picked it up on the first ring.

"Thanks for calling back, Mr. Revere. How you doing this morning?"

"You don't want to know."

"You're probably right," he said with a laugh. "Listen, I'm gonna be looking into the Pawlovsky case, and I could use your help."

There was no expression in his voice, nothing beyond a professional civility, and why would there be? He was a homicide cop; this was all in a day's work. Pawnshop proprietors were in a class with convenience-store operators and all-night-gas-station managers: easy marks.

"I'd like to if I can," I said.

"Well, that's just fine." I got the impression that he was toying with a pen, or a paper clip, or shuffling papers on his desk. "Now, I've looked over the statement you made to Officer Bando last night, and as far as that goes, it's quite clear, very helpful—"

"I'm surprised to hear it. I don't remember being too coherent."

"—but there are a few things I wanted to ask you about. You were an acquaintance of the deceased, right?"

"That's right," I said, after the moment it took to digest the unsettling phrase.

"And Lieutenant Harrigan thinks you might be the Revere who's worked with our Major Case Unit before, is that right, too?"

"Yes, it is. On some art-theft cases."

"Well, that's good, I'm hoping you can give us some assistance here. Now, there's a safe in the back of the Pawlovsky establishment, are you familiar with that?"

"Yes."

"When was the last time you saw it? I mean, before the events of last night."

"About an hour and a half earlier. Four o'clock. We opened—"

"Do you remember if it showed signs of tampering?"

"You mean like scrape marks, or—"

"That's right."

"No, I don't think so," I said. "It was pretty beat up, but just generally from age. Why, are you saying—"

"I'm saying that if what you're saying is accurate, someone worked real hard on jimmying it open after you saw it yesterday, and it's a pretty good guess that it was the guy you ran into. We can't tell for sure whether he ever got it open or not, and I was hoping you might know what Pawlovsky had in it. A lot of times, if we can get a good description of what somebody steals, it gives us a lead—"

"Of course I know what was in it, and obviously he *didn't* get it, or I would have seen it on him."

71

"Get what?"

"The painting."

"What painting is that, Mr. Revere?"

"What painting— You mean I didn't explain about the painting in my statement?"

"No, I can't say that you did."

I realized that I must have been even more out of it than I'd thought. "Sergeant, this is important. If you open up that safe—"

"It's open. We got into it this morning."

"And there was a painting in there, right? A man in black."

"Yeah, there was. I got it in front of me right now. Look, I'm starting to think we'd be better off talking here at Schroeder Plaza. Are you in good enough shape to come down?"

"I can make it. When?"

"Sooner the better. I can have a cruiser pick you up in five minutes. Or do you need any time to get ready?"

I laughed in spite of myself. "No more than six hours or so."

"Come again?"

"Give me forty-five minutes," I said.

SERGEANT DETECTIVE RON COX was a leathery, rawboned, rangy man of fifty who looked like a hardscrabble Dust Bowl farmer from the thirties; so much so that he seemed out of place in his contemporary, color-coordinated office in the spanking-new police building. A man who had seen everything, he was politely sympathetic about my swollen, banged-up

72

face, but it wasn't long before he got bored and started sneaking looks at whatever he had on his computer monitor. But he gave me his full attention when I got to the part about what the painting was worth. First he stared at me, and then at the painting, which was propped against an avocado file cabinet that some interior decorator had decided went with the russet-brown paneled walls. "You're kidding me, five million bucks?"

"That's a conservative estimate," I said. "It could bring a whole lot more, given the right buyer."

"Oh, shit," he said, reaching for his telephone. "I better see if it's been reported stolen from anywhere."

"It hasn't," I said. "I checked with CIAT in New York. They don't have any record of it. Neither does Interpol."

"Oh, yes?" He put the phone down. I could see that he didn't know what CIAT was but wasn't about to admit it. I could also see that he didn't approve of my doing things like checking with Interpol.

"My theory," I said, "is that it's been salted away overseas for years, maybe decades, maybe even since the war, and that it came over here fairly recently. From Russia, probably."

"Mm." He wasn't too crazy about my having theories either.

"That'd be my guess anyway," I said, trying to make amends.

"The fact that a Russian pawned it doesn't mean it just arrived from Russia, Mr. Revere."

"No, but I was thinking about the bag he had it in."

According to Simeon, I explained, Brodsky, if that was really his name, had brought the picture into the shop in a large canvas valise decorated with a floral design—a favored container for smuggling paintings into and out of countries without being spotted. The painting, minus its frame and stretcher, would be placed against an inside wall of the valise and a layer of cloth, also decorated with some complex, busy design, would be sewn over it, forming a sealed, invisible pocket. Then the suitcase would be stuffed with clothes, toiletries, whatever. The designs on the inside and outside would make it difficult for X-ray machines to pick out the painting, and the canvas material of the valise would bend and give under pressure without revealing that there was one more layer of canvas—a five-million-dollar layer—hidden between the inner and outer walls.

"Is that so," Cox murmured, looking at me from under tobacco-colored eyebrows. I got the impression that if this kept up, he might yet consider taking me seriously. "So where do the Russians come in?"

"There were some markings on the back that showed it'd been looted by the Nazis in 1942. One possibility is that it was grabbed in turn by Russian troops at the end of the war and that it's been hidden away over there all the time."

"And it shows up now because the Russian mafia's gotten into the act now?"

"Exactly."

"And the guy who pawned it, who was he? Some kind of mafia underling? A courier, maybe?"

"Yes, maybe, why not?"

He shrugged his shoulders, unconvinced. "It doesn't—"

"And don't forget that...that ape that came back to get it. He was Russian, too. I noticed his accent before, when he came in about the violin. He could have been mafia, too."

"A Russian accent, huh? You're positive? Couldn't have been Polish? Latvian? Bulgarian, maybe?"

He had a point, and I smiled. "Well, if you're going to put it like that, I suppose it could have been Serbo-Croatian for all I know, but doesn't it make sense that—"

"And even if it was Russian, so what? Didn't you tell me most of Pawlovsky's customers were Russian? So why should these guys be any different?"

"No reason, except for a five-million-dollar painting that happened to be sitting in the safe at the time."

"All right, tell me this: Why would this mafia courier you're talking about take a hundred bucks for something worth five million? And according to what you told us, he only wanted a thousand in the first place. How do you explain that?"

That was the question, all right. The going price among black-market art fences was 5 percent of estimated market value. That was a quarter of a million dollars, probably a lot more. And stolen-art receivers in Boston and New York weren't exactly hard to find if you had a few connections. Did the Russian who carried it into the shop not know what he had? Possible, but prodigiously unlikely.

"Here's this painting," Cox went on. "It disappears for fifty years—I mean, fifty *years*?—and then it gets unloaded in some junky pawnshop? For a hundred bucks? Why?"

I stiffened. Simeon Pawlovsky's shop wasn't "some junky pawnshop," I wanted to tell him. Only, of course it was.

"Sergeant, I don't have any idea," I said. "But the guy who came back for it obviously knew it was worth something. Enough to kill Simeon over it. And come damn near killing me."

Cox sighed, dropped the ballpoint he'd been fiddling with, and leaned back in his chair. "And then there's another thing: Okay, assume both these guys worked for the mafia, and the mafia decided it made some kind of mistake and wanted the painting back. Wouldn't you think the guy who pawned it in the first place would just come on back with his ticket and get it out of hock? Wouldn't that have been a whole hell of a lot easier?"

All I could do was shrug and shake my head. I didn't have any answer for him.

"No theory, huh?"

I laughed. "No theory. I'm afraid you're on your own there."

"Well, I'll tell you the truth, Mr. Revere. What you've been telling me is damn interesting, and I'll see that we look into it. But—Look, Pawlovsky was a friend of yours, and it's only natural for you to want his death to *mean* something, to be significant, if you understand what I'm saying. But I see a lot of these things, a lot, and ninety-nine times out of a hundred they turn out to be just what they look like. Some shithead druggie needs a few hundred bucks, and he sees all these rings and jewelry in the store, and nobody but this old crippled guy in the place—"

"Are you serious? You don't think it had anything to do with the painting? You think that was just a coincidence?"

"Look at it this way. Shithead walks into store to rob it. Sees young, healthy guy there—you—and takes off. Comes back later to do the job when the old man's alone. And of course he'd try to get into the safe, wouldn't he? Where else would the most valuable things be? So—"

"Sergeant, this guy was wearing a suit and tie. How many people breaking into a pawnshop for drug money wear suits and ties?"

"All right, maybe it wasn't drug money; that was just an example. All I'm trying to say is that the last thing we need to do right now is bring in World War Two, and Hitler, and the Russian mafia. Believe me, I've got more than enough on my plate as it is. Let's try and keep things simple, okay? At least for a start."

He straightened up with a tired smile and held out his hand, ready to move on to someone or something else. "Don't worry, you can be sure we'll do everything we can to nail this guy. I want to thank you—"

"Sergeant, can you tell me some more about...I don't really know how Simeon died. Was he...was he beaten to death?"

He settled back again and sighed. "That's about it. We don't have the M.E.'s final report yet, but it's fairly clear what happened. There's some pretty bad abdominal bruising, a detached collarbone, and probably some busted internal organs. Fists, probably. I'd guess the creep tried to beat the combination out of him."

"God," I said miserably. "Oh, dear God." I leaned my forehead on my hand, feeling sick.

Because it *was* my fault. Cox might not think so, but I knew in my heart that it was.

"He was an old man," he said in an effort to be kind. "It wouldn't have taken much."

"Sergeant," I said unevenly, "there's got to be something I can do to help with this. Broken ribs are no big deal." (I can lie when I need to.) "If there's any way that I can assist, anything at all I can do..."

He looked at me inquiringly, lips pursed, but I didn't know what I had in mind any more than he did. All I knew was that I was shaking with remorse and guilt and that I longed with all my heart to be Simeon's avenging angel.

"Well, I suppose it might help if you could tell me, you know, a little more about the painting," he said vaguely. "It couldn't hurt. Who knows, maybe this is the one case in a hundred."

I knew this was basically a benevolent sort of make-work, but I jumped at the idea. "You mean the provenance—where it came from, who owned it before, that kind of thing?"

"Sure, yes, that kind of thing. You said the Nazis took it in 1942. Well, who'd they take it from? For that matter, who's had it since? You said it *could* be the Russians, but do we know that for a fact?"

Far from it. The information in the López-Rey catalogue had been no help. Sure, it had translated a few of the markings on the back of the canvas, but the most recent entry in the catalogue was a 1902 sale, and even that didn't tell us who'd bought it. It was a century-old dead end.

"In a word," I said, "no."

"Well, is it something you could find out about?"

"I could sure try," I said.

"That's fine, Mr. Revere," Cox said, happy to be getting me out of his hair at last. "That could help a lot, you never know."

I didn't think for a minute that he believed it, but that didn't matter to me. I desperately needed a sense of doing *something,* and this was it. A long shot, but I owed it to Simeon. And as Cox had said, you never knew.

With all the careful preparation that was already becoming second nature, I slowly stood up, or rather levered myself with the help of the desk to a reasonably vertical position. "If we're done, I'll go on back to the research library at the museum right now and get started."

I almost laughed, imagining how dumb that sounded to him. What's the first thing you do when you need a murder solved? Head for the research library at the art museum. Obviously.

But Cox, a nice guy at heart, nodded benignly. "That's good. You do that, Mr. Revere."

CHAPTER 6

First, though, I had the squad car drop me back at my apartment, where I lunched on half a jar of applesauce and one suspect banana, the only food I had that didn't require the opening of a can or a sealed jar, which I didn't dare tackle. Then I used the telephone to arrange to have my car, left in front of the pawnshop the previous evening, driven to the garage I rented on Exeter. I knew by now that I wasn't going to be doing any driving of my own for a while. Another telephone call to arrange a taxi to the museum, and two more codeine tablets to head off the pain, which I could feel hunkering down inside me, waiting for the four-hour relief period to pass and just hoping that I'd forget to take my pills. An hour later I was back at the Hunt Memorial Library, at the same table I'd used the day before, where I managed to put in three hours of research (unproductive) before I had to quit because I couldn't sit upright anymore without wincing.

Much of the next day was spent at the library, too, and the next, so that Friday afternoon, three days after Simeon's death, I was still there, spent and aching, with a depressingly large jumble of thoroughly perused reports and monographs heaped in front of me, no wiser than I'd been when I started. I'd been poring over some fifty-year-old books and articles dealing with the activities of the famed MFA&A—the Monuments, Fine Arts, and Archives Unit—an Anglo-American organization of hastily commissioned art experts created by the United States Army at the end of World War II. Their job had been to fan out over the smoldering, still-dangerous European continent, ferreting out and then restoring to the rightful owners, whether individuals or institutions, the huge hoard of Nazi art plunder. It had been tremendously successful, a prodigious and unprecedented task of investigation, logistics, and Eliot Ness-like integrity that remains one of the justifiably proud achievements of American and English military history.

This is not to say, however, that their prose style was anything to write home about, and three hours of immersion in the stuff had left me with eyeballs glassy and mind benumbed. All without finding a single reference, even an indirect reference, to the *The Count of Torrijos*.

And why, you may well ask, would I have expected to find one in the MFA&A material

81

anyway? If it was the Russians and not the British or Americans who recovered the painting in 1945, as I was guessing, why wasn't I looking through the Soviet records? But the sorry fact is that whatever loot the Russians got their hands on had been summarily relooted by them, gone straight back to the Soviet Union as war booty, and stayed there, most likely in a museum, or a KGB warehouse, or the home of some high-level Party apparatchik.

Naturally enough, the Soviet authorities had not been anxious to publish reports on the operations of their aptly named Trophy Brigades, so my only hope-growing slimmer by the hour-for coming up with any kind of lead was to go through the American material on the off chance that they had come across the painting at some point before the Russians had gotten hold of it, or else that my guess was wrong and the Russians *didn't* get hold of it. Anyway, what choice did I have?

But I felt like the drunk in the old joke, down on his knees under a street lamp, feverishly searching for his keys. A passerby, stopping to help, asks him where exactly he thinks he might have dropped them. "Over there," the drunk says, pointing to a dimly lit stretch of sidewalk halfway up the darkened block. "Well, then why are you looking for them over here?" the passerby asks. The drunk pauses to direct a pitying look up at him. "And jusht how," he asks, "am I shupposed to find 'em inna dark?"

Like the drunk, I had been looking where there was light, and like him I hadn't found anything. Now I was down to my last few listings in the computer catalogue. I filled out the request slips and went to the desk.

The librarian, with plenty of time to see me hobbling toward her, greeted me with an arch look. "Do you mean we still have something you haven't checked out, Dr. Revere?"

"Amazingly enough, Valerie, yes. But this is the last batch, I promise."

She raised her eyes toward the chandeliers. "God be praised. All right, it'll be about ten minutes."

"Fine. I'm going to get a cup of coffee. You can leave the stuff at my table."

"Assuming I can find room."

The tall, tart-tongued Valerie Zwirn and I were old friends. I was a known quantity at the museum, having worked there first as associate curator and then as curator of Northern European paintings for three years before concluding that museum administration wasn't for me. That had been a few years after concluding that entrepreneurship wasn't for me, and a few months before concluding that university teaching wasn't for me. Finding my life's work was proving a little elusive, but no one could say I hadn't been trying. And if nothing else, I was getting better, or at any rate faster, at deciding what *wasn't* for me: four years as a businessman, three years as a museum administrator, nine months as a professor. I call that progress.

Trish, my ex-wife, probably wouldn't agree. She had married me when we were both graduate students at Boston University, she in sociology, I in art history, and when I stumbled on a way to (barely) keep body and soul together by selling Italian Renaissance art posters by mail-talk about niche marketing-she had been all for it. Amazingly, the mail-order business took off to the extent that I had to drop out of school to run it, in partnership with two other young go-getters. But despite its amazing success it was all luck on my part; I was never quite sure of what I was doing right and never very happy at it. I kept trying to understand how I'd become a businessman, of all things. To be sure, it wasn't a bad life, but it wasn't my life.

So, against Trish's judgment, I insisted on selling our interest in it for a ridiculously large amount of money (I'm still living, reasonably comfortably-well, quite comfortably-off my share of the income from the resulting investments) and went back to school at the age of thirty-four to complete my Ph.D., filled with enthusiasm for seventeenth-century painting and eager to embark on my life's career as a curator, or so I thought. Six years and two jobs later, when I decided not to renew my teaching contract at Harvard, my ambitious, goal-directed, justifiably fed-up wife of eight years decided she'd had it. We separated last year and were divorced a few months later. I wasn't happy about it, but I didn't argue either. I mean, who could deny that she had a point?

In the museum's second-floor restaurant I ordered coffee and a slice of hot apple pie with cheese to go with my pain pills and moped, hardly for the first time, about my state of mind since Trish had left. The fact was, I'd just about had it with her, too, particularly after she'd become a "certified organizational development facilitator" and had started giving and taking "enabling workshops" one or sometimes two weekends a month. I know, I know, that doesn't sound so bad, but, you see, she brought the stuff home with her, and how long, after all, can you go on living in amiable companionship with someone who sits across the breakfast table from you and earnestly tells you that your problem—or rather, one of your problems—is that you have never had the courage to nourish your inner soil properly? And goes on from there, in all seriousness, to expound on the appropriate "fertilizers" and "nutrients" that are needed?

So the time had come to part, and yet there was no arguing with the fact that I'd been in a black funk ever since. There had been a time when I'd been head over heels in love with Trish, and although that time had passed, nothing had ever replaced it, and the divorce had left me numbed and aimless. In the year and more since then, my relationship with Simeon-those chats, the occasional walks-had helped me over the roughest spots in a way that I hadn't really been aware of until after he was dead. I'd been under the impression that I'd been stopping in because he was the one who needed a friend, but now I wasn't so sure.

In any case, there was no doubting that Simeon's death was the first thing in all that time to really touch me, to move me to any kind of meaningful action, if you could call my progress so far meaningful. I'd been getting lazy and reclusive, my eating habits had gone to hell (I'd put on twelve pounds in ten months), and I hadn't been able to regroup my resources enough or summon up enough energy to get my life going in any particular direction. I hadn't especially wanted to, when it came down to it.

Having concluded this stimulating and productive bout of self-exploration, I took the long way back to the library through my old domain, European Paintings, stopping for a few moments in front of the two fine, glowing Velàzquezes in the Koch Gallery to clear my mind and make myself remember that it was art I was researching, not yellowing old army documents.

When I got back to my library table, I found the new pile neatly stacked and waiting for me. With a sigh I settled slowly into my chair and opened the topmost volume.

Two hours later, my eyelids drooping and my reserves just about drained, I came upon my first clue, the first indication that maybe I was on the right track after all: a brief, tantalizing footnote-an aside, really-in a 1950 article in the *College Art Journal* by a one-time MFA&A officer. In writing about the postwar recovery of a large religious canvas painted by Velàzquez, he noted, "For an even more intriguing story involving two other paintings by this artist, viz., *The Count of Torrijos* and *The Countess of Torrijos,* see RG 239, CIR 64."

That, I knew, meant U.S. Army Records Group 239, Consolidated Interrogation Report 64. Wide awake now, I scribbled the words and numbers on a slip of paper and went painfully to the desk once more.

Valerie looked at it and shook her head. "Sorry, you've finally hit on something we don't have."

"I know you don't, but the National Archives does. You can order Xeroxes from them. I'll pay the costs."

"Oh, I think we can work something out for you," she said. "You're one of our best customers."

THAT WAS FRIDAY. ON Monday I was back at my table with a single quarter-inch-thick sheaf of photocopied papers in front of me. The resourceful Valerie Zwirn had even had them bound in an Acco binder. The typewritten label pasted on the front was oversized to accommodate the oversized title:

Records Group 239. Records of the American Commission for the Protection and Salvage of Artistic and Historic Monuments in War Areas. Consolidated

Interrogation Report No. 64.
Respondent, Dr. Erhard Haftmann,
Chief Registrar, Altaussee Mine
Repository, Altaussee, Austria.
Interrogation Conducted at Special
Interrogation Center, Altaussee, During
the Period 10-21 June 1945. Subject:
Truckload No. N30, Unaccounted for.
(Appendix: Inventory of Contents.)

It was the inventory I wanted to see first, so I flipped past the body of the report, turning directly to the appendix, which had been translated from the German records.

And almost at once I found what I had been looking for:

Velàzquez, *The Count of Torrijos*. 94 cm. X 63 cm. No signature. "El Conde de Torrijos" inscribed at bottom. Repaired knife-cut(?), upper left, damage not considered significant. December 1942.

Bingo. At long last, bingo. It was the same painting, all right, and it was the Americans and not the Russians who had found it after all, which meant that they had disposed of it and kept records, which meant that there would be at least the beginning of a trail leading forward, not back, from World War II; a place to start, maybe even people to talk-I paused in mid-self-congratulation. What was that in the title about something "unaccounted for"?

But the title wasn't any clearer on the second reading than on the first. Uneasily I opened the report to start at the beginning. The interrogation had been conducted by a Captain Singer, and on page two it got down to the meat of it:

CAPT. SINGER: You said earlier that on April 19 one truckload failed to arrive with the convoy from Neuschwanstein?

DR. HAFTMANN: One consignment, yes.

CAPT. SINGER: And how did this come about?

DR. HAFTMANN: It was a time of terrible confusion and disorder. I was expecting thirty-five consignments, but only thirty-four arrived. The convoy master could not explain.

CAPT. SINGER: And of what did this consignment consist?

DR. HAFTMANN: Paintings, mostly acquired in Austria and France. It included a Giorgione, a Hals, several Velàzquezes, some of the Venetian masters....Naturally I have the bill of lading and inventory that were prepared at the place of embarkation. ;obSee appendix.;cb You understand, at the time of which we are speaking, order had completely broken down. It was a great tragedy, there was no one to exercise control.

CAPT. SINGER: Please tell me the eventual outcome of this incident.

DR. HAFTMANN: There was no eventual outcome. The consignment never arrived. I had neither the authority nor the means to hunt for it. It disappeared, that is all. A casualty of the war. If you had any idea of the tremendous, the enormous, difficulties...

I put down the report. Obviously the codeine wasn't doing my mind any good, because it had taken me all this time to finally figure out what I was reading about. This was the celebrated Lost Truck, the single truckload of masterpieces that had somehow gone astray between its wartime storage point in Mad Ludwig's Neuschwanstein Castle and its destination, the vast, bombproof underground caverns of the Altaussee salt mine high in the Austrian Alps. In the art world it was a famous story. The Nazis, reeling and near defeat, had frantically worked to hide their stolen treasures from the invading Allies. Truck convoys loaded with the cultural wealth of the Western world had poured into the mine compound in an unending stream, adding their loads to what was already the most phenomenal hoard of art ever gathered in one place.

But with Russian troops encroaching from the east and the British and Americans closing in from the south, the vaunted efficiency of the Nazis had broken down, giving way to tumult and disarray. Records were lost, objects miscatalogued. Frustration and confusion had run high.

In the commotion, sometime during the afternoon of April 19, 1945, one truck, its driver, and its priceless payload had vanished in a snowstorm. Without a trace.

"Unaccounted for."

It hadn't taken long for it to become the object of articles and conjectures by journalists, conspiracy theorists, neo-Nazis, victims'-rights groups, charlatans. "The legendary Lost Truck," it was endlessly, tiresomely called, and for a decade or two, before it dropped from the popular imagination, rumors of its treasures being glimpsed in Prague, or Tokyo, or Moscow, or Berlin frequently turned up, briefly making the newspapers before petering out to nothing.

In fact, only one of the pieces had ever been seen again. In 1995 the Hermitage Museum in St. Petersburg, in a celebrated (and temporary) burst of Russian openness, had put on an exhibition of a small portion of the art seized by them in 1945, which had lain in secret storage ever since, unknown to all but a very few government officials. (Even the director of the Hermitage had been kept in the dark.) I had been working at the Museum of Fine Arts at the time and had gone with a planeload of American curators to St. Petersburg to see the show. One of the fifty paintings, a brilliant, near-abstract oil by J. M. W. Turner of a colossal storm at sea, had been quickly recognized as part of the Lost Truck's payload, but the Russians had denied all knowledge of any lost truck, refusing to provide any further information at all. And so, along with everything else, this marvelous work had gone back underground when the exhibition closed, never to be seen again.

And now this: *El Conde de Torrijos,* only

the second object ever to surface from the truck. A Velàzquez, no less. As an art historian, I couldn't have been more excited.

But as a detective, I'd struck out. I still had no idea how the painting had found its way to Simeon's shop, or why, or who the Russian was who had brought it in, or where it had been since April 19, 1945. What's more, I had run out of places to look; the Lost Truck was as lost as it ever was.

And as for being an avenging angel, I was a complete bust.

CHAPTER 7

Or maybe I wasn't. The more I thought about it after I got home, the more I thought that maybe I wasn't a total bust, maybe I had come up with something after all.

If nothing else, I now knew that the only two paintings from the Lost Truck that had ever been seen again both had Russian connections. Didn't that make it a pretty good bet that the entire shipment had fallen into Soviet hands in 1945? And if that were so, then wasn't it possible that, by finding out more about one of them, I might come up with something useful about the other? If, for example, I could discover how that Turner had found its way to the Hermitage and where it had been all these years, then I'd have at least a start to put me on the track of the

Velàzquez. And as it happened, I thought I had a way I could do that.

When I'd been in St. Petersburg for the exhibition in 1995, I'd gotten to know Yuri Minkov, one of the younger assistant curators and an all-around good egg. He, I, and fifteen others from half a dozen countries had made a highly convivial night of it over caviar, piroshki, and vodka at the old Metropole restaurant. We'd sat across from each other, and although his English wasn't much better than my Russian, we both knew enough German and French for us to get on well enough, especially after the fourth round of vodka.

Yuri was one of Russia's lively new breed of art curators, born twenty-five years after the end of the Second World War and a devoted fan of Hootie and the Blowfish. For Yuri the Nazis were schoolbook history, about as relevant as the invasion of the Mongol hordes in 1237. As far as he was concerned, Russia was long overdue to return its cache of wartime art booty to the families and institutions it had originally been looted from—even the Germans— and let the past be the past. This was not the view of the government or of his museum superiors, however, and when the show closed, the paintings had vanished again with very little having been revealed about them.

But I'd been impressed with Yuri's attitude, and with his openness in front of a patently disapproving senior curator. And so

I hoped that he'd be willing to talk to me now, especially if he understood why I was asking questions.

Given the eight-hour time difference between Boston and St. Petersburg and the fact that Yuri had no telephone at home, I had to wait until the next morning to call him at the museum. It took me three tries to get through to the Hermitage, followed by fifteen minutes of yelling "angleeskee" into the telephone and getting cut off twice in the process before I was connected with someone who could speak English and then, finally, with Yuri. Making clear what I wanted was tricky, not only because neither of us was speaking our native language but because I thought it likely that our conversation was being monitored and I didn't want to be too explicit. About a year after the 1995 exhibit I'd heard that he'd been reprimanded for expressing views contrary to official policy, and I didn't want to get him into trouble again.

All the same, I think I was able to get through to him what it was that I was after, and he responded with enthusiasm to the idea of seeing me and maybe even showing me a few pieces I hadn't seen before when I got there. Unfortunately, I told him, that wouldn't be for another three weeks, which was how long it took to get a Russian visa; not necessarily a bad thing in my case, because the doctor had told me it would be another three or four weeks before I became a reasonably mobile human being again.

"Ve itt lawts piroshkis!" Yuri said, treating me to his limited but vigorous store of English. "Ve trinkh lawts vwawdka!"

"*Da, tovarich. Dosvidanya,*" I said, returning the compliment and pretty much exhausting my Russian repertoire.

When I replaced the receiver, I realized that I'd done it at almost normal speed, without even a wince.

I had begun to mend.

"MAY I SPEAK TO Ben Revere, please?" The voice was female, assertive, unfamiliar. I thought it might be someone from the travel agency that was handling my trip to Russia.

"Speaking."

"Mr. Revere, this is Alexandra Porter." A vaguely peremptory rise at the end, as if I were expected to know the name.

"Yes?"

"I'm Simeon Pawlovsky's niece? Or his grandniece, to be technical."

"Oh...yes, hello." It had been over a week since Simeon's death. The murder had been heavily on my mind since then, but I hadn't done anything about it since calling Yuri a couple of days earlier. In the first place, I was in no condition to do anything. In the second place, until I went off to Russia, what was there to do?

"I believe we would have met last week. At least Uncle Simeon told me you'd be coming to dinner with us. He did invite you, didn't he?"

"Oh, yes, that's right, he did. I...I was looking forward to it." It wasn't only that I didn't have the nerve to tell her I'd turned her uncle down cold, but after what had happened, what would have been the point? Also, I didn't have the nerve.

"I'm sorry about your uncle," I said. "I liked him a lot." That much was true anyway.

"Yes, he felt the same about you." Her manner was direct, her voice a little too loud. A junior executive on the rise, wanting to make sure she was taken seriously, I thought. I guessed that she was in her mid-twenties, probably fairly attractive, and not lacking for self-esteem. "Look," she said, "the reason I'm calling is that I'd like very much to talk to you about him. Do you suppose we might get together?"

"Well...okay, sure." Not the most civil response in the world, but aside from feeling too lousy for socializing, I wasn't feeling any too keen on assertive women, attractive or otherwise. I mean, I'm all for self-affirmation and so forth, but Trish had had enough of the stuff to last me the rest of my natural life and then some.

"Are you free now?" Alexandra Porter asked. Demanded.

"You mean this minute?"

"Yes. Well, unless you're tied up, of course."

I glanced into the living room, where I'd plumped up a couple of pillows on the sofa to make a daybed for myself in front of the TV. On the coffee table next to it was my dinner, a bag of chili-and-cheese-flavored Fritos and half a bottle of screw-top Chianti. (Yes, I know, a moderately assertive Puligny-Montrachet would have been the preferred accompaniment, but I was unaccountably out of Puligny-Montrachet at the time.) When the phone rang, I had been lying back tossing chips into my mouth and absentmindedly watching a skeet-shooting tournament from Spain on ESPN.

"No, I think I can make the time," I said. I hoped she couldn't hear the television. "Um, would you like to meet for a cup of coffee? A glass of wine?"

"That's fine. You name the place."

"Well, where are you calling from?"

"I'm just finishing up at my office. Anywhere would be fine. Someplace near where you live. You're in Back Bay, aren't you?"

"Yes. All right, there's an Italian restaurant on Newbury, near Fairfield. Outdoor tables—"

"I know the place-it's called Ciao Bella, right? Fifteen minutes?"

"Better make it thirty."

I hung up and went reluctantly into the bedroom to take off the sweats I was wearing and put on a shirt and a pair of chinos. People sure do change, I was thinking. Once upon a time the prospect of meeting an interesting-sounding new female over a glass of wine would have put a sparkle in my eye and a tune on my lips.

Now, all things considered, I'd just as soon have watched the skeet shooting.

CHAPTER 8

The avenue I live on, Commonwealth, is a broad, stately thoroughfare lined with handsome, turn-of-the-century apartment buildings (most of which, like mine, are now broken up into smallish condos), and with a parklike, lushly treed mall running down the middle, complete with pensive bronze statues of eminent personages—Alexander Hamilton, Leif Eriksson, William Lloyd Garrison, to name a few—at each corner. It was designed to look like an upscale Parisian boulevard, and it does. Right around the corner and down the block, however, is sprawling Newbury Street, as American as they come, with wall-to-wall restaurants, cafés, boutiques, and art galleries at street level, apartments for college students and not-yet-upwardly-mobile young professionals above, and on the sidewalks a never-ending flow of street life ranging from the trendy to the eccentric to the downright wacko.

Given my rather deliberate tread these days, I had allowed fifteen minutes to walk the block and a half to get there, but I surprised myself by making it in less than ten, arriving early. So I lowered myself into a chair at one of the sidewalk tables, ordered a glass of Chianti, and sat back to observe the Newbury fauna, always an absorbing occupation, and to wait for Simeon's niece to appear.

I'd been expecting a young exec on the

rise, a businesswoman with an attaché case, someone lean and tightly put together, compact and decisive in movement and posture—a younger variant of Simeon, I suppose; or maybe of Trish, come to think of it—so that when the big, strapping, leggy woman in delicately faded, neatly pressed blue jeans, white knit shirt, and yellow summer sweater knotted casually around her waist loped in, I gave her no more than a stranger's distant half-smile and kept looking up the street, searching—so I thought—for Alexandra.

But she was better at this than I was, coming straight up to my table. "Hi, I'm Alex. Thanks for meeting me."

I'd missed her age, too, by a decade; she was in her thirties, not her twenties, a robust, outdoorsy kind of woman, more milkmaid than executive, more handsome than pretty. Junoesque was the term that came to mind. Or maybe Amazonian, if you were feeling unkind.

"Hiya, Alex, nice to meet you," I said, indicating by this attitude of insouciant nonchalance that of course I'd recognized her on the spot.

She caught the waiter's eye. "Can I get a white wine, please?" With a sigh she sat down opposite me. "Whew, hot." She didn't look hot, she looked as if she'd just stepped out of a cool shower.

"Sure is, but not too muggy, fortunately. August can be a killer when it's humid."

"Not just August. We've had heat waves in

the middle of September. Remember last year?"

"Yes, but it's been a cool summer so far. Maybe it'll hold."

"Let's hope so."

So much for nimble, witty banter. She looked at her hands. I looked at my wine-glass and—surreptitiously—at her. She had a wide mouth, an oddly appealing ski-jump nose that didn't go with her telephone personality and somehow kept making me want to smile, and wide-set gray-green eyes, all of which went surprisingly well together. If I hadn't known about her Russian background I'd have tabbed her as Swedish or Norwegian. Her straight, streaky-blond hair was loosely pulled back and tied into a simple ponytail, your basic, clean-cut Thomas Jefferson look. Large, capable hands, with nails cut short and unpolished. And no wedding or engagement ring. That perked me up—I mean the fact that I'd noticed; it's always nice to realize you're still alive enough after all to show some interest.

"First of all," she said abruptly, "I'd like to thank you for what you did—what you tried to do—for my uncle last week. Sergeant Cox told me you'd been hurt, but I didn't realize..." She gestured in the direction of my face, which was in better shape than it had been a few days ago, but was still puffy and bruised, with two glossy, swollen black eyes.

"Me, hurt? Not at all; my head always looks like an eggplant."

Either she didn't hear me or she didn't find it worth laughing at. "How well did you know my uncle?"

"Not that well, really. I'd stop by to say hello once in a while, that's all. We met a couple of years ago, over a stolen painting that had shown up in his shop." I shrugged. "And we just seemed to hit it off."

Why, I had never been quite sure. I guess I liked his self-sufficiency and his funny good sense. And, I suppose, the fact that he sounded so much like my dimly remembered grandmother and grandfather—tiny Bubbe with her dowdy, ink-black wig, and the kind but imperious Zayde—who had fled Russia even longer ago than Simeon had, in the bad old days of the Romanovs; bad for the Jews anyway. As for what Simeon had liked about me, I couldn't say. I think part of it must have been that I represented a kind of walking American Dream to him. A penniless, barely literate young Jew escapes over the Turkish border from Russia in 1912, one step ahead of rampaging Cossacks—and two generations later his grandson has a Ph.D. after his name, knows his way around art museums and good society, and is even treated with respect and deference by a big-city police department.

Not that a little wasn't lost in the process. "Bubbe" and "Zayde" were now pretty close to the sum total of my Yiddish, and my Russian was nonexistent (Zayde wouldn't allow it to be spoken in his presence). My religious education had ended at thirteen with my bar mitzvah—which my far-from-religious father put me through mainly to pacify Zayde—after which I could hardly wait to get everything I'd learned in Hebrew school out of my mind as quickly as possible, at which effort I'd been successful.

"Did you know about his life?" she asked. "I mean, before he came to America."

I shook my head. "I know he came from Novgorod. That's about it."

"Yes, that's right, Novgorod. We still have family there, did you know that? My cousin is actually the deputy mayor there now." She smiled. "Simeon still can't believe a Jew could possibly be deputy mayor. He says..." Her eyelids lowered; the sentence died away. She'd forgotten he was dead, something I understood because I kept doing it myself.

"I know," I said gently, "it's hard to accept."

It didn't take her long to collect herself. A sip of wine, a little sigh, and she was her competent self again. "And after he left Novgorod?" she said. "He didn't tell you about that?"

"It's not the kind of thing he talked about to me."

"No, it's not the kind of thing he talked about to anybody. My Uncle Simeon had quite a life, though."

And over our wine and a plate of fried calamari that we ordered to go with it, she told me about it. It took half an hour. The barely touched calamari grew cold.

Simeon had been a young soldier, hardly

more than a child, in the Russian Army during World War II. Captured by the Germans during the terrible fighting at Smolensk, he had spent most of the war in Mauthausen, a German concentration camp specifically reserved for Soviet prisoners and other persons officially classified as *Rückkehr unerwünscht*—"return not desired"—where conditions were unspeakable even by Nazi standards. Still, he had managed to survive, only to return, sick, starving, and in rags to a victorious Russia that didn't even acknowledge his return, let alone desire it. There were no parades, no commendations, no stipends for Simeon and his hundreds of thousands of fellow prisoners of war; the Moscow government formally refused to admit that any Russian soldier would have been cowardly enough to give up rather than die for the motherland.

It had taken him two years to get his health back. He had married a nurse and gone to work in Novgorod, first in a shoe factory and then in a glove factory, where he eventually rose to assistant manager of production. Somewhere along the line, however, he was accused of "deviating." He was tried, convicted, and sentenced to two years in a so-called mental institution followed by six years' hard labor in a penal factory in Siberia, where his leg was accidentally broken in five places by a stamping machine and he later lost half of his right foot to frostbite.

In 1963, soon after being freed, he had

fled Russia with his family, escaping through Poland and East Germany to Israel. But he had arrived alone and broken. His wife and fifteen-year-old son had been killed by border guards in the final desperate dash from East to West. It was a loss from which he never fully recovered, physically or emotionally.

Five years later, with the help of his nephew, Alex's father, he had come to the United States and had worked as a bathroom attendant and janitor, living with Alex's family when she was a little girl and saving almost everything he earned beyond paying for his room and board. Two years after that he had moved out, opening the pawnshop and settling into a solitary residence in the seedy rooms behind the store. He had never found the heart to remake his life in any significant way, but ten years later, his gift to Alex when she started college had been a check for ten thousand dollars.

Tears trembled on her eyelashes a couple of times as she spoke, but she brushed them away with a fingertip before they welled over. When she wound down, we had the waiter take the soggy calamari away and ordered some more wine. She smiled at me for the first time, a sweet smile, almost shy. Her mouth was wide, her teeth large and square, with one front incisor very slightly overlapping the other, but it was an attractively feminine smile all the same, fresh and healthy-looking, like everything else about her.

"Thanks for letting me run on like that. You're a good listener."

"Why did you tell me all that?" I asked.

It came out more disagreeably than I'd intended, but as I said it I realized that I was in fact feeling disagreeable. Disagreeable, chagrined, sullen—I didn't know what else. I was genuinely upset over having thought that I'd known the man and yet known nothing of the awful afflictions he'd lived through. I hadn't known and I hadn't been interested enough to ask or even to wonder; for me he'd been a sweet old guy running a pawnshop, period. And more than that, I was embarrassed that my own pampered, self-indulgent life had been so free of tragedy and despair and his so filled with them.

And then, naturally, I was annoyed at Alex for being the cause of my feeling like such a complete crud about it all.

At my tone, her smile disappeared. "I thought you might be interested," she said coldly. "I was under the impression that he meant something to you." It was as if an iron shutter had come clunking down over those clear, gray-green eyes.

Terrific, I thought, good going. Benny Revere, charmer. "I only meant that you must have something in mind," I said, smoothing the waters, but not much. "Is there something I can do?"

"Yes, as a matter of fact. I've been talking to Ron Cox at the police department. He puts a good face on things, but I can see they're not getting anywhere."

"Well, there's not much to go on."

"He told me you've been helping with the investigation. I thought perhaps—"

"Helping with the investigation is over-stating it," I said modestly. I told her what I'd found out about the Velàzquez and about my call to Yuri.

She looked at me expectantly, waiting for more, but of course there wasn't anything else. "And that's it?" she said. "You're not doing anything else? You haven't done anything since?" Alex wasn't exactly silver-tongued herself.

"Such as what?" I asked testily. (Now I was mad in addition to everything else.) "I spent three days in the damn library, aching every minute. I told the police everything I found out. I'm going to St. Petersburg just as soon as I can get a visa. What else would you suggest?"

"Simeon was murdered here," she said coldly, "not in St. Petersburg."

"So?"

"So I'd think the place to look would be here."

"Look? For what?"

"I don't know—clues, leads....I'm no cop, you're supposed to be the cop."

I blinked. "*I'm* a cop?"

"He used to talk about you a lot," she said, her expression softening a little. "You meant a lot to him. He was really proud of you. I remember an article he cut out of the paper to show me. 'Museum's Paintings Back Home, Thanks to Boston's Art Cop.' That was you."

"Take my word for it," I said wryly, "it's not the same kind of cop."

She frowned at her wineglass, slowly rotating it on the table. "Do you know why Sergeant Cox thinks Simeon was killed? Did he tell you his theory?"

I nodded. *Shithead robs pawnshop.* "A simple, everyday burglary that went wrong," I said. "Nothing to do with the painting."

"Yes, but you know that's not true."

"Alex, I don't *know* anything, and neither do you. For all we do know—"

She stared incredulously at me. "Are you seriously suggesting that my uncle wasn't murdered because of your precious Velàzquez?"

I glared back at her. *My* precious Velàzquez? "Wait a minute, don't you think this is getting a little—"

"Look, I'm not interested in getting into an argument with you. My only point is that Sergeant Cox may know all about murder, but he doesn't know beans about art and he doesn't care. He's going to be looking in all the wrong places, don't you see that?"

"No, I don't see that." I did, of course, but she'd riled up my contrary impulses. "And anyway, *I* don't know beans about homicide investigations, so I'm following up the only way I know how."

"By going to St. Petersburg to ask somebody some questions about a Turnbull—"

"Turner."

"—that was stolen fifty years ago, for God's sake, and has probably been in Russia ever since? Pardon me, but the connection seems a little tenuous."

"Sure it's tenuous," I said hotly, "you think I don't know that? It'll probably be a complete waste of effort, but I'm willing to spend my time and my money trying it precisely because Simeon *did* mean something to me. And, forgive my saying so, but I don't hear you coming up with any better ideas." The damn woman had really gotten my goat.

I expected her to respond in kind, but instead she merely looked at me with a pitying sort of smile, just to indicate I'd let her down, then stood up, put fifteen dollars on the table to cover her share, and held out her hand. "Well, thanks for talking to me anyway."

Ordinarily, being old-school, I would have insisted on picking up the tab, but this time I didn't. I had a hunch it just would have set her off again. "Alex," I said, taking her cool, dry fingers, "you couldn't want Simeon's murderer caught any more than I do. Believe me, I'll be doing everything I can. And I wouldn't sell Cox short."

She smiled at me, not really unfriendly now, only distant and ready to be gone. "Good-bye, then. And good luck."

Feeling thoroughly ill used and out of sorts, I finished my wine, levered myself painfully up from the chair, and started on the long, slow, one-block trek to my apartment.

CHAPTER 9

Two more weeks passed. My Russian visa came through; I was cleared to arrive in St. Petersburg as of September 19, another five days. Meanwhile, time dragged. A couple of articles about the painting appeared in the paper, and then the story, in the nature of such things, disappeared. The police made no apparent progress. Sergeant Cox never got in touch with me again. While my ribs slowly knitted, I frittered away my time, eating junk food, getting no exercise, watching too much baseball (but no ice dancing yet, knock on wood), drinking too much wine every evening, going to bed every night angry at myself for wasting another day of my life, and swearing that I was going to get organized for sure when I got back from Russia. Or to put it another way, things returned to normal.

However, I did manage, by dint of intermittent episodes of self-discipline, to keep rolling on the nearest thing I had to steady work, namely, *Samuel van Hoogstraten: The Illusionist of Dordrecht,* my book on the capable but obscure Dutch painter whose chief claim to fame was having been a student of Rembrandt's.

Actually, "keep rolling" is a slight exaggeration. Hoogstraten had been one of the subjects in a Dutch painting exhibition I'd curated when I was at the museum, and in a momentary fit of egotism I had afterward signed a contract to turn my catalogue notes and a subsequent article into a book for Sfumato Press, an art publishing house almost as obscure as Hoogstraten himself. The advance was $850 (to be paid on acceptance of the manuscript), and as the months wore on, my interest, never exactly passionate to begin with, had waned, until now I worked on the thing perhaps six or eight hours a week, usually in the afternoons. It wasn't as if I needed the money, after all—I could easily live, in the not-overly-lavish manner to which I was accustomed, on the income from my art-poster investments and an occasional windfall from a consulting job. And it sure wasn't as if the art world was champing at the bit for a new Hoogstraten monograph. When it came down to it, as I knew all too well, the reason I was still working on it at all was that it would have been more trouble to look into breaking the contract than it was to keep plodding away.

Anyhow, I was plodding away early one afternoon when I heard the mouselike scratchings of the fax machine across the room. As always when working on Hoogstraten, I was easy to distract, but you have to let these bossy machines know who's in charge, so I ignored it and took my own good time finishing up a paragraph while a sheet of paper stuttered its way out of the machine, flopped into the tray, and lay waiting.

It was a formal letter, not a fax form, with a letterhead consisting of a crest with a two-headed eagle and the words *Albrecht, Graf Stetten,* in Gothic lettering. No address.

Graf. Count. How about that, first the Count of Torrijos and now the Count of Stetten. Suddenly, I was up to my eyeballs in counts. I settled back into my chair to read it.

My Dear Dr. Revere:

I have read with great interest the news accounts of the Velàzquez portrait that has recently come to light in Boston. I was particularly interested in the role you played in identifying it and in your knowledgeable references to the lost truck from Altaussee.

It is my belief that this painting, like the others on that truck, was confiscated from my family's Paris residence by German occupation forces in December 1942. At that time they removed a total of seventy-three paintings, including major works by Giorgione, Hals, Poussin, Tintoretto, Goya, Watteau, and others, for which I have been searching without success since the end of the war. You can imagine my excitement upon reading about the Velàzquez.

More exciting still, yesterday I was contacted by a Czech art dealer who claims to have in his possession a second painting from my father's collection (in fact, the companion portrait to *El Conde de Torrijos*), which he has offered to me, assuming that satisfactory terms can be reached. I wonder, therefore, if you might be willing to assist me in a preliminary assessment of its authenticity? This would necessarily involve a brief visit to the Continent. Naturally, I would expect to pay all costs, as well as a reasonable fee for your assistance.

You may reach me by telephone or fax at my Salzburg residence: 43-662-84-85-71. I do hope this matter interests you.

Yours sincerely,
Albrecht von Stetten

You bet the matter interested me; how could it not? I'd put in years of research on the theft of art in the Second World War; how could I pass up the chance to actually play a part in its recovery? Even if I'd never known Simeon Pawlovsky, I'd have jumped at the chance.

But of course I had known Simeon, and it was Simeon that was at the front of my mind now. It could hardly be a coincidence that not even three weeks after Simeon was bludgeoned to death over a painting from the Lost Truck, up pops another one—the only two, aside from the Turner in the Hermitage, to show up in half a century. Surely, surely there was a connection between them. By taking Stetten up on his offer I could work on finding a link to Simeon's murder from two opposite directions—forward from the past by means of the trip to St. Petersburg, and backward from the present by helping Stetten with his painting. Neither one of them the most direct route to finding a murderer, perhaps, but despite Cox's reservations I was as sure as ever that the Velàzquez in Simeon's safe was at the heart of what had happened to him. That had been the one thing on which Alex Porter and I had been in agreement.

I read the letter again while going to the kitchen to touch up my coffee. "The companion portrait"—that rang a bell. Hadn't the *catalogue raisonné* made some reference to *El Conde de Torrijos*'s having been painted as one of a pair? I'd have to go back to the library if I wanted to see the *catalogue*, but at least I had the MFA&A report right there in my desk. It took me only a second to open a desk drawer, find my neatly labeled Velàzquez file—I might not be the most focused person in the world, but I'm organized—and pull out my copy of the MFA&A report on the Lost Truck. I turned quickly to the inventory.

And there it was, right below *The Count of Torrijos*.

F-8. Velàzquez, *The Countess of Torrijos*. 93 cm. X 63 cm. No signature. *La Cond^a de Torrijos* inscribed at bottom. December 1942.

A quick scan of the other entries showed that everything on the truck had indeed been acquired by the ERR in 1942. The total number of artworks, however, was 106, not the 73 that Stetten had mentioned, so there had been other people's paintings aboard too.

I dialed an international line and called

Stetten's number. The receiver was picked up on the fourth ring.

"*Guten Abend. Hier bei Graf Stetten.*" The voice was bossy, the tone gruff but proper. The butler? Well, why not? If counts couldn't have butlers, who could?

"*Guten Abend,*" I said. "*Ich möchte ich mit Graf sprechen, bitte. Hier ist Benjamin Revere aus den Vereinigten Staaten.*"

Don't be too impressed. You can't very well be a curator of Northern European painting without knowing some German, and I can understand the spoken and written language, even scientific German, fairly well, but my accent, so they tell me, is pretty atrocious. Some German-speakers have even said that they have trouble understanding it, but no doubt this was in jest.

Fortunately for us both, Count Stetten's English was more than adequate: cultivated and only faintly accented with a pleasing, sophisticated Continental overlay. "Dr. Revere, is that really you? This is Albrecht von Stetten. How good of you to call so quickly! May I hope that my proposition appeals to you?"

He had a thin, timid voice with a slight, pleasant hitch of hesitation in it. I pictured an elderly curate in a Victorian comedy, apple-cheeked, cheerful, innocent, and ever so slightly befuddled.

"It certainly does," I said.

"Excellent. You'll take the job then?"

"Well, I do have some questions—"

"Yes, of course you would. As to the matter of your fee—"

"It's not that, it's just that I'm not sure you're getting the right person. There are some top-notch authorities a lot closer to Salzburg than I am, and, you know, I'm not particularly known as a Velàzquez expert."

"Oh, I know that," he said, laughing. "You're known as a Hoogstraten expert, isn't that so?"

That caught me by surprise, because it told me that this was no spur-of-the-moment contact on his part. He'd taken the trouble to find out about me before getting in touch. On the one hand, I was flattered. On the other, who wants to be known as a Hoogstraten expert?

"I understand that you're also something of an expert on Nazi plunder," he went on, "and that should be a good thing. But the most important thing is that you are the only recognized art authority who's had the opportunity of examining the companion portrait in the last fifty years. In this case, I think such experience is invaluable, don't you?"

Yes, I did, come to think of it. I, alone in the art world as far as either of us knew, was in a position to compare the physical aspects of the two pictures—the colors, the amounts of fading or darkening, the backings (including the labels and markings), the canvases themselves, the overall condition of the works. When you're trying to judge the authenticity of a painting that was originally done as one of a pair, that's a lot of handy information.

"Well, that's true," I said, happy to let him think he was arguing me into it. "Look, can you tell me a little more about what's going on? You said you'd been approached by a Czech dealer?"

"Yes, that's right, a Mr. Zykmund Dulska. I've had him thoroughly looked into."

In one day? I thought. Clearly, Count Stetten had some pretty good resources for looking into people.

"The fellow seems to be a highly reputable dealer with an established business in decorative and fine arts in Prague. It seems he found the piece tucked away in a lot he bought at auction several years ago and only recently discovered its worth. Somehow he learned that it had come from my family's collection and contacted me at once. He wants only to do the right thing, you see. All he's asking is a finder's fee."

Talk about setting off an alarm bell. Not too many art dealers, established or otherwise, go into that shark-infested business because they are possessed of a desire to "do the right thing." And from what I've seen, "finder's fees" usually turn out to be no more than a socially acceptable way of saying "ransom."

The thing is, crooks can find it extremely difficult to unload high-profile stolen art (and any Velàzquez is going to rank as high-profile) on the legitimate market. As a result, they are sometimes forced to go back to the original owner and offer him his property back—for a consideration.

On the other hand, a finder's fee can also be nothing more than what a perfectly upstanding citizen asks as honest recompense for his time and effort in reconnecting a piece of art and its owner. I just can't think of any recent examples, that's all.

"And how much does he want?" I asked.

"How much does he want?" From the blank way he said it, I knew that this was the first time the subject had crossed his mind. "Well, I don't know, really. We didn't discuss it." He paused. "Is it likely to be much?"

"I don't know. Several thousand dollars for sure, probably considerably more. A lot depends on how much he paid for the painting himself." Or rather, how much he claims he paid.

"I see. Hmm. Well, as long as it's no more than...well, I'm sure I'll be able to manage it." But he sounded concerned, which wasn't really surprising. It's been a long time since princely wealth and princely titles necessarily went together. He coughed gently. "Perhaps I'd better ask what *your* fee will be, Dr. Revere."

"Generally, I charge a thousand dollars a day, but—"

"No, please, I can certainly afford that. As long as it doesn't involve too many days, of course."

"If it's a problem, I'm sure we can work something out."

"My dear friend, I was only joking. I don't see why a day or two shouldn't do it, do you? So, are we in agreement? You'll take me on?"

"I will, yes. Did you want me to fly to Prague, then?"

"Oh, we won't be going to Prague. I don't tolerate the stresses of international travel very well these days—the humiliating debilities of age, I'm afraid. So Mr. Dulska has agreed to bring the picture to Vienna. We can meet him there."

More alarm bells. "To Vienna? How does he expect to get it through customs?"

"Customs?" Apparently this was another subject it hadn't occurred to him to give any thought to. "To tell you the truth, I don't know. But that's what he's offered to do, so I suppose it's his problem, not ours, yes? Now, as to timing: Would there be any possibility that you might come this week? I know it's very soon, but I can't begin to tell you how anxious—"

"I can come." Hoogstraten had been waiting three hundred years for his monograph. He could hold out a little longer.

"On Friday? That is to say, perhaps you could fly to Vienna on Thursday so that we could meet with Mr. Dulska the following morning? I can book a room for you at the Imperial."

Friday would work out fine. My Russian visa was good as of Saturday, the very next day, so if I allowed two days for Vienna to be on the safe side, I could fly from there to St. Petersburg on Sunday and meet Yuri on Monday. Perfect. The only thing that worried me a little was that, this being Tuesday, I would have only two days to get my Velàzquez expertise up to snuff, but then we'd already agreed that Velàzquez expertise wasn't the number one priority at this stage. Later on, assuming it passed our initial inspection, the lab experts could have their go at it.

"I'll be there," I said.

"Ah, that's wonderful, thank you."

"But you have to understand: All I can do is make a stab at saying whether or not it's authentic. Even if it is, that won't prove it's really the same painting that was taken from your family's collection. There's no way I can help you there."

"My friend, you let me worry about that."

"Fine. And I assume you'll have some legal help with you?"

"Legal help? Will I need a lawyer?"

"I think it'd be a good idea. These things have a way of getting complicated in a hurry."

He hesitated. "All right, I shall. Ah..." He cleared his throat. "As to Friday evening, do you happen to like opera?"

Well, I do and I don't. Verdi, Puccini, Donizetti, sure, I can float all night on those lush, lilting melodies. But five minutes of Wagner (let alone five hours) and I'm clawing at the arms of my chair. Still, it was obvious that the guy was dying to go and he wanted company. I took my chances and said yes.

"Oh, that's wonderful, wonderful," he said warmly. "They're performing *Rigoletto* at the Staatsoper."

(Whew.)

"I haven't been in years," he chattered happily on. "I don't get into Vienna much anymore, you see, and even then it's unpleasant to go to the opera by oneself. Now the season's just begun, so tickets are hard to come by, but I'll do my best. Good-bye, good-bye!" he sang in his reedy, lively voice. "Until Thursday. And *thank* you!"

I didn't know if he was more excited about his Velàzquez or his Verdi.

CHAPTER 10

This time I spotted her from a block away as she crossed Gloucester Street with the WALK light, her long, confident stride distinguishing her from the slouching, end-of-the-workday mob that crossed with her. We'd been hit with one of our muggy September heat waves after all, the nasty kind that comes after everyone has begun to hope that the worst of the summer is finally past. After-noon temperatures and humidity both had been in the mid-nineties for a week, steam-bath weather, and yet there she was, stepping lightly along at the end of a sopping day, a fresh thoroughbred in a mob of straggling dray horses.

Having never tolerated the heat very well myself, I considered this display of fitness unseemly, almost a personal affront. But the truth is that, despite the naked athleticism, I was pleased to see her. A dozen times since our distinctly unspectacular meeting two weeks earlier she'd popped unbidden into my mind. More than once I'd replayed our conversation, starting over again from the beginning and giving myself lines that would have done a better job of explaining where I was coming from and been a lot snappier to boot. She needed some better lines, too, so I gave her some as well.

What was surprising about this was that I'd come away from the encounter with a rankling sense of irritation and injustice. Alex had struck me as overbearing, obstinate, closed-minded, and generally exasperating. And then something changed. I'm not sure what it was, but all of a sudden one morning I wasn't exasperated anymore, except with myself for having cut such a feckless figure. For Alex I found myself making excuses: What had seemed overbearing seemed on second thought to be forthright, what had been obstinate was now steadfast and self-possessed. More than that, I found myself remembering with pleasure that amusing, upturned nose, those wide-set, gray-green eyes, the general clean-cut look of her. And especially the cool pressure of her fingers when we shook hands at the end. Had a tremor run through me at the time, or did I only imagine that it had?

In short, what I was doing was mooning over her, and I couldn't remember the last time a woman had gotten me doing that. I don't mean to imply that I'd been celibate since separating from Trish— far from it (well, not as far as all that, actually)—but I'd never been able to get comfortable with the modern mating dance, and, without ever consciously deciding to do it, I'd been gradually dropping out. The early years of my marriage had been wonderful, and I hadn't ever expected to be out on the circuit again, so I hadn't paid much attention to the changing mores of the unattached set. Now, either I'd been out of circulation too long or the rules had changed on me while I was married, or both. Or maybe, just between you and me, I was starting to think that having sex wasn't worth the rigmarole that went along with it if you were single.

Also, take it from me, there are some extremely strange females out there.

Anyway, as soon as I'd finished talking to Stetten, I opened the local telephone book, found a number for one "A.R. Porter" of Brookline, and dialed it, holding my breath and hoping that it was the right number. Happily, it was. I told her it appeared I had another project that might conceivably shed some light on her uncle's death after all. If she was interested, I said nonchalantly, did she care to meet me again at Ciao Bella to hear the details?

She did, and now here she was. I was at the same table as before, this time with a white-wine spritzer. She sat down opposite me and ordered a club soda with lime. Amazing. She looked cool as a cucumber. In fact, she looked *like* a cucumber: dark-green linen jacket on the outside, pale green knit shirt and pale green slacks on the inside.

No small talk this time. "Are you working with the police again?" she asked.

"No, I'm on my own."

Then, playing up the more exotic and glamorous angles, I told her about the telephone call from Stetten and my upcoming trip to Vienna.

She wasn't exactly bowled over. "'Count'? Who goes around calling himself 'Count' these days?"

"Well, it's different in Austria."

"Why? There isn't any more Austro-Hungarian throne. The Habsburgs haven't been around since, what, 1914, 1918? He sounds like some kind of shyster to me."

"No," I said, summoning up what little wind was left in my sails, "a lot of the old nobility have kept their titles over there. Besides, he never actually referred to himself as a count; it was on his letterhead, that's all. There wasn't really anything phony about him, or stuffy either. He sounded like a nice guy."

"But?" she said, hearing the misgiving in my voice before I realized it was there myself. And it was. I did have reservations.

"But," I said, "I have to admit that there's an oddball quality to the whole deal."

"In what way?" She looked at me over the rim of her glass. Her green eyes, showing some interest now, seemed flecked with hazel pinpoints, with no gray at all, and so clear that the pupils were like enameled black circles on green glass. Splendid, I thought, that was the word for her. How could I not have noticed the first time?

"Well," I went on, "take the fact that the dealer is bringing the painting with him to Austria. That's pretty strange."

"Why? You said Stetten doesn't like to travel."

"But how does this guy expect to cross the border with a fantastic piece of art like that? The only way I know of to do it without a government-approved bill of sale—which he can't have, because, aside from everything else, he hasn't sold it yet—is to smuggle it. With the open borders these days, that isn't too difficult, but why would a 'reputable, established' dealer want to risk it at all?"

"I see."

"And then this vague understanding about some undetermined finder's fee." I shook my head. "That isn't the way you do these things."

"So you *do* think he's some kind of phony, then?"

"No, I wouldn't say that. He didn't come across as a con man to me. I liked him."

"Well, of course you did. What kind of a con man would he be if he came across as a con man?"

I laughed. "Hard to argue with that."

She sipped her club soda, then put it down, frowning slightly. "Ben, this isn't...you're not going to be in any kind of danger, are you?"

I couldn't have been more delighted with the question. Maybe I had failed to convince her that my mission was particularly exotic, but now, quite inadvertently, I had her believing that it was perilous. And perilous had it all over exotic.

I toyed with my glass and smiled. "No, I don't think there's anything to worry about." Clearly implying: Yes, of course there's danger involved, great danger, but it's nothing I can't handle, and anyway I don't want you worrying your pretty little head about it.

She was still frowning. "Ben, tell me something, will you? Why are you doing this? Do you get paid a lot?"

That made twice in two sentences, and only twice all told, that she'd called me Ben. This, I thought happily, was palpable progress. At the same time, a tiny, cautionary voice somewhere deep in my brain wanted to know what I was doing counting the number of times she murmured my name. I was a divorced, case-hardened forty-year-old, not some addled teenager who had yet to be burned.

"It's not the money," I said. "There isn't that much money involved. I'll charge Stetten a thousand bucks a day, the same as I would anybody else."

She stifled a laugh. "A thousand dollars a day isn't much money? It doesn't sound bad to me."

"If I consulted five days a week, fifty weeks a year, yes, you bet. But I don't do it fifty *days* a year, or even half that." Or want to either. "Besides, half the time I do it for customs, or for the cops, and mostly I do that for free, and as for Stetten, I'm not really positive he can afford it, and if he can't—"

"Why, then?"

"Alex, Simeon was killed because he was keeping a multimillion-dollar painting in his shop when he shouldn't have. I knew that was a lousy idea at the time, and if I'd tried a little harder I could have gotten him to let me put it someplace else. But I didn't try harder."

She leaned forward, eyes narrowed. "Are you saying you *knew* somebody might—"

"No, no!" I said, shocked. "Jesus, of course not, how could you think that? I was just generally concerned about the painting, that's all. It never crossed my mind that— But what's the difference what I was concerned about? No matter how you cut it, I'm responsible for his death."

"That's putting it a little strongly. You didn't kill him."

"I could have saved him."

She shook her head. "No, blaming yourself doesn't make sense. The safe was locked, right? The man who killed him never got it open. How could he have known for sure whether or not it was in there? Even if you'd taken it to the museum or wherever you wanted to, he'd still probably have *thought* it was there, and Simeon would still be dead."

"I don't think so. Simeon would have opened it for him; the guy would have seen it was empty."

"Maybe not. My uncle could be stubborn."

"Look, let me put it this way. Knowing your uncle helped me through a hard time in my life. He was a good friend; I just wish I realized it more while he was alive. And now he's dead on account of me—no, don't try to tell me that's not so—and I just feel I owe it to him, that's all. That's why I'm taking Stetten's offer. That's why I'm going to St. Petersburg, too." All of which was true, wholly and sincerely true.

She was studying me without saying anything, sizing me up, trying to figure out how straight I was being with her. She must have come down on my side, because after a moment she smiled and relaxed against the back of her chair. A Hare Krishna group was going by on the sidewalk in their saffron robes, chanting and jingling and looking happy as clams at high water. Sipping our drinks, aware that we'd crossed a barrier and were now something like friends, or at least not adversaries, we watched them snake and jiggle their way out of sight.

"What do you do for a living anyway?" she asked. "Are you in museum work?"

"No, I was a curator at the Museum of Fine Arts for a few years, but...well, I left there a couple of years ago."

"Really? I would have thought that was about as good a job as you could get in that world."

"It was, I suppose, but...I don't know, it wasn't for me. Not for the rest of my life."

"And now...let me guess. You're a professor, am I right?"

"No, not exactly. I did teach at Harvard last

year—in art history—but...well, I quit there, too."

"Just like that? You walked away from a faculty position at Harvard?"

This was starting to sound like a conversation with Trish. "Well, you know, it wasn't tenure-track anyway."

"So what *do* you do? When you're not consulting at a thousand dollars a day."

"I'm writing a book," I said, then headed her off before she could follow up. "What about you?"

"Oh, I'm in educational administration."

"Really? So is my ex-wife." A clever interjection to let her know that I was unattached, on the off chance that Simeon had failed to mention it. "What do you do, specifically?"

"I'm director of admissions at Boston University."

"Really? You work at BU? So does my ex-w—"

Oops, not so brilliant that time. Trish was the last person in the world I wanted Alex talking to; in particular, about me. I cleared my throat. "Anyway, getting back to—"

But she wouldn't let me get away with it. "Your ex-wife works at BU? What's her name?"

I fidgeted, but there was no way out of it. "Trish Calder," I mumbled. "She's associate dean of students."

Alex's pretty eyes popped open wider. Her jaw didn't exactly drop, but if she'd been sipping her club soda at the time, I'm sure she would have sprayed it over the table. For a good

128

five seconds she just stared at me. "You're Trish Calder's husband?" she stammered at last. "You're...?"

"That's right," I admitted. "The Prototypical Dysfunctional Male."

She dissolved into laughter, throwing her head back and hooting. "I'm sorry," she said when she'd calmed down. "I'm not laughing at you—"

"Of course not. Why would I think that?"

"No, really." A last little explosion of giggling made her put her hand to her mouth, but she stifled it and took a deep, restorative breath. Ordinarily I don't much like giggling, but she was...well, *cute.* The funny thing is that ordinarily I don't like cute either.

"Really," she said. "It's just that, from what Trish said, I had a— well, a completely different picture of you."

"I'll bet. You and everybody else at BU. Are you and Trish pretty good friends, then?"

"We chat from time to time, but, no, I wouldn't say we're good friends. Mm-mm, no, not at all."

I took heart from that "no, not at all."

"In fact, we see things pretty differently. Trish—I guess I don't have to tell you this— is into regression therapy, and transformative healing, and rebirthing, and—"

"I know," I said curtly. "She wasn't always. And what about you? What are you into?"

She shrugged. "Just getting on with your life and doing your thing, I suppose. Digging in your heels."

"Me, too."

She couldn't resist a tiny flicker of the eyebrow at that, but what I'd said was the truth. It was just taking me a little time to get things sorted out.

"Say," I said, looking at my watch as if I didn't already know what time it was, "it's six-thirty. The pasta's good here, and there's air-conditioning inside. Why don't we—"

"I'm sorry, I can't, not tonight." She stood up to go, as fresh and unrumpled as when she'd come. "Perhaps we could do it when you get back." She hesitated. "Will you call me?"

I nodded, getting up too. "Sure thing." And then, just to make sure she didn't get the impression that there was the least little bit of personal attraction involved, "I'll let you know how it goes in Vienna."

"And St. Petersburg." She took my hand— my left in her right, which made it clumsy and impersonal. No tremors this time. "Ben... thanks very much for doing this. Even if nothing comes of it, you've made me feel a lot better."

"Good. But I hope something comes of it."

"And you will be careful, won't you?"

"You can bet I'll be careful," I said. "That zwiebelrostbraten they serve over there can kill you."

WHEN I GOT BACK to the apartment, there was a message from Sergeant Cox on the machine, asking me to call him at his office, or at home if I got back after six.

A child answered the telephone. "May I speak to Mr. Cox, please?" I asked.

"Just a minute," he said politely, then bawled, "Daaaddyyy! Tewaphone!"

In the background I heard Cox's voice. "Back in a second, hon," he was saying, presumably to his wife. Then, closer to the telephone, "Thanks, Pooh-Bear." What do you know, the sergeant had a life, too.

"This is Ben Revere," I said when he picked up the receiver.

"Oh, yeah, thanks for calling." He was still chewing. Wife, kid, dinner with the family— my barren condo suddenly looked awfully depressing. "Listen, I just wanted to touch base on a couple of things with you," he said. "This guy who pawned the painting with Pawlovsky in the first place—you want to tell me again what he looked like?"

"The one who *pawned* it? I never saw him."

"No, I know, but Pawlovsky told you, and you told us. But I want to check with you again. What do you remember about him?"

I searched my mind. What had Simeon... "Oh, that's right. He said there was a scar on his cheek...."

"Which cheek?"

I took a moment to conjure up an image of Simeon gesturing at his own face. "Right, I think. And part of his ear was missing."

"How tall?"

"That I don't know."

"What about his hair color?"

"No, I don't know that either— Wait a

minute, yes I do. Like hay, Simeon said. That'd mean blond, wouldn't you think?"

"Anything else?"

I poked in my memory for tidbits of the conversation with Simeon. "No, I don't think so. What's this about, Sergeant? Have you found him?"

"Yeah, you could say that." He lowered his voice to a rough whisper. "In a section of concrete sewer pipe west of Andover, with four nine-millimeter slugs in him. Dead about a week."

"And you're sure it's him?"

"You tell me. Listen to this." I heard him shuffling paper. "'Evidence of healed linear laceration,'" he read aloud, "'eleven-point-twenty-five centimeters in length, extending from the right nostril to the auditory meatus. Well-healed amputation of the right earlobe, healed crushing fractures of both nasal bones—'"

"Hey, that's right, I forgot. Simeon said he had a broken nose, too."

"Right, here's more. 'The body is that of a blond, well-nourished white male in his thirties, estimated living height and weight—'"

"He was small!" I exclaimed. "Right? A runt, Simeon called him. I forgot about that, too."

"There you go, then," he said with satisfaction. " 'Five feet four and one hundred and twenty pounds.' Fills the bill, doesn't he?"

"He sure does. Do you know who he is?"

"Not a clue. No identification on him. Has all the earmarks of a gangland thing, though.

More like an execution than a murder. Well, thanks for your help, Mr. Revere, have a—"

"Sergeant, are there any new developments on the case? On Simeon's murder, I mean?"

"Nothing else, only this. We'll see where it takes us." He paused. I heard him sucking a shred of food out of his teeth. "I should tell you, Mr. Revere, I'm starting to think maybe you're right, maybe there's more to this than I thought."

"You mean you think it might be about the painting after all?"

"That's right. By the way, I appreciate the report you sent me. Sorry I didn't get around to saying thanks sooner. You let me know anything else you find out, all right? Well, gotta go. We'll be in touch."

That raised my spirits. Cox seemed like a solid, workmanlike cop; it was a relief to think that he'd come around.

Later, in the kitchen, searching among the ambiguous packages in the freezer, looking for something for dinner, I found a triple-wrapped, rock-hard brick of something that gave every indication of being meat sauce, so I put it in the microwave, started up a kettle of water for spaghetti, and went to the cupboard to make myself a gin and tonic while I waited, except there wasn't any tonic and there wasn't any gin, so I had a vodka with club soda. No lime anywhere in sight, needless to say. The time was getting close when I would have to go shopping again.

I put in the spaghetti and leaned against the

counter, sipping vodka, watching the water come slowly back to a rolling boil, and asking myself if I truly, honestly thought that the presumed reappearance of Stetten's Velàzquez in Zurich was related to the appearance of the one that had shown up in Simeon's shop. If it was, that meant that, whatever was going on, two people had now been murdered over it. What was I getting myself into? It was starting to look as if Alex was right to be concerned; there might be more in Vienna to worry about than clogged arteries.

The "meat sauce" turned out to be mincemeat—raisins, apples, spices, and whatever else people put in there. What it was doing in my freezer was a mystery. I don't even like the stuff in a pie. Still, waste not, want not. I dumped it over the spaghetti and sat down to eat it while restudying the MFA&A's report on the Lost Truck.

I've had worse.

CHAPTER 11

In the middle years of the nineteenth century, when the rich but time-frayed capitals of Europe embarked on their grand civic-development projects, they were faced with an unprecedented difficulty. They had the resources, they had the backing of their governments, they had the public will. What they didn't have was a "look." The nineteenth century, so innovative in the arts and sciences, had forgotten to come up with an architectural style it could call its own.

So what were the monumental new buildings going to look like? The happy answer was to turn to the styles of the past, so that today's classic nineteenth-century boulevards-Paris's rue de Rivoli, Budapest's Danube Promenade, and, most of all, Vienna's Ringstrasse, created in 1857 when the city's encircling fortifications were pulled down-are glorious hodgepodges of everything that came before.

From where I stood at the window of my room on the fifth floor of the Hotel Imperial early on a sparkling Friday morning, showered, shaved, and reasonably sprightly after an all-night flight, it was all splendidly laid out for me like an educational diorama: "The History of Architecture at a Glance." Neo-Renaissance? There was the famous opera house, practically across the street, and the art museum and the natural history museum a few blocks to the west. Greek Revival? There was the Parliament building, straight out of ancient Athens. Neo-Gothic? Off to my left were the five needle-thin, newly cleaned spires of the city hall. To some, it added up to a grandiose, incoherent clutter, but, me, I loved it.

The hotel fitted right in, too, a stately, mustard-colored (Dijon, not Gulden's) building constructed in the 1870s in the neoclassical style that had been popular a century earlier (which, come to think of it, made it neo-neoclassical). I'd dined at this famous old dowager of a place once or twice on previous visits, and had drinks in the bar, but I'd never stayed here. When I'd come to Vienna as a graduate student, all I could afford was one of the seedy, anonymous pensions out in Josefstadt. Later, when I'd come on business for the museum, I'd been put up at the Sacher, which was one hell of a step up, but even that plush and venerable institution was no match for the Imperial, where my room, by no means one of the hotel's grandest, was fitted out in Dresden blue and white, with flocked walls, matching carpets, ten-foot ceilings, good-quality Empire-style furniture, and a mounded basket of fresh fruit.

So there I was, dopey from a night without sleep, dreaming away at the window and munching on some grapes. Physically I was feeling pretty good, but my mind seemed to be floating about four feet above my head, softly jogging against the ceiling. Partly it was the jet lag, of course, but, independent of that, I was suffering from an unsettling sense of unreality. After all those years of reading and writing about wartime loot and restoration, here I was, fifty years after the fact, caught up in the middle of the real thing for the very first time.

And yet it somehow felt less real, not more, as if I were playing at a game I'd invented for myself. Even the possibility of a connection to Simeon's death seemed-to use Alex's word-tenuous. It just seemed impossible, now that I was here, that anything in this glittering world could have any relationship to a thuggish murder in a humble Boston pawnshop that catered to old ladies who came in to pawn the same forty-dollar ring every month.

The discreet little *tap-tap* at the door was a welcome distraction. I walked across the room, treading comfortably in my socks on the thick carpeting, opened the door, and smiled at the slight, gray-haired, faultlessly groomed man standing politely before it.

The great international hotels of the Continent have a lot of things in common, regardless of the country, and one of them is a certain species of hotel manager-not the annoyingly supercilious managers of the more expensive chains but a more genteel, more old-fashioned type, a distinct and dying breed that the intrepid and knowledgeable traveler recognizes in an instant: mature, refined, helpful, courteous, and self-effacing. Ten years ago they were still wearing gray-striped trousers, waistcoats, and cutaways with a carnation in the lapel. Today they are more likely to be in conservative business suits. But this one was a pleasant throwback; a midnight-blue blazer, almost black, replaced the cutaway, but everything else was the same: gray-striped trousers, dove-gray waistcoat, diagonally striped black tie perfectly knotted and held in place with a gray-pearl tiepin. And a fresh red carnation in his buttonhole. I glanced at his feet, hoping for spats, but there he let me down.

"Yes?" I said in German. "Can I help you?"

"I certainly hope so," he said, looking up at me with mild, friendly eyes of milky blue. "I'm, ah, Stetten?"

I sighed. The Intrepid Traveler scores again.

ALBRECHT, GRAF STETTEN, BROKE open a crusty roll, showering flakes onto the tablecloth, and spread a delicately scalloped rondel of butter on a quarter of it. "I've asked my lawyer to meet us in half an hour," he said a little nervously, "because I thought that we-you and I-should have an understanding between ourselves before we meet with Mr. Dulska. Don't you agree?"

I started getting nervous myself. Art collectors are a peculiar and finicky breed, and when an "understanding" is mentioned before a meeting like this one, what's likely to follow is something along the lines of "Now, if you determine that it's authentic (or valuable, or what I'm looking for, or worth three times what the seller thinks), whatever you do, don't let on. Just let *me* know by lifting your left eyebrow twice, while crossing your left leg over your right, and flexing the second joint of the fifth finger of your right hand. Discreetly, of course."

Once, if you can believe it, it happened the other way around. I was working with a passionate collector of Dutch realist landscapes and we were going to look at a purported van Ruisdael that she'd set her heart on, but just before we entered the dealer's showroom, she grabbed my sleeve and burst out, "If it's not really a Ruisdael, I don't want to know! Don't tell me!"

It was her money, so I shrugged and went along (you do that a lot when you work with art collectors), but I couldn't help wondering what she was paying me for. I mean, if what you want is *not* to be told something, why not just hire some kid at five dollars an hour to do it, or rather not to do it? However, as it turned out, it was the real thing, so I could be honest, the dealer could make his sale, and the collector could get what she wanted. Everybody was happy.

Stetten's "understanding" was almost as unusual. "If you believe it's authentic, I hope you'll simply come out and say so. If you believe it's not, I hope you'll say so as well. I don't want you to be coy, I don't want you to 'protect' my interests. Honestly, I don't, Dr. Revere. No games, no prevarication; just your honest, objective judgment. Do you think we can agree on that?"

"Completely." I was much relieved.

"And if you see that I'm making a blunder of some kind, which I'm afraid is likely, I hope you'll come out and say so, too, and not worry about sparing my sensitivities."

"Agreed," I said, liking him more by the minute. "You must be quite excited about this. When was the last time you saw the picture?"

"On the tenth of December, 1942," he said without hesitation. "In Paris. We had an apartment in the Seventh Arrondissement, on avenue Charles-Floquet, just off the Champ-de-Mars. I was twenty-six years old."

He bit into his roll. We were in the Café Imperial on the ground floor of the hotel, surrounded by what passes for understated elegance in Vienna: mirrored walls, gorgeous burled-wood wainscoting, heavy chandeliers, scurrying, whispering waiters in tuxedos. We had been served a breakfast of croissants, rolls, cold cuts, cheese, and coffee-and for Stetten a boiled egg. While I spread a roll of my own with kräuterkäse, the wake-up-your-taste-buds-in-a-hurry breakfast cheese they like here, I did some quick calculating. Twenty-six in 1942...that made him eighty-one or eighty-two now, yet I had taken him for a man fifteen years younger, what with that glossy, pink-cheeked, healthy skin and those lively blue eyes. But now, looking again, I could see that his shirt collar was too roomy for a neck grown scrawny, that his gray-white hair and short-cropped, almost invisible white mustache, while carefully groomed, were listless and scant. And that the backs of his thin, elegant hands, those unforgiving betrayers of age, were knotted with dull purplish veins as thick as earthworms.

"Your family lived in Paris during the war, then?" I asked.

"Yes, my father was one of those who saw the German menace to Austria for the horror it was. In 1938, just before the Anschluss, he gathered together his most beloved paintings, put the rest in storage here in Austria, and moved us-my mother, my brother, Rolf, and me-to Paris."

140

"You avoided the Nazis by moving to *Paris*?" I didn't mean to say it, it just came out.

He smiled. "It may not have been the best choice."

As we ate, he told me more. The family business had been founded four generations earlier, on confections and tobacco, but it had been Stetten's grandfather Konrad who had really created the Stetten fortune with his invention of a cigarette-manufacturing machine in the 1890s and his subsequent near-monopoly of cigarette-making in Austria-Hungary. Konrad had also been the one who had acquired the bulk of the family's art collection, passing his love of art and of acquisition down to his son, Stetten's father, an even more dedicated collector.

Having eaten lightly but steadily while telling me this, Stetten now began using the back of a tiny egg spoon to crack the egg, methodically rotating the egg cup a few degrees at a time to get to a fresh surface. "For my father, you see, art was more important-more real in a way-than life. He lived for his family and his pictures, nothing else. When they took the pictures, they took his life, really."

He began to peel away bits of brown eggshell with buffed and manicured fingernails. On the little finger of his right hand was a gold signet ring with a crescent formed by a double-headed eagle; the same crest that I'd seen on his letterhead.

"They came while we were having our dinner," he said, then seemed to become

141

absorbed in dislodging a particularly stubborn bit of membrane from the egg white.

"The Nazis?" I prompted softly.

He separated the membrane and wiped his hands with a napkin. "The Nazis, yes. Oskar-our man-came in during the fish. We could see that he was frightened. He was an old fellow, his voice was shaking. 'The Gestapo,' he told my father. Poor man, he could barely get the words out." Stetten looked up from his egg. "Of course, a person living in today's world...you can have no idea of the feelings such words could convey."

"I can imagine," I said humbly.

"Oh, my dear friend, I hope not. In any event, my father put down his fork. 'At this hour?' he said"-and Stetten's voice took on a deeper, weightier tone—"exactly as if he had been informed that some thoughtless shopkeeper had come to present a bill at an inconvenient time. 'You may tell them that I will see them after dinner.'"

At last Stetten began to spoon up the egg in tiny mouthfuls; no salt, no pepper. "Oskar placed at my father's elbow a pewter salver on which there was a piece of paper. Later I learned that it was a search-and-seize order, but my father barely gave it a glance. 'Put them in the drawing room and make them comfortable,' he said. 'You may offer them something to drink.' And poor Oskar did, though he could hardly walk. My mother wept through the rest of the dinner, but my father made us finish....You know, they prepare boiled eggs

142

to perfection here. I'm going to have another. Are you sure you wouldn't like one?"

I shook my head, my appetite long gone. "And they waited?"

"Oh, yes, they waited. I could hear them muttering-the lowest type of Bavarian accents, no breeding. I was able to catch glimpses of them from my chair-those perfectly cut uniforms, the swastikas, the beautiful boots. Probably the best clothes they'd ever owned. Even their cologne, I could smell. They were impatient, but yes, they waited. You see..." And he paused, as if deciding how to put something in the easiest way for me to understand. "They recognized in my father someone superior to themselves. We Germanic peoples are very attuned to such nuances."

"And what happened?"

"Ah, the rest of the story isn't so inspiring. My father was arrested, and the paintings were taken away."

"Simply taken? Not even a pretext of payment?"

"At that point it wasn't necessary," he said matter-of-factly. "My father's primary business partner had been classified as an enemy of the state, and that was all the pretext they needed."

"He was Jewish?"

"Jewish? No, of course not."

"A member of the Resistance?"

"Florian? Hardly. No, he was a Mason. Ah, you didn't know the Freemasons were 'enemies of the Reich,' too? Oh, yes, the Nazis were very generous about bestowing such labels. Florian-poor, good-hearted Florian-died at Auschwitz, in the gas chambers."

"And...and your father?" I steeled myself, not sure I really wanted to hear the answer.

Stetten finished his egg and wiped his mouth. "My father was taken to a holding center near the Gare de l'Est," he said, and as he did, something shivery moved along my spine. To hear him talk about these things in that pleasant, neutral voice somehow made them all the more horrible. "There he was held for four days, at the end of which time he was found beaten to death, the unfortunate victim of unknown assailants. The commandant, who expressed his profound regret, refused us permission to see his body. Much later I learned that during those four days my father had steadfastly refused to sign an instrument legally ceding the paintings to the Third Reich."

Not a catch in his throat during the entire ugly recital, not the minutest variation in tone, not even a subtle hint of irony at phrases like "profound regret" or "legally ceding." There was nothing at all to show what he might be feeling other than an unnatural (or was it natural?) erectness of posture. "As for the rest of my family—"

"Sir," I interrupted, "it's really not necessary—"

"No, it's all right, I'd like you to know. It's been such a long time since I've talked about these things."

So, fascinated and appalled, I listened.

Two days after the report of the senior Stetten's death, the same two Gestapo officers, accompanied this time by a pair of French policemen, came to the apartment and escorted Frau Stetten to ERR headquarters in the plush Hotel Commodore on boulevard Haussmann, keeping her for a day and a night. There, using persuasions that she would never speak of to her son, they convinced her to sign the same "legal" document that had unsuccessfully been offered to her husband.

With the Nazi version of due process satisfied, the Stettens were then shipped back to Austria, where more legalisms ensued. The family's cigarette factory and other holdings were ceded to the state for the duration of the war, and the two-hundred-year-old family residences near Melk, Austria, and Csorna, Hungary, were signed away as German officers' quarters, while the Stettens were permitted to keep the top floor of their town house on the outskirts of Vienna for themselves.

Albrecht and his brother, Rolf, were quickly drafted and sent to the Eastern front. Rolf died of blood poisoning at Stalingrad. Albrecht was bayoneted in the throat in the first action he saw, and was reassigned as a stretcher-bearer. When he later suffered a ruptured lung during a mortar attack near Smolensk, he was hospitalized for three months, dismissed from the army, and sent back to Vienna, where he found his mother, once a celebrated society beauty, disheveled, emaciated, and drifting in and out of sanity. A few months later she dashed blindly out into the street in her nightgown during an early-morning bombing. Running after her, Stetten was terribly injured yet again, lying for two days in the rubble before they got to him, his pelvis crushed by falling masonry. His mother's body was never identified. The end of the war found him in a filthy, overcrowded hospital ward, physically wrecked, emotionally numbed, and the sole remaining member of his noble family, the last of the long line of Stettens. He was twenty-nine.

There isn't too much you can say after a story like that, so I just picked mechanically at my food, sunk in what was getting to be a familiar feeling: a half-thankful, half-ashamed sense of unearned and fantastic good fortune-of having, in a world of misery on every side, simply been born at the right time and in the right place.

Amazingly, Stetten's eyes twinkled. "Oh, dear, now I've gone and depressed you. I think we'd better change the subject." He gave the table a brisk double tap to announce a shift in mood and looked around us. "Let me see...have you noticed anything extraordinary about this breakfast room?" He asked it as brightly as if he'd spent the last twenty minutes describing his summer in the Alps.

I let out my breath and shook my head, more than ready to talk about something else.

He gestured at the other tables, each with a single person or a quiet couple at it, all using their knives and forks in the concise, delicate European manner, like surgeons excising a gallbladder. "We're all sitting down and being served, like gentlemen and ladies. Isn't it nice? We might be back in the last century. This, my friend, may be the only first-class hotel in Vienna, perhaps in the world, that hasn't succumbed to the crass grotesquerie of the breakfast buffet. Where else can you go at this time of the morning without having to witness hordes of brutish, bulging gluttons piling their plates with food?" He dabbed his almost-invisible mustache with his napkin and made a droll, mock-horrified face. "And then going grimly back for more, like drowsy, sated lions returning to the bloody carcass, because it's still there."

He smiled cheerfully at me. "And what's your opinion about it, Dr. Revere?"

"What's my opinion?" I said, laughing. "My opinion is that if I could speak English like that, I'd be a happy man."

That made him laugh too. "You must remember that I've been at it longer than you have. My first visit to London was in 1930, many years before you were born. I was educated at Cambridge."

With the somber mood broken, we had a last cup of coffee and went out to the handsome lobby to find Leo Schnittke, Stetten's attorney. Stetten used an old-fashioned silver-headed walking stick. Not so much as a cane, like Simeon's, but as a sartorial accessory; like the rest of his costume, dapper as could be but a couple of generations out of date.

Was there an element of phoniness in all this *fin-de-siècle* folderol? Was it too good to be true, could there be a con job going on here, as Alex suspected? I admit that I gave it some thought. Stetten was simply too perfect a count, a casting director's dream in speech, deportment, dress, and manners. In the end, however, I decided not. For one thing, he was just too good at it; it came too naturally. I couldn't believe he was playing a part. Besides, although he had been trying to be amusing (and succeeding) when he was going on about breakfast buffets, I sensed that behind the clever words he was speaking from the heart. If he'd had his way, we *would* have been back in the last century, and the peasants would have been where they belonged, huddled around their hearths eating blood sausage and boiled cabbage and not bellying up to eggs Benedict at fancy buffet tables all over the world. The Count of Stetten, I was pretty certain, was a genuine, deep-dyed member of his caste, a blue-blooded dinosaur who had yet to resign himself to the rise of the plebeians-especially when they encroached upon the sensibilities of the more refined.

Leo Schnittke, waiting for us near the marble-columned main staircase, wasn't much younger than Stetten, a portly man with world-weary, disillusioned eyes set in blue-black sacs, heavy, drooping jowls, and a wispy, near-colorless goatee that made him look like a venerable sage on a twelfth-century Chinese vase. Or would have, if not for the well-chewed stump of an unlit cigar in his mouth and an undisguised expression of testiness, impatience, and general superiority on his pouchy face.

"*Tag,*" he said shortly, bowing stiffly when Stetten introduced us, but pointedly leaving his hand in his pocket and not extending it, which was unusual in this part of the world, where males shook hands at every conceivable opportunity. He also didn't bother taking the cigar out of his mouth. I wondered if he was miffed at not having been invited to breakfast with us.

"So where is this Dulska?" he asked Stetten in German.

"I don't know, but we'll soon find out."

At the reception desk Stetten's bona fides as genuine aristocracy were persuasively confirmed. When at first the young clerk haughtily began to explain that he wasn't at liberty to give out the room numbers of guests, he was hissed aside by the scandalized day manager (in full-dress morning coat, I'm happy to say). Herr Stumpf apologized profusely on the hotel's behalf, and after expressing his great pleasure in seeing the Count again after so long an absence and hoping that the Count was well, that the Count was entirely satisfied with his suite, and that the Count would let him know the instant he required anything, however minor, he informed us that although Herr Dulska was registered in suite 400, he had engaged the private Württemberg sitting room for the morning, a most charming room, and was awaiting us there. We would find it on the mezzanine, should the Count and his friends care to take the elevator to that floor.

Stetten accepted these servilities courteously but absentmindedly, musing aloud as we walked to the elevator. "There was a time when I used to stay here three or four times every month, but that was before...well, before." He fingered a veined, honey-colored marble wall affectionately, almost proprietorially. "Did you know that it was the Emperor Franz Joseph himself who dedicated this hotel? My grandfather attended the reception. Afterwards, it was the only hotel in Vienna at which His Majesty would stay. Other monarchs shared his preference. It was Edward VII's favorite hotel as well. And Victor Emmanuel III's-I was at a private dinner in his honor here."

"Mm," I said. A scrap of information that I'd picked up somewhere went floating through my mind: As Führer, Adolf Hitler had a favorite Viennese hotel, too, at which he also invariably stayed.

Guess which one.

Under the circumstances, I thought I'd just as well keep it to myself.

CHAPTER 12

Zykmund Dulska, the art dealer who wanted only to do the right thing, brought to mind a spiteful bullfrog. He was one of those uncomfortably swollen people who seem to have too much blood in their bodies, a spongy, fat-faced man with goggling eyes that wouldn't stop jumping around. At the door he greeted us effusively in English, the only language all four of us understood, and bowed us toward a table on which coffee, tea, and enough fruit, bread, and rolls to feed the Chicago Bulls had been meticulously arranged on linen so white it hurt to look at it. His Czech accent-or, as Sergeant Cox might point out, what I took to be a Czech accent-was heavy, his voice a liquorish gargle that didn't go with all the fluttering.

Stetten responded for the three of us. "Thank you very much," he said civilly enough, although I could see that he was about as taken with Dulska as I was, "but perhaps we might see the picture?"

Dulska leaped heavily to obey. "Of course, of course, certainly, *Exzellenz*. At once."

At the far end of the room, illuminated by northern light streaming through the opened velour drapery of a ceiling-high window, was an easel covered with a dark cloth. Dulska lumbered to it and dramatically snatched the cloth away, watching Stetten as if he expected him to gasp or clutch his chest.

All he got out of him, however, was a quiet "Well, well," followed by thirty seconds of studying it at room's length with the gentlest of smiles on his face, his head cocked to one side, hands clasped atop the walking stick. I didn't have a clue as to what he was thinking, and I was sure that Dulska didn't either.

Unlike the picture in Simeon's shop, this one was still in its frame, and even from twenty feet away I could see that it-the frame-wasn't authentic. Gilded and elaborate as it was, it was of a type that hadn't come into existence until the nineteenth century, long after Velàzquez's day, and not in Spain but in Germany at that, where it was produced for foreign, mostly English, consumption. That wasn't necessarily a bad sign-old frames often got replaced when they developed rot or were damaged-but you couldn't call it a good sign either. The important question in this case was, Was this the same frame that had been on Stetten's father's painting in 1942? I couldn't imagine his remembering, but I thought I ought to ask anyway.

"Do you recognize the frame?"

He smiled. "Let's have a closer look. It's handsome, isn't it?"

Well, it was time to do what he had asked and be honest. "Yes, extremely handsome, but I'm afraid—"

"That it's not original," he finished for me. "Yes, I know. According to my father, it was made in Munich only in the last century, but with great attention to detail, if not to historical accuracy."

What did you know about that? Maybe his memory had something going for it after all.

"I forget the name of the maker," he said. "Kantner, Kastner... Now, wait a second, there used to be..." He went around the easel to the rear of the picture. "Yes, here it is."

I looked at the small, dulled brass plate nailed to the back of the frame: ANTON KANT-MANN IN MÜNCHEN, it said. BOGENGASSE 9. Stetten's fifty-five-year-old recollection was on target.

He returned to the front and, frowning, ran his hand over the carved grape leaves at the lower-right corner. "Also, there should be a-ah, here. You see where this sprig has been broken off and regilded? My father told me I did that when I was a child. It seems I hit it with a toy hammer. I have no memory of doing it. Well."

He stepped back from the painting and nodded at me, which I took to indicate that (a) I was now expected to do my thing, and (b) whatever I said wasn't going to make much difference because he'd already made up his mind. Had he reached his decision wholly on the basis of the frame? That seemed a little naïve, to put it mildly. And he'd barely given the picture itself a glance.

While Dulska stood fidgeting to one side, Stetten stood smiling to the other, and a scowling Schnittke chewed on his cigar, I took a good look at the painting, front and back. Stetten didn't take long to get restless. "What do you think, Dr. Revere? Can you give us the benefit of your opinion? Would you like more time?"

No, I didn't need any more time. I'd barely needed the ten minutes I'd taken. For three days I'd been poring over photographs and descriptions of the *Condesa de Torrijos*, not only at the museum in Boston but by way of the Internet and a quick run down to New York to the unparalleled art library at the Frick Museum. I was reasonably sure I'd seen everything that had gotten into print about it in the last hundred years, and a lot that hadn't made it into print as well. Besides that, I had the formidable advantage, as Stetten had pointed out, of having examined its companion portrait, *El Conde*, only a few weeks earlier.

Stetten had mentioned one criterion: the frame. I had a hundred of them burned into my mind, and every one of them quickly told me that the sober, gloved matron in black with the mantilla, the fan, and the wonderfully rendered jeweled cross dangling from one wrist was the real thing, another authentic and beautiful Velàzquez. And I, like Stetten, was equally sure that it *was* the companion painting to his father's *Count of Torrijos*, stripped from the wall of their Paris apartment in 1942, its last known whereabouts the back of a renegade German truck that had disappeared into an Alpine spring blizzard in April 1945.

This was clear not only from the matching size, treatment, and condition of the two pictures but from the back of the *Condesa*'s canvas, on which the various symbols and markings were almost exactly the same as those on the back of the one in Simeon's shop, which meant that the two had shared a common history, as you might expect in a

154

pair of portraits made as a set and then passed down through generations of art-loving collectors. There were only a few differences. Instead of *Osuna 127/6*, this one said *Osuna 126/ 6*, which was obviously the number assigned to it at the 1843 "Osuna sale" mentioned in the *catalogue raisonné* entry on *The Count of Torrijos*. And instead of the *ne-2* that had been stamped on the first painting, there was now an *sr-4*, but neither symbol meant anything to me beyond the fact that it had been applied by the Germans; the angular Gothic lettering gave that away. The *ERR* was there, too, although there was no German inventory tag.

Otherwise, the backs of the two pictures were near-duplicates. The possibility that some forger or crook had faked these markings wasn't quite nil, but it was close. Where would he have gotten the information to reproduce them so exactly? The backs of paintings weren't described in *catalogues raisonnés,* and even the meticulous German records hadn't mentioned them, let alone illustrated them.

So I was pretty certain that this was it, but when you're a thousand-dollar-a-day expert, you can't just look at something for ten minutes and deliver your verdict. If you do, people feel as if they're not getting their money's worth, which sounds silly, but I understand where the feeling comes from. I can remember Bubbe's complaining that traveling by air was for crazy people; not because it was dangerous but because it wasn't worth the extra cost compared to going by train, because on a train at least you spend some time, but on an airplane you're there before you know it.

Same thing.

So I started running on about *pentimenti* and glazes, about the marvelously adroit, feathery brush strokes and the sure-handed blending, about the lack of a signature (again, a good sign in this case) and the plain but superbly done background, and so on and so forth, until I noticed that Stetten, while observing me with a certain fondness, had stopped paying attention. I finished my sentence, whatever it was, grinned, and reached to shake his hand.

"Congratulations, sir, I think you've found your father's-that is, your-painting."

I had forgotten about Dulska, but now he uttered a relieved grunt and brought his fat-fingered hands together. "Well, well, gentlemen, I'm glad that's been settled so readily. Now perhaps you'll join me in a cup of coffee and we can come to terms."

Here's where it gets interesting, I thought. For a guy who was just doing the right thing, who wanted no more than a finder's fee to cover his own costs, who had no personal stake in the matter, he was awfully keen to wrap things up.

At the table he fussed over us, or rather over Stetten. ("Croissant, *Exzellenz*? Rolls, *Exzellenz*? I can personally recommend the gooseberry preserves, *Exzellenz*.") But under that unctuous toadying I thought I could detect a man who didn't have much use for Albrecht, Graf Stetten, and his kind. And not much for me either.

Stetten accepted coffee and a croissant from Dulska but made no move to consume them. Schnittke and I were left to pour our own coffee. I sat next to Dulska. Stetten and Schnittke sat across from us.

"You mentioned terms, Mr. Dulska," Schnittke said. He had an unpleasantly blunt way of speaking, with an odd, flat way of sounding his vowels that rang a bell, that reminded me of someone I knew, but that I couldn't quite place. Everything he said sounded like a challenge.

"Why, yes," Dulska said. He looked from one of us to the other and sucked in a nervous breath of air that puffed out his pigeon breast. Beads of perspiration had come out on his forehead. "Yes. I believe that, ah, mm, one million American dollars, that is to say, ten million Austrian schillings, would be fair, yes?"

If he was talking to me, the answer was no. I thought a million dollars was outrageous. Not as a price for the picture, no. But as a finder's fee?

Stetten was taken aback, too. "Why, why..."

"Impossible," Schnittke said curtly. "Out of the question. If that is the sort of figure you have in mind, we may as well all go home right now."

That launched Dulska into an excited, rambling harangue that had him picking at his already untidy collar and stuttering with earnestness. Surely we understood that he had gone to great trouble and expense in this matter. He was asking only what he himself had paid, expressed as a percentage of the amount he had given for the total lot in which the painting had been found-plus a small, indeed a ridiculously small commission to reimburse him for his expenses since then, and a reasonable adjustment for inflation. And surely the count could see that the painting would bring far, *far* more than a million dollars on the open market.

"Maybe so," said an unimpressed Schnittke, "but Count Stetten is not interested in the picture in order to place it on the market."

"No, indeed, far from it," Stetten put in.

No, of course not, Dulska replied, that went without saying, that was understood; it had been a mere figure of speech. But the count must realize that there had been certain essential monetary considerations, that one did not cross the Czech and Austrian borders with such a painting without ensuring beforehand that its way would be, shall we say, smoothed? That was not cheap.

Schnittke, cigar wedged in the corner of his mouth, merely looked at him without comment. Stetten glanced nervously at me for help, but I didn't see how I could guide him on this. Was it worth a million dollars? Yes, at a million dollars it was a bargain. On the other hand, why should he have to fork over a million bucks for his own painting? Besides, who knew if he had a million dollars to fork over? All I could do was shrug. He was going to have to decide this one on his own.

Stetten licked his lips and opened his mouth to speak, but Schnittke tapped his wrist and leaned over to say something lawyerly in his ear. They whispered together for a few seconds, and Stetten, looking nervous, nodded.

It was Schnittke who spoke. "We are prepared to go as high as one hundred thousand dollars," he said, taking the cigar out of his mouth for the first time. "One million schillings."

"One hundred—" Dulska's lips went in and out like a guppy's. "No, really, you must be reasonable. If I wanted to *sell* the picture, I could ask five times as much, ten times as much, surely you see that, but I want no profit, I seek only to do the right thing."

There it was again. This guy wanted nothing more from life than to do the right thing. "Five hundred thousand," he blurted. "I'm sorry, I cannot take anything less."

"If that's your position," Schnittke said, gathering together some papers that he had come in with and beginning to slip them into an attaché case, "there's nothing more to discuss. Go ahead and sell it, and good luck with it."

Pretty heavy-handed, but it struck me as the right approach to take with someone like Dulska. Schnittke knew-we all knew-that for whatever reason, and many came to mind, Dulska couldn't sell it at market value. If he could have, he would have, and the four of us wouldn't have been sitting there haggling over a finder's fee.

Dulska's turn again. "Perhaps I could—Wait a moment...." He scribbled a few calculations, probably sham, on some hotel notepaper. "Yes, it might be possible. I believe that I could accept three hundred thousand dollars if it were—"

Schnittke made a restless motion with his hand. "We're wasting our time. Albrecht, let's get out of here. If you want my opinion, this fellow—"

Stetten held up his hand. "One moment, Leo. Mr. Dulska, I'm afraid you may have been misinformed as to my resources. I'm not a rich man. I can't pretend that I am other than eager to have this picture, and if I had a million dollars I would gladly—Yes, Leo, don't look at me like that; I would."

Schnittke grumbled something under his breath and chewed on his stogie some more, staring at the table. I wasn't sure, but it seemed to me that the cigar, which he'd never lit, was an inch shorter than it had been when we started. He ate the damn things.

Stetten continued, "While you've been speaking, Mr. Dulska, I've been thinking of just how much money I can raise without turning myself into a pauper."

Dulska watched him expectantly. Schnittke continued to emit disapproving sounds from somewhere down around his belt.

"I am prepared to pay you a finder's fee of

one hundred and twenty-five thousand dollars, no more."

"But, *Exzellenz*—"

"And even that may take me a few days. I'm afraid I can do no better, Mr. Dulska. I hope you can see your way to accepting it."

Schnittke shook his head in sad disapproval but said nothing. Was it a routine they'd worked out between them, a sort of good-cop/bad-cop attack to put Dulska on the spot? Maybe, but Stetten didn't strike me as the devious type. On the other hand, Schnittke did. And he *was* a lawyer.

Planned or not, it worked. Dulska, his head down, nodded. "Very well," he said, sounding as if he were choking on a fish bone.

That surprised me. A hundred and twenty-five thousand dollars was only about half the price that the painting would be likely to bring on the black market. Apparently Dulska not only couldn't sell it on the open market, which was understandable because it was Stetten's painting after all, but he couldn't even unload it illicitly at a decent cut-rate price. *Why not?*

"Very good, thank you," Stetten said. He sounded calm and self-possessed, but I could see that his hands were trembling. "Leo, if you would work with Mr. Dulska to prepare the necessary papers—Dr. Revere, did you say something?"

Not exactly. I'd meant to issue a sober word of caution, but it had come out as an unprofessional squawk. I was flabbergasted; I couldn't believe what I was hearing.

I took a sip of cold coffee while I collected my thoughts and settled down. "I was only thinking," I said with admirable calm, "that it may be a bit early to finalize things. There are a few important questions to resolve."

"Questions?" Dulska said peevishly. Apparently he felt that at the price he was getting we weren't entitled to any questions.

"Questions of provenance," I said.

Stetten's white eyebrows went halfway up his forehead. He had his Velàzquez within his grasp at long last, and he was terrified that I might rock the boat. "Provenance? But-but, my dear friend, the provenance is impeccable; it can be verified from the mid-eighteenth century, from, from 1765, to the day my father bought it in 1912. I don't...I have documentary..." He flapped his hands uncertainly.

"Sir, who owned it in 1765 isn't the issue you have to worry about. What I'm talking about is its provenance *since* your father bought it."

"Since...? But what possible difference can that make? It was stolen from our home in 1942. Surely you don't doubt...you don't doubt—" For the first time he looked like a man in his ninth decade, befuddled and petulant.

"No, of course not," I said as gently as I could, "but who's owned it since then? Where's it been for the last fifty years? How many times has it changed hands? How do we know someone else—someone other than Mr. Dulska, I mean—doesn't have title to it?"

"Yes, but you don't seem to want to under-

stand." By now petulance had gained the upper hand, stiffening his spine a little. "The painting was taken from us by Hitler's thugs. Who has or has not possessed it since that time has no relevance."

Until then I hadn't been able to decide for certain how savvy Stetten was or wasn't when it came to the way the art market worked. Now I knew. He was a babe in the woods.

"Well, I'm afraid you're wrong there," I said reasonably. "If someone, somewhere along the line since then, bought it in good faith—that is, not knowing it was stolen property—he'd be able to assert a legally valid claim to it, too, especially if whoever he'd bought it from had *also* come by it in good faith."

"But surely his claim wouldn't take precedence over mine."

"I'm sorry, but you can't be sure of that. Ever since the war, the courts have had people fighting out just this kind of case. On the face of it, you'd have to say that both claims would be valid. Sometimes the decision goes one way, sometimes the other."

Dulska uttered what he must have thought was a reassuring laugh. "Ha. Ha. Gentlemen, gentlemen, I can give you my word that there is no such problem here, none whatever."

"That's fair enough," Stetten said. "If we have your assurance—" Schnittke, who had been listening keenly but saying nothing for the last few minutes, interrupted him. "No, Albrecht, Revere makes an important point. He's right to be concerned." I actually got an approving little nod from him, and then he turned to the sweating art dealer. "What about the provenance then, Dulska? Our art expert is right. We'll need more than your word."

"Ah. Well. Yes. Well, naturally, the records of the immediate postwar years are somewhat confused, but I can assure you that the gentleman-a *very* prominent Belgian gentleman of impeccable family-who owned the artworks of which this is one, did indeed purchase the painting in good faith, knowing nothing of its history or even of its real value-it is not signed, remember-in the mid-1950s, and owned it until the time of his death, when I successfully bid on his collection at auction-also in good faith, I need hardly add. That, I am afraid, *Exzellenz,* is all that is known of its provenance since it was taken from your home."

"Well, then," Stetten said with relief, spreading his hands as if that took care of that. But it didn't; not by a long shot.

"Mr. Dulska," I said with appropriate severity. "In the first place, I think we need to know the name of this prominent Belgian gentleman of impeccable family."

Dulska looked suitably shocked. "Ah, I'm afraid I'm not at liberty to provide this information. Professional ethics don't permit me to reveal his name."

Sure, I thought, that and the shady dealer's typical worry that if he disclosed his real source, we might very well cut out the middleman.

"And in the second place, I'm afraid we're going to need some proof that *you* have title to the painting."

Dulska lifted his chin and pursed his fleshy lips to let me know that his feelings were wounded. "I have papers that would satisfy you, of course, but I did not think to bring them with me at this time. I assumed we were operating as gentlemen, in an atmosphere of mutual trust."

I just looked at him. Schnittke took the cigar out of his mouth again for the purpose of uttering a short laugh.

"I could have them here tomorrow if that would be satisfactory," Dulska said stiffly. "Say, three o'clock?"

"How about having them faxed?" I asked.

"It will take time to collect them. Tomorrow is the best I can do."

"Leo?" Stetten said.

Schnittke ran stubby fingers through his wispy beard. "All right," he said grudgingly, a man who didn't like giving in on anything.

"Then that's what we'll do," Stetten said, taking charge again. "You'll get in touch with Mr. Schnittke tomorrow, when you have the papers?" He looked ready to go; he'd begun fidgeting in his chair.

Dulska nodded sulkily, a misunderstood man (who was trying only to do the right thing). "Yes."

"I'll be going, then, Albrecht," Schnittke said. "I have things to do. You know where to find me. Gentlemen." We stood up and bowed to each other. Once again, Schnittke chose not to shake hands. Dead cigar stuck in his face, he waddled out like a grumpy bear with berries on its mind. Stetten, obviously restless himself, reached for his walking stick, anxious to follow him.

But there was one more point I wanted to raise, even if Stetten had had enough. "Mr. Dulska, I'm sure—"

Stetten cut plaintively in. "Is there such a thing as a toilet in here, Dulska?"

I realized that it hadn't been restlessness that had been making him fidget but pressure on the bladder, not something most men in their eighties are able to put off for very long.

"Of course, *Exzellenz*." Dulska bowed him toward a set of double doors at the rear of the room, sat down, and returned his attention to me.

"You were saying?"

"I'm sure you know that this wasn't the only painting confiscated from the Stetten family. There were seventy-odd others taken at the same time and also known to have been on the Lost Truck. I can't help wondering if you might possibly have some information on those as well."

With the exception of those moist, protuberant eyes, which never stopped their darting and shifting, he became stone-still. "Why should you think I would have such information?"

Bingo; I'd hit on something. "I don't really know," I said, trying not to let my excitement show. "*Do* you?"

"And if I did? It would be of interest?"

"Well, of course it would."

"Even if the provenances were not 'impeccable'?"

"Mr. Dulska, if you have any information at all—"

He shushed me with his hand as Stetten came back through the double doors. "*Later.*"

By the time Stetten and I left a few moments afterward, Dulska was affable and obsequious again, but I had the unsettling feeling that those fervid, froggy eyes were taking in my every gesture, every nuance, as if he were filing them away for future reference.

If I ever ran into him on a lily pad, I was going to have to watch my back.

CHAPTER 13

It was almost noon when we left Dulska. Stetten, looking frail, retired to his suite, explaining that inasmuch as we'd had a late breakfast and it was going to be an unusually long day for him, he would skip lunch, rest during the afternoon, and then order a light, early dinner from room service. We agreed to meet in the hotel lobby at six-thirty, half an hour before *Rigoletto*'s curtain time.

That left me with six hours to myself, and I did just what you'd expect somebody like me to do with himself when he has a free afternoon in a place like Vienna. Without even having to think about it, I headed, the way a cow heads for the barn, for the Kunsthistorisches Museum, Vienna's superb treasure-house of art. But at the entrance I had a change of heart. The trouble was, I had some serious thinking to do, and I knew from experience that the riches of the Kunsthistorisches would have me hurrying greedily from Holbein, to Rembrandt, to Brueghel, to Dürer— so many painters, so little time!—as overstuffed, wild-eyed, and rapacious as one of Stetten's buffet groupies. Besides, it was bound to be, because it always was, swarming with visitors.

What I needed was someplace not quite so stimulating, something more conducive to placid cogitation. So with my mind running in a museum groove, I went instead into the Naturhistorisches Museum, which faces the Kunsthistorisches in a twin building— twin palace, if you like—across the wide green lawn of Maria-Theresien-platz.

It turned out to be a good choice. The Naturhistorisches has its areas of charm (the tiny Venus of Willendorf in its little, out-of-the-way glass case, for example), but no one has ever called it overstimulating. It is what a museum used to be in the days before "hands-on exhibits" and "interactive learning experiences," full of roomy nineteenth-century cases, each with a complement of moth-eaten alligators, or lions, or hyenas. Miles of rows of beetles, butterflies, and bees, each mounted on a single pin and with its own faded, curling little label in Latin. Vast, ornate galleries lit only by a dim, dusty daylight. And not an educational diorama in sight.

It didn't take long to find a bench in a quiet corner of a quiet gallery with a dozen twenty-foot-long cases in which, lined up in mind-numbingly regular rows, rested one specimen each of what must surely have been every kind of coral known to man. There, lulled into a reflective state by slowly revolving columns of sunlit dust motes, the only moving things in sight, and knowing that I was unlikely to be disturbed by rowdy gangs of coral enthusiasts, I gave myself over to thinking about what was bothering me.

Not Dulska, as you might expect. I mean, sure, the guy was a shyster, but how much thinking did that take?

But what about Stetten? What was he?

One minute—most minutes—I liked him. The next I found myself pulling back. A big part of it was that "count" business. It wasn't that I wasn't used to titled aristocrats either. When you work for a major art museum, you work with big-time art collectors, and when you work with big-time collectors, you're bound to run into the occasional peer of the realm. The ones I'd met had ranged from a lord-of-the-manor English viscount who firmly believed that the decline of Western civilization had begun on August 10, 1911, when the House of Lords lost its right of absolute veto, to a twenty-five-year-old German baroness with a butterfly tattoo on her shoulder, a ring through her belly button, and a passion for motorcycles and motorcycle racers.

But Stetten was almost too good to be true.

When I was with him, I felt as if I were in the middle of a Sigmund Romberg operetta. Every time a waitress had approached our table at breakfast, I'd expected her to burst into song. Well, I told myself, Stetten was my first Austrian count, and maybe that made it different.

But there was more than that. Why had he been so ready to seal the deal with Dulska? He'd haggled a little about the amount of the finder's fee—or rather, Schnittke had—but he'd wanted to ignore the really crucial aspects in terms of potential legal battles in the future: the provenance and the proof of Dulska's ownership. Unless Dulska himself had legal title to the painting or was acting as agent for someone who did—and that was yet to be settled—he had no right to sell it, or transfer it, or do anything else with it.

No matter how naïve Stetten was, it still seemed incredible that, if not for my objections and some timely support from Schnittke (who didn't really seem to know a hell of a lot about buying paintings himself, but was at least quick to grasp the issues), he would have let Dulska skate right by those all-important particulars. For that matter, why *was* he so naïve? If he'd been chasing down his father's art all these years, you'd think he'd have learned a little about the business. I'd assumed he was a collector in his own right, but maybe not.

And what about his reaction to the painting, or rather his nonreaction? Why had he shown next to no interest in a picture for which he'd

170

been searching for the last five decades? The frame, yes, but the painting? He'd hardly looked at it. Even allowing for the fact that he wasn't the collector his father had been, you'd think he'd have said something—remarked on some aspect of it, or just stood there basking in its glow, or even gloated over it a bit. Something...

That was as far as I got before a combination of jet lag and those mesmerizing dust motes did me in. When I woke up with a jerk that hurt my neck, I was slumped on the base of my spine, head tipped back against the hard marble wall, mouth gaping in mid-snuffle. I felt like hell. The clock on the wall said 4:55; barely time enough to get a bite on my way back to the Imperial, brush my teeth, and dress for the opera before meeting Stetten in the hotel lobby.

For all the answers I'd come up with, I might just as well have spent the time jogging between the Dürers and the Holbeins.

"MR. REVERE?"

Even if I hadn't been half expecting the call, the throaty voice would have been easy to recognize.

"What can I do for you, Mr. Dulska?"

I was in the bedroom of my suite, about to leave to meet Stetten. But I'd just been thinking about Dulska, about that whispered "*Later*" when Stetten had returned from his visit to the bathroom. It had gone in one ear and out the other at the time, so it wasn't until I was idly changing clothes that I grasped what it meant—which was, of course, that he wanted to discuss the other looted paintings not with Stetten, or with Schnittke, but with me. Alone. And that, in turn, had to mean Dulska had thought that was the way I wanted it, too, that I had purposely waited to raise the subject until Schnittke had left and Stetten was out of the room, that I had some ulterior, personal motive in mind.

In other words, Dulska was under the impression that I was bent.

"Are you alone?" he asked while I was still reflecting on this astounding circumstance.

"Um, yes."

"You know, I've been thinking about our conversation this morning," he said with a treacly negligence that came across as fake even over the telephone. "I thought it might be interesting to continue it. Are you free? Would you care to join me in my suite for a drink?"

"Sorry, I have an appointment."

"A little later, then? Say, eight o'clock?"

"No, I'll be out for the evening—"

"Mr. Revere, no more games!" he blurted, surprising me with his vehemence. Apparently the guy was convinced that everything I said had a hidden meaning. He was also jumpy as hell.

"Mr. Dulska, how about just saying what you have to say?"

He breathed in and out, a long, noisy breath through his nose, then was silent for a few seconds. When he spoke, it was quietly, but with a lockjawed intensity. "As it happens, I do have information about certain other missing paintings. I know, in fact, where they are and who has them. And I know that this person—you understand, I cannot name him—is now interested in disposing of them. Would you be interested in hearing more?"

Would I be...but I needed to make sure that I was tracking before I got in any deeper. "You're talking about some more of Stetten's missing paintings; that's right, isn't it?"

"I'm talking about *all* of them."

All of them? Practically the entire contents of the Lost Truck? Giorgione, Tintoretto, Hals, Goya...The idea was enough to drop me into a chair. Coming as it did from the mouth of a slimy customer like Dulska, I wouldn't have given it a moment's credibility—except that he'd already produced the Velàzquez, hadn't he, so who could say what else he might have up his sleeve? Maybe even, I realized with a prickle of excitement, the whys and hows that had brought the companion Velàzquez to Simeon Pawlovsky's shop and ended in his death.

"Why not offer them to Stetten, then?" It seemed like what a bent person in my position would want to know.

"For reasons of his own, this gentleman prefers not to do business with Count Stetten," Dulska said smoothly. "But he has authorized me to act as his agent in offering you a generous commission for your help in locating a dependable buyer—a discreet buyer, if I make myself clear." An oily silence, and then, "A *very* generous, very discreet commission, I can tell you."

He waited for my response, breathing noisily into the phone, while I scrambled for something to say that sounded as if I knew my way around dealings like this.

"Exactly how much money are we talking about here?" I asked. It was hard to see how I could go wrong with that.

Dulska liked it, too. "A great deal," he said with an unpleasant laugh, as if he now knew that he had me in his pocket. "When would you like to discuss it? I must tell you that time is of the essence."

"Well, I'm about to leave for the opera with Stetten. I don't see how I can break that. I should be back by ten-thirty."

"You'll come to my suite?"

"I don't think so. What about the bar?"

"Wouldn't my suite be more private?"

Definitely, which was why I wanted to meet in the bar. I was all too aware that I was swimming—dog-paddling was more like it—in unfamiliar waters here. For all I knew I was being set up for something, and I didn't want Dulska, whom I trusted not an inch, ever to be able to claim that he and I had met anywhere but in a public place.

"The bar, I think," I said.

"If you insist. Shall we say eleven?"

"Eleven it is."

"Oh, and Mr. Revere? It goes without

174

saying, yes?—nothing of this to our friend the count, eh?"

"Not a word," I said.

I DIDN'T SAY A word either; not because of Dulska's warning but because I didn't know what Stetten's reaction might be. He might have wanted to call in the police or confront Dulska himself, and I didn't want anything to happen that might bollix up whatever was in the works. I don't believe I was being disloyal to Stetten; my commitment to him concerned *The Countess of Torrijos*, and I intended to fulfill it. The rest of the paintings were another matter. In the end, assuming that they were really his, it would be a pleasure to do everything I could to see that they got back to him. But for the moment my interest was bigger than Count Stetten's rightful patrimony—bigger, if I'm going to be honest, than getting to the root of my friend's death. Because if Dulska was telling the truth (or some version of the truth), I now had a one-of-a-kind chance to pick up the scent of a stolen collection of irreplaceable, culturally priceless masterpieces that the world at large had thought lost forever. I couldn't pass it up.

At some point Stetten would have to be brought into it, of course. And the police; I had no illusions about continuing the charade with Dulska for very much longer or about chasing down the paintings on my own. But not yet. If I went to the police now, what would I tell them? I didn't know where the paintings were or who had them. When it came down to it, I didn't even know whether Dulska knew or was merely spinning some scam of his own. Dulska himself would simply deny what he'd said, and that would be the end of that. The paintings would slip back into whatever black hole they'd been in until now, and who knew when they'd surface again?

Or if.

*R*IGOLETTO WAS A FLOP.

Stetten had gotten us terrific seats in the nearest of the five horseshoe-shaped, gilt-and-white rungs of boxes in the opera house, but I couldn't concentrate on the music for thoughts of my upcoming meeting with Dulska. And the black-tied Stetten, who began the evening as chipper as could be, reminiscing lovingly about the glories and grandeur of Vienna in the days before the war, fell into a carping, biting mood almost as soon as we entered the great opera house, finding fault from beginning to end. The tenor was "a poor, thin stick of a Duke" (as I would have realized if I'd ever heard the great Richard Tauber in the role). The soprano looked more like a fashion model than a serious singer. (I should have seen Schwarzkopf's Gilda.) The orchestra, once the glory of the Staatsoper, was shamefully ragged and undisciplined. (If only I'd heard them in the glory days of the great Karl Böhm.)

176

Even the audience failed to meet his standards. "In my day," he said as we looked down on them between acts, "the fat, ugly women were all on the stage and the pretty ones were in the audience. Now it's the other way around. I call that a net loss." I don't doubt that he would have had something to say about the scarcity of evening dress in the hall, except that I was wearing the disreputable, mystery-fabric sport coat that I travel with because it never wrinkles.

Afterward we walked the three blocks back to the hotel along Kärtner Ring, its glossy shops closed but its streets still filled with pedestrians. Stetten walked slowly and precisely, now using his stick like a working cane, putting his weight on it at every other step. For the first time I noticed a limp, a hitch in the way one of his hips worked. The opera had left him in a melancholy, reminiscent mood, and he began to talk about his father's collection. At one time, he said, there had been well over four hundred paintings in the family residences at Melk and Csorna. His father had bought the Csorna castle—well, a country house, really, but everyone called it "the castle"—specifically to hold the overflow. When the family moved to Paris, all but the seventy-three paintings that went there with them had gone into storage in Austria.

"And what happened to them?"

"Gone. A few were legitimately sold. Mostly they were confiscated by the Nazis while we were away. When we came back, there was nothing—only some meaningless 'receipts.'"

"But weren't any of them recovered?"

"If you mean, were they returned to Austria, yes, some were. After the war, as you know, the Germans delivered a good many art objects to the Austrian government for return to the individual owners. However, it didn't always work out that way."

He paused to lever himself down from the curb to cross a street. I almost offered him my arm, but I knew he wouldn't like it. "I long ago gave up hope of seeing any of them again," he said, and then gave me a wry smile. "It seems I was unable to satisfy the court's documentary criteria."

He didn't have to say any more. Austria's approach to the restitution of artworks stolen by the Nazis from its citizens—most of them Jews, unlike Stetten—was notorious for foot-dragging, ineptitude, and outright meanness, right up there with Switzerland's similarly venal treatment of Holocaust victims' claims to wartime bank accounts. For forty years after the war Austria had stored the returned works of art in state museums and government storehouses, categorically refusing to consider any claims. Only in 1985, under scathing international pressure, did the Parliament pass legislation allowing previous owners or their heirs to file claims for their property.

Even then the "documentary criteria" were daunting. Claimants, who weren't allowed to view the works themselves, had to provide either exact descriptions or impeccable evi-

178

dence, such as appraisals or sales records. After four decades, with most of the original owners dead, not many could meet the requirements. There were notorious cases in which claims were turned down because the estimated size of a painting—last seen in the 1940s—was off by a centimeter or two. As a result, only about 10 percent of the holdings were ever returned; the rest were auctioned in 1996, with the proceeds finally going (grudgingly) to Holocaust-victim agencies.

Not a pretty record, but Austria and Switzerland had hardly been the only ones. Even brave France, it was turning out, had plenty to be ashamed of, let alone Russia and the Eastern European countries. And it was by no means only wealthy collectors like Stetten who were being stiffed. Many of the claimants were poor, not rich, seeking the return not of a stately collection but of a dining-room commode that had been in the family two hundred years, or a single portrait that had hung in the living room. Sons and daughters of people who had been gassed to death at Auschwitz or Dachau were routinely turned away because they could produce no death certificates for their parents. Wretched stuff, enough to shake anybody's faith in humanity's penchant for doing the right thing when there were profits to be made for doing anything but.

By the time we reached the hotel, my spirits were as low as his, so that I was more than ready to say good night. I freshened up in my suite and came back downstairs at 10:55, five minutes before I was due to meet Dulska. There was some kind of hassle going on in the lobby—hurried, snappish policemen, gesticulating clerks— but the Imperial's bar was far enough away from the traffic to be peaceful. I ordered a glass of barack, the pungent, apricot-flavored liquor that I'd never been quite certain I liked, but which I order when I'm in Vienna anyway because I had it on my first visit. Then I sat down to wait for Dulska.

At 11:10 he hadn't yet arrived. I assumed that he'd been worried about seeming a little too anxious and had decided to make me wait a bit to prove he wasn't. But when he hadn't shown up by 11:25, I started to get itchy. Apparently he'd decided that we were going to meet in his suite after all, whether I liked it or not. At first I was annoyed, but it didn't take me long to conclude that, inasmuch as he was holding all the cards, the only thing I could do was go along with him.

I remembered the hotel manager's saying that morning that he was in suite 400, so I went through the lobby—tranquil enough now— and took the mirrored elevator to the fourth floor. When I came out, my way was blocked by two policemen in summer uniforms—light-blue, open-necked shirts with red epaulets, green military caps and matching pants, and handguns in flap-covered holsters on their belts. One of them, tall and sinewy, stepped away from the corridor wall against which he'd been leaning and blocked my way.

"Kann ich Ihnen helfen?"

180

I told him that I was on my way to speak with Herr Dulska, the gentleman in room 400.

"*Ein Moment, bitte,*" he said with a nod, then spoke a few rapid words to his colleague, who went to an open doorway at the far end of the hall, hurrying back with a middle-aged officer whose spiffy uniform included a black tie and a green tunic but no sidearm. This, I was informed, was Polizeibezirkinspektor Pirchl, who wished to ask me a few questions.

Pirchl, a squash-faced man with a watch-yourself-I'm-in-charge-here manner, looked me up and down with his hands clasped behind him. "*Amerikaner?*"

I nodded and told him who I was. "And you are a 'business' associate of Herr Dulska's?" he asked in German, with a heavy, caustic emphasis on "business."

This man is not too taken with me, I thought. I couldn't tell whether it was just something that went with the job or it was me in particular that he didn't like. Or maybe *Amerikaners* in general.

I shrugged. "Not really, no." Not the world's greatest comeback, but what was there to say?

Fortunately he didn't pursue it, but I didn't like the way he was looking at me. "Come with me, please," he said abruptly, turning on his heel and quick-marching me to the open door. Nope, I thought, it's me, personally.

In the front room I could see men in uniform and civilian dress bustling around. "Walk only on the paper," Pirchl said at the door. "Put your hands in your pockets so you touch nothing." Then, with a quick look at me, "You don't mind looking at a dead body?"

Christ, I thought, not another dead body.

But it was, of course, and of course it was Dulska. He was in shirtsleeves, trousers, and socks, lying on his stomach on the floor of the bedroom, his arms caught under his body, his head twisted enough to one side for me to recognize him. I'd been right about his having more than enough blood. His white shirt was drenched from shoulders to belt with it, and there was more soaking blackly into the pale carpet around him, like dark wine into a sponge cake. There were only a few flecks of it on his face, but something pinkish and unsettling protruded from between his lips; after a moment I realized that it was a denture that had been displaced and lodged half in, half out of his mouth. I closed my eyes and turned away.

Pirchl touched my elbow and motioned me back through the front room. "The paper, the paper," he snapped when I almost cut across a corner of carpet that hadn't been covered by the four-foot-wide strip of glossy brown paper.

"So, is it the man?" he asked in the hallway, with a sort of careless impatience.

"Uh...yes, it's him...yes."

One patronizing eyebrow lifted. "Do you need to sit down?"

"No."

It wasn't only that I didn't want to give him the satisfaction either. Amazingly enough, as sordid and pathetic and ugly as the scene in there had been, I didn't feel the need to. The truth is, I wasn't feeling much of anything beyond disappointment and frustration: There went my lead to the paintings; there went my lead to Simeon's killer. But there had been no stomach-twisting lurch of disgust, no urge to retch, not even any queasiness to speak of after the first look at him.

I guess you can get used to anything.

THE WUURTTEMBERG SITTING ROOM, where Stetten, Dulska, and I had met that morning, had been taken over as the police command post, and it was there that I was asked to go over in detail my business with Dulska. Even with the help of an interpreter it got a little dodgy when I tried to explain to Pirchl that whereas I was pretty sure Dulska was a crook, *I* most certainly wasn't, and that my only purpose in agreeing to a late-night, private appointment with him had been to lead him on. Eventually Pirchl seemed to accept it, at least for the moment, but naturally that got me onto explaining about Stetten, the Velàzquezes, Simeon, and all the rest of it, which took a long time and irritated him with me that much more. He was one of those people with a natural knack for making you feel that there were a hundred incredibly pressing, much more important things

183

demanding his immediate attention, if only you weren't taking up his time with your trivial and pointless maunderings.

Somewhere near 1:00 A.M. a policeman came in to report that the painting was nowhere to be found; not in Dulska's suite, and not in the hotel safe either. Hardly surprising, but depressing all the same. After that, it took another hour before they turned me loose. Pirchl told me that I would have to review and sign my statement at central police headquarters no later than noon that day. Once there, he said, I should expect to remain for a while because Polizeioberstleutnant Feuchtmüller would no doubt wish to speak with me about this matter, as would someone from the American consulate.

By this time I didn't give a damn who might want to speak with me, or why, or when. My head could have been stuffed with cotton batting (and felt as if it were) for all the good it was doing me. I was practically ready to weep with exhaustion. Aside from its having been an extremely long, strange day, I'd been awake all of the previous night on the flight to Vienna, which meant I hadn't slept in about forty hours, except for a bit of uneasy snoozing in the museum. And with a raging case of jet lag on top of that, my circadian rhythms were still slogging along on Boston time, six whopping hours out of whack. Besides, it had been less than four weeks since I'd had my ribs broken and I had yet to come around to feeling 100 percent whole again, even before all this.

I mean, poor me.

CHAPTER 14

I have a hazy recollection of stumbling into my room, kicking off my shoes, and falling into bed, but that's about it. My brain had shut down. All the same, utterly zonked or not, I popped wide awake at a little before 3:00 A.M., having slept one hour, with a jumpy feeling in my muscles and a hollow feeling in my stomach that told me I was finished sleeping for the night whether my brain liked it or not. The hollow feeling wasn't from hunger. I was jet-lagged, at loose ends, lonesome, and even a little homesick—which is to say, about normal for the first night in a foreign country, when you're all alone, and it's three o'clock in the morning, and you can't sleep because your biological clock doesn't know what time it is. And that's without a new murder thrown in.

What I needed was the sound of a friendly voice, but it was coming home to me with increasing clarity that my list of friends was pretty short, especially with Simeon gone, and that it didn't extend to anyone who would have been pleased with a 3:00 A.M. telephone call. So I got up, took a shower, which got the coating of grime off but didn't do much else, switched into a pair of pajama bottoms, and flopped into an armchair to smoke one of my bimonthly cigars and mope.

Give Alex a call to let her know how things were going? No, not at this time of the morning. Besides, I didn't really have anything to tell her. Sure, all sorts of exciting things had happened, but so what? Stetten's Velàzquez was gone, and I wasn't any closer to learning anything even vaguely linked to Simeon's murder. The truth was, I suddenly and contritely realized, that I'd hardly thought about Simeon all day, or so it seemed to me now. The brutal death of that good old man had been shoved aside by golden visions of buried Goyas and Gainsboroughs and pipe dreams of glory: LOST MASTERPIECES DISCOVERED BY FAMED BOSTON ART COP.

Shit. I sat there a while longer, penitent and ashamed, weary of the now-soggy cigar—as bad as Schnittke's—but smoking it down to a disgusting black stub anyway as a kind of self-punishment. It was a full half hour before I realized that I had my times mixed up—it was only 9:30 P.M. back in Boston. (I told you, my brain had shut down.) I picked up the phone and dialed before I could change my mind.

THE MUFFLED SOUNDS OF chewing told me that she'd answered before she was quite ready. Then a gulped swallow. "Hello?"

"Alex, hi, this is Ben Revere. I'm still in Vienna. I—"

186

"Ben, hello! This is amazing, I was just having some pickled herring and thinking of you."

What is there to say to that? "That's nice," I said. "I think." Whatever it meant, I was cheered. Not only was she thinking of me, she sounded glad to hear from me.

"No, I mean I was sitting around noshing and reading the *Globe,* and here was this article about the Velàzquez on page two."

"Which Velàzquez?"

"Simeon's, the one here in Boston. It mentions you, too, but the main thing is, your friend the count isn't the only one who's saying it's his. All kinds of other people are claiming that it really belongs to them."

"That's not too surprising. The shysters come crawling out of the woodwork on something like this. But possibly some of them are telling the truth."

"How can that be? I thought it belonged to your friend the count."

"What is this with my 'friend the count'?"

"Well, does it or doesn't it?"

"It does, but it might also belong to someone else—somebody, say, who bought it after the war, thinking it was on the up-and-up, and owned it for maybe ten or fifteen years, and then had it stolen from him. Well, he'd have a legitimate claim, too. It'd be complicated; nobody would really be at fault, and he'd have been every bit as genuinely ripped off as Stetten."

"I suppose so," she said dubiously, "but that

sounds like lawyer talk to me. As far as I'm concerned, what matters is who it was stolen from in the first place. Hey, it's the middle of the night over there. What are you doing up?"

"Well—"

"Let me get my coffee. Then I want to hear what you've been up to." In a few seconds she picked up the phone again. "Okay, I'm back."

"Coffee with pickled herring?" I said.

"Coffee *after* pickled herring."

"Who eats pickled herring at nine-thirty anyway? It's unnatural." As if I were in a position to criticize weird eating habits.

Alex laughed, and I got a sudden, clear image of her bigmouthed, scoop-nosed, streaky-haired beauty, and her long, strong legs and big hands, and the way she threw back her head and let go when she laughed, with a honk like Julia Child's. What was really odd about this was that, until now, I'd always thought my taste in women ran to the small-boned and delicate. Live and learn. *What are you wearing right now?* I wanted to ask. *Is your hair still in a ponytail?* But of course I didn't.

"Aahh," she said, gulping coffee. "So tell me: How did it go?"

"Not real well, I'm afraid."

"Well, on a scale of one to ten."

"On a scale of one to ten? Ohh, mm...minus two hundred and fifty, I'd say. The dealer's dead and the painting's disappeared." I figured I might as well get it all out at once. "Oh, and the Vienna police suspect me of something, but I'm not sure what."

I heard her cup come down on a table with a whack. "The— Are you serious?"

And so I told her all about it, and it wasn't nearly as bad as I'd imagined. "Ben," she said with gratifying concern, "this is really getting— I mean, that makes three people that have been killed just since this began, do you realize that?"

"It's been pretty hard not to notice, but I still have a few apples in my basket. I'm not ready to give up yet."

"Listen, Ben, I don't know how to say this—I know that I'm the one that's been pushing you all along to get involved in this, but now...people getting murdered all over the place, and you in trouble with the police....I'm starting to think you were right. This is police work. Maybe you should just leave it to them and come home, don't you think?"

"Not a chance," I said resolutely.

Okay, I was posturing a little, but it wasn't just swagger. I'd meant everything I'd ever said about Simeon. I had a date in St. Petersburg, and I damn well intended to keep it. And somewhere along the way another idea had belatedly occurred to me. The Altaussee mine was still a working salt mine but a tourist attraction as well, with its own historical museum. They were bound to have some World War II records—maybe even somebody still around who had worked there at the time—so there might well be something of interest to be learned. Certainly it was worth the day or two it would take me to get there

189

and back from Vienna after I returned from St. Petersburg.

I heard a barely audible cluck of the tongue from Alex's end after I told her this, and then a sigh. "You'll promise to be careful, though?" Then, as if regretting having shown too much concern, "It'd be a real pain to have you on my conscience."

"Don't give it a thought. I know exactly what I'm doing, sort of."

"I can't tell you how reassuring that is. Oh, before I forget— have you talked to Sergeant Cox lately? Has he told you who that dead body is, that they found in the pipe?"

"*Who* it is? No, have they identified it?"

"Yes, he says that it's someone named Dmitri Korolenko, and that he was a courier for the Moscow mafia. Simeon had him pegged right. Apparently he flew into Boston from Moscow only one day before he...before it happened."

"So it's true." I leaned back in my chair, musing. "A professional courier for the Moscow mafia really *did* come all the way to Boston to pawn a five-million-dollar painting for one hundred bucks."

"Yes, but why?"

Indeed. The old question again.

CHAPTER 15

I don't remember getting back into bed after talking to Alex, but I must have, because that's where I was the next time I woke up, at 8:50 A.M. It took me four or five foggy seconds to realize that what had jarred me awake was the trill of the telephone on the table at the far side of the big bed, and then at least that much time again to reach it, having to fight my way through the billows of an oversized down comforter that must have decimated the Central European goose population.

"Dr. Revere? It's Stetten. Did you hear? Dulska is dead!"

"Yes, I know."

"My painting is gone!"

"Yes, I know."

"I still can't believe it. I can't make myself believe it. It's terrible, I don't know what to do." He sounded dazed, as if he were rocking back and forth and wringing his hands in despair, or would have been if he weren't holding the telephone in one of them.

"Why don't we meet downstairs?" I suggested gently. "We can talk about it over a cup of coffee." Coffee was certainly what I needed.

"*Coffee?*" From his amazement you'd have thought I'd suggested brake fluid. "No...no, I don't want any coffee. I must leave at once. I don't wish to get involved in this." His voice, a little on the quavery side anyway, was shaking so hard you could hear the beat, like a vibrato on a violin string.

"But the police are going to want to talk to you. I've—"

"To *me*?" He was horrified. "No, I'm leaving, it's not my affair. It's too much to expect of me, of a man my age. I'm sorry I ever began this terrible business."

"But—"

"Your hotel expenses have been posted to my account," he said, not letting me get in a word, "and if you'll send the rest of your bill to me, I'll take care of it at once. Good-bye, good-bye, and thank you."

"No, wait," I said hurriedly. "What about all your other paintings? I've been thinking about them, and I've come up with a few ideas that might just lead—"

"I'm sorry, I can't discuss it, I have to go. Good-bye, good-bye," he cried again, and the receiver hit the cradle with a bang.

By THE TIME I'D showered and eaten a room-service meal of juice, coffee, rolls, and cheese, it was almost eleven-thirty and time to get over to police headquarters. Pirchl had offered to send a car for me, but I decided to walk instead. Every cop in the Württemberg room had smoked without stopping, and I felt the need to gather in a few lungfuls of fresh air before being submerged in what was bound to be a similar fug at the police station. I also wanted to walk, to swing my arms and legs at a good clip for a while, something I hadn't done for far too long, and the station's location off Schottenring on Deutschmeisterplatz would give me a brisk half-hour stroll through the heart of Old Vienna, just what I needed to clear my lungs, and my head as well.

But before I left, I put in a call to Christie Valle de Leon at CIAT. It was early in New York, not yet 6:00 A.M., but Christie was one of those people—surely the only one in the art world— who like to get to work at that time, at least when the weather's good, so that they can get something done while things are quiet. Of course, she also usually left for the day at three, so she wasn't completely crazy. Sometimes she wouldn't even pick up the phone before nine, but this time I was in luck.

In less than five minutes she filled me in on the claimants that Alex had told me about. There were five altogether, none of whom had been identified in the news releases, but Christie had looked into them herself, as I'd assumed she would. Three of them, in her opinion, were mere opportunists with no more claim to the painting than she had. Of the remaining two, one was a Hungarian art dealer named Szarvas, and the other was a Viennese named Nussbaum, both of whom raised troubling questions and made potentially persuasive cases. I wrote down their names and addresses, listened to the few facts she could tell me about them, and left for the police station in a more optimistic mood. Nussbaum's address placed him about a mile from where

I was at that moment, and Szarvas was in Budapest, where I had to change planes on the way back here from St. Petersburg anyway. So I had two brand-new leads to follow— if I could convince them to talk to me. I put in a quick call to Nussbaum's number to see if I could arrange a meeting, but got no answer. Calling Szarvas in Budapest was bound to take some time, so I put it aside until later and headed off through the old section of the city for Deutschmeisterplatz.

In the dozen or so years I'd known Vienna, it had changed not at all physically. The same broad boulevards and narrow cobblestoned streets, the same pleasant, stately open spaces, the same splendid hotels and cafés. In other ways, things were different. As always the city was awash in posters advertising concerts of Strauss and Mozart, but now they were fighting a losing battle for space with notices of appearances by Joe Cocker, U2, Jewel, and David Bowie. There were also a lot of homegrown bands with names meant to sound like famous English or American groups: the Gruesome Babies, Tommyboy, Anal Chickens, Beastly Sneakers. Or maybe they *were* famous English or American groups, what do I know?

The tourist population had altered, too. There still seemed to be plenty from Rome, Munich, and Paris, but now, with the Iron Curtain gone, the rows of boxy tour buses pulled up at cultural shrines and group hotels were more likely to be from Bratislava, Moldovia, and points farther east, and the clumps of people sticking close to their Slavic-speaking guides wore the mistrustful expressions of country folk who'd been warned to keep one hand on their wallets when they were in the big city. ✗

By the time I reached Schottenring, the northernmost segment of the Ring, which is actually six sides of an octagon that more or less encircles the inner city (the curving Danube Canal serves as the other two sides), the monuments, the tourists, and the posters had thinned out. Deutschmeisterplatz itself was a square plot of worn grass, deserted except for a couple of elderly dog-walkers, with a few benches and a weather-and pigeon-stained monument to the exploits of an eighteenth-century Viennese garrison. The only building of any size that faced it was a handsome, five-story, late-eighteenth-century "palazzo" in the Florentine style, with a façade of "rusticated"—rough-textured and deep-jointed—stone blocks. There was nothing about it to suggest from any distance that it was police headquarters, but beside the tall, ornate, wooden double doors—the original ones, if I wasn't mistaken—an inconspicuous red-and-white sign made it clear that I'd found the right place.

BUNDESPOLIZEIDIREKTION
WIEN
BEZIRKPOLIZEIKOMMISSARIAT
INNERE STADT

The left-hand door opened to a cobble-stoned inner courtyard, where a policewoman in a guard shack directed me to a second-floor counter. There, in an antiseptically clean waiting room with magazines and a wall-mounted television set in one corner, I was asked by a receptionist with braided blond hair to wait. I watched a dubbed *Magnum, P.I.* episode for a while, wondering, not for the first time, why it was that European dubbers gave all American leading men a deep, sonorous voice. Every time the real Tom Selleck went "hee-hee-hee," the voice on the TV went "harr-harr-harr."

After a few minutes an efficient-looking cop in a crisp, faultlessly fitted green uniform came out with my typed-up statement and waited, shifting from one foot to the other, while I read and signed it, then politely asked me to continue waiting. I returned to Magnum, who had just run into one of his friends in a Honolulu dive. ("*Harr-harr, T.J., wie geht's?*")

"Ben Revere, am I right?" somebody asked in plain old American English, Upper Midwestern variety.

I looked up to see a rumpled, overweight man of fifty in a lumpy tweed sport coat that reeked almost visibly of pipe tobacco, baggy slacks with bulging pockets, and an exhausted tie twisted into a skinny knot. Above the knot was a fleshy, friendly face with a bulbous red wine-bibber's nose.

"That's right," I said, standing. "And

you're...? Oh, are you from the consulate?"

"Lord have mercy, no, I'm Polizeiober-stleutnant Feuchtmüller."

"I...you're...I beg your pardon?" The man looked as if he couldn't be from the same planet as the spruce, sleek Viennese cops I'd seen so far.

He took pity on my confusion. "All is explainable. I'm half American—my mother's from Green Bay, Wisconsin, in the Land of the Round Doorknobs. My full name's Alois McGuffey Feuchtmüller, and, as bizarre as it may seem to you—as it seems to me some-times—I really am a genuine Polizeiober-stleutnant in the Office of the Federal Directorate-General for Public Security, Organized Crime Division. On my honor. Am I not, Greta?"

"Ze rreal ssing," the blond receptionist agreed.

CHAPTER 16

Policemen must not trust one another's interrogative skills, because they're always asking you to tell them what happened, no matter how many times you've told it before, and Polizeioberstleutnant Alois McGuffey Feuchtmüller was no exception. For a good hour I talked while he muttered in his snuffly voice from time to time, asked an occasional question, smoked a foul, sooty pipe, and took no notes whatsoever, unless his doodles of ducks and swans (chickens and turkeys?) were a secret code. I told him about everything pertinent that had happened to me in Vienna, and about Simeon and the Boston Velàzquez. The history of the Lost Truck particularly intrigued him, and so I dredged up every fact, hypothesis, and reasonably plausible speculation I'd ever heard about it while we sipped coffee and then Cokes in his stuffy office—more like a college professor's than a cop's, what with books piled on every flat surface. The furniture was gray steel and Naugahyde, the walls pale green, the floor linoleum-tiled. I felt right at home, as if I were back in my old non-tenure-track cubicle at Harvard. Even the book titles were professorial: thick tomes in German and English on sociology, political theory, and economics, most of them with multiple torn-paper markers sticking out of them. A funny cop, I thought.

At one o'clock he reamed out the pipe for the third time, emptied the ashtray—thoroughly nasty by now—into a wastepaper basket, and made his first declarative statement in some time: "Lunchtime, my friend, what do you say to going and getting something to eat?"

"Sounds great," I said. "Here I've been in Vienna for over twenty-four hours now, and I've yet to meet my first wienerschnitzel."

Under tangled gray eyebrows his eyes lit up. "Oho, do I know the place for you."

• • •

TEN MINUTES LATER WE were at the Café Schottenring a few blocks from police headquarters, seated under a green awning at a sidewalk table. Boxed junipers more or less shielded us from passersby and from the steady hum of automobile traffic on the Ring. Our orders had already been taken. I had ordered the *schnitzel mit pommes frites*, while Alois—mercifully, he had told me to call him Alois after hearing me mangle "Polizeioberstleutnant" a few times (to say nothing of "Feuchtmüller")—had asked for the salad plate. He was, he sorrowfully explained, watching his waistline.

Obviously his proscriptions did not extend to beer, inasmuch as each of us had a generous stemmed goblet of Gösser Bier, the velvety, justly famous Viennese brew, in front of him. Alois downed a third of his glass in two luxurious swallows, licked his lips, leaned back, and rolled his eyes with contentment. "Now then, this Dulska: Was he telling you the truth? Do you think he really had access to all of Stetten's missing paintings?"

I shrugged. "Maybe. Everything else about this is weird, so why not that, too?"

"How much do you know about him, Ben? Ever run across him before? Heard of him, I mean?"

"No. According to Stetten, he was a reputable dealer, but—"

Alois's wheezing laugh cut me off. "'Reputable.' Not the word I'd choose."

199

"But he *was* an art dealer?"

"Oh, yes, that was one of his businesses, all right, but he's been involved, one way or another, with the Moscow mafia ever since the Wall came down. He does jobs for the Chetverk crime family— it means Thursday, by the way, don't ask me why. Front man, fence, go-between, you name it. He's the only reason they've put me on the case, y'see."

"Not really, no," I said. "Aren't you just investigating the murder?"

"Good heavens, no, that's Pirchl's job. Do I look like some sort of homicide detective? Can you imagine them giving me a gun? Who would be safe? No, I'm a member of the investigative wing of the organized-crime bureau." I was beginning to detect the slightest of Viennese accents in his speech, more a matter of meter than pronunciation.

"I didn't realize Austria had much of an organized-crime problem."

"It didn't until recently, if you mean the homegrown variety, but you know, we share three borders with what used to be the Soviet bloc, and they do, they most certainly do. And now we do, too. Is Klaus Loitzl a familiar name to you?"

"No."

"Well, Klaus Loitzl is to Viennese crime what John Gotti was to New York City crime, if that helps. He was a big boss in East Berlin when it was East Berlin. When the Wall came down, he moved to Vienna, to greener pastures. The organized-crime bureau was formed a few years ago to try to deal with Loitzl and his people, but also with the more general intrusion of East European gangs. My own specialty happens to be the Russian mafia. I thought you understood."

I shook my head.

"True," Alois said, "I am a policeman now, of a sort, but until three years ago I was a happily obscure professor of socioeconomic theory with a specialty in applied Western Marxist doctrine and a particular interest in Soviet post-Communist reform or the lack thereof."

A professor. Ah, now, that explained things.

When the waiter came with our food, Alois watched hungrily as my plate was set down, the golden veal cutlet hanging over the sides, the tawny French fries fragrant and perfectly crisped. He looked so forlorn that I offered him some.

"No, thanks," he said mournfully, "I have a hard enough time keeping my weight down as it is."

If a Viennese saladteller was his idea of a diet plate, it was no wonder. Anybody would have had a tough time keeping his weight down lunching on the four hefty mounds on his plate: thickly sauced German potato salad, curried creamed chicken, beef in cream sauce, and chunks of wurst in some kind of rich, mustardy gravy. The only thing with fewer than two hundred calories per mouthful was the layer of leaf lettuce on which it all sat. And that, naturally, he never touched.

As we ate—and once he got going, he attacked

his "salad" with good cheer—Alois gave me a quick course on the Eastern European crime wave that had followed the Communist collapse and had yet to slow down. In part, it seemed, it was a matter of logistics. The East-West borders that had been fiercely controlled until 1989 were now wide open, and the poorly paid border guards, when they weren't overwhelmed by the flow, were easily bribed by anybody who wanted to haul anything across—drugs, alcohol, forged currencies, Kalashnikovs, Strontium-90...or Old Masters paintings.

And within the borders of countries that had been ruled by Communist governments, hatred and fear of the police still ran high, so that Western methods of going after organized crime were usually outlawed: no police wiretapping, no bugging devices, no "sting" operations, no undercover agents, no cutting deals with little fish in order to catch the big ones. As Alois put it, it would be a long time before the Poles, the Czechs, and the rest of them truly understood that it was possible for a democratic society to use modern police techniques and still remain a democracy.

These factors, along with rising standards that had made Eastern Europe a lucrative new target, had combined to produce something new: an international, borderless criminal underground, in which rival syndicates competed with and killed off each other in intertribal warfare that made 1920s Chicago look like a playpen. Last year, Alois said, there had been a summit meeting in Kraków, where Czech, Russian, Polish, and Hungarian gang lords, trying to hold down the fraternal bloodshed, worked out formal rules of engagement and cooperation. And even the Japanese Yakuza, the Chinese Triads, and the Colombian drug cartels, sensing money to be made, had now gotten into the act in Eastern and Central Europe.

But Alois's baby was the Russian mafia, and in particular the Moscow crime families, the region's most ruthless and effective criminal organizations—no surprise, since much of their leadership had more or less transferred straight out of the KGB. And where Zykmund Dulska was involved, the Russian mafia was sure to be involved.

Which was why he was on the case.

"Another beer?" he asked hopefully when the food was gone and he'd wound down his lecture.

"Why not?" The first one had gone to my head, I was pleasantly full of wienerschnitzel, and I was feeling expansive for the first time in months.

"One more question, Ben. You said you never told Stetten that Dulska called you about making a deal on the side. Are you sure you didn't tell anyone else? On the telephone, perhaps...?"

"Uh-uh, no."

"And you're absolutely positive you didn't imply it to Stetten in some way? Inadvertently?"

"I don't see how. He didn't stop griping about the opera long enough for me to get a sentence in."

"So the question is—assuming that was the reason he was killed, which may or may not be the case—how did anybody manage to find out about it between six-thirty, when he called you, and eight o'clock or so, which Pirchl tells me is the approximate time he died. Quick work, wouldn't you say?"

"I don't know, compared to what?"

"You know, the usual way the Russians deal with this sort of, ah, disloyalty, is to send a hit man, a contract killer, in from Moscow and back out on a plane, all in the same day so that it's next to impossible to trace. By the time anyone finds out the victim is dead, the killer is back sleeping in his own bed. In this case, obviously, there was no time for that sort of arrangement. The killer would already have had to be in Vienna. All we have to do is figure out who it is."

"Alois, you're not seriously thinking it was Stetten, are you?"

"I don't know, am I?"

"But it's impossible. We were in a box at the opera until well after ten. He was sitting right next to me the whole time."

"Stetten himself, all right, but you wouldn't expect him to do it with his own hands, would you? These things can be arranged."

"But why would *Stetten* want to have Dulska killed, for Christ's sake? Dulska was his only link to the painting."

"A telling point," he said amiably. "On the other hand, isn't it at least theoretically possible that Stetten now *has* the painting? That it was Stetten who had him killed for just that purpose? It would have saved him a million and a quarter schillings; a great many people have been killed for less. Ah, I see from your expression that the possibility hadn't occurred to you."

"Not until now, no." But even as I said it I realized that I wasn't telling the truth. It had occurred to me, all right; I'd just pushed it down to a subliminal level. I didn't like thinking that Stetten might be a murderer. "Alois, if you think he might really be involved, why haven't you talked to *him*?"

"But we have. I had a discussion with him this morning. Charming man. We managed to put him on the eleven twenty-two to Salzburg, only two hours after the train he intended to take."

"And do you suspect him? I mean, really suspect him?"

He shrugged. "Early days yet, friend Revere." He looked up with evident pleasure as the waiter set down our refilled goblets, then downed a healthy swallow and wiped foam from his upper lip. "Aahh." He was one of those people who made whatever he ate or drank look wonderful.

"Let me ask you something, Alois," I said, sipping my own beer and still thinking about Stetten. "I can't help wondering about him. The guy is like something out of 1860. Is he really a count, do you know?"

He pondered. "Let me answer that in two words. Yes and no."

I smiled. "Well, I'm glad to have that cleared up."

"Albrecht, Graf Stetten, is a genuine count, a *royal* count in fact, a lineal descendant of the ruling Habsburgs, great-grandnephew of Emperor Ferdinand I and Anna of Sardinia, grandnephew of Felix Ludwig and Amalia of Saxe-Meiningen-Hohenlohe, and currently sixty-second in line for the throne of Austria."

"I'm impressed."

Alois went on, "The catch being, as may have occurred to you, that there *is* no throne of Austria." With a fresh glass in front of him and with his stomach full, he was feeling expansive, too.

"You know, I think I did notice that, yes. That's why I'm asking."

Alois settled himself more solidly in his chair and cleared his throat, shifting visibly into professorial mode.

"The controlling legislation in this matter is the Habsburg Law of 1919, subsequently written into the Austrian State Treaty of 1955, which banishes all members of the Habsburg family from Austrian territory unless they explicitly renounce dynastic pretensions and accept the status of loyal private citizens, which Stetten did many years ago. The upshot is that, although technically the term 'count' no longer has legal meaning, Stetten is entitled to use it if he wants to—as long as it's for amusement purposes only, so to speak."

Having delivered himself of this explanation, he got out his pipe and pouch and started on his personal version of the pipe-lighter's lengthy ritual, using a brown, tobacco-cured thumb to press the stuff into the bowl of the pipe. "Now let me ask you something. This collection that Stetten's father put together— I gather it's quite good?"

"It's a lot better than good."

"But before this started, you hadn't heard of it?"

"That's right."

"Well, why not, if it's so extraordinary? I'd have thought it would be famous."

"No," I said, "and it's really not that surprising. Look, if you don't count the collections in a handful of the world's top museums— the Met, the Louvre, the Uffizi, the Hermitage, the National Gallery, a few others, maybe—most Old Masters are in private hands, not public collections, and—I'm guessing now—I'd say that nobody but the owners has any idea where half of them are, and that's a conservative estimate. There's no law that says dealings in the art market have to be made public, and a lot of sellers, let alone buyers, prefer to keep things private. Why would you want the whole world to know you have a million dollars' worth of art hanging on your living-room walls?"

"Mm. All right, let's move on." He got the pipe into his mouth, in the process adding another sprinkling of tobacco shreds to his lapels, and noisily lit up, flaring a wooden match with his thumbnail, the way they do in old movies. "You know the way the art market works, Ben. In your opinion, just what was our man Dulska up to?"

"Well, assuming that you're right and he'd been acting for the mafia in this, I guess he just figured he could do better on his own and that I could help him find—"

"No, I don't mean about his calling you, I mean what was he doing in the first place? He certainly couldn't have anticipated making a deal of his own with you; you weren't even in the picture when he contacted Stetten. So just why did he come to Vienna?"

"You mean you *don't* think he was working for the mafia?"

"No, I do think he was working for the mafia. Let me put it this way, then. What were *they* up to?"

"You've lost me."

"You said the picture was worth five million dollars, *nicht wahr*?"

I nodded.

"So why would they be willing to let it go for one million— for a hundred thousand, when it came down to it? These are not people who are known for their generosity or their readiness to compromise. Damn." His pipe had gone out; he set about relighting it.

"Well, Stetten was the legitimate owner; why would he agree to—"

"But why deal with Stetten at all?" he said, narrowing his eyes against the acrid, self-generated fog spiraling around his head. "Why not sell it to somebody who'd pay what it's worth? After all, that's obviously what Dulska was trying to set up with you, so why bother going through the rigmarole with Stetten at all?"

It was the same question that had occurred to me, and the best answer that I'd been able to come up with so far was that Dulska or his bosses had been afraid to offer it on the open market for fear that Stetten might hear about it, raise a stink, and perhaps bring the law down on them; the Old Masters marketplace, private or not, can be an extremely gossipy world. And as for fencing it in the criminal market, selling it to a fence would have brought only 5 percent of value—10 at most; say, five hundred thousand dollars. (Then again, Dulska wouldn't have had to sell it to a fence, because according to Alois he *was* a fence, an international one, and as such, you'd have thought he'd have had sufficient contacts among the unscrupulous to get at least a couple of million dollars for the painting.)

In other words, I didn't know.

"Neither do I," Alois said.

From the reflective way he said it, I thought he might have some ideas of his own, but if he did, he didn't share them with me.

We ordered a *Kännchen* of coffee to round off the meal, and as Alois stirred a second spoonful of sugar into his cup he said casually, "So will you be going home now?"

"Not yet, no. I really don't see how I can just take off and let things rest as they are. There are still a few things I can do on this side of the Pond."

"Such as? I sincerely hope you're not thinking of doing a little independent police work of your own."

"No, of course not."

"And you're not working for Stetten anymore, are you?"

"No, I'm fired; as of this morning I'm on my own, but there really are some things I can do, and I'm afraid if I just go back home and forget about it, there'll never be any answers."

"Oh, I don't know. We have a pretty competent police force here, and Pirchl's like a bulldog once he gets his teeth into something."

I had no doubt of that, but Pirchl's job was finding out who killed Zykmund Dulska in the heart of Vienna. His interest in the murder of an elderly Boston pawnbroker was zilch. I knew Sergeant Cox was plugging away on it back home, but I had a growing conviction, strengthened by Dulska's death, that the answers were here in Europe, not in New England.

I told Alois about my plans: fly to St. Petersburg the next day to talk to Yuri Minkov, then to Budapest to talk to Szarvas, the Hungarian art dealer who was claiming that the Boston Velàzquez was really his, then back to Vienna to talk to Nussbaum, who claimed that the Boston Velàzquez was *his,* and then, at some point, to the mine at Altaussee to learn whatever I could learn there.

"I've heard of cold leads," Alois said with a chuckle, "but this is in a class of its own. You're researching the Second World War. What are you hoping you're going to find out?"

"I don't know. Do you always know what you're looking for when you're asking questions?"

"Hardly ever. Well, I wish you luck. And I wish I could do something about your friend's murder."

"It's not only Simeon," I said. "I'd still like to help Stetten if I can, and maybe I can head these claimants off at the start and save everybody a lot of trouble and expense. According to the director at CIAT, the one in Budapest is a crook, a shady art dealer who puts in claims like this all the time—and manages to win a fair proportion of them. Unfortunately, the courts don't always come up with the right decision."

"I'm truly distressed to hear that. But look, what are you going to do if their claims *are* legitimate? What if these people, or the one here in Vienna at any rate, made a good-faith purchase somewhere along the way, not knowing the painting's history, and is the innocent victim of a theft himself? Wouldn't he have as good a case as Stetten?"

"Yes, he would, but at any rate, his claim isn't legitimate; neither of them is. Both of them are claiming that the Nazis confiscated the painting directly from them in the 1940s, which is impossible."

"No; at least one of them has to be lying."

"They're both lying, Alois, or if they're not, then at the very least they've got the wrong painting in mind; that can happen, too, after fifty-plus years. But *this* one was taken from Stetten's apartment by the Germans in 1942, along with seventy-two others."

"That's possible." He looked at me shrewdly. "It's also possible that Stetten is lying."

I poured us both some more coffee from the *Kännchen,* remembering Stetten's calm, straightforward narration of the night the Gestapo came, and of the terrible events that had followed. "I don't think so."

"Well, it's up to you," Alois said. "Personally, I think you ought to go back home, or at least stay clear of Vienna—of Austria—for a while. You get on Pirchl's nerves, I'm afraid."

"Yeah, well, he doesn't do anything for mine either."

"Yes, but *you* can't haul *him* in for questioning anytime you feel like it."

"What's he got against me anyway? As far as I can tell, he just doesn't like my looks."

"Well, that happens to be true, he thinks you look too American. But be fair, there's a little more than that. You did, after all, come to a foreign city and make a clandestine midnight appointment—"

"Eleven o'clock, not midnight."

"—with a known mafia operative to discuss dealing in contraband art of enormous value."

"But I explained all that to him—about twenty times."

"And struck him as glib and overly facile, with an answer for everything."

"Of course I had an answer for everything, why wouldn't I have an answer for everything? I was telling the truth."

Alois smiled. "I don't think you quite understand the way a policeman's mind works."

He'd started to worry me. I put down my cup and leaned across the table. "Alois, surely he can't think that I—what?—murdered Dulska and then hopped on the elevator and came back up there with the body lying on the carpet and the place crawling with cops? I'd have been out of my mind."

"No, I'm sure he doesn't believe you're a murderer, but he does seem to think it's possible that you may be, shall we say, 'involved' in some way."

"That's absolutely crazy!"

"Actually it isn't. Put yourself in his place. You say that, aside from the Turner in the exhibition at St. Petersburg, these two Velàzquezes are the first paintings from the truck to surface since the war."

"As far as I know, yes."

"Two paintings only. Coming to light in two different manners, on two different continents, with two entirely different casts of characters."

"Yes..."

"Except for one person: you. You've wound up smack, kerplunk, at the center of things both times. You, and only you."

"Well, yes, but...I think it's..."

"To what, a person of Pirchl's mode of thinking would ask, do we attribute this? Mere innocent coincidence or"—his expressive eyebrows went up and down—"a meaningful and perhaps sinister confluence of events? It makes one wonder, *nein*?"

"Alois, you're really making me nervous here. Do *you* think I'm involved?"

"I do not," he said promptly, for which I was grateful, "but it's Pirchl you have to worry about, and you'd be better off in Boston, where you wouldn't be so much on his mind."

"No, I'm not going back." I made it sound firm, which it was.

"Well, it's your funeral," he said cheerfully. "You'd better let me know where you'll be, and I'll pass it on to the inspector. And if you turn up anything useful or need me for anything..." He gave me his card, first scrawling his home number on it, and pushed himself to his feet. "Well, back to saving humanity from itself. Good luck, Ben. Keep in touch."

I sat there a few minutes longer, finishing the strong, good Austrian coffee and thinking over what he'd said about sinister confluences of events.

It made you wonder, *ja*.

CHAPTER 17

When I got back to my room, the amber telephone-message light was flashing. Pirchl on my case already? Just what I needed to make my day complete.

But the recorded message wasn't from the police. "Dr. Revere? Stetten here. I'm sorry about the bother this morning, I'm sure you understand. Well, then. You said something about locating my other paintings, I believe? I'm extremely interested to hear what you have in mind. You have my number, yes? Call when you are able. I'm anxious to— Well, please call."

Stetten's thin voice was animated and cheerful, about as different from the tone of his flustered call of the morning as a voice can be. Whatever else you said about him, the old guy sure could change moods in a hurry. In the short time I'd been in Vienna I'd seen him go from affable patrician to imperious monseigneur to terrified old codger, with a few stops in between. And now, presto chango, here he was, airily dismissing the morning's "bother." I just hoped my recuperative powers would be that good when I was in my eighties.

When I called his number I got a busy signal, so instead I set about trying to get the telephone number of Szarvas, the shady Hungarian art dealer Christie had told me about, but coping with the Hungarian information operator was miles beyond me, as I thought it might be, so I went down to the long-distance booths in the lobby, where I could get some help from the clerk in charge of them. With her assistance I got through to the art gallery in Budapest on the first try, and although Szarvas himself, the man I wanted to talk to, didn't speak English, an assistant did. I explained what I wanted to talk about, and he said fine, come on over, and gave me the name of what he assured me was a superior hotel practically next door to the gallery. I told him I'd be there on the morning of the following Tuesday.

I had the concierge rearrange my flight schedule to let me stop off for a night in Budapest on the way back from Russia, then put in another telephone call to the other claimant, the one in Vienna, Mr. Nussbaum, but for the second time got no answer. Then, back in my room, I tried Stetten again.

This time he picked it up. "Dr. Revere? Ah, I was hoping it was you. How are things in Vienna?"

"About as well as could be expected," I said, not knowing what else to answer. "I understand the police spoke to you this morning."

"Yes, yes," he said offhandedly. "There wasn't much I could tell them. Well, then, tell me, what do you have in mind? You mentioned a plan to find my other paintings?"

I sank into the armchair beside the phone. "Well, I don't know that I'd go so far as to call it a plan, but I've been thinking about a few things that might be useful. First of all, there's the other painting from the Lost Truck that's already shown up—"

"Yes, the other Velàzquez, the one in Boston."

"No, I don't mean that one, I mean the one that turned up a few years ago in the Hermitage exhibition."

"Hermitage exhibition!" he exclaimed. "But I knew nothing about this. Which one was it?"

"It was a Turner seascape."

"A what? A Turner, you said?" The excitement left his voice. "No, I don't believe we had any Turners. I'm sure we didn't. Father never had faith in the English school. I'm afraid that's no help at all."

"Not necessarily. The Nazis took seventy-some-odd paintings from you—"

"They took seventy-three."

"But there were a hundred and six on the truck. So some of them came from elsewhere."

"Elsewhere?"

"Other collections."

"Did they really?"

"You mean you didn't know that?"

"No, I didn't. But how does it matter? Why would I be interested in someone else's pictures?"

"Because by talking to the people at the Hermitage I might be able to establish a trail back to the truck itself, to the rest of the paintings—including yours—and then, with a little luck, follow it forward again to wherever they are now."

"Ah," he said after a moment, "I think see what you're driving at."

"There are some other possibilities, too." I told him that I intended to visit the Altaussee salt mine, and that other claimants to the Boston Velàzquez had popped up in Budapest and Vienna and that I planned to try to see them, too.

"Yes, Leo told me others had come forward. I was concerned, but he says there's nothing to be worried about; our case is very, very strong. Do you...you do agree, don't you?"

"I'm sure Mr. Schnittke's right," I said reassuringly, not that I thought there was ever nothing to be worried about in a case like this, "but all the same, I don't see how it can hurt to talk to them, and it might do some good."

"By all means, see what you can do with them; I leave it to you. Now, listen, are you done in Vienna for the moment? Why don't you come to Salzburg for a day or two? We can talk all this over more thoroughly. And there's something I want very much to show you."

So I wasn't canned after all; that was nice. "Sure, all right."

"Can you make it tomorrow? Or even this evening? There's a flight every hour."

"No, I can't. I have an eleven-o'clock flight to St. Petersburg tomorrow morning, and I'll be there and in Budapest for the next few days, so Wednesday would be the earliest."

"Wednesday, then. And, Dr. Revere? It

seems to me that you'll be doing a great deal more than you bargained for. Would fifteen hundred dollars a day plus expenses be appropriate?"

I have to admit that I gave this a moment's consideration, but only a moment's, and in the end I came down on the side of right. It was Simeon I was doing this for, not Stetten—Simeon and myself—and I damn well ought to be the one paying for it, even if it scuttled my budget for the next six months, which it just about would. "Thanks very much," I said, "but these next few days are on me. If you like, we can go back to the old arrangement when I show up in Salzburg."

"Oh, but at least you'll let me take care of your expenses. I have an account with the Hotel Kempinski in Budapest. I can—"

"I appreciate it, sir, but I insist. I've already booked my room at the Duna."

"The Duna?" he said doubtfully. "Are you sure it's good? You have to be careful with hotels in Budapest."

"It'll be fine for me. I don't really need anything fancy."

"As you like," he said stiffly. I suppose I'd hurt his feelings. Well, I'd soothe them when I got to Salzburg in a few days.

Tomorrow, Russia.

CHAPTER 18

St. Petersburg was freezing, which should have come as no surprise. After all, there it sits on the Gulf of Finland, only five hundred miles south of the Arctic Circle, under lowering, slate-colored skies for three out of every four days, and pierced through by broad, twisting canals that act as funnels for the bone-chilling winds whistling in off the gray water. It was thirty degrees Fahrenheit when I got there, and although it wasn't snowing at the moment, it looked as if it might start any second. This was only September 22, bear in mind, and the clothes I'd brought with me from Boston had been packed with Central Europe in mind, not northern Russia.

So the first thing I did, after checking in at the Grand Hotel Europe—a *real* budget-buster, but the only place in St. Petersburg that had its own water-purification system so that you could brush your teeth without worrying about an invasion of *Giardia lamblia,* the intestinal parasite that had laid me low in 1995—the first thing I did was to run over to the huge Gostinny Dvor shopping complex across the street to buy a coat by means of sign language. I came within a millimeter of getting one of the sleek, sexy, gangsterish leather jackets that were so popular here, but finally, standing in front of the mirror, I concluded somewhat sadly that it just wasn't me. I settled instead for a puffy, tan, hip-length parka with a detachable hood, very ordinary. I don't think that was really me either, but it was probably in the ballpark.

Then back to the hotel, with its smiling, friendly staff; long, gleaming marble corridors; dark, plush curtains; and an all-around air of decadent, pre-Revolutionary opulence, as long as you didn't count the scowling security guards at the door and the high-tech metal detector you had to walk through to get into the place. I suppose at least part of the idea was to give guests a sense of security, but somehow it didn't work that way.

My flight from Vienna had been delayed, then canceled, so that I'd had to wait around the airport for five hours before getting a later one, and I hadn't arrived in St. Petersburg until after seven, totally bushed. Now it was almost nine, too late to do much of anything (anything that I was interested in doing) but have a drink and something to eat and go to bed.

This being another first night in another foreign country, bombarded with alien customs, accents, and smells, I was feeling lonesome and a little off center again (with as much international hopping-around as I do, you'd think I'd take to it more naturally, but no, I always have a spell or two of the heebie-jeebies, usually at night). I went down to the hotel bar—the site of predinner drinks with Yuri and the rest of the crew a few years ago—found a table for one, and ordered a Baltika beer, which is pretty good and also comes in a squat, brown, Budweiserlike bottle that is comfortingly reminiscent of home.

The Grand Bar, living up to its name, had polished cherrywood wainscoting and Art Deco reliefs, a ten-foot-high stove tiled in green porcelain at each end, and windows bordered with stained glass that looked out on the department stores and public buildings of Nevsky Prospect, which is St. Petersburg's answer to the Champs-Élysées and just about as old, having been laid out in 1710. Not far from me a pianist in a tuxedo slumped at a grand piano like Oscar Levant, cigarette dangling from his mouth, casually riffing his way through sets of George Gershwin and Neil Diamond. Get rid of the porcelain stoves and change the view out the windows a little, and I might have been in one of the big hotel cocktail lounges on Fifth Avenue, an ambience that suited me fine.

The waitress brought my beer, poured a little, and set down a bowl of fat cashews to go with it (I should think so, with the beer at seven bucks a pop). The place was crowded, mostly with middle-aged, ruggedly good-looking men. Maybe it was the mood I was in, but a good third of them looked like mafiosi to me— slicked-back hair, black turtlenecks, Armani blazers, and with a svelte, showgirl-gorgeous twenty-year-old, sometimes two, at each table. Another third looked like would-be mafiosi—slicked-back hair, black turtlenecks, Armani blazers...but no showgirls. Most of the other people seemed to be German tourists, along with a sprinkling of Americans. The Germans were drinking beer and pretending not to stare at the mafiosi, the Americans were drinking cocktails and pretending not to stare at the showgirls.

Me, I was too tired to stare at anybody. Rather than finding a restaurant, I stayed where I was, treating myself to another beer and the Russian equivalent of tapas—black and red caviars, minced onion, chopped egg, and sour cream, and a stack of silver-dollar-sized blini to pile them on.

My meeting with Yuri was set for ten o'clock the next morning, and I tried to outline in my mind the questions I needed to ask. Instead my thoughts kept drifting back to Stetten: I was still having a hard time knowing what to make of him. The complete turnaround after Dulska's murder—"I'm out of here, don't call me, I'll call you" at nine o'clock in the morning, followed by "What's your plan, I'm all ears" at two o'clock in the afternoon—was hard to fathom.

And I was puzzled about something else. According to Stetten, he'd been assiduously hunting down his pictures for decades. Wouldn't you think he'd have heard about the Turner that had been shown at the well-publicized Hermitage exhibition? I would. Wouldn't you think he'd already have known that the Lost Truck had carried other paintings besides his father's seventy-three? I would. So why had they come as surprises when I'd told him?

It wasn't that I didn't trust him; I was pretty sure he'd been leveling with me—but only as far as he'd gone. More and more I was getting the feeling that there were pieces missing, things going on behind the scenes that I wasn't being let in on.

Whatever it was, there was just something about it all that wouldn't hang together. And something—*something*—about Albrecht von Stetten and his quest that didn't quite compute.

THE NEXT MORNING THINGS looked brighter, partly because I'd finally had a good, long night's sleep and partly because the threat of snow had disappeared and the day had dawned warm and golden. I breakfasted in my room, then left my puffy new parka in the closet and walked down Nevsky Prospect and across the splendid Palace Square to the Hermitage, where I got in line with everybody else waiting to get in.

For my money, the Hermitage is the most beautiful museum in the world. I'm not talking about the collection, which is not shabby either, but about the building itself, or rather the five interconnected, eighteenth-century buildings that make it up, especially its centerpiece, the vast and beautiful Winter Palace. Except for some dismal interior rooms and courtyards that weren't often seen by strangers, it had been meticulously, ornately restored to what it must have looked like two centuries ago, with extravagant quantities of gilt, semi-precious stone, carved marble, and lavish stucco work and molding. In a country not known for big spending on public works, it was amazing.

The problem, from my perspective anyway, is that the place itself is such a knockout that it keeps your eyes in a constant state of gogglement—"Holy cow, look at them there chandeliers!" and "Good gosh, will you look at that there ceiling!"—and overwhelms the art that you thought you were there to see. You can't help feeling like a *muzhik* fresh in from the country, with ox dung still on your boots. I can't anyway, so that by the time I'd made it past the ticket booth and into the entrance hall, with its fantastic marble grand staircase, and approached the regal, upright woman at the information desk, I would have been tugging my forelock, if I'd had a forelock.

"Yuri Minkov," I said, expecting to have to repeat it a few times, but apparently she was expecting me, because she got on the telephone at once, and a minute later a slight, scholarly young man—not Yuri—came up politely. Murmuring something in Russian, he gestured with a pair of taped, horn-rimmed glasses for me to follow him to an elevator that took us up to the second floor. There I was quickly walked through a string of dazzling galleries— one of them, if I remembered correctly, being the White Dining Room, where the Bolsheviks had barged in and seized power from the provisional government in 1917—to a handsome, balconied, wood-paneled library that I didn't remember seeing on my earlier visit.

In the anteroom just beside it was an inconspicuous door. The young man bowed me through and removed himself, leaving me in a cluttered room with books and old-fashioned card-catalogue drawers scattered over a library table at which a couple of elderly women with rubber finger-thimbles mumblingly counted through mounds of catalogue cards, rubber-banding them into packets of fifty or so. Wedged into one cramped corner was a wooden desk, and at it was a large-featured, rather fierce-looking woman of fifty in a stark, classically cut black suit, very erect, with penetrating dark eyes and striking, ruler-straight black eyebrows that almost but not quite met over a nose like the prow of a ship. Quite handsome, really, if you went in for the Greek-Fury type.

"*You* are Dr. Benjamin Revere?" she asked in English, not flatteringly.

"Yes."

She looked me over as if she doubted it. "I was expecting to meet with older man."

"And I was expecting to meet with Yuri Minkov."

"That is impossible. Assistant Deputy Curator Minkov has been called away to other duties. My name is Curator Dr. Mrs. Galina Kuznetsova. I, myself, will tell you everything you would like to know."

Permit me to doubt, I thought with sinking

heart. It was clear that, between the time I'd telephoned Yuri and now, the heavy hand of Russian officialdom had come down. I just hoped he wasn't in big trouble on my account.

"You may sit," she said.

I looked around, but I didn't see where. The only spare seat was a low stool at the table where the two women were mumbling over the cards. I suppose Curator Dr. Mrs. Kuznetsova intended for me to drag it over to her desk and then sit, or rather squat, more or less at her feet. I did not care for this scenario; I'd gotten over my *muzhik* phase back in the entrance hall.

"Not much room," I said.

"My office is too small for so many people," she said. "Here we don't have grand offices such as in your American museums and universities."

I made a try at being agreeable. "Obviously you've never seen the non-tenure-track cubicles at Harvard," I said with a smile.

No response.

"Perhaps there's someplace else we could meet?" I didn't want to offend her—that is, I couldn't afford to offend her—but I was not going to get talked into cowering before her on that stool.

Mrs. Kuznetsova didn't like the idea, but what could she say, that there was no room anywhere in the colossal complex of the Hermitage for two people to get together? "Perhaps outside in garden," she allowed, rising from her chair. "We will not be having so many more days like this one, and St. Petersburg is one of most beautiful cities in world, don't you agree?"

AS WE WALKED TO the elevator through the spectacular Malachite Room, I made an innocuous, appreciative remark about it.

"Yes, is very beautiful," she agreed, and I thought maybe I'd scored a point.

She openly studied me a little more, and then, when we got into the elevator, she asked with blunt curiosity, "What is your ethnic?"

"Russian, actually. My grandparents were born in Russia."

"Yes?" she said with interest. Another point scored. "What place in Russia?"

"Pinsk."

"Byelorussia," she muttered with disdain. It looked as if Pinsk had lost me whatever gains I'd made. "And what was family name?" She uttered a short laugh. "Not Revere."

"No, Rawidowicz, but that was too much for the officer who made out the passenger manifest on the way to Ellis Island. He liked Revere better."

"Like great hero, Paul Revere."

"That's right."

Mrs. Kuznetsova sniffed. "One should not change one's name. One should be proud of heritage." And then, even more ominously, "Rawidowicz—to me it sounds Polish."

But by the time we emerged from the building a few moments later, she had apparently decided that we were more or less kinsmen anyway, despite the Polish-sounding name and the dubious Pinsk connection.

"You will call me Galina," she commanded.

"And you will call me Ben," I replied in kind.

CHAPTER 19

Not that I'd admit it to her, but Galina was right about St. Petersburg's being one of the world's great places—a rarity, a venerable, grand-scale city that is all of a piece. Almost every building in the inner city is Russian Baroque, having been built between 1700 and 1800, on broad, generously laid-out boulevards, so that when you're out in the street it's easy to imagine yourself as a tiny figure in wig and breeches in one of those eighteenth-century "bird's-eye" architectural paintings. The whole thing is all the more impressive in that this city, so European and cosmopolitan in its ambience, had been constructed out of whole cloth—literally from nothing, like Brasilia—in freezing boglands more than a thousand miles from anything resembling a European city at that time.

It had been pounded to bits during the long, horrific siege of Leningrad in World War II, of course, but the Soviets had done a good job of rebuilding in the fifties. It was starting to look just a little tacky around the edges again, but show me a city that doesn't look tacky around the edges. The trick is not to look at the edges.

She was right about the weather, too. The sun was shining, and the temperature was pushing sixty. In the public garden that ran along the River Neva between the Hermitage and the Admiralty, we weren't the only people taking advantage of the last of the good weather. People sat on benches with eyes closed and pale faces turned up to the sun, pairs of chatting women pushed baby carriages, amateur artists with easels and paint cases daubed away at their renderings of the Winter Palace or the Neva.

While we strolled, stopping now and then to watch one of the painters at work, I told her why I was there and what I hoped to learn. It was obvious almost at once that I wasn't going to have any success getting across to her what anything in the Hermitage could possibly have to do with the death of an old man in Boston, so I switched my rationale to Stetten's case, figuring that would make more sense to her. In retrospect, it was not a smart move. After listening for five minutes, walking with her head down and her arms folded on her chest, like a man, she interrupted with a burst of impatience.

"What is it exactly that you wish from me?"

Telling Yuri would have been easy. Telling Galina wasn't so simple. I mean, I couldn't very well say, "Inasmuch as you folks exhibited one of the missing paintings from the Lost Truck a few years ago, I was wondering if you might-with no attempt at deception, of course-also happen to have the rest of them hidden away in the basement at the moment, despite all your denials over the years?" No, I didn't think that would go over very well.

"I have a list of Mr. Stetten's pictures with me," I said carefully. At least I was smart enough not to use Stetten's title with Galina. I know a fire-breathing Bolshevik when I see one. "I was hoping that you might look at it and tell me if you have any idea at all where any of them are or what might have happened to them."

She stopped walking. "And why should I know such a thing?"

"Well, the Turner seascape in your 1995 exhibition was from the same German shipment, so I, um, thought..."

She started walking again. "I have no interest in helping Germans recover their art collections. It is true, yes, we admit it freely, that certain art materials seized by Soviet government in Great Patriotic War are still in keeping, but these we regard as legal exports, rightful compensation for unparalleled German atrocities."

That was the current government line, all right. In 1997 both houses of parliament had passed a bill nationalizing all works of art brought back to the Soviet Union by its armies. Boris Yeltsin, feeling the sting of world condemnation, had vetoed it, whereupon the parliament, not so worried about world opinion, promptly overrode his veto, making it law.

"Mr. Stetten is Austrian," I said, "not German."

"Oh. Austrian, not German. I see. I beg your pardon, such a very great difference. And in the war, what did this not-German do? A courageous leader of the Resistance, no doubt? He killed many Nazis, of course?"

"Galina, Stetten was no Nazi; far from it. They murdered his father, they stole his house, his collection." That was the best I could do. In point of fact, Stetten had told me that he'd fought on the Eastern front as a conscript in the Austrian Army. If he'd killed anybody at all, it would have been Russians.

My reply was brushed aside. "The Austrians, the Germans, they are the same race, the same people; the Hun. Everything they put their fingers on they destroyed or else they took away. Do you know how many of our art pieces are still missing, even now? Two hundred thousand of them that the Germans stole from us, so why are you coming to me about Russian people stealing art?"

"Who's coming to you about—" But I stopped myself before I made a complete hash of things. "I only meant to say that Mr. Stetten, like many other Austrians, was a victim of the Nazis, too. They plundered his art just as they plundered the art of Russia. It was the same thing."

Galina abruptly halted again. "You think so? No, you are wrong. The art of Russia, the art most precious to us, our native art, they considered worthless. In 1941 alone, the first year, they destroyed more than two hundred Russian museums. Destroyed, you understand? Nothing looted, nothing saved. Destruction for pleasure of destruction."

"That's awful," I said.

"Yes, awful. Here in this beautiful city, the walls, the mirrors, the wonderful statues inside the palaces were shot for fun with machine guns, smashed in pieces. At Petrodvorets—Peterhof—they destroyed for pleasure the machinery of the wonderful cascade fountains, they took away the golden statues to the smelting furnace, right in front of the eyes of all the watching people. Animals! And at the end, when they ran away, what was left they burned or took with them to Germany...yes, and to Austria! Yet you come here and ask me to *help* them?" She stared at me, breathing hard through her nose.

I said nothing. I didn't have the stomach to make the obvious argument about two wrongs not making a right, not when I was faced with the raw conviction that had painfully thickened her voice and made the tendons on her neck stand out like straws. More than that, although I disagreed with the Russians' stance on the return of their art loot, I didn't have any trouble at all understanding their point of view.

"And I do not even mention," she said, "the terrible human sufferings, which you cannot begin to imagine, that they, these invaders, brought on us. In Leningrad-St. Petersburg-more than six hundred thousand dead of starvation, of freezing, of disease."

"Galina," I said meekly, "I'm just trying to

get information on behalf of one thoroughly decent man, not the German or the Austrian government. I'm not talking about repatriating—"

"Repatriate!" she said hotly. "Here is not a question of repatriation. To repatriate means to accept idea of legitimate ownership by Germany. We do not accept that, never."

"But I'm not saying—"

"Besides, many, many art objects we already returned to German museums in 1957, including famous Pergamum altar."

"To East Germany, you mean."

"Of course, to GDR. Altogether, one and one-half million objects we give back. That is enough. Is for German people to return two hundred thousand missing art pieces now, not for Russia to return."

That depended on which side you were on. The Russian Trophy Brigades had made off with over 2.5 million pieces of art from Germany. As Galina had said, they had returned 1.5 million to their satellite in 1957. That left over a million items still in Russia, many of them not from German museums at all, but the property of blameless victims like Stetten, looted-prelooted, so to speak-by the Nazis. Since 1990 Germany and Russia had been engaged in prickly negotiations over who owed what to whom, but so far little had come of them.

I was beginning to lose hope but gave it another try anyway; I'd come a long way, and I hated to give up.

"I appreciate what you're saying, Galina, believe me. Still, if—Well, just on the possibility that Mr. Stetten's art is somewhere in the basement of the Hermitage or—"

Galina stiffened. "We do not keep art in basement. We have proper storage, completely scientific, better than U.S." With a huff, she started us walking again.

"At end of war," she said forcefully, "was much confusion, many things burnt, destroyed, lost. By taking objects safely back to Russia we have kept them from terrible ravages of war. Am I not correct?"

Was she not correct, I thought with a sigh. That question, in its essence, was what was known in the trade as the Elgin argument: If we had not stolen (removed, confiscated, appropriated, seized) this painting (etching, engraving, statue, tapestry), would it not have been ruined (destroyed, lost, mutilated, corrupted) by the vicissitudes of war (climate, neglect, ignorance, barbarism)? In one form or another, this argument had been in use for two hundred years, by scoundrels and world-renowned institutions alike, ever since the Earl of Elgin carried off to England two hundred feet of glorious marble frieze that he'd stripped from the face of the Parthenon, claiming that he was saving it for posterity against the ravages of the Turks.

And the reason this particular argument had been around so long was that, like most arguments that have been around for a long time, it wasn't easy to refute. The fact is that

Elgin, vilified at the time by British public opinion and since then by almost everyone else as well, probably *did* save those irreplaceable marbles. The Turks who were in charge, Greece being part of the Ottoman Empire at the time, didn't give a damn about the glories of ancient Athens (neither did the local Athenians, for that matter) and were, in fact, happily using the convenient Parthenon for explosives storage and target practice (not at the same time, but even so, it wasn't doing the frieze any good).

Moreover, neither the Greeks nor the Turks had raised any objection to his carting the sculptures off, which he did with their official blessings and only after paying heftily for the privilege. A few years later, in 1816, he sold them—at a substantial loss, or so he claimed- to the British Museum, where an enormous gallery was built for them and where they still remain.

And I don't think that anyone who knows much about it believes for a minute that they would *not* have been lost (destroyed, ruined, mutilated, corrupted) had he left them on that hilltop in Athens. Still, as a modern-day rationale for making off with other people's property, it no longer held water, as it shouldn't. To say that it's all right to take art from people who can't take care of it is uncomfortably close to saying it's all right to steal somebody's car if he doesn't bother to wash it. Civilized nations can no longer get away with the Elgin argument, but at the same time many of the old disputes continue unresolved. Greece and England have been squabbling over those marbles for decades, but despite the recent increase in volume of the Greek complaints, I wouldn't bet on their going back to Greece anytime soon.

The last thing I wanted was to get into a similar squabble with Galina. Besides, as far as it went, she was right: The Russians had rescued a lot of art from destruction. The problem lay with what had happened to it afterward. And as far as *owing* the Germans some payback, she had a damn good case there, too.

There were some Gypsies begging along the outskirts of the park, mostly women with babies slung on their backs and grimy, skinny, big-eyed children clutching their skirts. One of the kids, a boy of eight, ran up to me and started grabbing with scabby hands at my pocket, my sleeve. "Hey, meestair! Jeengle-change, meestair? Please, jeengle-change?"

I began to reach into my pocket, but Galina stopped me and, with a sudden motion and a snarl, as if she were going to hit him, sent him running. "To these people you don't give. Parasites."

I cringed a little—the kid looked hungry, and he'd flinched as if he really expected to be hit— but let it go. I had enough things to differ with Galina about.

But a few yards farther along was a white-haired old woman on her knees, her head bent, with a cigar box in front of her that had a couple of cardboard images of icons in it.

"To her, you give," I was instructed. "This old babushka, she lived through the Siege."

Obediently, I leaned down and put a ten-thousand-ruble note—about two dollars—into the box. It had to be far more than she was used to getting, but she snatched it up and stuffed it in the pocket of her coat without ever looking at me. There were other elderly women like her kneeling on the cold, dirty sidewalks along Nevsky Prospect, shabby, kerchiefed, equally pathetic, all with their cigar boxes or cigarette cartons of icons, all utterly passive, never raising their eyes above the knees of the passersby, rocking back and forth, crooning to themselves and crossing themselves endlessly, like zoo animals caught up in a routine they couldn't stop. They were the reason for the wad of rubles I kept in my pocket when I was in St. Petersburg; it was impossible to walk past one without giving something.

"And what did you give to her?" Galina demanded as we turned and walked back toward the museum.

"Ten thousand rubles."

She nodded her approval. "Is good, Ben."

"Galina," I began, heartened by getting back into her good graces a little, "all I'm trying—"

"No," she said, stopping again. "I am sorry. You are not bad man. But I do not help you. I do not help Germany."

"But, look, surely you'd agree that you can't hold individuals responsible for the actions

238

of their governments. Surely you see that there are some individual Austrians, some individual Germans, who were just as—"

"No, I do not see. I see it was Germans who attacked us, not us them." She held her hand out to me. "Good-bye, I must work. I am sorry you come for nothing."

That is one tough cookie, I thought, watching her stride manfully back through the park toward the museum, but admirable, too, in her own way. If Galina Kuznetsova were on any of those Russian-German commissions, Germany would never get back a single piece of art.

In any case, she was certainly right about my having made the trip to St. Petersburg for nothing beyond a rousing argument, which I'd lost hands down. On my dejected way back out of the park I came across the group of Gypsies and beckoned to the kid who'd come up to us before.

He approached like a dog that wasn't sure whether he was going to get a treat or a kick. "Jeengle-change?" he inquired from a safe distance.

I held out five thousand rubles. Delighted, he plucked it out of my hand and with the kind of sudden, dark, gleaming laugh that was going to slay the girls in another fifteen years, scampered off to the women.

That made me feel a little better. "Is good, Ben," I said to myself.

CHAPTER 20

My flight to Budapest didn't leave until 8:00 P.M., but I couldn't think of anything useful to do in the interim, so I spent the afternoon in the Hermitage as a tourist, lunching on a hamburger and potato chips at the museum's Koka Kola Kafe, which looked depressingly like every other museum cafeteria in the world. As I walked back to the Grand Hotel at a little before five, Yuri was on my mind. Galina's appearance in his stead clearly meant that he wasn't considered reliable when it came to spouting the party line, and although the days when his freedom might have been endangered for such a thing had passed, I hoped I hadn't put his job in jeopardy, especially for what had turned out to be nothing.

As I was crossing the lobby of the Grand, a clean-cut, smiling young man in neatly creased, buff-colored slacks and a crisp, striped Oxford shirt with a button-down collar got up from a chair wedged into an out-of-the-way niche between two pillars and approached me. I could tell that he'd been there awhile, waiting for me to show up.

I stopped. "Yes?"

The smile broadened. "Hey, Ben! Is me!"

"Yuri, I didn't recognize you!"

The last time I'd seen him in his off-duty persona, he'd been wearing a Hard Rock Café T-shirt and baggy shorts, with an earring (the clip-on kind) in one ear, green dye (the

240

rinse-out kind) in his hair, and a funny haircut. I think the idea was to look like a punk rocker. Now, it seemed, he'd gone in for the preppy look (with considerably more success), and had done some filling out as well, so he looked less boyish, less soft. He also looked cheerful and happy, not at all like a man in big-time hot water, which I was happy to see.

"So, how was your meeting with the Dragon Lady?" he asked, pumping my hand up and down.

"Not too bad, except that she wouldn't tell me anything. Listen, Yuri, I haven't gotten you in a lot of trouble over this, have I?"

"No, only a little, don't worry."

Now, this doesn't come close to reconstructing our actual conversation, you understand; I've had to take some liberties. Remember, we were communicating in four languages at the same time: German, of which I knew a lot and he knew a little; French, of which I knew a little and he knew a lot; Russian, of which he knew a lot and I knew next to nothing; and English, of which he knew next to nothing and I knew a lot. So our dialogue, while its gist was as indicated, wasn't a bit like the model of concision and linearity described above. To spare both of us-you and me-the pain and the laughter of a literal transcription, I'm honing it into something along the lines of comprehensible speech. Anyway, to appreciate the real thing, you'd have had to be there.

He was proud of having found me. "I

remembered the problem you had with your stomach the last time," he said (sort of), "so I figured this was where you'd be staying. I want to talk to you, but I don't want to hang around the Grand. Too many people I might know. There's a string of little restaurants on Kanal Griboyedova, practically around the corner, where the *apparatchiks* never go. You want to have dinner?"

Sure, I told him, as long as it wouldn't turn into the standard Russian dining-out experience, which never ended before eleven, and seldom as early as that; I had an eight-o'clock plane to catch.

"No problem," Yuri said, this time in perfect English. Surely by now this has to be the most ubiquitous American phrase in the world, having overtaken even "okay."

The restaurant we decided on was a Russian-Ukrainian place that Yuri said smelled particularly good (it smelled like boiled cabbage to me). Called the Ukrainskaya, it was, at any rate, atmospheric, with a dejected-looking balalaika duo playing sweet, mournful Russian folk music and waiters in rolled-up shirt-sleeves and dirty white aprons.

Yuri ordered us a kind of high tea made up of a lot of small, individually served courses that kept coming and coming: a thick soup of sturgeon and marinated cabbage, three kinds of piroshki, red and black caviar served with chopped eggs and onions (it's hard to find a meal without caviar in St. Petersburg), and open-faced sandwiches of smoked salmon and thick-sliced cucumber and tomato on brown bread plastered with half an inch of butter. All served with a pot of Russian-style tea, i.e., very hot and very weak.

While we grazed our way through this, I explained to him, in more detail than I had on the telephone, what had brought me there and what I was trying to find out.

And this time, this time it seemed I'd hit pay-dirt.

"I know about those paintings," Yuri said, first looking around to see if anybody was listening in.

"About Stetten's paintings?"

"About *all* the paintings that were on the truck."

That started my heart pounding. I sat up straight and put down my salmon sandwich. "You know where they are?"

He nodded gravely. "You mustn't say where you got this information, Ben."

"Of course not, you have my word."

It was a complicated tale, not made any simpler by our language difficulties. At the war's end, it appeared, the truck and all its contents had been captured by the Trophy Brigades somewhere in eastern Austria. Some said that it had been taken directly from a captured German convoy, others that it had come to them by way of a unit of Austrian partisans; Yuri didn't know which story was true. Once back in Russia, the paintings went to a central collecting point in Moscow, along with everything else the brigades had "liberated," and there they had stayed until 1947 or 1948, at which time some of the materials were distributed to Russia's major museums. Of the hundred and six paintings on the truck, six had gone to the Pushkin Museum, three to the Hermitage, and two to the Tretyakov. The others were put into a KGB warehouse in Moscow.

He smiled, pleased with himself. "And that's the story."

Everything but the punch line. "But where are they now?" I asked. "There aren't any more KGB warehouses. There isn't any more KGB."

Yuri started to squirm. "But I thought you asked me what happened to them at the end of the war."

"Well, I did, but what I really need to know is who has them now."

"*Now?*" He shook his head. "No, that you do not want to know."

"Yuri, please—"

"Ben—"

By now the noise level in the restaurant, which had been steadily going up, had just about gone off the scale, so in addition to our polyglot-language problem we were having trouble hearing each other. Dining out in Russia is unlikely to be a quiet affair under any circumstances, and as the evening wears on, it gets noisier. Partly it's because the entertainment inevitably grows louder-the balalaika duo had been replaced by a rowdy (and apparently raunchy) floor show with disco lights-and partly because of the incredible amount of vodka the diners put away. Every table but ours had a liter bottle of Smirnoff, Stolichnaya, or Sinopskaya sitting on it in an ice bucket. Every few minutes a waiter would come, unscrew the cap, and slosh the stuff into four-ounce tulip glasses, filling them to the brim as if it were wine or mineral water. And the noise would go up another notch.

It didn't seem to bother Yuri, who was either used to it or deafened by frequent exposure to it, but it was giving me a headache, so I suggested we leave. Out in the blessedly quiet street I started in on him again as we began walking back toward the hotel. "Yuri, this is really important to me."

"Ben, do I have to put it into words? You must know what happened to them-the same thing that happened to anything else in the KGB repositories that could bring a price."

Yes, I knew. He meant they'd fallen under the control of the mafia. When the KGB had been disbanded, its displaced members hadn't taken long to find another place that was practically tailor-made for their specialized skills: the newly hatched Russian mafia, which quickly took the place of the old KGB as the most powerful and feared institution in Russian society. High-level KGB officials moved with ease into high-level mafia positions and never left. And with them went much of the KGB's treasure storehouse of weapons, drugs, booze, and art.

"If you mean the mafia," I said, "yes, I

guess I already knew that, but it doesn't get me anywhere, there's nothing I can do with it. I need specifics. I need—"

He shook his head. "Ben, I'm sorry, I can't tell you any more." We had reached the corner of Nevsky Prospect. We were both hunched and shivering; the temperature was dropping fast. I noticed that Yuri, hugging himself, hung back, out of the range of the bright street lamps.

"But you do know more?"

"I can guess more, but it would be too dangerous to talk about it. These men are *killers,* don't you know that? It's freezing, I'm going to turn around and go home now. I'm starting to think it was a mistake to talk to you at all."

I put my hand on his arm to stop him. "Yuri, don't say that. You know I'd never do anything to put your life in danger."

He looked startled. "*My* life? Who's talking about my life? I'm talking about *your* life. Ben, listen to me. Don't pursue this. There are things it would be very bad for you to know. You don't know what you're up against."

At least, that's what I thought he was saying, or trying to say. Now that I think about it, how would I know for sure?

CHAPTER 21

The Hungarian language is not related to any of the Romance languages, or to the Germanic, the Slavic, the Italic, or any other member of the Indo-European language family. It is (so Alois Feuchtmüller had told me) a member of the Uralic family, subfamily Finno-Ugric, branch Ugric, formal denomination Magyar. Its closest—almost its only—relatives are Ostyak and Vogul, which are still spoken in a few parts of Siberia. As a result, Hungarians have only each other to talk to. Save for the occasional visiting scholar of Finno-Ugric, foreigners who arrive in Budapest can rarely speak more than a few phrases of phrase-book Hungarian. By the same token, Hungarian vacationers who want to be understood on their foreign travels are pretty much limited to the general vicinity of Irkutsk.

It's Alois's theory that this has made them grumpy in their dealings with visitors, over and above the expectable general grumpiness of Eastern Europeans only now emerging from a grim and repressive political system.

Maybe, maybe not, but it was certainly true that the ones I ran into, from the moment I arrived at Budapest's Ferihegy Airport, were a dour bunch. The customs and passport-control people, the taxi driver who drove me to the hotel, the English-speaking hotel receptionist—all were impatient and unhelpful, and the first two, in their plain gray woolen uniforms, had been subtly, sullenly threatening, so that by the time I got to my second-floor hotel room a little before midnight, I was feeling edgy and paranoid, over and above my usual first-night-in-a-foreign-country jitters.

The Hotel Duna wasn't doing anything for

my mood either. The minute I walked into the place, I knew that I was in one of the old State Tourist Authority hotels of the Eastern bloc—I'd been in them before, in Prague and East Berlin—now probably privatized but otherwise unchanged in atmosphere and appearance. If you've ever been in one of these places, you know what I mean. The building itself was typical Brezhnev-era style (otherwise fondly known as Neo-Brutal), a drab, cubical hulk with a façade of cement-colored cement. The lobby areas were shabby and neglected, with linoleum floors that smelled of disinfectant, and packed—even at midnight—with frazzled-looking tour groups huddled in clumps, waiting for—well, I'm not sure what they were waiting for. The night staff was overbearing, disgruntled, and pointedly slow. And the air was full of sinister, unanswered mysteries: Who was the bald man in the black suit who leaned against the counter sucking on a toothpick and writing something in a notebook every time anybody got on the elevator? What were the cashier and the security guard sniping at each other about under their breath? Why was the chambermaid crying behind the laundry cart?

My room had two narrow, low-to-the-floor beds, a round table with no ashtray but many cigarette burns (could these facts be related?), and an unobstructed view of acres of railroad yards with standing freight trains, open boxcars, and rows of tracks, all illuminated by lurid, purple-white lights that cast hard shadows and made the place look like an embarkation point for Buchenwald. All it needed were a few patrolling Wehrmacht guards with slavering Dobermans straining at the leash.

In all, it wasn't a view that recommended itself to me, so I called down to see if I could upgrade to a room in the front, looking out on the cobblestoned streets and handsome houses of Castle Hill. The reply was a single contemptuous word: "Impossible." I heard the clerk laughing to himself as he hung up the telephone.

I hung up, too, then drank a glass of bottled water in the bathroom, scowling at the multilanguage "welcome" sign pasted to the door.

WELCOME IN BUDAPEST

We hope you have a pleasant stay of enjoyment in Hotel. Here are some "tips" to mach your stay more enjoyable.

—You should carefully check restaurant bill. Mistakes are often being made.

—It is adwisable to carry only small amount of money in wallet or purse, with most money elsewhere in case of robbery.

—Due to bad experiences, best to carefully lock door of room always. Hotel Duna cannot be responsible otherwise.

—You should check hotel bill carefully before leaving premises. Refunds and complaints can not be possible.

ENJOY YOUR WISIT HOTEL DUNA!

Next time, I said to myself, next time I'd let Stetten pick my hotels for me.

IN THE MORNING THE people-be-damned approach so charmingly reminiscent of the old Evil Empire continued. At the door of a corridor leading to the breakfast room a formidable woman who was checking names off on a list stopped me and held out her hand. "Card, please."

"I'm sorry?"

"You have buffet card?"

"I don't know about any card," I said. "I'm a guest here."

"What group you are with?"

"I'm not with a group."

"You are not with a group?" She sounded stunned, as if this were the first time such a thing had happened in the history of the Hotel Duna, which it may well have been.

By now twelve or fifteen people, all wearing tour-group cards, had piled up in an impatient line behind me, and the woman with the checklist decided it might be best to let me by, even if I wasn't with a group, and in I went to breakfast.

You know that scene in prison movies where the inmates all start yelling and banging their forks on their plates? Well, that's what the noise that came bouncing off the walls at me sounded like, and the scene itself was almost as riotous. There were some big tables in the center, and around them were mobs—"groups"— of people, three and four deep, all wearing tour-group cards, struggling to get at the food and shouting warnings or encouragement to their compatriots in a Babel of broad-voweled East European languages, plus Japanese, German, and (I think) Finnish. Every now and then somebody would fight his way back out of the crowd, ducking from underneath the tangle of arms and triumphantly clutching in both hands an impossibly loaded plate that was practically a buffet table unto itself.

I was thankful Stetten wasn't with me. With his attitude toward buffets, he would have had a heart attack on the spot. Personally, I'm a buffet fan myself, but this was too much even for me. I managed to spot a little-used dessert table off to one side and went to it to get myself a shot of coffee and a prune pastry that I took out to the lobby and ate there under the disapproving stare of the woman with the check sheet, who looked at the tooth-pick-sucking guy near the elevator with a meaningful lift of her eyebrows and tilt of her chin: *You see? I knew there was something wrong with this one.*

The prune pastry wasn't half bad, though, and I went back for another. But I didn't have the nerve to eat it under that stony glare, so I took it with me to munch on while I went out to beard Attila Miklós Szarvas, better known, according to Christie, as Attila the Hun, and for good reason.

Szarvas had owned his gallery—with the frighteningly unpronounceable name of

Mügyüjtök Aukcióház—for more than fifty years, and no one knew how old he was, although it was documented that he'd been arrested in Italy as far back as 1926 for exporting stolen art, and in Brussels in 1929 for trying to peddle fake Michelangelo diaries. That meant he was a nonagenarian for sure, and for at least seventy of his ninety-some years he had been an art dealer of less than stainless repute. During the Second World War he had willingly and profitably assisted the Nazi authorities (Hungary, like Austria, had signed up as a German ally early on) in their systematic looting of private and institutional art, and in the Soviet occupation he had just as readily (but probably not as profitably) worked with the Russians. Since the collapse of the Soviet bloc he had been engaged in one dubious transaction after another, sometimes getting himself fined, once or twice being jailed for a while, but almost always coming out of them richer than he'd been when he went in.

In the last few years he'd made a semiprofession of filing claims for works of art that he said had been taken during the war, either from him or from the families of clients he was now representing. He'd been a principal in at least two dozen civil suits, in four countries, had won at least five of them outright, and had squeezed a rewarding financial settlement out of another ten. And now it looked as if he'd trained his sights on Stetten's Velàzquez.

Not a man to be taken lightly, Attila the Hun.

THE MÜGYÜJTÖK AUKCIÓHÁZ (CHRISTIE thought it might mean "Collector's Auction House") was, as promised, three blocks from the Duna, on Krisztina körut, a commercial, middle-class street of small shops, some of which had signs in the new pan-European language that is nowadays equally likely to be found in Moscow, Dubrovnik, London, or Paris—and probably Ulan Bator and Pyongyang, for all I know: 0–24 MINI MART, OPTIKA FOTO, MARLBORO, TOTO LOTTO. These were enough to make me feel at least minimally at home among the bewildering array of Hungarian signs: ÉLELMISZERBOLT, CUKRÁSZDA, BORTÁRSASÁG (to judge from the goods in the windows: groceries, pastries, and wines, in that order).

Szarvas's gallery, next to the pastry shop and filled with the luscious scent of warm almond paste coming from it, was a warehouselike spread of small bays that was more like an antiques mall than an art gallery, crowded with old dish sets, flamboyant gilded mirrors, and 1930s furniture, as well as the usual assortment of muddy nineteenth-century oil paintings and anonymous marble busts and statuary. The most expensive item I saw, a bronze table sculpture of a saddle-weary cowboy à la Remington, had a tag on it with a price of 265,000 forints, or about $1,500.

At the rear of the main room was a first-rate Empire desk at which a neatly dressed man with a thin fuzz of orange hair sat alertly, hands folded on the desktop, like the manager of a local bank overseeing his domain.

"Good morning, I'm Benjamin Revere," I told him, hoping that he was the English-speaker I'd talked with on the telephone.

He was, and I was rewarded with the first genuine smile I'd gotten since arriving in Budapest, as well as a flurry of courtesies. Wouldn't I sit down? (No, thank you.) Would I care for some tea or coffee? (No, thank you.) Was I happy with my room at the Duna? (No comment.) Would I like a small glass of Unicum, Hungary's national drink? (No, thank you.) Or perhaps—

I had to interrupt him to get more than three words in. Thank you, no, I told him, but it would be nice if I could speak with Mr. Szarvas.

Alas, Mr. Szarvas was not on the premises. He had expected me at nine, not at ten (I chalked this up to the everyday vicissitudes of translation). He had waited for me until nine-fifteen and had then left, but if I went to the street market at Ecseri Piac, I could speak with him there. I would find him in the leather-goods aisle, playing chess.

"But I don't speak Hungarian. How do I communicate?"

"Don't worry, there will be someone."

"Fine, I'll go right now. What directions do I give the taxi? Could you write them down for me?"

"Oh, everybody knows Ecseri Piac," he said, "but don't take a taxi, it will cost you a fortune. Public transportation is not only cheaper but faster. Just walk two blocks to your left, to Deák Ferenc ter and take the Metro Line Number Three—be sure you don't go toward Újpest-Központ but toward Kóbanya-Kispest, and get off at Határ út. Then take the Number Fifty-four bus to Ecseri Piac, only a five-minute ride. That's all there is to it. Only, make sure you don't take the bus going to Boráros ter. It sounds confusing, but it's really very simple. And it will cost you only sixty forints."

I thanked him profusely for his help, left the shop, and immediately got into a taxi.

Well, wouldn't you?

ECSERI PIAC, ON THE outskirts of the city, was a vast, crowded enclave of patched asphalt pavement with four long metal sheds running side by side down the center. The hundred-yard-long spaces between the sheds were roofed with grimy Plexiglas, forming covered aisles filled with tables and stalls selling everything from framed, hand-tinted photographs of Lenin and Stalin, to old automobile engines and carburetors piled willy-nilly in rusting heaps, to cuckoo clocks, to delicate porcelain figurines running the gamut from Jesus Christ to naked ladies. There were tables with forty pairs of bright new shoes, each with a printed price tag, as in a real shop, while a few yards away someone else was trying to sell a single pathetic pair of worn overshoes and an old purse.

The sellers ranged from elderly, snuff-taking Mustache Petes who sat at folding tables with collections of war medals or old coins to snazzy, miniskirted bleached blondes overseeing racks of gleaming belts and trendy boots. Away from the sheds, along the market's perimeter, were shadier-looking operators, men selling rings, or watches, or icons, or jewelry from the hoods of cars or even out of their pockets. Some simply stood there looking stealthy, with no goods at all on display, but obviously conducting some kind of unwholesome business. If there were any police around, I didn't see them.

Adding to the general hubbub, there was a carnival going at the far end of the sheds, with rides and shooting galleries and games of chance.

Finding Szarvas was easy. As the man in the gallery had said, one of the aisles was devoted to leather goods, mostly new, mostly bomber jackets like the one I'd almost succumbed to in St. Petersburg, and soft, thigh-length, belted coats. At a folding table set in a nook at one side of this fragrant aisle, wedged in among racks of buttery-looking, cocoa-colored coats, sat an old man with a red flower in the buttonhole of his gray blazer, a colossal sapphire ring on one pinky, and a face amazingly like that of Ramses II—the mummy of Ramses II, I mean, after he'd been dead about three thousand years—hollow-cheeked, parchment-skinned, and beak-nosed. He was playing chess with a much younger man while a dozen other people, all male, stood around the table watching.

As I came up, I saw that one of the men beside the table seemed different from the others, standing humbly with his baseball cap in his hands and nervously, expectantly, watching Szarvas. Szarvas, meanwhile, appeared to pay no attention to him, pondering his move, scratching his liver-spotted scalp and stroking a clean-shaven chin. Shaking his head, he shifted his knight, then said a few quick words without looking up from the chessboard.

The waiting man looked stricken. He opened his mouth to protest, but a brusque word of warning from one of the others instantly stopped him. Still clutching his cap, he backed off a step and slunk away down the aisle, between the coatracks. Someone else stepped forward into his place and began to speak in a soft voice, sounding like a man going to his execution.

At that point I realized there were two distinct groups around the table. One of them was composed of men like the one who had just left—humble, imploring, respectful, and standing in a ragged line. Those who had caps or hats held them in their hands against their chests. Those who didn't have caps looked as if they'd have been holding them if they'd had them. The other subgroup was made up of dangerous-looking men in their twenties or thirties, in soft, expensive leather jackets like the ones on the racks. They all seemed to come from the same mold: handsome, square-jawed, lizardy, with long, carefully combed black hair and mostly with gleaming black sunglasses. They looked like the male models you see sketched in the newspapers leaning casually against motorcycles, modeling the very sort of jackets they had on.

Whatever passed for a mafia in Budapest, I knew I was seeing it in action: the *padrone* holding court at his chess table, the supplicants coming to beg favors or forgiveness, the vigilant ring of lounging bodyguards. Szarvas moved another piece, a pawn this time, and muttered a few more words. This time they were favorable, because the man who had approached him looked as if he were going to faint with relief, but the moment a flood of grateful words began to pour from his mouth Szarvas dismissed him with a negligent wave of his hand. The man immediately shut up, bobbed his head—I thought for a moment that he was going to drop to his knees and kiss the old man's ring—and left.

Before the next person in line could shuffle into his place, I stepped forward. "Mr. Szarvas—"

One of the lizardy guys mumbled something—probably the Finno-Ugric version of "hey"—and stepped into my path, his fingertips against my collarbone, his eyes inviting me to do something stupid.

I held my hands up, shoulder height, to keep him off. "Look, I'm just trying—"

He shoved with both hands, sending me back a few steps.

"Now, look—" I said with as much dignity as I could.

Whatever would have come next was interrupted by a couple of clipped syllables from Szarvas: "Tibor!"

Tibor moved aside a little, but remained, as they say, in my face. Szarvas made a quick, graceful gesture at me with his pale, tapering fingers, like a conductor encouraging his chorus: Go ahead, sing.

"Is there anyone here who speaks English?"

No response. I put my hand to my chest and addressed Szarvas. "Benjamin Revere."

Nothing.

"America."

Nothing but simple curiosity all around. I was a variant in the afternoon's entertainment, no more. "Telephone," I tried, miming. "From Vienna? Painting? Portrait? *Porträt?*"

The guys in the leather jackets were starting to lose interest. The one barring my way looked devotedly back at Szarvas, like a puppy dog who couldn't wait to please. *Would you like me to beat the shit out of this guy for you? Would you like me to kill him for you, huh?*

"Velàzquez?" I said. "*Vay-lahss-kayss.*"

Finally, results. Szarvas said something to one of the leather jackets, who took off running, in a couple of minutes bringing back a smooth Continental type, a sharpie in pilot's sunglasses, with a flashy, expensively tailored suit jacket draped, capelike, over the shoulders of an open-throated, lavender silk dress shirt that showed a thick-linked gold chain around his neck. He listened to Szarvas's instructions with bowed head, then spoke to me.

"I am János, Mr. Szarvas's counselor-at-law. I will interpret, yes?"

"All right," I said, pretending I had a choice.

"Come."

Only when he reached around behind Szarvas, undid a brake, and began to push did I realize that the old man was in a wheelchair. Without speaking we navigated down the crowded aisle, an easy task because shoppers melted respectfully out of the way of the wheelchair as soon as they saw who was in it. Occasionally some out-of-towner who didn't know who Szarvas was would be jerked out of our path by someone else who did. We rounded the end of the long shed, only a few yards from the bustle and clamor of the carnival, and went back down the next aisle a little ways to what was apparently János's office, a cubicle in one of the sheds, separated from the kitchen of a hopping snack bar next door only by a plywood partition that didn't reach the metal roof, so that the place reeked of fried food and old grease. The furniture consisted of a few chairs and a dark, heavy old office desk with an insert in the top. My Uncle Sol—Zayde's brother—who had a store that sold kitchen curtains, had had one like it and it had enchanted me as a child. If you pulled up on a handle in front, the insert turned smoothly over and a lovely, clunky, upright Underwood that was bolted to the underside came up, all ready to use.

János rolled the armchair that was behind the desk out of the way and pushed Szarvas's wheelchair respectfully into its place. Then he motioned me into one of the two armless wooden chairs and took the other for himself.

He removed his sunglasses, wiped them with a folded handkerchief, and put them back on. "Mr. Szarvas would like to know who you are and whom you represent."

Fair enough. I explained, once again using my connection to Stetten as the rationale, because to tell a man like Szarvas that I was there on my own, or in the interest of a murdered friend in Boston, would have meant nothing to him and probably cut no ice with him even if it had. Szarvas, showing no reaction, asked a question in a shrill, whispery voice.

"What Mr. Szarvas would like to know is what you have in mind."

Well, that was harder. The original idea was that I'd simply show up in Budapest, ask a few questions, gather a little information, and be on my way. With luck, maybe I'd pick up something that fitted in somewhere in helping make sense of Simeon's murder—but that was a long shot, because everything Christie had told me about Szarvas suggested he was a faker who had never really been within a mile of the Boston Velàzquez and therefore couldn't know anything about it. Still, you never knew. In any case, I'd thought that perhaps I'd be able to give Stetten a hand by showing Szarvas the error of his ways or at least send him sniffing off in some other direction.

But nobody told me, for God's sake, that I'd be dealing with the Big Kahuna of the Budapest mafia, along with his slick, smooth counselor-at-law. I decided that a more proactive approach was called for. Put 'em on the defensive, let 'em know you're onto them, and see what comes of it. There were certain obvious risks in putting a mafia kingpin on the defensive, of course, but I really couldn't see Szarvas having his goons work me over, let alone do me in, over this. Not that Tibor wouldn't have been willing.

"What *I'd* like to know," I said, "is what Mr. Szarvas has in mind by claiming a painting that doesn't belong to him."

János pretended that he didn't quite get the whole message. "Mr. Szarvas wishes the return of his painting, of course. What else?"

"Does he understand that Count Stetten can produce evidence that the painting is from the Stetten collection?"

This time János did translate, and Szarvas responded volubly, motioning to János to go ahead and tell me what he'd said.

Mr. Szarvas, János said, understood that very well. He had no intention of contesting Count Stetten's claim that the painting was from the Stetten collection and had been stolen by the Nazis; he was perfectly willing to stipulate as much.

"Well, then, how—"

"What Mr. Szarvas *is* prepared to contest is the count's claim that the painting should be *returned* to him."

"I'm afraid I don't understand," I said, although I was afraid I did.

Szarvas spoke rapidly, pausing after every few phrases to let János translate and watching me with hooded eyes, rheumy but keen, to gauge my reaction. Sometimes he'd nod vigorously or gesture at me while János talked, as if to drive home a point: *There, you see? Isn't it so?*

His story was this: As one of Budapest's most knowledgeable prewar dealers, he had served as art adviser to the German military commander of the city late in the war. In that capacity—

Szarvas held up his hand to interrupt and rat-a-tatted a few more words, motioning to János to pass them along.

Surely I understood, János translated, that under the Tripartite Pact Hungary had been allied with Germany from 1940 on, and that in March 1944 the country had been occupied by the German Army in hopes of countering the Soviets, who were advancing from the east. Szarvas, like everyone else in Budapest, had merely been doing his best to get along with the German military, who were, after all, the legally constituted government. He had not been, had never been, a traitor to his country.

"Yes, I understand that," I said.

But I also understood that the term "art adviser" glossed over something a good bit darker. Christie had told me that part of his "advice" to the Germans had consisted of providing them with information as to where hidden, Jewish-owned art, legally defenseless from plunder by the state, could be found, and that for this he had received a standard commission of 25 percent of value. This, it seemed to me, was stretching the meaning of "doing his best to get along" to its outer limits.

As a dealer, János continued, Szarvas sold art to the Nazis himself, and sometimes bought it from them, and in 1944 he had purchased the Velàzquez for the equivalent of six thousand dollars from a Gestapo captain, who claimed it had been given to him by an Austrian doctor in appreciation for saving his life. Shortly afterward, however, the new German military commander "temporarily requisitioned" it as decoration for his residence on Castle Hill. In early 1945, when the Russians finally reached Budapest, the German Army units put up a fierce resistance. The bombardment had been terrific. Every bridge in the city was blown up, more than a quarter of the buildings were destroyed, and Castle Hill, the jewel of Budapest and the center of the German presence, was blasted into a charred, sprawling ruin.

Szarvas had naturally assumed that the Velàzquez had been burned to ashes with everything else—until two weeks earlier, when someone had called to his attention an article describing the incident in Boston. He had followed up with a little research and was now certain beyond doubt that the painting in question was the one the German commander had taken from him. He recognized that Stetten had a valid claim, but he, too, had a valid claim and would be happy to let the courts decide the matter.

It was what I'd been afraid of; the good-faith-purchaser argument I'd warned Stetten about. Szarvas was claiming, in effect, that in 1944 he had had no way of knowing that the painting had previously been Stetten's and no reason at the time for disbelieving the Gestapo officer's story about having received it as a present. The fact that Stetten could prove it had been taken from him in no way affected the fact that it had also been taken from *him*, Szarvas. He was, like Stetten, a mere innocent victim, blameless and well-meaning, and he deserved recompense.

I was beginning to see why he was so successful at winning these cases. Who could know for sure what had or hadn't happened to a painting *after* the Nazis got it? With all the transfers, thefts, losses, and confusion that went on during the final years of the war, there was no such thing as a credible provenance covering that time. Szarvas's story was next to impossible to disprove.

"I'm sure you see the justice of Mr. Szarvas's case," János said, smiling. "You see what we are looking for."

I did indeed. His professed desire for the painting's return was strictly pro forma; old-fashioned boilerplate. What he was looking for was money, a settlement to keep the case out of the legal tangles in which he could enmesh it for years. He had a good chance of getting it, too, and nothing to lose.

Just in case I *didn't* get it, however, János made it crystal clear. "We realize that the painting has great sentimental value to Count Stetten, and Mr. Szarvas has no wish to deprive him of this. If an arrangement that reimburses Mr. Szarvas for his losses can be reached, we would be happy to see Count Stetten have the painting."

"I see. Well, you may have quite a job convincing a judge that a painting Mr. Szarvas got from a Gestapo officer in 1945 was bought in all innocence—"

"In good faith, yes; a good-faith purchase."

"No, not a good-faith purchase. You're a lawyer. You know that for it to be a good-faith purchase the buyer has to be unaware that the object might have been stolen. Are you seriously expecting a judge to believe that 'one of Budapest's most knowledgeable dealers,' a man who worked day in, day out with the Nazis— the art adviser to the German commandant himself—had no idea of what was going on all around him, that it never occurred to him that the painting might, just might, have been taken away from someone else?"

János translated. Szarvas snorted and waggled his fingers in an imperious gesture. János jumped from his chair to provide an ultrathin cigarette from a silver case and light it with a silver lighter. In a moment, the musky, sickish smell of expensive Turkish tobacco was added to the fast-food smells in the little room. Szarvas drew a few short puffs, holding it European-style, between thumb and fingertips with his palm turned up, and puffing the smoke out of his mouth like a man blowing out birthday candles. Then he began to talk again in his rapid-fire, herky-jerky manner, pausing every few seconds to take another pull while János caught up.

János's translation was first-person, straight from the horse's mouth. "I will be frank with you. It is true that I had some suspicions concerning these and other artworks that I bought from the German military. Perhaps they were war loot, perhaps not. I had no way of knowing. You could not ask such a question. What *did* I know? I knew that the chances of these precious things being destroyed or lost was enormous if left in German hands. There was at that time serious talk that the Nazis would destroy everything rather than let it fall into Allied possession. I was determined, in the small way granted to me by God, to prevent this from happening."

You really had to hand it to the guy. First, the good-faith-purchaser argument. Then, if that didn't do the trick, the always reliable old Elgin argument, appropriately updated. Not only had Szarvas been an innocent victim, he had been trying to save Western civilization.

"Perhaps you would be good enough to convey Mr. Szarvas's position to Count Stetten?" János said.

"Yes, I'll do that, but I'll also tell him what I think of it."

János was untroubled by this. "Of course," he said smoothly, "Count Stetten would have to take into consideration the fact that the six thousand dollars paid at that time is no longer relevant. The painting's market value has appreciated many, many times beyond that. In filing our claim we estimated the value at one billion, four hundred thousand forints. That is eight million dollars."

"You've already filed a formal claim?"

"Yes, yesterday afternoon, before a judge here in Budapest."

"In Budapest? But the painting's in Boston. It was *found* in Boston."

I'd had the impression all along, from the way he watched me when I spoke, that Szarvas understood a little English, and now he confirmed it.

"Found, Boston," the old man said. "Lost, Budapest." Then, looking me right in the eye, he went into a long, shrill, merry cackle.

I knew exactly why he was laughing, and it was bad news for Stetten. *Where* a case like this is heard is crucial. In the United States the law leans toward the original owner of a stolen work of art. Let's say that you're browsing through the newspaper one day and you see a photograph of a painting just sold at auction for, say, fifty thousand dollars, and you recognize it as one that was stolen from you years before. Let's say you then come forward to claim it, but the new owner refuses to go along, claiming in turn that he or she bought it in good faith from a legitimate auction house, which acquired it from the estate of a reputable collector without knowing anything of its past. He asserts, honestly enough, that he's not a thief, and that he put out good money on it, just as you did.

Armed with ample proof of your previous ownership, you take the buyer (and maybe the auction house) to court. Do it in New York or Boston and the chances are that you'll get your picture back and the new buyer will be out fifty thousand dollars, despite having purchased it in all innocence.

But put the same case on the docket in Hungary or any other Continental European country and you're probably going to be out of luck, because the law is almost certainly going to come down on the side of the good-faith purchaser. You may (or may not) get your picture back, but if you do you're probably going to have to reimburse the buyer the fifty thousand dollars he shelled out for it. Both perspectives have their merits, but Stetten's chances of getting his picture back—and doing it without having to fork over a large pile of money to Attila the Hun—were tremendously greater in the States, something of which Attila was all too obviously aware.

Still chuckling happily, he motioned to János to start his wheelchair rolling again and gestured to me to come along. We walked back out into the aisle and started around the end of the shed, with people once more parting like the Red Sea before Moses. Szarvas jabbered earnestly at János, periodically stopping to let him translate.

"Mr. Szarvas asks me to tell you that he is not interested in a long and expensive courtroom battle any more than Count Stetten is." He had to shout to be heard over the organ-grinder music from the rides and the crackling *pop-pop-pop* from the shooting galleries. "He hopes that Count Stetten will agree that it would be best for all concerned—"

Szarvas held up his hand. "Ah..."

János paused, waiting for him to continue, but Szarvas's head fell forward and he slipped, twisting, out of the wheelchair. János snatched clumsily at his arm but couldn't stop him from slumping to the pavement with his shriveled legs bent almost double. Szarvas's beaky face was tilted up, the eyes open and fixed. On the expensive gray material of his blazer, just above the red carnation, were two small holes six inches apart, welling with thick, dark fluid.

CHAPTER 22

For perhaps half a second we both stood there, frozen. The people around us were equally transfixed, caught in midsentence or midgesture, staring at the old man bleeding onto the ground. Then everyone's nervous system switched on at once and the living-picture tableau erupted into violent life. People screamed, and ducked, and scattered. Because of the continuing *pop-pop-pop* from the galleries, no one knew if the shooter was still at it or not.

János dived into the crowd, and I fought my way after him, figuring that he'd have a better idea than I would of the best place to be at a time like this. Racks of merchandise were being knocked over and sale items—plastic containers of bottled water, antique religious pictures, shoes—were rolling and bouncing underfoot, tripping people up. Ahead of me János rounded the end of the shed and turned into the leather aisle, and I followed. As I turned the corner after him, I looked back to catch a last glimpse of Szarvas and saw that apparently nobody else had been shot. Szarvas and his empty wheelchair, a pathetic little grouping, were at the center of an otherwise empty, near-perfect circle, fifteen feet in diameter and expanding fast.

Ten yards down the leather aisle and presumably out of the line of fire I slowed up. Now that it was becoming clearer that only one person had gone down, the atmosphere had more excitement than fear in it. At least half a dozen times I heard Szarvas's name whispered in tones of awe as word spread of the momentous thing that had happened. Some of Szarvas's lizard-men were beginning to fan out through the crowd, moving fast and looking dangerous as hell with their mirrored sunglasses and their semiautomatic pistols in hand. Near the chess table where Szarvas had been playing, János was talking excitedly to three of them, who were nodding and listening closely.

"János!" I shouted from twenty feet away.

"What's happened? What is this about?"

He turned to me with a look of amazement. Assuming that he was under the impression somehow that I'd been shot too, I called, "I'm all right, I—"

But he wasn't listening. He was jabbing his finger in my direction and yelling at the three hoods. Even if I'd been able to hear him, I wouldn't have been able to understand the words, but there was no mistaking the meaning. *There he is!* he was telling them. *That's him, the one that killed Szarvas!*

I skidded to a stop. "No! I had nothing to do with—"

But all three of them, raring to go, pulled handguns from under-the-arm holsters. I think one of them actually fired, despite the crowds, but the crackle from the shooting galleries made it impossible to tell. Fortunately, right beside me there was a kind of alleyway that led to the next aisle—they had them every fifty feet or so—and I ducked into it at top speed, coming out into what seemed to be the musical aisle—balalaikas, ancient gramophones with big horns, banjos, accordions. As I turned into this, I caught a brief sight of the first of the three hoods pounding after me, semi-automatic waving. With people parting before me as magically as they had before Szarvas, I ran the fifty feet to the next alleyway and turned into it, not left to the next aisle down but right, back toward the leather aisle, hoping they'd never expect me to do that.

Once there I took a right turn, away from

the chess table, which seemed to be the center of operations, then dodged into a makeshift dressing area among the leather jackets on display, no more than a cleared space big enough for one person, with a dime-store, full-length mirror propped against one of the clothing racks. The proprietor of the stall started to object, but I treated him to a ferocious snarl, modeled on Galina Kuznetsova's approach to the Gypsy kid in the park. It worked fine; he clamped his mouth shut and jumped back, his hands raised submissively.

Pressed into this space I was able to use the mirror to see what was going on behind me. Aside from the general commotion, there was nothing. I counted to five, and still nothing happened. Had it worked, then, had they not realized that I'd turned back into the leather stalls? I let out my breath in a whoosh and began to step out into the aisle, but jumped back just in time, when one of the gun-waving hoods shot out of the alleyway and into the aisle about twenty feet behind me. Anxiously I watched him in the mirror while he took a long look both ways, up and down the aisle. *Go left!* I willed him powerfully. *Do not go right! Do not even* look *right!*

He went right, of course, and I wedged myself farther yet into my little coat-bordered niche. There were people standing next to him who had seen me run into the space, and when he threw a curt question at them I thought, That's it, it's all over. But they only shook their heads and shrank back into the stalls, bug-eyed and mute.

Nevertheless, gun drawn and ready, he came cautiously down the aisle, a step at a time. Even in the wiggly mirror and with hanging coats and jackets blocking my view, I could see him clearly, a dark, thickset young guy who moved with his arms out from his sides, like a weight lifter. Dense, close-cropped black hair, clipped black mustache, eyes hidden behind a pair of those mirrored glasses, shirt open halfway down his chest with a mat of curly hair showing. I realized it was Tibor, the one who'd been ready to destroy me before he'd even thought I'd done anything. Christ.

Two more steps and he must have thought he heard something, because he whirled suddenly, the gun extended in front of him, left hand steadying the right wrist, and fired twice into a little dressing area exactly like mine. This time I could hear the sound of the shots over the background noise, and I could clearly see his hand jump with the recoil.

I don't know whether some poor soul was standing there innocently trying something on and took two bullets intended for me, or whether Tibor merely wound up assassinating a suspicious-looking leather coat, but I do know that perspiration popped out all over me, running into my eyes and pooling at the small of my back.

While Tibor checked to see what damage he'd done, I gave some thought to bolting, but I knew I didn't have a chance of making it without getting shot; he was only a dozen feet from me, and I had to cover thirty feet to reach the next corner. I also thought about bolting in his direction, hoping to surprise him, knock him off balance, and keep going, but he looked awfully solid, and with that big black gun in his hand I didn't see how I could get away with it. If I was going to get out of this at all, I was going to have to fight my way out, and to do that I was going to need a weapon.

Luck was with me. At my side there were a couple of three-foot-long wooden rods leaning against a carton—sturdy, inch-thick poles that fitted into the racks to hold the hanging coats and jackets. I closed my hand around one of them and quietly brought it to my side. My back was to Tibor, but in the mirror I could see him checking out whoever/whatever he'd shot, then continuing to advance, the gun held out stiffly in front of him. Firing it had excited him, made him jumpier. One inching step…I could hear the sole of his shoe scrape softly over the pavement. Two steps… He was out of the mirror's angle of vision now, but from what I'd seen already I knew that the gun was going to arrive before he did, so I fixed my eyes on the place where it was about to appear, wrapped both hands around the pole as if it were a baseball bat, and held my breath.

The gun didn't arrive. The aisle was deathly quiet. I got the horrible, tingling feeling that he knew I was here—perhaps he'd seen my feet or caught a glimpse of me in the mirror— and that in another second he would pump two, or three, or four bullets into and through the layers of coats that separated us. The muscles in my neck were about to snap with tension.

I stepped out into the aisle, and Tibor jerked back. I brought the rod slashing down on the barrel of the gun, which fired—I didn't know where the bullet went—and spiraled halfway out of his hand, spinning on his trigger finger. Again I swung at it, but this time I missed completely, almost losing my balance as the pole bounced off the pavement. Tibor, looking as scared as I was, was still fumbling with the gun, trying to get it into shooting position. This time I didn't bother with his hand. I whipped the rod up from the ground with both hands and caught him hard, under the jaw, uppercut-style. His teeth clicked solidly together, and I saw his eyes glaze a little, but he held on to the gun, even managing to get it properly set in his hand. But he was slower now, a little dazed, and before he could rightly aim it in my direction, I whacked him one more time, sideways, over the left ear and temple. He stumbled back a step, wavered, and, with a great sigh, as of air escaping from a balloon, he fell on his face.

I watch enough boxing to know that when a struck fighter falls forward onto his face, he's not getting up for a while. I knelt quickly and pulled the gun from his curled fingers, looking up again just in time to see a young-ster break from the knot of onlookers and run back down the aisle, yelling at the top of his lungs, toward where I assumed János still was. I didn't have to understand Hungarian to know he was shouting the news.

That meant I didn't have much time, and I didn't expect to be lucky twice in a row. I turned to the rack behind me and slipped on one of the creamy brown bomber jackets that looked like the ones the hoods were wearing, threw a wad of Hungarian money on the table, and headed up the aisle, away from where János probably was. On second thought I ran back, knelt again, pulled Tibor's mirrored sunglasses from his face—his eyelids were twitching, but nothing else was moving—and got them over my own eyes. Then, shoulders hunched and head down, I took the next alleyway and ran two aisles over, to the rusty-automobile-engine-and-carburetor section.

Once there I straightened up, made sure the sunglasses sat straight on my nose, showed the gun, and generally did my best to look like one of the lizardy guys who were out looking for me. I prayed that I wouldn't have to use the gun. Number one, I didn't want to kill anybody. Number two, if it required anything more esoteric than pulling the trigger, I wouldn't know how to do it.

As I got to the end of the aisle—the far end, near the carnival—one of the hoods saw me from a distance and called something. Keeping my head turned away, I replied with an elaborate shrug and kept moving, but not too fast. He didn't come after me, and he didn't shoot me. I started to think I just might make it.

Once in the carnival crowd I tossed the gun into a garbage can and just kept sauntering toward one of the exits, expecting a bullet between the shoulder blades any second and flinching every time a shooting gallery rifle went *pop*. At the exit I jumped into a cab at the taxi stand and said, "Hotel Duna." But before it was quite out of my mouth it came to me that Szarvas's people knew that's where I was staying, so it was out of the question. They could kill me there as easily as here; probably more easily.

"No," I told the driver, "Ferihegy Airport," saying it enough times and trying enough pronunciations so that he finally got it.

AN HOUR LATER, WITH my pulse rate finally calming down, I was on my way to Vienna on Austrian Airlines Flight HO-39, trying to make sense of what had happened. Why would János have leapt to the conclusion that I had engineered Szarvas's killing? And who *had* engineered it? And why? In a way, I knew that he was right; that is, his boss was dead because of me. To assume that he'd been killed for some reason that had nothing to do with me, while I just happened to be around, was stretching things beyond credibility, especially considering what had been happening to just about everybody else I'd been talking to lately. Had someone been afraid that Szarvas might tell me something they didn't want me to know? But what? Szarvas's claim to the painting was patently false, so what was there for him to tell me? Were they afraid he'd make some kind of deal with me, as Dulska had tried to do? But about what? He had nothing to offer; he was trying to *get* money, and get it for nothing.

And who were "they"? Could it conceivably be Stetten? He was the only one—well, aside from Alois Feuchtmüller and Alex—who knew I was going to be meeting with Szarvas. Although, come to think of it, I was sure I'd never mentioned Szarvas's name to him, only that I was going to see a Hungarian art dealer.

No, I didn't see how, and not just because I liked him and it went against my instincts. All Stetten had to fear from Szarvas was a phony court case that might or might not cost him some money, and you didn't go around having people killed to avoid that; not at this early stage, when there was plenty of time for threats (I mean lawyers' threats) and negotiations, and you didn't know if it would ever really come to a head—as most such cases did not. Besides, Stetten had encouraged me to see Szarvas; if he'd been worried about it, why wouldn't he have tried to talk me out of it?

No, it had to be the mafia. Who else was there that would have an interest in these paintings? Who else would have the resources to follow me around from country to country, or tap my phones, or do whatever they'd been doing to know where I was going, and then, with almost no notice, have a sharpshooting assassin at the ready there at Ecseri Piac? And he was sure as hell a sharpshooter; those two closely spaced holes above Szarvas's carnation left no doubt about that.

Which still left me with the "why," and I couldn't come up with even a decent guess. They didn't want me to learn something about something; that was what Yuri had implied, and it was the best I could do, but it sure left an awful lot of questions. For example, if I were such an irritant to them, why didn't they just bump *me* off, instead of going after everyone I was talking to? You'd think it would be simpler; more cost-effective, too. Whatever the answer, it meant that if I didn't want to get anyone else killed, let alone me, either I was going to have to drop the whole thing and go home, or else I'd have to be a whole lot more careful than I'd been up to now. I resolved to be a whole lot more careful.

When the flight attendant offered a glass of wine, I practically snatched it out of her hand, sinking gratefully back into my seat and assessing my current situation in more immediate terms. My unplanned departure from Budapest had left me with no luggage, no toiletries, and none of the clothes I'd brought with me other than what I had on my back.

But I wasn't complaining. What I did have was the most important thing: an intact, unpunctured skin. Also my wallet with credit cards and money, and my passport (God bless those ugly little pouches you wear around your waist).

Not to mention a nifty new leather jacket that was going to bowl them over in Back Bay.

CHAPTER 23

Europe is a small continent. Although I felt as if I'd already lived through three days' worth of excitement so far that day, it was only one-thirty in the afternoon when the plane landed in Vienna. The first thing I did was telephone Mr. Nussbaum, the hard-to-get Viennese claimant to the Boston Velàzquez. Still no answer.

The second thing I did was to hop in a cab and go to the big Marks & Spencer department store on Mariahilfer Strasse, where I outfitted myself with everything from toothpaste to trousers, plus a shoulder bag to carry them in. By this time I wasn't sure what shape my MasterCard account was in, so I put it on Visa and hoped for the best. Apparently there was still some money there, because they let me out of the store with three hundred dollars' worth of their wares.

I tried Nussbaum one more time and again failed to get him, then called Stetten to tell him I was back from Budapest sooner than I'd expected, and perhaps I might come up to Salzburg to see him today, a day early.

"That will be a pleasure," he said warmly. "And how was Budapest? Did you have any luck?"

"No, not really." Just escaping with my life by the skin of my teeth, that was all.

"And St. Petersburg?"

"I'll tell you all about it when I see you."

"Wonderful, I'll book a room for you at the Altstadt. Or would you prefer someplace else? The Goldner Hirsch? They're both excellent."

"No, don't bother," I said. "I'm perfectly happy staying at any—" It occurred to me just in time that the last time Stetten had chosen a hotel for me, it had been the Imperial in Vienna. The last time I'd picked for myself, it had been the Hotel Duna.

"Well, all right, thanks," I finished. "The Altstadt'll be fine."

"Good. Now, my address is Rainerstrasse Seventy-seven. I'll see you this afternoon, then."

"I'll be on the next plane."

*R*AINERSTRASSE SIEBENUNDZIEBZIG," THE CABBIE said, pulling to the curb.

I looked dubiously out the window and asked him if he was sure. Receiving only a pained, over-the-shoulder look in reply, I handed him fifty schillings to cover the forty-schilling fare from the Altstadt and stepped out onto the sidewalk.

The thing was, the living quarters I'd dreamed up for Albrecht, Graf Stetten, were on the wooded, exclusive slopes of the Kapuzinerberg, overlooking the lovely clock towers and belfries of Old Salzburg; one of those faded but enchanting châteaus with a quiet, walled garden—a sort of Austrian version of *la petite grand-mère*'s villa in *An Affair to Remember*, you know?

282

But Rainerstrasse, while no more than seven or eight blocks from the base of the Kapuzinerberg, was in a different world, a noisy commercial street full of snarling trucks and huge, jointed, hissing buses. Not run-down or poor, no, but as nondescript as could be. Never once had Julie Andrews pranced down Rainerstrasse with her brood of von Trapps. There were no quaint, hanging, wrought- iron signboards, no charming, sculptured fountains, no pretty, yellow-fronted baroque architecture. Just anonymous, shop-fronted apartment buildings that might have been ten years old or a hundred and fifty; with all that pea-soup-green gunite on them, who could tell?

Number 77 was no different from the rest, a plain five-story building with a dusty cutlery shop on the ground floor. Next to the apartment entrance was a brass panel with names, buzzers, and a speaker. The top name was STETTEN. I pressed the button.

"*Wer ist da?*" came from the speaker. Not Stetten's voice.

"Benjamin Revere," I shouted at it.

"I will open the door for you," the voice said grudgingly in German, as if, personally, he didn't think it was such a hot idea. Ah, Stetten's snooty butler, or valet, or whatever he was. "You will please take the elevator."

"What floor?"

"This is a private floor, there is no button. I will see to it that the elevator brings you here."

A buzz, a pop, and the front door unlocked. I walked down a poorly lit, not overly clean hallway to a glass-paneled elevator about the size of a fairly roomy coffin. I might have had space for a duffel bag in there with me, but that would have been it. Another pop, a thump, a hum, and the elevator began ascending in a wire tunnel that ran up through the hollow of the stairwell. The other floors were like the entrance hall—dim, carelessly maintained, and without signs of residents. When the elevator stopped at the top, I was in the dark, staring at a black metal surface on the other side of the glass. This turned out to be a heavy door, which was opened by a sallow, balding, wide-hipped man wearing a canary-yellow smock over a suit and tie. Graying hair slicked back, close-set eyes a disapproving gray. Jeeves, I presumed.

"Bitte, kommen Sie herein, mein Herr. Ich heisse Georg."

I stepped directly into a surprisingly large, high-ceilinged living room, where I was asked to make myself comfortable while *den Herrn Grafen* was informed of my presence. As Georg left, I noticed that, although perfectly turned out otherwise, he was shuffling along in felt bedroom slippers.

The room was fitted out with worn, comfortable furniture—two big sofas upholstered in soft, cream-colored leather, several armchairs, pale tapestry carpets on a wooden floor, and a dining-room table and four chairs set in an alcove under a Meissen chandelier. And lots of florid, nineteenth-century bronze statuary now doing time as bases for table lamps.

All of it handsome and of good quality, but almost all of it scruffy. The couches sagged, the carpet was threadbare, and I wouldn't have tried sitting down in one of those rickety dining-room chairs if you'd paid me—notwithstanding the fact that I was pretty sure they were from the shop of Johann Valentin Raab, the great nineteenth-century Würzburg furniture maker, and worth maybe twenty thousand dollars apiece in decent condition. But even in twenty-thousand-dollar chairs, if they're not taken care of, the glue eventually dries up, shrinks, and falls out of the joints.

None of this was really surprising. Stetten was old money, not new money, and I had learned during my curatorial days that old money didn't usually go in for conspicuous consumption. If anything, it was conspicuous nonconsumption they liked, driving old clunkers and walking around with holes in the elbows of their coats. This had been particularly true with the Boston old rich, where a penny-squeezing Yankee stinginess had been considered a positive virtue—that is, as long as you were rich enough not to have to be stingy, if you see what I mean. A colleague at the museum had put it perfectly: "When I walk into a house and see good paintings on the wall, I can smell money. But when I see tatty old carpets on the floor under them, I smell *real* money."

Whether Stetten had "real" money or not, I wasn't sure; his taste in hotels indicated that he did, while his dickering with Dulska over the relatively modest price of the Velàzquez suggested that he might not. But one of the interesting things I'd learned in Boston is that old money looks like old money even when it isn't there anymore.

Stetten's apartment fit the picture, except for the paintings on the wall. There weren't any, other than two or three ancestral portraits, crudely done. But there were plenty of small pairs of antlers mounted on shield-shaped wooden tablets, with plaques identifying the place, the date, and the hunters (Stettens in every case, some going back to the nineteenth century). And there were old family photographs, dozens of them, hung in irregular tiers on the walls, set one behind the other on the lamp tables, crowded into bunches on the mantel. None of them, as far as I could tell, had been taken less than sixty years ago. There were men in spiked Prussian helmets and straw boaters, women in ankle-length crinolined dresses or neck-to-knee woolen bathing suits; pictures of laughing, long-dead people taken in Paris, in Monte Carlo, in front of snow-bound Bavarian chalets, on the giant Ferris wheel in the Prater. I picked out a twelve-year-old Stetten in a short-trousered sailor suit, complete with ribboned cap, sitting erectly between a distinguished man and a beautiful, full-figured woman with upswept hair, whose hand rested lightly on young Albrecht's. They were in front of a studio backdrop of sailboats scudding over the waves under a bright sun.

My scalp tingled. A mausoleum, I thought.

Stetten's world, the world he'd cared about, had stopped for all time on March 13, 1938. Anschluss day.

Given this line of thinking, it was almost spooky to see a smiling, healthy, living Stetten come into the room, cheeks aglow and thin, graceful hand extended in greeting. He was wearing a crushed-velvet burgundy smoking jacket and a beautifully arranged ascot with a black pearl tiepin, God bless him, and he looked just great.

"There you are, Ben! May I call you Ben? I feel we've been through enough by now."

"Of course. I wish you would."

"And I'm Albrecht."

That was a relief, because until now I'd been avoiding calling him anything. I'd tried "Count" a couple of times, with all good intentions, but it just wouldn't make it out of my egalitarian American mouth. I guess my name isn't Revere for nothing.

"Come out onto the terrace, we'll have some tea and talk. Georg!" he called, pointing to a set of French doors that led onto the slate-tiled terrace. *"Tee, bitte."*

Georg responded with what looked to me like a for-God's-sake-will-this-person-never-stop-bothering-me eyebrow shrug before he went grumbling to do his master's bidding. This, I thought, is not a man who is happy in his work. But if Stetten found anything disagreeable in the performance, or even noticed it, he gave no sign. I supposed it was an old relationship, worn into deep ruts like a long-standing marriage that's turned sour but is too ingrained and familiar for the parties to do anything about.

Once out on the terrace, under an awning, I saw that Stetten's apartment wasn't as badly situated as I'd thought. True, the building entrance was on grubby Rainerstrasse, but the rear, where the terrace was, looked down on the Mirabell Gardens from a perfect distance, close enough to provide a fine view of the intricate, elegant hedges and flower beds, but far enough away to mitigate the effects of the third-rate garden statuary. (Yes, even the artists of the baroque era could produce crappy art on occasion, a thought that should give hope to us all.) Beyond the gardens the view continued over the river and the roofs of the Old Town to the looming fortress, and farther on to the rolling green hills of the Salzach Valley. And from here the noises of the street were no more than a remote rumbling. No, not bad at all.

When we had settled into a couple of padded wrought-iron chairs and Georg had left us alone after bringing out hot tea, cookies, and finger sandwiches, Stetten poured the tea and leaned forward expectantly. "Now, then, my dear friend, how did it go? I'm all ears."

"Albrecht, let me ask you something first. Did you tell anybody at all that I was going to Budapest?"

"Tell anybody? No."

"Not your attorney?"

"Leo? No. Why do you ask?"

"Not Georg?"

"*Georg?* Of course not. What's the matter?"

"Who else besides Georg and Leo knew that you were negotiating for one of your paintings?"

"No one at all," he said, beginning to get jittery. "Whom would I tell? Now, what's the matter? Tell me."

I told him. Delicately, because I knew that he upset easily, but there was no way to make what had happened anything but frightening: Yuri's warning, Szarvas's murder, my near-murder. Especially when added to what had gone before: the deaths of Simeon and Dulska.

It shook him up, all right. Under normal circumstances Stetten was a pink-and-white-complexioned old guy with a healthy-looking rosy spot on each cheek. But as I gave him the details, I could see the color leaving his face. The area around his lips turned a sickly blue-white. In a way I was relieved to see it. No one could fake a reaction like that; Stetten couldn't have known anything about what had happened in Budapest.

Still, I was nagged by the feeling that he knew *something* more than what he'd told me. "Albrecht, I need you to tell me the truth. I need to know what's going on."

He looked honestly confused. "You need *me*...?"

"Did you know Dulska worked for the mafia?"

His eyelids whirred. "Dulska?"

"Yes. You had no idea that it was really the mafia you were dealing with? Please, be honest. A lot of people have died."

"Ben, I give you my word, I had no idea. Are you sure about this?"

"Positive."

"The mafia..." He shook his head, then asked suddenly: "But then—who killed him?"

"His bosses, probably."

"But why?"

"He tried to set up a deal with me on the side, cutting you out of the picture—and, more important, cutting the mafia out of the picture. That's why the police think they killed him, and I agree with them."

"A deal with you?" he asked slowly. "For my painting?"

"For all your paintings."

"*All—!*"

"Whether he could really pull that off or not I don't know, Albrecht. But I'm guessing he could."

His fingers went nervously to his trim, white mustache while he pondered this. "But if that's so, it would mean that the mafia has them all, wouldn't it?"

"Yes. Albrecht, do you have any idea at all why Szarvas might have been killed?"

"No, I've never even heard of— I promise you, no. Ben, why didn't you tell me that Dulska was trying to arrange a deal with you?"

"I couldn't. You left the next morning. There wasn't time."

Okay, not exactly truthful. I could have told him easily enough when we were at the opera, but I hadn't, for fear that he might foul things up before they came to a head. However, I thought I'd better not say this. I didn't want *him* to start suspecting *me* of something.

By now a little color had returned to his face. Those cheery pink disks weren't back, but at least he no longer looked like a corpse. He picked up a tiny shrimp-and-mayonnaise sandwich and absentmindedly put it in his mouth; I doubt if he knew he was chewing anything.

"The mafia..." he murmured again. I could practically hear the cogs turning in his head. On the whole, I believed what he'd told me, but I was still dogged with a hunch that he was holding something back, that the whole mess somehow made more sense to him than it did to me. It was as if he knew enough about what was happening and why to be good and scared, but not enough to know what was really going on.

"Albrecht, is there anything else that I ought to know? Please. I'm doing my best to help you, but I feel as if I'm all alone in the dark."

He looked as bewildered as I was. "I don't know anything. I don't understand what's happening either." He began to reach for the teapot, but his hand was trembling and he pretended that he'd only been flexing his fingers. "Will you pour?"

I poured us each a second cup of Earl Grey from a beautiful little nineteenth-century pot decorated in French cloisonné enamel into equally old, almost equally precious cups of acorn-and-oak-leaf Staffordshire china. The pot was dented, the cups and saucers as chipped as cafeteria tableware. Old money.

He held his cup in both hands and sipped; I could see the strength flow back into him.

"Albrecht, how well do you know Leo Schnittke?"

He looked up sharply. "You suspect Leo of being in league with them?"

I shrugged.

Stetten put the teacup down with a hand that had steadied. "Leo Schnittke has been my attorney since 1958. For forty years I've trusted him with my accounts, with my properties, with every business transaction in which I've been involved. He has never let me down. He is a little blunt sometimes, that's true, but he's a man of tremendous integrity. I would willingly entrust him with my life. I trust him as much as anyone I've ever known—as much as I trust you."

Whom you've known for all of five days, I thought. Still, I had the feeling that his assessment of Schnittke was on target: a tough, crusty lawyer, but a straight one, and loyal to his client.

"And Georg?" I said, first making sure we were out of earshot. "Would you entrust him with your life?"

He smiled a little. "As a matter of fact, yes. Don't be misled by his manner. Georg is from Leipzig, a distant cousin on my mother's side. It was I who got him, his father, and his sister out of East Germany in 1971. He's been with me ever since. He would never betray me, never. Besides, he knows nothing of this."

If that was true, if the bad guys weren't getting their information about where I was and what I was doing from Stetten, or Schnittke, or Georg, then that meant that they were literally trailing me around from place to place, which was pretty much what I'd surmised anyway. What I didn't know was why I should be that important to them.

"Ben, what you've told me is terrible. I don't want to put you in any more danger. I think you should—"

"No, I want to continue. It's not only for you, Albrecht. I want to get to the bottom of this if I can. The man who was killed in Boston—he was a friend—I could have prevented it...."

"I understand," he said gently. "And *will* you get to the bottom of it?"

I don't know. I have two more leads to follow up. Tomorrow I'm going to go out to the Altaussee salt mine to see if I can learn something. Would you like to come along? It can't be much more than a couple of hours' drive."

He shuddered. "*No!*"

I could sympathize with that. "And then, assuming I can get hold of this other claimant in Vienna, I'll want to talk with him."

"Truthfully, it's hard for me to see how that can be of any help."

"Well, I just don't want to leave anything unexplored. But that's basically my affair, not yours. I certainly don't expect you to be paying my—"

He held up his hand. "No, I don't want to hear that. We've been through this once already. Anything you do is also in my interest, and I will pay for your valuable time and your invaluable assistance. This time *I* insist. Believe me, I can afford it."

"Okay. Thank you, I appreciate it."

"No, it's you who are doing me the favor. I don't think you can have any idea what it means to me to think that after so long a time we may be getting close to my father's paintings—that they've survived all these years."

"Don't get your hopes up too much, Albrecht. If the mafia really does have them, I don't have to tell you that they're not going to give them to you because you ask them in a nice way. And if they don't have them—" I hesitated, then decided I'd better say what I'd been reluctant to put into words. "Then for all we know, they might be lost, or destroyed, or stored away and forgotten in somebody's attic in Omaha or Stuttgart. A lot of the war loot didn't make it through, you know."

He smiled. "If they can be found," he said simply, "I know you'll find them, Ben."

He was so optimistic, so transparently trusting, that it made me feel a little anxious, even guilty. Finding them was only the first step, I told him, treading lightly. Even if we were lucky enough to locate some or all of them, he would be facing an uphill battle from there. Look at all the claimants that had come forward for the Boston Velàzquez alone. How many would there be for seventy-three equally valuable masterpieces? As in everything involving big money, there would be a horde of charlatans disputing Stetten's claims and willing to go to court about it, just as Szarvas had been. How did he expect to prove that the paintings were really his? What about those "documentary criteria"? Did he have sales slips for any of them?

No, no sales slips, he said—rather airily, I thought.

Insurance records?

Well, no, not to speak of.

Restorers' bills?

Sorry, none of those either.

He'd been holding back a smile, but now it broke brightly through. All right, I thought, what have you got up your sleeve? I put down the little triangle of egg salad and toast that I'd just picked up from the broken Stafford-shire serving plate (broken, not merely chipped; a two-inch-long crescent had cracked off the rim). "You're not going to sit there and tell me you can identify all of them by means of scratches on the frames, or marks on the back, or something else you remember from fifty years ago, are you? Because—"

At that the smile erupted into a ripple of laughter that made him toss his head back. "My dear friend, I have a confession to make. My memory isn't really very good at all. And it's not improving with age."

"You could have fooled me. You remembered

the name of the frame maker, you remembered that brass plate on the back—"

He held up his hand to stop me. "I want to show you something. I think it's time for you to see it. I'll be right back." At the door he looked playfully over his shoulder. "Don't go away now."

CHAPTER 24

I made good use of the couple of minutes Stetten was gone, wolfing down two one-bite egg-salad sandwiches, two of smoked salmon and cream cheese, and three dried-cherry cookies. Buying clothes and catching the flight to Salzburg had precluded any chance to get lunch, and I'd been talking too much until now to dig in. Done eating, I went to stand at the terrace's balustrade and contentedly played a fixed, tripod-mounted telescope over the town. The Salzburg Landestheater was on the edge of the gardens, not very far away, and the lens was strong enough to let me see what the current production was: *Wer hat Angst vor Virginia Woolf?* If the play translated as well as the title, I thought, it'd be a great show.

When Stetten returned, he had with him a zippered loose-leaf binder, which he placed on the flat stone railing that topped the balustrade, then carefully opened. The pebbled leather binder, once probably a pliant black, was ashy gray, cracked and rotting, and the pages it contained were yellow and humpy with age and intermittent moisture, the corners curling, the loose-leaf holes frayed. Mostly, they were covered with the faded, uneven printing of an old manual typewriter that had punched pinholes in the letters here and there, but there were some black-and-white photographs, too.

Stetten flipped pages until he found the one he was searching for. "How well do you read German?"

"A lot better than I speak it."

"Look at this, then." He tapped the page just below its middle. I took the binder from him and read the paragraph he indicated:

Frame. 106 cm. X 76 cm. Manufactured by Anton Kantmann, Bogengasse 9, Munich, probably between 1870 and 1885 (maker's plate on reverse). The style is not appropriate for the picture, being an imitation of sixteenth-century naturalistic Siennese frames, with many fantastically carved birds and animals, and therefore predating Velàzquez by some fifty years in its design. Aside from natural deterioration, the only damage is the fracturing of a small leaf at the lower-right corner....

It went on in this vein for another ten lines, a meticulous description of everything that could possibly be said about the frame on the Velàzquez that Zykmund Dulska had brought to Vienna. I glanced up, puzzled. "Albrecht, what is this? What am I looking at here?"

"Please, examine the rest first. Take your time. More tea?"

I took his advice, sitting down with another cup of tea and going through the binder, if not painstakingly (there were 245 densely worded pages), then carefully enough to understand just what it was I was holding in my hands: nothing less than a detailed, comprehensive set of descriptions of the paintings—fronts, backs, and frames—that had been looted from Stetten's Paris apartment, each of them diligently researched and scrupulously annotated. A catalogue to end all catalogues.

Sitting there leafing through the thing, I became aware in a way that I hadn't been before of just what a fabulous collection I was dealing with. Hals, Poussin, Goya, Van Dyck, de La Tour, Gainsborough, Copley, David...My God, what would it be worth now? Two hundred million, three hundred million dollars? Maybe more, if the general quality approached that of the two I'd seen for myself so far. Incredible to think, assuming they still existed, that these wonderful pictures had been hidden away for over fifty years. And even more incredible— hardly conceivable—to think that I, of all the people in the world, might be the one to track them down and maybe bring them to light.

Or was I just spinning a wishful fairy tale for Stetten's benefit and my own? I wasn't sure myself.

The format was the same for each picture: a full-page, decent-quality, black-and-white photograph, followed by three, four, or five pages of rigorously researched, scrupulously annotated narrative: measurements, materials, condition, description, and critical interpretation, all put down in exacting, sometimes excruciating, detail.

And the proprietary markings on the backs were set down as well; symbols other than numbers or letters were carefully drawn by hand. Sometimes the meanings were listed as "unknown," but many had detailed attributions assigned to them, sometimes several possible attributions. Some had lengthy explanatory notes that tracked them back two hundred years and more. The only markings not referred to were the rubber-stamped letters and numbers that the Nazis had put on them, which showed that the notations had been prepared before 1942. Altogether, it was as exhaustive a compendium of information on the paintings as you could hope for, more even than an art museum would have in its records.

"Okay, I've looked at it," I said, looking up at him and brushing crumbs of leather off my lap. "I'm impressed. Now tell me what this is and where it came from."

He spoke with his back to me, leaning against the railing and gazing across the rooftops toward the distant hills. "These are my father's records, a lifelong labor of love. They were made in the twenties and thirties.

I found them after the war at the family house in Melk, in the cellars, under the rubble. Wonderfully thorough, aren't they?"

"That's putting it mildly," I said. "I've never seen anything like it." "Oh, yes?" He turned to look at me. "Do you think they might prove useful in pressing my claims, then?"

"Useful...!" I said before I realized that he was chortling away with his chin tucked down into his ascot, having his little joke.

"Hm, yes," I said, going along with it, "I suppose you might say that."

Indeed he might. There was information here that, to my knowledge, had never been recorded anywhere else; not in any *catalogue raisonné*, not in the MFA&A reports, not in the ERR records. There was only one place it could have come from, and that was from personal, detailed knowledge of the paintings themselves, all seventy-three of them. Added to everything else, it was tangible confirmation that they had once really belonged to Stetten's father. It was more than confirmation; it was as close to solid proof as you could get when you were dealing with war-looted art; better than some dubious provenance or some easily forgeable bill of sale from a defunct dealer. Without some enormously convincing evidence to the contrary, any court of law in the world would accept Stetten's claim to the collection.

Which raised a question. "Albrecht, what about those other paintings you tried to get back from the government? Something like four hundred, didn't you say?"

"No, something like three hundred and fifty were taken by the Nazis, but most disappeared for good. Only thirty or so were ever returned to the Austrian government. Those were the ones I filed for."

"But you couldn't convince the officials they were yours." I'd been sitting a long time, so I got up and moved to the railing beside him, both of us looking out over the gardens.

"The officials," he said dryly, "were not easy to convince."

"I know that, but I don't understand how they could possibly give you any trouble if you had material like this."

"Ah, but I didn't. All I have are the contents of this album, seventy-three paintings. These were my father's most precious possessions, the ones we took away to Paris with us. Unfortunately, he didn't go to such lengths with the others. Or it may be that he did, and they've been lost. I don't remember ever seeing them."

"Damn, that's a shame."

"My dear friend, don't look so gloomy," he said. "Were you under the impression that life is always fair?" He patted the binder. "These, these are the ones that mean the most to me, and with you to help, I have new hope that they may yet be found."

"Let's hope so," I said, not very confidently.

"And after all, don't forget that I still have my own collection to comfort me."

That came out of the blue, a complete surprise. "You do? But I thought everything had been—"

"No, no, I have quite a sizable collection still. I've had the wall between the sitting room and one of the bedrooms knocked out to make a gallery. Would you like to see it?" His eyes had lit up, something that invariably happens to collectors when they have the chance to show off their things to an appreciative audience. And the pink was back in his cheeks.

"Very much."

"Excellent. It's getting a bit chilly out here in any case."

We walked through the big living room with a sprightly if limping Stetten, *sans* cane, leading the way, past an old-fashioned kitchen in which Georg was skulking noiselessly about with his sleeves rolled up, then down a hallway with more family photographs, to a room closed off by a heavy pair of velvet curtains instead of a door.

"Now, will you let me go in first and adjust the lighting? I want it to be right. You know how important the proper lighting is."

He slipped in between the curtains, and I could hear him fussing and talking to himself on the other side. "Ah," he said after a minute, "that's perfect. Come in, Ben!"

CHAPTER 25

I parted the curtains and stepped through. Don't ask me what I was expecting. Probably something English—Turners, or Constables, or maybe Hogarths—or else an Impressionist collection. You know, a son's rebellion against his father's taste for the Old Masters, and so forth. Well, this was a rebellion against his father's taste for the Old Masters, all right, but there weren't any Turners or Constables.

I found myself standing in a strange, semi-darkened room with a gray-blue floor, dusky olive walls, and a ceiling painted a silvery aquamarine. The indirect lighting that Stetten had been fussing over was a dim, seawater green with perhaps one or two rose-colored bulbs hidden away somewhere to cast a diffuse, sunsetlike glow. The result was to make me feel as if I were standing on the bottom of a giant aquarium—an effect not lessened by the objects on display. There were thousands of them: miniature helmeted divers, some of them battling octopuses or alligators; tiny shipwrecks; pert, Kewpie-like mermaids—hundreds of mermaids—and bathing beauties; and little, hollow castles and lighthouses; and wrecked ships; and treasure chests with gold spilling out of them; and Chinese pagodas and Japanese *torii;* and porcelain snails and seashells and fishes and starfish. Altogether there must have been five thousand such things, none of them more than six inches high and most of them less. Some were displayed on shelves along the walls, some in cases, some in water-filled but fishless aquariums of their own.

As far as I could tell, there wasn't anything in the room worth more than $4.99.

I could see Stetten off to the side, watching me with nervous anticipation. I stood there staring dumbly around, searching for something nice to say. Everything looked as if it had been picked up at a dime store or a seaside souvenir stand. "It's..." I ran my tongue over my lips. "It's astonishing. I've never seen anything like it."

"Do you really think so?" he said, touchingly pleased. "I value your opinion, Ben."

"Absolutely," I said. "It's beautiful, Albrecht, really beautiful. And the way you have it displayed!" What the hell, in for a dime, in for a dollar, and who was I hurting?

"You like aquarium furniture?"

"Sure I do." At least now I had a name for the stuff.

"The lighthouses—they're particularly wonderful, don't you think so?"

"The lighthouses, yes. Definitely, the lighthouses. Wonderful."

He moved fondly to a six-foot-high case full of the things. "I don't mean to boast, but I honestly believe this to be the finest collection of Spanish bisque miniature lighthouses in the world. Not the largest, you understand—Nobutaka in Kyoto has the largest collection; I'd be the first to admit that—but the finest. I'll stand by that."

"Mm," I said.

"Do you know what their function is? They were designed as places for baby fish to hide so the bigger fish don't eat them. Interesting, isn't it? And some of them are aerators to keep the fish from drowning, which seems an odd thing to have to worry about with fish but is nonetheless true. As for the mermaids— Oh, and did you notice these little seals with the balls balanced on their snouts? So delightful. They were made in the early 1880s; not so easy to find anymore, I can tell you. Look, look here, the balls spin if you..."

This was a Stetten I hadn't seen before, passionate and melting at the same time. Everything about him had softened as he spoke— his eyes, his voice, even the dry creases around his mouth. The pink on his cheeks was brighter than ever. He was like a man raving about his children or his long-lost first love.

He took me through the collection, talking nonstop and shining with something close to bliss. The seals with the balls on their snouts were worth over five thousand dollars, not that you could find them anywhere these days because there were only about two hundred in existence, and the Spanish bisque lighthouses brought two thousand dollars each. I made appreciative noises, of course, but, personally, I still wouldn't have given five bucks for anything in the place.

"Albrecht," I said when we were back in the living room, with me sunk into one of the low, cream-colored sofas and Stetten on a thinly padded armchair that would be easier for him to get out of, "may I ask you something?"

"Certainly, my friend," he said, ruddy with the afterglow of his mermaids and lighthouses. He held up a cut-glass decanter. "A cordial?"

"Yes, thanks."

Stetten filled two glasses and gave one to me. "*Prosit.*"

It was caraway-flavored Kümmel, another of the spicy Continental liqueurs that sit so queerly on the American palate. I sipped, set the glass down, and leaned forward (not an easy thing to do on that soft, sagging sofa), steepling my fingers in front of my chin while I looked for the right words.

"It's easy to see how much you love your collection," I began.

He looked suddenly alarmed, as if afraid that I was about to find fault with it.

"And I can certainly understand why," I added to his relief. "But at the same time...well, I get the impression that the paintings don't mean that much to you."

He looked hurt. "Ben. Why do you say such a thing?"

"No, offense, Albrecht, but they just don't seem to affect you the same way. Watching you in there with that, um, aquarium furniture, you were a different man. That seal with the ball

306

on its nose made you light up in a way that *The Countess of Torrijos* never did."

He laughed quietly. "Well, I have to admit you're right about that. It's true that I don't have my father's passion for paintings as paintings. I don't really know that much about them—or care that much about them as such, if it comes to that. And their monetary value means very little to me."

I wondered if that could be because he'd never computed what they were worth. Surely he couldn't be rich enough to be that casual about three hundred million dollars. "Then why am I here?" I asked. "Why are you investing so much effort into getting them back?"

He put his glass down. "Is that a serious question, Benjamin?"

He pronounced it the European way, Ben-*ya*meen. It produced an unexpected tug, because of course it was the Yiddish way, too, and that's how Zayde had said my name. Zayde, I suddenly realized, would have been younger when he died than Stetten was now, yet at the time he had seemed like Abraham the Patriarch.

"Yes, it's a serious question."

He stood up with his glass, went to the French doors to the terrace, and looked out over the town and the hills. "I wonder if I can make you understand," he said as if he were talking to someone out there. A lethargic bluebottle fly that had managed to outlast the summer bumbled on the pane near his face, but he didn't seem to notice. After a few moments, without turning from the doors, he began to speak.

"I don't want them because they're beautiful paintings, or even valuable paintings," he said in the same quiet, neutral tone that his voice had in the Café Imperial, when he told me about what had happened to his family during the war. "I want them because they are my father's beloved paintings, taken from him at the cost of his life. I want them because by recovering them I recover a precious piece of my family's past that was stolen from me. My memory, my identity, are in those pictures. And—well, I want them because it's *right*, Ben. If I can really recover them, you see, I will have attained, on behalf of my dead family, after so many years, the only justice I can still hope for."

Delivered by an actor in a movie, it would have made a mawkish, uncomfortable speech, but from Stetten, said in that simple, almost throwaway manner, it made the hair on my neck stand up. I wanted to apologize for having asked the question in the first place.

"Forgive me, I didn't mean to make a speech," he said, still looking out over the town.

"I—that—I'm sorry I asked. I should have understood what they mean to you."

He turned from the window, blinking. I could see that he was more moved than his voice had let on. "I may know very little about the art of painting, but those pictures I love with all my heart."

As always, he refused to stay sentimental for long. "Almost as much, in fact, as my Spanish bisque lighthouses."

THE HOTEL ALTSTADT WAS in the most picturesque part of Salzburg, right on Judengasse, one of the main pedestrian streets. A brewery in medieval times, it still had old stone arches, wood-beamed ceilings, and fifteenth-century stucco work poking picturesquely out here and there among the many twentieth-century mod cons. If not quite in a class with the Grand Europe in St. Petersburg, it was nevertheless pretty swank and would have been out of my league if I'd been the one paying the bill. My room had a pleasant little window alcove on the quiet side of the building, overlooking the Salzach River, which flowed behind the hotel through the heart of the town, and it was there that I sat for what was left of the day, watching the copper roofs on the far bank turn a glowing orange-yellow as the sun fell, replaying the day I'd just had.

It took a lot of replaying: the meeting with Szarvas and János, Szarvas's murder, the wild chase through Ecseri Piac, the heart-stopping confrontation with Tibor, the flight to Salzburg, the fantastic catalogue that Stetten's father had prepared, the many sides of Stetten himself....Some day. Was it possible that not even twelve hours had passed since I'd been eating prune pastries at the Hotel Duna's funhouse buffet?

Thinking of food made me realize that all

I'd had since then were some finger sandwiches and cookies out on Stetten's terrace,
which made me realize that I was as hungry
as a wolf. I walked downstairs and out into the
narrow streets, bustling even at 8:00 P.M. with
tourists, crowded shops, and restaurants. It
was impossible to go two steps without the smell
of schnitzel, gulasch, or Salzburger nockerl in
one's nostrils, but what I sought was nour-
ishment for the spirit as well as the body;
good, familiar, honest, all-American food.
Pizza.

I found it, too; a thick-crust pepperoni
pizza at a tiny place with picnic tables out on
the sidewalk, just around the corner from
Getriedegasse 9, Mozart's birthplace. I shared
a wooden trestle table with a lively group of
Austrian soldiers in fatigues, clinked pewter
beer steins with them, and returned to the Altstadt in an optimistic and self-assured frame
of mind.

When I got back, I called Alex's number in
Brookline.

"Alex, hi. Listen, I wonder if you could do
something for me—"

"I'm fine, thank you for asking."

"Sorry," I said, laughing. "I've had sort of
a long day. I guess I'm a little stupid. How are
you?"

"Still fine, thanks, how are you? *Where* are
you?"

"In Salzburg. I'm spending some time with
Stetten."

"Ah. Is he— Well, you can tell me about it

in a minute. What was it you wanted me to do?"

"Stop by my place and pick up some stuff for me. I'll be going up to the Altaussee mine the day after tomorrow, and I realized it might be useful to have the MFA&A material on the place with me. It's sitting right on my desk in a blue binder. Records of the American Commission for the Protection and Salvage of Something Something Something."

"How would I get in?"

"Ring the downstairs buzzer for Rochelle Blackburn. I'll tell her to expect you. She'll have a key."

Come on, I thought, at least ask me why Rochelle Blackburn has a key to my condo, show that much interest. (Rochelle was the sixty-two-year-old building manager.) But no, she wouldn't.

"All right, and do what with the file?"

"Fax it to me at the Hotel Seevilla in Altaussee. Got a pencil?"

"Just a second. Yes, go ahead."

I gave her the fax number and the country code. "There are forty or fifty pages, so it'll take a little time, but I have a fax machine right there. Make yourself some coffee. There might even be some cookies in the freezer; you can defrost them in the microwave."

"All right. And you need it by when? Now? Tomorrow?"

"No, the day after. I want to stay in Salzburg another day. He's got this incredible catalogue of his paintings that his father made, and I want to spend one more day with it."

"All right, Ben, will do. Now, seriously, how are you? How's it going?"

"Well—are you sure you really want to know?"

"Of course."

"Okay, you asked for it. Where was I the last time I called?"

"In Vienna. You were about to go to St. Petersburg."

"Right. Well, I've been to St. Petersburg, where I had a strange but interesting visit and got very little information, but all kinds of dire warnings from Yuri Minkov. I also went to Budapest—"

"Budapest? Hungary? Why?"

"One of the claimants you told me about lived there; I thought I might learn something."

"And?"

I took a breath. "And he turned out to be a mafia bigwig who was shot to death right in front of me in this huge flea market, and I only managed to get out of there alive by clubbing a mafia hood in the chops, disguising myself as a bad guy, and running like hell for the airport with the whole Budapest mafia right on my tail. I had to leave all my clothing, my luggage, everything, behind."

There was a very long silence at the other end. "You know what's really weird?" she said at last. "I believe every word you've just told me."

"You should, it's true."

"When did all this happen?"

"This morning."

"This...! My God, and the day's not even over yet."

"Bite your tongue. I've had all the excitement I can handle for one day."

"Ben," she said soberly, "what's going on?"

I settled myself in the armchair a bit more comfortably. "This may take a little time," I said.

CHAPTER 26

The two-and-a-half-hour trip from Salzburg to Altaussee, through the Lake District, is one of the most beautiful drives in the Austrian Alps, which is to say, one of the most beautiful drives anywhere: craggy, glacier-topped ridges and pyramidal peaks above you every which way you look; rolling, impossibly green pastures; humpy, forested hills; tiny hamlets clustered in the very bottoms of valleys as if they'd slid down the steep sides and come to rest there; and sky-blue mountain lake after mountain lake, each with a picturesque village on its shore. Heaven.

But Lake Altaussee is one of the smaller lakes and Altaussee itself one of the less picturesque hamlets, lacking the usual *gemütlich* village center and arranged instead into a long commercial strip along the main road. At the lakefront, where the road ends, things are better: leafy, sun-dappled paths alongside the water, rustic pensions, fish restaurants, and the lake itself, crisscrossed by small tour boats and towered over on three sides by walls of granite rearing straight up from the water's edge a thousand feet and more.

The Seevilla, shaded by a stand of trees, sits right at the shore, a pleasant country hotel with forty or so rooms-making it the village's largest-whose claim to fame is that Johannes Brahms once lived there. At the reception desk the first thing I did after checking in was to ask in German if there were any messages for me. There weren't.

"Are you positive? I was expecting a fax."

"No, sir, I'm very sorry, there's nothing."

Something bumped against my elbow. I'd been noticing that the person next to me wasn't giving me much space—a foreign tourist, I figured; Austrians and Germans are generally pretty good about not crowding you—and now I looked down to see my MFA&A report on the Altaussee interrogations—not a fax, but the actual blue binder, complete with oversized label—being slipped along the counter under my forearm.

"Would this be what you're looking for?"

I turned in astonishment, and there she was in a blue linen blazer, a striped boat shirt, and beige slacks, leaning easily against the counter and laughing, a wisp of streaky blond hair hanging prettily down over her forehead.

"Hello, Ben."

"Alex...what are you...how..."

"Special delivery. I brought the report you wanted. Also a fax that was in your machine. I tucked it inside."

I took it from her, then started laughing, too. I couldn't believe she was standing right there next to me. "Hey, you look great!"

"So do you. Is that your Hungarian-gangster jacket?"

"Neat, isn't it? I wish I knew what I paid for it. Hey, what are you doing here? How did you get here so fast? I just talked to you the day before yesterday. You were in Boston."

"Yes, but they have airplanes now, you see. I flew out of Boston last night."

"What, you went up and found the report and then you thought, Well, I suppose I could fax it, but why not jump on a plane to Europe instead? Just like that?"

"No, not exactly just like that. I got a midnight red-eye out of Logan, arrived in Vienna at noon, flew to Salzburg, got a train to Bad Aussee, and took a taxi here, beating you by about twenty minutes."

"But—"

"Look, I do this kind of thing all the time. My brother's a United pilot, I travel for next to nothing. I go to Paris or London for the weekend all the time. And BU's very flexible about my schedule as long as it's not crazy season."

"Yes, b—"

"Ben, I can't tell you how touched I am that you're so glad to see me."

I grabbed her hand and pulled her away from the openly interested reception clerk. "Alex, I couldn't be more glad. There's absolutely nobody in the world I'd rather see. I'm just bowled over, that's all."

She gave my hand a slight return squeeze. "That's better."

"That being said, I want you to take the first bus, train, and plane out of here tomorrow morning and get the hell home."

"Because it's dangerous?"

"Because it's dangerous. I'm not sure you really grasp that this is the mafia we're—"

"Are *you* getting the hell home?"

"No, I'm not, but don't forget, I owe something to Simeon."

"And I don't? Look, I want to be part of this, too, Ben. Simeon was *my* uncle, not yours. I loved that man, and I'm not going to sit around in Brookline anymore waiting for occasional reports to trickle in from the front. You can understand that, can't you?"

"I can understand that."

"Also, my mother's family is from Austria and I'm betting I speak better German than you do, so I might even turn out to be useful. All right, are we done arguing?"

"All I'm—"

"Not that it matters, because I'm not going back. Now, are there any other questions?"

"Yes," I said. "What are you doing for dinner?"

AFTER I'D SENT MY things up to my room, we walked into town to the Gasthof Engel, which the hotel clerk recommended to us as having the most authentic regional cooking in Altaussee. The little restaurant, part of a mom-and-pop guest house, had a pea-graveled terrace in back, with huge banks of impatiens and a few tree-shaded wooden tables covered with blue-checked cloths. Alex was delighted with the menu.

"I'll say it's authentic! Look, they have stinkerknödl."

"My goodness, doesn't that sound appetizing."

"As a kid I hated it, but, gosh, it brings back memories. They're sort of fried potato dumplings filled with Limburger cheese or something. You eat it with roasted onions. My Aunt Rachel was famous for it. You could smell it from four blocks away."

She ordered it, too. I was willing to go along with the old-country mood, but not that far. I asked for liver dumplings and sauerkraut, which I actually like. When the stinkerknödl arrived, Alex immediately cut into it with her fork, and out with the steam came what had to be the Mother of All Dirty-Socks Smells; four blocks was an understatement.

"Tell me," I said, leaning as far away from it as I could get, "why do they call it stinkerknödl?"

Tentatively, she tried a little on the tip of her fork.

I watched her move it around on her tongue, trying it out on different taste buds. "Well?"

"It's awful," she said with a happy grin. "Exactly like *Tante* Rachel's."

During the meal we talked a little bit about what had been happening-but there wasn't much to tell because I'd brought her up to date a few days ago and nothing new had happened yesterday-a little about her multi-leg trip to get here, and a little about Austrian cuisine, eventually reaching one of those awkward junctures where the chitchat seemingly dries up and blows away. We pushed our plates to one side and folded our napkins and set them on the table and sipped what was left of our wine and murmured "Mm."

"So," I said.

"So."

"Um, how about telling me something about yourself, Alex? You already know all about me."

"I do?"

"Well, you're friendly with Trish. I'm sure she's given you a warm and objective assessment of my background and personality."

"That's true," she said. "I happened to mention to her last week that I'd met you, and she said she's been giving you a lot of thought lately."

"I don't know how happy I am to hear that."

"No, wait, it was interesting. She told me all sorts of fascinating things about you that I hadn't realized before. Such as..." Her eyes suddenly crinkled up; she laughed and bit her lower lip. "Such as..."

I grimaced. "Do I really want to hear this? Do I have a choice?"

"For one thing, I learned that you've always resisted sorting out the yin and yang aspects of your personality. That's why you never have any firm opinions and you're such an indecisive fence-straddler about everything."

I put down my wine. "Well, now, just one cotton-pickin' minute. I wouldn't say—"

"I'm quoting; no offense. But you know what else she told me? And this is really interesting-that you've never, not even once, made a genuine effort to enter into a frank and open dialogue with your sexuality."

I burst out laughing. "That one I can't argue with."

"Also—"

"Please," I said, raising a hand. "How much self-improvement can I absorb at one sitting? Can we get on to you for a while?"

"That's only fair," she agreed. "What would you like to know?"

Plenty, I thought. Have you ever been married? Is there anyone in your life now? Did you really come to Altaussee strictly to be part of whatever it was that was happening here, or did I, personally, have anything at all to do with it? What exactly do you think of me, really?

"Well?" she said. "Isn't there anything?"

I cleared my throat. "How long have you been at Boston University?" I asked.

HAVING HOPELESSLY DEMOLISHED OUR saturated-fat allowance for the month anyway (in Austria you do that by the end of breakfast), we went ahead and got another local specialty for dessert: Mohr im Hemd, a superrich chocolate sponge cake slathered with hot whipped chocolate and then buried under a mountain of whipped cream. Incredible; why didn't these people all weigh three hundred pounds?

While we worked through a *Kännchen* of coffee and shamelessly cleaned our plates-polished is closer to the truth-Alex talked about herself. I learned that she'd majored in sociology at the University of Massachusetts and had started on her master's degree but had quit partway through to take a job as registrar at a community college on Long Island. There she'd finished up her master's at the state university in Stony Brook, but in educational administration, and after three more years at the community college she'd landed the job with BU.

Along the way she'd fallen in love once (if you didn't count teenage crushes), or maybe twice; she still wasn't sure. She'd lived with the second one, a lawyer, for a year. They'd split up, amicably, about a year ago and were still good friends. She liked men, and her social life was fairly active, and why she'd never gotten married she couldn't say. It seemed like a good idea in the abstract, but for some reason she'd never been able to imagine being married to anyone she knew without either laughing or shuddering, neither of which seemed like a promising sign.

All this didn't come without some pretty subtle probing on my part, you realize, and it had taken a while to get to this point. In the meantime it had grown dark, and I could see that she was starting to flag, which was natural enough, considering that she hadn't slept the night before and had spent the entire day on the road. For the first time I saw something vulnerable in her face, the smallest of fatigue tics in her cheek, just under the left eye. And damned attractive it was.

"What do you say we call it a day?" I suggested.

"No more questions left?" she said with a tired smile.

Yes, I had some questions left. What did she mean by "good friends"? What the hell did "fairly active" mean?

"Nope," I said.

"That was fun, Ben," she said when we got outside. "Thank you. I enjoyed it."

"Me too. I *am* glad you're here, Alex, I-well, I'm glad."

I think we both knew that we'd moved to a different level in our relationship. Not deeper, necessarily, but easier, closer, more comfortable. For four hours we'd been steadily in each other's company, talking almost without stopping, not about murders or stolen art but about ourselves and each other, and whatever else was at hand or came to mind. It had all been so casual and random, like the desultory talk of old friends, that we'd slipped into imagining that's what we were, and, although it felt fine, it was going to take some getting used to.

I took her arm, highly conscious of the fact

that it was the first time I'd touched any-thing other than her hand, and started us toward the hotel.

She held back. "I go the other way."

"But the hotel is—Aren't you staying at the Seevilla?"

"No, I'm down the other way, at the Pen-sion Obermayr. We're not all on expense accounts, you know."

"Is it all right?"

"About what I expected. The room's just big enough to hold a bed and a bureau, with a bath-room down the hall. And the view is of Frau Obermayr's string-bean and tomato garden. But it's clean. How's your room?"

My "room" was an airy bedroom and a big sitting room, with a fireplace, a shining, well-equipped bathroom, and a pleasant balcony overlooking the lake and the mountains.

"Pretty posh," I said.

"Ah," she said soberly. "Well, I should think so."

A pretty ambiguous statement, if you asked me. What did she mean by it? I was teetering on the edge of suggesting that she come spend the night at the Seevilla with me-I almost thought that was what she might have been hinting at-but I didn't know how to put it. *Oh, say, I have an idea. I have lots of room at my place, so why don't you stay the night with me? I'll sleep in the sitting room and you can have the bed-room. Or you can sleep in the sitting room and we'll get a nice fire going in the fireplace for you to sleep by if it gets chilly.* Would that sound as sappy to her as it did to me? What about a simple, carelessly tossed-off *Why don't you stay the night with me?*-and leave the interpretation to her. How would she take that? What would she think I meant? What did *I* think I meant? You see, it was already getting tricky.

Did I want her to come and sleep with me? In principle, yes, sure, what do you think? But now, tonight? Well, there I didn't know. I liked her a lot, I liked the way I felt when she was around, and I was happy with the way we were getting to know each other. Would sex at this point spoil that? (That is, assuming she was interested.) Yeah, actually, I thought it just might.

Or then again, it might not. In the end I kept quiet about it and walked her to her pension, which wasn't bad-looking at all, a two-story house built in the Tyrolean style, with a steeply pitched roof, carved wooden balconies, and geraniums spilling from a dozen window boxes. I told her to sleep as late as she wanted to and give me a call when she woke up. We'd have breakfast somewhere, then drive up to the salt mine and see what was to be seen.

We bade each other a slightly stilted goodnight, followed, after a moment's hesitation and one false start, by a blameless hug and then an old-friends-style kiss on the cheek, made even more clumsy because we hadn't figured out which of us was supposed to aim for which cheek, so that we wound up bobbing heads at each other like pigeons doing a mating dance. But that made us laugh, which was a nice way to end the evening.

Walking back to the Seevilla in the dark, I felt like three different people, angry with myself for being so namby-pamby, pleased with myself for behaving like a gentleman, and relieved with myself at managing so far not to screw everything up. What I wanted to happen, I still didn't know. I was beginning to think Trish had a point. Maybe what I needed was a frank and open dialogue with my sexuality. In fact, I'd be highly interested to hear what it had to say for itself.

CHAPTER 27

In the morning I put in another call to Mr. Nussbaum in Vienna, and this time I finally got him. He'd been in Badgastein for a week, he explained in German, taking his annual spa cure, and he was apologetic about having missed my calls. He came across as a decent sort, nothing at all like his deceased fellow claimant Szarvas, and the impression I had was that he was probably honestly confusing the Boston Velàzquez with some other painting; hardly surprising after a half century or so. An honest mistake. If so, it meant that he would know nothing of value relating to Simeon or Stetten, but I thought that an hour spent with him might save him, as well as Stetten, a lot of unproductive time and money, and he very cordially agreed to see me when I got back to Vienna.

"Thank you very much," I said. "I should be there tomorrow— no, make that the day after tomorrow. Could I come by about three?"

He switched to English. "Tell me, what kind of accent is that? American, Canadian?"

"American. I'm from Boston."

"Is that so? I was five years in Chicago, living with my son and his wife. Twice we went to Boston. A wonderful city, so much history, so much culture. You're lucky."

"Well, Vienna's not too bad on those scores either," I said. "Is three o'clock okay, then?"

"I'll be here."

"Oh, and one more thing? Would you please not tell anyone that you're going to be seeing me?"

"Why not, what's the secret?"

"I just think it would be better. It's important; I'll explain later. Will you give me your word?"

"Sure, you can have my word. Who would I tell anyway, my dog?"

"That's good," I said. "Thanks."

He sounded like a nice old coot. I didn't want to get him killed.

CONTINUING OUR CARDIOLOGICAL BANZAI charge of the evening before, Alex and I brunched on rostbratwurst and rolls, with Eskimo Pie bars for dessert, sitting on high stools at a sausage stand on the main road.

"Listen," I said, unwrapping my ice cream, "I can't imagine that we'll need more than a couple of hours up at the mine. What are your plans for the next few days?"

"I don't know. What *are* my plans for the next few days?"

I liked that answer a lot. "Well, I finally got hold of Mr. Nussbaum in Vienna this morning, and I set up a meeting with him for the day after tomorrow. You might want to be there, too."

"The day *after* tomorrow? Vienna's only a one-hour flight from Salzburg. We could be there tomorrow morning."

"Well, that's my point. There's no real hurry on this. I sure could stand a day off, and I was thinking it might be fun to drive there instead of flying; it's beautiful country, and it's only a couple of hundred miles, even going the slow route. We could follow the Danube Valley most of the way, and there's a terrific little village right on the river, an old fortified town named Dürnstein with some wonderful old inns. There's a ruined castle there that you can climb around in, where Richard the Lion-Hearted was imprisoned for a year. Do you know the legend of Blondel? Well, that's where it happened, Dürnstein...."

It's an old habit. When I get nervous, or anxious, or unsure of myself, I tend to blather. It never helps, of course, but I do it anyway. And Alex wasn't helping either. She was just munching away at her second bratwurst and watching me prattle. I could feel my forehead getting hot.

"Anyway," I said offhandedly, as if it couldn't matter less (I'm sure it fooled her), "what do you think? How does that sound?"

She licked mustard off her pinky. "It sounds," she said, "just fine." And then she gave me the prettiest smile you can imagine, with her eyes as well as her mouth.

"Great," I said, and over me, like a warm, welcome cloak settling on my shoulders, came the feeling that I was onto something good, that maybe the gods were with me again. That I'd turned a corner.

To GET TO THE Altaussee salt mine, you turn off the village's main street at the SALZBERG-WERK sign, then drive a thousand feet or so up into the mountains on a steep but well-engineered, paved road. At the mine there's a big visitors' parking lot with a separate area for tour buses, a pleasant little picnic area with a few tables, and several buildings, the largest of which is the entrance to the mine and also houses a small museum on the upper floor.

Leaving our rented Saab in the lot, we went first to the museum, in hopes that there might be old records we could look over, but found it shut tight. Then to the administrative office in one of the outbuildings. Ditto, nobody home. The only staff we could find were a couple of youngsters in the ticket office, where you paid to go on the tour, who said they knew nothing at all about the workings of the mine, past or present, and suggested that our best bet would be to take the 11:00 A.M. educational tour, on which a knowledgeable guide would be able to answer all our questions.

So with two dozen other people we went into a dressing room to put on coveralls over our clothes, then followed the lantern-toting guide into the mountain and down through the rock-cut tunnels and galleries. We slid down a hundred-foot-long miner's slide, we watched an entertainingly spooky sound-and-light show at an underground lake, and we broke off pieces of the gleaming, rust-colored walls around us to taste them and see that they were indeed salty. We learned that salt had been mined in these caverns since Roman times and that the process was still going on only a few hundred yards away. We learned that the salt had to be washed out of the rock with water, and that the annual output of brine produced in this manner was 2.3 million tons, from which 460,000 tons of salt resulted. We learned that almost all of this output was for industrial purposes such as porcelain manufacture and metallurgy, with only 7 percent purified into cooking salt. We learned the pros and cons of solar evaporation, bore-hole brine procedure, and multiple-effect vacuum evaporators.

Of the mine's role as the greatest repository of looted art in the history of the world we heard nothing.

I mean nothing, not a word. Zero. And when we'd put questions to our guide—Could he tell us which particular caverns had housed the paintings? Could he tell us how they'd been protected against the underground moisture?—he had shaken his head and said he didn't know anything about any paintings. And probably he hadn't; he was about twenty-five years old.

Yet in these caverns had been well over ten thousand major works of art. They had formed the core of what was going to be Hitler's pan-Germanic Führermuseum at Linz, the future cultural heart of the thousand-year Reich. Among them had been some of the world's most revered masterpieces. The fabulous Ghent altarpiece known as *The Adoration of the Lamb,* painted by Jan and Hubert van Eyck (or maybe only by Jan; nobody's sure) in 1432 and long venerated as Belgium's most precious art treasure, was there in a room constructed especially for it. The famous *Portrait of the Artist in His Studio* by Vermeer was there, as was the entire art collection from the Naples Museum—paintings by Titian, Rembrandt, Raphael, Claude Lorrain, Brueghel, Palma Vecchio—and the equally great personal collections of the Rothschild, Gutman, and Mannheimer families, alongside of which Stetten's collection was small potatoes. Michelangelo's masterpiece, the lovely marble Madonna from the Church of the Annunciation in Bruges, was there, too, having been carried off by the Germans in 1944 to "save" it from the "Allied barbarians" approaching the city. At Altaussee it had lain on a filthy mattress with a sheet of asphalt paper over it until the first MFA&A team had come tramping up the mountain in May of 1945, to be amazed at what they saw.

Only in a brochure that I'd bought at the bookshop near the entrance was there a single passing reference to any of this: "In the subterranean treasure vaults of the Altaussee salt mine, a large part of the European cultural heritage was protected against the turbulence of World War II." Otherwise known as Old Reliable, the Elgin argument.

"Talk about spin control," Alex said, handing it back to me. We were sitting at a picnic table in the sunny little park near the entrance, trying to get warm after the damp chill of the mountain's interior. "You'd think, after all this time, they could be a little more honest than that."

"Well, as far as it goes, it's true enough, I suppose," I said.

"What, that they were *protecting* all those things, that that's why they put them there? Protecting them for whom, for what? Tell me, what were they going to do with them after they finished 'protecting' them? And what did the people they took them from think about it?"

"Whoa, don't get excited, I'm only saying that what it says there is true—as far as it goes. The paintings were saved, weren't they?"

"Sure, because *we* saved them."

"Partly, yes."

"*Partly!*"

330

"Yes, partly. The Austrian Resistance had something to do with it, too, as you'd know if you'd ever looked into it." For whatever reason, the tour had put both of us on a short fuse. "The Nazis were going to blow up everything in the mine before the Allies reached it, did you know that?"

"Yes, I knew that."

"And do you know why they didn't, do you know who stopped it?"

"No, but something tells me I'm about to find out."

I ignored this. "Alex, what happened here at this mine was one of the great stories of the war. The bombs to do the job had already been delivered, ready to be detonated—eight five-hundred-pounders—only the Austrian mine workers themselves kept throwing one monkey wrench after another into the gears to prevent it from happening. If not for them, everything in the mine would have been destroyed, and there's no doubt about their risking their lives to do it either. It was sabotage, pure and simple. If the Nazis had caught on to them, they would have been executed for treason— or defeatism, which was just as bad."

"Well, good for them," Alex said tartly. "I guess I must have gotten it wrong when I read that the Austrians and Germans were on the same side."

"No, you did not get it wrong. They were on the same side, all right. Not only that, but the most rabid Nazi officials at the mine weren't Germans at all, but Austrians. And when it came down to the wire, the man who got the bombs out of there at the last minute and then sealed the mine entrance so they couldn't get back in wasn't some brave Austrian Resistance fighter, he was the German SS commander, of all people. Go figure."

"Go figure? What's that supposed to mean?"

Why are we arguing? I wanted to say, but I was fired up. "It means that it's not always so easy to tell the good guys from the bad guys, especially when you weren't there yourself and you don't know what they went through. There were a lot of sides to what went on at Altaussee."

And what was true of Altaussee was just as true of wartime Austria as a whole, I pointed out with heat. Depending on who was telling the story, you got a lot of different versions. Either Hitler had brutally annexed Austria after first engineering the killing of his opponents in the government...or he had peacefully entered Austria in his open Mercedes-Benz to the enthusiastic applause of huge crowds lining the roads all the way to Vienna. Either the Austrian population had vigorously embraced the loathsome Nazi racial laws...or they had resisted in every way they could, taking awful risks to hide Jewish friends and neighbors in their attics and basements. Either Austria had been a willing part of Greater Germany and its near-equal partner...or it had been a subject nation, ground down and oppressed by jackbooted invaders. Either they had endorsed Hitler's bizarre schemes of Germanic exaltation... or they had stubbornly resisted, taking to guns, bombs, and knives of their own. Either—

I caught myself and stopped. Somewhere along the line I'd slipped into professorial gear, not usually an indicator of good things to follow.

"All right, I buy all that," Alex said. "So the question is, Which is it, the 'either' or the 'or'? Were they good guys or were they bad guys? You tell me."

"But that's the problem. It's *all* true. At the end of the war the Allies themselves couldn't agree which side Austria was on. Were they occupying the country or liberating it? It made a huge difference in the way Austria was going to be treated. In the end they decided— not without reservations—on liberation: Officially speaking, Austria had been a friend, not an enemy."

"Officially speaking—!" She stopped abruptly, her head cocked. "Are we having a fight?"

"I think so."

"What about?"

"Exactly what I've been wondering."

"Well, I don't like it. Would you mind very much if we called it quits?"

"I would love to call it quits," I said. "I would pay good money to call it quits."

A business-suited woman who'd been standing nearby waiting for a break in our conversation came up to the table. "I'm Mrs. Hirsch, the tour manager," she said in cultivated German. "You are the people who were asking about the Altaussee treasure?"

At last, a living Austrian who'd heard of it. "That's right. We're trying to find out what we can about a number of paintings that were stored here during the war."

"Ah. Well, I'm afraid I know very little about it. It's Dr. Haftmann you should speak with. He was employed at the mine during that time."

"Do you know where we could find him?" I asked.

"I do. In the village, at the Hotel am See's restaurant, on the lakeside terrace, farthest table on the left. Dr. Haftmann is a man of habit. It is where he lunched every day except Sunday in 1944, and it is where he lunches every day except Sunday now. On trout from the lake. He comes early, at noon, so he'll be there now."

"Haftmann, Haftmann..." I said, trying to dredge up whatever dim association the name had for me. "Haftmann..." When it came, I sat bolt upright. "The MFA&A report!" I blurted in English. "The interview..." I switched excitedly to German. "You can't be talking about Erhard Haftmann?"

"That's right, Dr. Erhard Haftmann. You know him?"

"I know of him. He wasn't just an employee, he was the registrar."

"Yes, I believe that's correct. We don't pay much attention to all that here at the saltworks anymore."

"And he lives here in Altaussee?" I said. "I'd assumed he was German, not Austrian." I'd also assumed he had to be dead by now.

"Yes, you're correct, he's from Kassel, I believe. But after he retired—he was a university professor, you know—he came and settled here. That was twenty years ago. We still see him at the mine sometimes, although he rarely goes inside anymore." Mrs. Hirsch gave us a thin-lipped smile. "I believe the old fellow likes the idea of being near what was his great creation."

"Do you really want to go and talk with him?" Alex asked as we drove down the mountain.

"You bet."

"Why? What could he tell us that would be helpful? He never even saw any of the paintings. The Lost Truck never made it to the mine, remember?"

"Naturally I remember. That is why we call it 'lost.'"

"Well, why then? Or is this just intellectual curiosity?"

"Oh, I'm not sure how intellectual it is, but, yes, it's partly curiosity. How can we be right here and not bother to see him? How often do you get to talk to somebody who was actually part of the ERR operation?"

"How often do you want to?"

"And then, aside from plain curiosity, there are some symbols on the backs of the paintings that I'm hoping he'll be able to explain."

"Oh?" said Alex without much interest.

I had in mind two markings in particular: the *sr-4* on the back of the *Conde* in Simeon's shop and the *ne-2* on the back of the *Condesa* that Dulska brought to Vienna. I was certain

335

that they'd been put there by the Nazis, and I'd been wondering what they signified. Maybe, if I knew what they meant, they'd suggest some kind of lead. With everything else petering out, I was running low on possibilities.

The Hotel am See was a rambling, picturesque old place not far from the Seevilla. As we entered, Alex wisely suggested that Haftmann might be afraid to talk about his role during the old days if he knew that we had an interest in the restitution of the loot he'd been responsible for, so I came up with a story about our being researchers who were compiling a comparative study of art storage and cataloguing methods, nothing more.

"You'd better do most of the talking," she said. "He'll spot me as a fake the minute I open my mouth."

"Mm," I said, not really paying attention. To my knowledge I had never met an actual Nazi before, and I was trying to figure out how I felt about it.

CHAPTER 28

Say what you will about stereotypes, one thing you have to admit is that they turn out to be right on the money a lot of the time. Which can either be sweetly reassuring or damned irritating, depending on how you look at things.

In this case it was reassuring. Picture in your mind's eye a Nazi functionary. I don't mean

Gestapo or SS, but a diligent and loyal civilian, one of the army of midlevel officials industriously engaged in administering the meticulously organized bureaucracy necessary to the grand designs of the Führer and the Third Reich.

What do you see? A pinched, cold, arid face with thin lips and expressionless gray eyes, perhaps distorted by thick, round lenses, am I right? Not particularly sinister, not really very interesting-looking; the kind of man you'd pass in the street and never remember that you'd seen him at all. Thinning gray hair, gray suit, and pallid gray skin. A gray man altogether.

That was Erhard Haftmann to a tee, except that his hair was now white, not gray. I would have picked him out even without the advance information from Mrs. Hirsch. He was sitting by himself when we first saw him, dabbing at a spot of grease on the lapel of his brown loden jacket, using a linen napkin dipped in mineral water. His lunch had been finished, with the remains pushed to one side. By Austrian standards it had been frugal: a small, whole fish—no doubt the lake trout that Mrs. Hirsch had predicted— now surgically dissected down to its perfect little skeleton, along with string beans, parsleyed boiled potatoes, an untouched roll, and a glass of white wine, only half consumed.

When it was obvious that we were headed to his table, he glanced up with undisguised annoyance. Men of a certain age who are accustomed to eating alone at the same time, same restaurant, and same table every single weekday for decades on end generally don't like having their meals intruded upon. But once I gave him our cock-and-bull story about being interested in his cataloguing methods, he became guardedly civil, offering us cigarettes from a pack of Marlboros and inviting us to join him for coffee.

"I speak English," he said once he'd heard my German. "I think that would be better." You'd be surprised how often I hear that when I'm traveling. "Now, what is it you wish to know?"

Given our catalogue-researcher story, it didn't seem sensible to begin with the ERR symbols, so I started off generally, asking him how many objects had been stored in the mine at the end of the war.

"At the *end* of the war?" he said. "That I can't tell you. At one time we had over twenty-one thousand objects, but in the final weeks all order broke down. There was no discipline. I can't begin to describe the horror. The only accurate figures I can give you are the results of a census a few weeks earlier, which was limited to the material earmarked for the Führer's personal collection. Are you interested in this?"

I nodded.

"So," Haftmann said, and stared dimly at the prodigious wall of mountain on the far shore of the lake while he collected his thoughts. One of his eyes was inflamed and crusty, and he occasionally dabbed at it with a handkerchief. After a moment he drew a whistling breath through his nose and began abruptly to rattle off figures. "For the Führermuseum we safeguarded almost seven thousand paintings, of which more than five thousand were Old Masters. There were also approximately a thousand prints, one hundred tapestries, seventy sculptures, one hundred and thirty articles of armor, two hundred and fifty crates of rare books, eighty baskets and forty cases of smaller art objects, and thirty or thirty-five cases of ancient coins. In addition there were more than seven hundred paintings destined for the Führer's private collections at Berchtesgaden and Posen, as well as some sculptures and tapestries, the number of which I no longer remember."

Midway through, Alex looked at me and muttered out of the side of her mouth, "Is he reading, or what?"

I glanced at the table myself to see if he had some notes there, but of course he didn't, and anyway he had never stopped staring through his thick glasses across the quiet lake. Had this deluge of specifics been dumped on us by someone currently engaged in administering the operation, it would have been impressive. Coming from this aged man more than fifty years after the fact, it was astounding.

He sipped from his coffee cup, frowning. "Did I mention the two hundred and thirty drawings and watercolors?"

Beats me, I thought.

"I don't believe so," Alex said diplomatically.

"For the Linz collection: two hundred and thirty drawings and watercolors. And all of them, every single one of these precious objects, were perfectly preserved, duly recorded, and in its assigned place when the Americans arrived on May eighth. No museum could have cared for them better. And all this was accomplished, I remind you, in the face of severe budget and manpower restrictions—at times we had to resort to unwilling labor—and even in the face of overt opposition from certain highly placed officers."

It was as Mrs. Hirsch had said: Altaussee had been the towering achievement of his life. Behind the bottle-bottom glasses the gray eyes glinted as he waited for a response from us. But although Alex murmured something or other, I couldn't think of anything to say. I was in a sort of daze, stunned not just by the cascade of figures but by the magnitude of the wretchedness they represented. Stetten's father had been tortured and killed over his seventy-three paintings. How many more stories like that had gone into "collecting" the thousands upon thousands of things that Haftmann had just enumerated with such icy pride? How many people, for example, did you have to threaten, or torture, or murder to "collect" eighty baskets and forty cases of small art objects?

Not to mention the "unwilling labor" that had gone into storing it.

And here was this cool, unprepossessing, ancient little man swelling even now with self-regard over his part in it.

"And what was my reward for sacrificing my health, my marriage, to accomplish this?" he asked, clamping his invisible lips with remembered resentment. "I will tell you: When the Americans came, and I went voluntarily to meet them, to give them my assistance, I was arrested." He glared at us, the nearest Americans to hand. "Arrested! For three days I was held like a criminal, questioned every day from morning till night. I ask you frankly, was this justice?"

"Well, there was a lot of information they had to have—" I began.

"Tell me, how many people did I murder? How many Jews did I kill? No, my only crime was the preservation, when civilization was crumbling all around, of the world's greatest art, here in Altaussee. That was my terrible crime."

I really didn't want to get into a fight with him, but this was too much to take sitting down. "Dr. Haftmann, the only reason that art was in Altaussee was that it'd been looted, often by force and always by intimidation—"

"In wartime such things are bound to happen. Apparently you have already forgotten My Lai."

"—from the rightful owners. You can't expect—"

"You speak to me of rightful owners? And what of the art rightfully owned by the German people, what of that? Where is the fabulous art collection of Frederick the Great? In Berlin and Potsdam, where it rightfully belongs? No, in Paris, thanks to Napoleon Bonaparte. And what of the contents of the Austrian Imperial Gallery, flagrantly looted from Vienna in 1809? Of the collections plundered from Munich in 1806 by foreign soldiers? Where is the world's indignation over these outrages?" He spoke, not with outrage of his own, or even passion, but with a clipped, cold, fluent fury, like a fire-and-brimstone preacher laying into the doubting Thomases.

An unrepentant Nazi, a true believer; it seemed fantastic. Naturally I'd known that such people still existed, but I hadn't really *known* it, if you know what I mean, not down deep, not grasped that they got grease spots on their lapels, and had eye infections, and ate fish for lunch. I found myself watching his mouth as he spoke, the way I'd watch a talking snake, fascinated and repelled at the same time.

"From my own city of Kassel in 1807," he went on, "the French stole three hundred masterpieces: Titian, Rembr—"

I came out of my trance. "Dr. Haftmann, you know as well as I do what an old, old story that is. How did Frederick the Great come by his collection? Where did the Austrian Imperial Gallery get theirs?"

"I am speaking of Germanic works."

"You are? I think Titian might have been surprised to hear himself classified as Germanic. And what about the famous Correggio and the

Watteaus from Potsdam? Are they Germanic, too?" If it came to hectoring, I could get right up there with him. "Soldiers have been looting art for a thousand years, sometimes the same pieces, over and over again. That doesn't make it right, and it's certainly not an excuse for the systematic, government-approved looting of every piece of art that Hitler or Göring or Rosenberg—"

"And what would have happened if they hadn't been, as you call it, 'looted'?"

"As *I* call it? What do you call it?"

"Ben?" Alex said. "There's no point in fighting about it."

I already knew that; I just couldn't help myself. I mumbled something to Alex.

"But we're not fighting," Haftmann surprised me by saying. "We're having a hypothetical discussion, an academic debate, that's all."

The hell we are, I thought but managed not to say.

"I can tell you exactly what would have happened," he continued. "Much, perhaps most of it, would have been bombed, burned, destroyed in the war—gone forever, these priceless treasures. How could the possessors possibly protect them? It was we who saved them."

I responded with no more than a glum nod. I'd known that good old Elgin was going to get into the act somewhere, and as far as I was concerned, the issue, while hardly hypothetical, was certainly moot. Besides, the longer he went on, the less fascinated and the more repelled

I was becoming. All I wanted to do was finish up, get away from him, and find someplace to have a drink, or two drinks, with Alex.

"Dr. Haftmann," I said, "may we move to another subject, please? I've been able to study two of the pieces that were"—I made myself say "safeguarded"—"in the mine, and one of the things I noticed was a cataloguing code of some sort that was stamped on the backs. There was an *ne-2* on one, and an *sr-4*, I think it was, on the other. I was wondering if you could tell us their significance."

He jerked his head irritably, not much happier with me than I was with him. "They had no significance. They were merely a crude clerical notation, a system that the Paris ERR units used for a while to indicate the source of the acquisition; it had nothing at all to do with the way the objects were eventually catalogued at Altaussee. The system I used here, you see, my system, was not contextually based at all, but was derived from the broad historico-cultural principles first defined in Otto Kümmel's great work on the dispersion of Germanic art and its inevitable reclamation. To understand this system, it is first necessary..."

ON THE DRIVE BACK down to town Alex was quiet, looking out the window and watching the Alpine landscape slide by. It was more than pretty enough to hold one's attention, but I could tell that she was somewhere inside herself. During the last few minutes of our talk with Haftmann she had gradually grown pensive and dropped out of the conversation.

"What a horrible old man," she murmured now. "He'll give me nightmares tonight. I just want to go somewhere and get clean."

"Oh, I don't know. At least you have to give the old guy credit for sticking to his principles and not backing down just because the rest of the world thinks they're putrid. He can't be too popular. You notice he was eating alone."

It was meant to lighten things, but it missed the mark by a mile. "I knew it," she said, turning fiercely from the window. "I *knew* you'd say something to defend him."

I was dumbfounded; she was really angry. "I...Alex, I'm not—"

"Can't you just say he was a monster and let it go at that?"

"All right, he was a monster. He still is a monster."

"And I want you to say, 'The Austrians were Nazi allies in World War Two. They were on the same side.'"

Ah, so we were still on that. "All right, fine. They were. But—"

"No, without the 'but'! A simple declarative statement."

Whatever was bugging her, she'd succeeded in getting under my skin, too; she was good at that. "Alex, how about telling me what the hell is going on? What's bothering you?"

"Nothing's going on. It's just that— Oh, Ben, sometimes I wonder about you, I really do."

We had reached the bottom of the mountain, and I pulled the car over to the side of the road so I could look her in the eye and show her I was mad. "Because I said 'but'? Because I can see somebody else's point of view? Real life doesn't lend itself to nice, clean, declarative statements, Alex. Don't you ever see anything in shades of gray?"

"Do you ever see anything *but* shades of gray?" she shot back, and I could see she was close to angry tears. "Haftmann is a monster—but on the other hand you have to give him credit. The Austrians were bad guys—but not really. The Russians are wrong about keeping their trophy art—but they're not *really* wrong. Stetten should definitely get his paintings back—but of course other claimants have a valid point, too."

"But—"

"But, but, but, that's all you ever say. Ben, if everybody's right, then nobody's wrong, and I just have a hard time with that, that's all." She lowered her head and covered her eyes with her hand. "That's what's bothering me."

It was my turn to say something, but I just stared straight ahead with my hands on the wheel, resentful and wounded—and still trying to figure out what had happened.

"This is sure fun," I said meanly and as if to myself. "Almost as good as being with Trish."

I was ashamed even before I finished saying it, but the words of apology jammed in my throat and wouldn't come out. Alex stared at me, took a breath, and said, very calmly,

"Would you mind very much if I caught the train back to Salzburg this afternoon instead of going to Vienna with you tomorrow?"

"And then what? Fly to Vienna?"

"I don't know."

"Go home?"

"I told you, I don't know."

"If you go to Vienna, will you get in touch with me there?"

Silence.

"I'll call you when I get back home, all right?"

She was staring down at her lap. "All right."

"Alex…" I hardly knew what I wanted to say. "I don't know what we're fighting about; this isn't even about *us*. Look, you've come all the way out here, I'm glad you're here, and I don't want… I don't want to see this happen."

"Neither do I, Ben. I just think it would be better if I left." She still wasn't looking at me.

"Fine," I said, feeling as if my chest were packed with lead, "whatever you want."

"If you'll drop me off at the pension, I'll get my things and catch a cab to the station in Bad Aussee."

"You don't have to get a cab. I'll drive you to the station."

"That's all right, a cab would be easier."

"Suit yourself," I said, starting up the car again, and five minutes later, having said nothing in the intervening time, we made our brief good-byes.

Maybe, on second thought, I hadn't turned any corners.

CHAPTER 29

I felt miserable: angry, let down, and—this I wouldn't have expected—strangely rudderless and off balance. And even now I didn't have a clue as to what had started it, except that I knew it wasn't me.

Well, it wasn't. What did I do?

"The hell with her," I mumbled unconvincingly to myself as I turned the key in the door of my room after a late, solitary lunch. "Who needs her?"

The telephone message button was blinking; I banged it with my fist. The call had come in only ten minutes earlier. It was from police headquarters in Vienna, asking me to get in touch with Polizeiobersteutnant Feuchtmüller as soon as possible. Christ, what now? Well, at least it wasn't Pirchl who was after me. I sat down and dialed.

"Hello, Alois, it's Ben Revere. How'd you know where to reach me?"

"I'm a detective, am I not? Or at least I have detectives helping me, which is much better. I've just had a long conversation about you with a police captain in Budapest."

"Oh—you know about Szarvas, then."

"Yes, I know about Szarvas. Am I mistaken, or weren't you going to keep me informed from time to time?"

"Well, yes, and I meant to call you, but...Oh, hell, I'm sorry, Alois, I should have called you right away. It kind of got away from me."

"Mm. Suppose you give me your version now."

I did, including the various speculations I'd made about Szarvas's murder.

He listened without comment until I'd finished. "You know what the Budapest police think, don't you?"

"No, what do they think?"

"They think that you're an international crime boss who set up the shooting with a contract killer. They've issued a warrant for your arrest."

I waited for the rumbly laugh that would tell me this was one of his heavy-handed jokes, but it didn't arrive.

"Are you serious? I hope you're not serious."

"Oh, but I am."

"But...they only think that because...I mean, you know I'm not..."

"Yes, that's exactly what I told them, and I *think* that Captain Nagy was reasonably convinced of your innocence, although he did choose not to withdraw the warrant."

"Does that mean I have to go back there?"

I heard the click of his pipe against his teeth as it came out of his mouth. "Dr. Revere, if I were you I would not go within ten miles of the Hungarian border for the rest of my life—however long or short that might be."

"But if the police—"

"I'm not thinking about the police. The police will do fine without your help. The problem is, their local mafia appears to be suffering from the same misapprehension and is—understandably, under the circumstances—

annoyed with you. Unfortunately, I was unable to speak with them to set them straight."

"Christ," I said.

"But all is not bleak. We've been making a little headway here. We need to talk to you again."

"'We' being Pirchl?" I said, hoping otherwise.

And now his growly laugh did rumble across the two hundred miles between us. "Yes, actually, but don't worry, I think you and I can handle this between us. It should only take a few minutes. When can you be in Vienna?"

"I was planning to be there the day after tomorrow."

"That will do. I'll see you at the station at, say, three o'clock?"

"No good, I have an appointment with Mr. Nussbaum at three o'clock."

"Two o'clock, then. This will only take a few minutes."

"Okay, two o'clock. Alois—I'm not in any trouble with *your* people, am I? With Pirchl?"

"My son, when you're in trouble with Pirchl, you won't need me to tell you about it."

AT EIGHT-THIRTY THE NEXT morning I drove to the Salzburg airport, returned the rental car, and bought a ticket on the 11:00 A.M. flight to Vienna. Without Alex, the idea of driving slowly along the Danube Valley, let alone staying in a romantic old inn, had lost its appeal, and I thought I might just as well get myself to Vienna without delay.

I'd reached that conclusion about fifteen seconds after dropping Alex off at her pension the day before, but I'd waited until this morning to do anything about it, because I'd been hoping that sometime during the evening I would get a remorseful call from her, maybe even a tearful one, that would somehow chalk up the painful exchange we'd had to a misunderstanding and make everything right again. I was more than ready to be persuaded, but the call never came.

As soon as we were in the air, I telephoned Alois to tell him I'd be in a day early, and I was at his disposal. He had a lunch date he couldn't break, so we set up the meeting for one-thirty, which would give me a chance to check into the Hotel Imperial and leave my bag there. Then, looking for something to do, I pulled out the MFA&A report that Alex had brought. The first thing I saw when I opened it was a three-page fax that had been put in the front. Alex had mentioned it at the time, but I'd forgotten all about it. The cover sheet was from CIAT's Christie Valle de Leon, and it was dated four days earlier.

Dear Ben:
   This letter only came to my attention yesterday. I know it will interest you. It was sent to the Boston Police Department a little over a week ago.

Christie

The second sheet was murky from photo-copying, but still legible. It had been typed on plain paper, no letterhead, on a cranky manual typewriter that had seen better days, and it was from Mr. Nussbaum, the man I would be seeing in Vienna.

Prinz-Eugen-Strasse 24,
A-1030 Wien

To Whom It May Concern:

My name is Jakob Nussbaum. I am 77 years of age. I understand that you have found a painting called *The Count of Torrijos,* by Diego Velàzquez, and are searching for the owner. I have seen a photograph of this painting in the *Neue Kronen Zeitung,* and I believe that it may have been the property of my late uncle, Eberhard Nussbaum, who was the owner of the Galerie Eberhard in the First District of this city from 1931 to 1938, and who bought it at an auction in Brussels sometime in the 1920s.

At the time the Racial Purity Laws came into effect in 1938, the picture to which I refer was given by my uncle Eberhard Nussbaum to his friend, the French art dealer Paul Cazeau, for the purpose of saving it from being confiscated. Shortly after this, the Galerie Eberhard was Aryanized and my uncle and I were sent to the labor camp at Lublin with those of our family who were still living.

After the war (my uncle died in the

camps), I learned that Paul Cazeau took the picture to Paris with him in 1938, where it was hidden from the Nazis with other paintings belonging to Austrian, French, and Dutch Jews, in a secret room in the cellar of the Galerie du Cloître, which I understand was located on the place Vendôme. But in 1942, the Gestapo learned of the existence of this room. Paul Cazeau was arrested and made to confess under torture whom these paintings belonged to. They were then taken away by the ERR, and this brave and good man was sent to Theresienstadt, where he died.

I never heard again of the painting until now. Since my father's entire family was killed in 1939–1944, I am the only relative to Eberhard Nussbaum who still remains alive. Therefore, I would like to submit a claim to this picture. I would appreciate it if you would tell me how I should go about this.

Respectfully,
Jakob Nussbaum

I was sweating by the time I finished. *Racial Purity Laws....My uncle and I were sent to the labor camp....My father's entire family was killed in 1939–1944....* Another truly wretched life story to put into perspective the petty bitching and whining that I'd been doing all my life. And I was supposed to see this guy, this nice guy, tomorrow and tell him to forget it, that he had to be mistaken, that the painting wasn't his? I felt my resolve slipping. Maybe I could call the whole thing off. This was just make-work on my part, after all; it wasn't what Stetten had hired me to do.

Christie had written a few paragraphs diagonally across the bottom, then, running away with herself (as she often did), continued them on another sheet when she was out of room.

> A lot of this checks out, Ben. There really was a Galerie Eberhard in Vienna in the 1930s, and also a Galerie du Cloître on the place Vendôme in Paris. And the owner, Paul Cazeau, was definitely arrested by the Nazis for helping Jews and is believed to have died in the camps.
>
> On the other hand, if Count Stetten can really prove his ownership, then this version can't possibly be accurate. All the same, the letter strikes me as credible. My guess would be that his *story* is true, but that he's thinking of another painting (all he's seen, apparently, is the one newspaper photo).

That's what I thought, too, but what she had to say next opened up a new angle.

> You know, there are still some unclaimed paintings from World War II that could easily be confused with a Velàzquez, and I've been wondering if one of them might

354

be the one he's talking about. I'm thinking in particular of a portrait that the French government has been holding, unclaimed, ever since it was returned by the Germans. It's unsigned, but is almost certainly by the young Juan Bautista Martínez del Mazo, and is possibly a student exercise based on *The Count of Torrijos,* which makes sense because, as you know, Mazo was a pupil of Velàzquez's. Mazo is also believed to have done a similar study of *The Countess of Torrijos* at about the same time, so they may have been workshop productions made to order for some of the Torrijos kinfolk. At one time they were both believed to be Velàzquezes, but that was a hundred years ago.

These aren't exact copies, you understand—the man's goatee is darker, and he's looking rightish, not leftish, and there's no book in his hand, but it's close enough to make anybody stop and think. And—get this—all anybody knows about it is that it came into ERR possession IN PARIS, SOMETIME IN 1942!—SOURCE UNKNOWN! As far as I know, in all these years nobody's ever put in a claim for it.

So—could this possibly be what Nussbaum's talking about? It's probably wishful thinking on my part, because I'd like to help him if we can; it's obvious from his letter that he isn't getting any competent legal advice of his own. Wouldn't it be wonderful if it turns out to be true?

So if you do talk to him, would you see what you think of him? Maybe he can provide some helpful details. If you think there's something there, put him in touch with me. It could be that CIAT could give him some assistance. (But don't get his hopes up! You know what the odds are.)

Still, stranger things have happened. What do you think?

What did I think? I thought it was a great idea. Cheered by the possibility that I might at long last be able to do a deserving, living human being some actual, concrete good, I settled back and asked the flight attendant for another cup of strong, good Austrian Airlines coffee.

"ACTUALLY, I DIDN'T WANT to ask you anything, I wanted to show you something," Alois said, seated behind his desk and puffing away at a curving, carved meerschaum pipe, handsomer than the stubby little job I'd seen him with before, but equally foul. He pulled open the crammed top drawer of the desk, rooted around through dog-eared cards and papers, ballpoint pens, and pipe cleaners (some used), and located a sheet of paper folded in half. "What do you think of this? I'm afraid it didn't reproduce very well."

I spread it out to see what looked like an enlarged ID photo, possibly from a passport, of a brutal, nearly cubical head set on a neck like a tree trunk. It was a good thing I'd put down the coffee I was sipping, because otherwise I'd have gotten it all over Alois.

"It's *him*! This is— He's the one who, who killed Simeon, the one who— Alois, who is this? How did you get this picture?"

Alois snuffled with pleasure, his shoulders shaking. "I thought you'd be pleased!"

"I don't know if 'pleased' is the right word," I said, staring at the blunt, heavy-jawed face and feeling a ghost-twinge in my left side, where the pry bar had made contact.

"This illustrates what superior investigative work can accomplish," Alois said complacently. "It was your description of him that made me begin to wonder, and now I find that I was right. The gentleman's name is Janko Golubov."

Good name for him, I thought. He looked like a Janko Golubov.

"Otherwise known as the Hammer," Alois said.

"Gee, I wonder why that is. What is he, a mafia killer, a—"

"A hit man, yes, and a highly specialized one, one of those fellows who flies into a country, does the deed, and is on his way back out within two hours. Now, do you recall my mentioning the Chetverk gang?"

"I think so. A Moscow crime family?"

"Yes, the one that Zykmund Dulska was associated with. Well, it's also the one that uses Golubov. So you see, we've started to narrow things, to tighten the noose a little. Naturally, I'll want to tell the police in Boston about all this. Do you have a name for me?"

"Sergeant Cox. I'll give you his number."

I was beginning to get excited, to take heart. We *had* accomplished something, I thought. Simeon's killer; we knew who he was, we knew his name, we knew who he worked for. Maybe those crushed ribs and endless weeks of brushing my teeth in slow motion had served a purpose after all. "Do you know where he is now? Can you find him?"

"Not yet. People generally know where he was after the fact, when it's too late."

"Is that right? He didn't strike me as all that bright." Persuasive, though.

"Perhaps not, but he's effective enough at what he does," Alois said.

My hand rose on its own to the still-tender area on my left side. "No kidding," I said. "Tell me about it."

A FEW MINUTES LATER I emerged blinking into the autumn sunlight and looked at my watch. Two o'clock. On the spur of the moment I called Jakob Nussbaum's number from a post office pay phone.

"Mr. Nussbaum, this is Ben Revere. I'm in Vienna a day early. Do you suppose we might meet today instead of tomorrow? Would right now be okay?"

"Why not, one day's as good as another. You know my address?"

"Prinz-Eugen-Strasse Twenty-four."

"That's right, it's on the corner of Plössl-gasse, not far from the Belvedere. You can find it?"

"I know just about where it is. I'll see you shortly. And, sir? I hope you understand: I'm not here either as Mr. Stetten's advocate or as your adversary. I'm just interested in seeing that—well, that the right thing gets done, that—"

"Yes, yes, you don't have to explain, I trust you. All right, I'll see you at— No, wait, that's not so good. Two-thirty, when the weather's nice, I go for a walk in the Belvedere gardens with Wittgenstein. I have to; the old fellow depends on me."

"Oh. Well, in that case it'd probably be better if we just waited—"

"I tell you what. Why don't you meet us in the gardens? It's a beautiful day, we can talk there. We'll be by the big fountain at the top, you know, the one with Hercules pulling on the poor alligator's mouth? It's a beautiful view of the city from there."

"Yes, but—"

"We'll be on a bench. With us, it's more sitting than walking anyway."

"Well, but wouldn't you rather—"

"Don't worry, Wittgenstein won't mind."

CHAPTER 30

Wittgenstein, being a miniature bearded Schnauzer of contemplative mien, had no objection whatever, but lay placidly at our feet, his head resting on his forepaws in measured reflection, while Jakob Nussbaum, a spic-and-span old man in a buttoned-up, bright-yellow cardigan sweater and a cornflower-blue bow tie, told me what he remembered about the painting.

It wasn't much. He'd been only sixteen in 1938, when he'd last seen it, and although he'd been working part-time in his uncle's gallery, it was only in the nature of after-school sweeping and straightening up. He couldn't remember if the subject's beard was light or dark, or say for sure whether he was looking left or right, or if he had a book or anything else in his hand, or how "finished" the portrait was. And this was after seeing a photo in the papers only a week ago. All the same, he stuck to his guns. The minute he'd seen the photograph, it had jumped out at him.

But was he sure it was a Velàzquez? Could it have been painted by Juan Bautista Martínez del Mazo? Well, about that he didn't know. He was pretty sure his uncle had said Velàzquez. Mazo he'd never heard of. But whatever it was, it was one of the two pictures his uncle had given to Cazeau, the Parisian dealer, in 1938, before things had gotten really bad.

"*Two* pictures? What was the other?"

He shook his head. "That I can't tell you. My uncle didn't keep it in the shop, so I never saw it. By a Frenchman—the name's on the tip of my tongue. Lebrun, was it? Delacroix? Le Nain? I'm not sure, I can't remember. But who's this Mazo fellow? Where does he come into it?"

"I'll explain that in a minute. But is there anything else at all you can tell me that might help identify it? Do you have any recollection of the frame, for example? Do you know who your uncle bought it from? Did he ever tell you anything about it, other than that it was by Velàzquez?"

No, no, and no, he shook his head, and then, as if coming upon something he'd forgotten long ago, "Wait, it was one of a pair that Velàzquez made, is that any help? There was a woman, too...."

My ears pricked. Christie had said that there *was* a pair, that Mazo had made studies of both of the Velàzquez portraits. I started to get excited on Nussbaum's account. "And your uncle owned both of them?"

"No, no, I didn't mean that. He always *wanted* the other one, because it was the other half of the set, you see, they belonged together, a man and his sister, I believe. Or maybe it was a man and wife? But the fellow who owned it, I can't remember his name, also Jewish, also an art dealer, wouldn't sell it. In fact, he kept trying to buy Eberhard's. They were always in competition, bitter enemies."

He turned his thin, clean-shaven face up to

the September sun, eyes closed. "Not so bitter, really. It was this man who was a friend of Paul Cazeau's and put my uncle in touch with him, which was a very great favor, and a lucky thing, because a few months later the gallery was Aryanized, and that was that." He looked at me. "You understand the term—'Aryanized'?"

"Yes, I do," I said, dropping my glance to the dog. Aryanization had been the Nazi policy, officially applied in countries under German domination, of forcing all Jews who owned businesses to "sell" them to Gentiles, thereby morally and aesthetically cleansing Europe of the dread influence of Jewish culture—and materially increasing the assets of non-Jewish merchants, a benefit that did not escape the notice of the local business communities.

Nussbaum nodded, his hands folded quietly in his lap. "I'm sorry, young man," he said kindly, "I know it's not such a pleasant subject. I didn't mean to bring it up."

I shook my head with something like awe. This made twice in the last week—Stetten had done it my first day in Vienna—that one of these resilient, upbeat old geezers who had been through the tortures of the damned had apologized for depressing me by mentioning it.

He smiled at me. "I know what you're thinking. You're thinking, How can he bear to live here, right where it all happened, among these very same people"—he gestured at the strollers, the baby nurses, the old people on the benches—"who didn't do anything to stop it from happening? Am I right?"

"You're pretty close," I said.

"It's a good question," he agreed. "Let me tell you a story. My father had a young friend, Dr. Luckner, a pediatrician, a very kindly, gentle man; he died only a few years ago. Well, when the Nazis came, he saw a Jewish woman who was being mauled by hooligans commit suicide by jumping under a tram. People applauded. This was in the heart of Vienna. He was appalled, shocked. After a few days the Jews began to be rounded up and to disappear. Dr. Luckner couldn't claim ignorance; he could see as well as anyone what was happening. And what did he do about it? Nothing. He tried to live his life quietly, treating his patients, doing no harm to others, dealing as little as possible with the new authorities, making no trouble for himself or his family. Was he therefore a bad man? In his place, would I have done differently?" He gave me a gentle smile. "Would you?"

"I don't know." I shook my head, filled with admiration for this tolerant old man.

"Of course, it took me a little while to get so philosophical about it. Thirty-five years, to be exact."

He had moved through several labor camps during the war, managing through blind luck and good health to avoid being sent to an extermination center, and ending up in Kielce, Poland, at the war's end. He was twenty-three at the time, and went to South Africa, where some distant relatives on his mother's side lived. There he had gone to college and become a teacher, teaching mathematics and philosophy for almost thirty years. When he retired, he'd tried living near his son-in-law in Chicago for a while, looking for someplace that felt more like home. And ten years ago he'd reached the conclusion that the only place that would feel like home was home.

"So back I came. And it was the right decision."

"As long as another Hitler doesn't show up."

"Hitler's not coming again." He leaned down to scratch behind the dog's ear. "Is he, Wittgenstein? Ah. Sussman."

"Pardon?"

"Sussman, that was his name—Eberhard's competitor, the one who owned the other painting we were talking about. Raoul Sussman. Also dead, of course, him and his whole family. They went in the first roundup. Us, we were luckier, we went a little later. So what do you say we go back to my apartment for a cup of coffee? I'm ready to put my feet up. You can tell me about this Mazo while we walk."

HE SURPRISED ME BY accepting without argument the possibility that the painting might be by the little-known Mazo rather than by the great Velàzquez.

"What would it be worth?" was what he

364

wanted to know as we came out of the gardens onto Prinz-Eugen-Strasse.

"I don't know—whatever it would bring. With a painter like Mazo there's really no such thing as market value. But probably a fair amount."

"But not five million dollars?"

"No, not five million. I'd guess a hundred thousand, maybe even two hundred thousand."

"That's not chicken feed. Invested, it would do the trick. What do you think, Wittgenstein? Liver twice a day."

The widowed Mr. Nussbaum and his dog, it seemed, now lived, in comfortable enough circumstances, on a combination of his pension and the largess of his son-in-law, a Chicago building contractor. His hopes for the painting, if he got it, were strictly financial: that it would allow him to provide for himself without being dependent on them.

"I can't take from them anymore. Besides, it would be nice to buy them a present now and then," he said wistfully, "instead of being a drain on them, not that they would ever bring it up."

His apartment, a corner set of rooms on the third floor, was very Viennese—full of knick-knacks, Oriental rugs, varnished surfaces, and dark, overstuffed chairs and hassocks, but with a light, modern kitchen in which, as promised, he brewed us some coffee in a French coffee press and brought it out to the living room with a few straight-from-the-carton cookies arranged on a tray, which he set out on a coffee table. Wittgenstein, for his part, got a piece of knotted rawhide, to which he immediately and single-mindedly turned his attention.

Nussbaum sank into the armchair opposite mine, got his feet up on the hassock, and listened, visibly affected, while I told him about CIAT and Christie Valle de Leon's offer of help.

"How wonderful, what a kind person. And you, too, thank you! I'll get in touch with this woman right away."

"That's fine, I'll fill her in." I was feeling pretty good myself.

We grinned self-consciously at each other, embarrassing ourselves, and Nussbaum poured some more coffee. "What do you think of the view?" He gestured with his chin at the corner windows, and I got up to look.

One of the windows faced the Belvedere Palace's grounds across the boulevard, and the other looked up Prinz-Eugen-Strasse to its origin at the World War II Russian War Memorial (or the Tomb of the Unknown Plunderer, as it was wryly referred to by the Viennese). Even now it was an elegant residential street with several embassies on it, but it had suffered heavy bomb damage during the war, so that for every beautiful, nineteenth-century apartment building still left—and Nussbaum's was one of them—there was now a plain, flat-fronted concrete box as well.

"Nice," I said.

Nussbaum came to stand beside me. "That's a building I never get tired of looking at."

"This one right across the street?" It seemed an odd one to never get tired of: one of the anonymous cubes from the 1950s, with six rows of identical, rectangular windows. The sign out front declared that it was headquarters for a local employees' organization.

"That's Prinz-Eugen-Strasse Twenty-two. In that building, or rather in the one that stood there before, was the Bureau of Jewish Emigration...as they chose to call it." I heard something like a little sigh escape him. "Colonel Eichmann's headquarters."

Eichmann's headquarters. I stared at it, at the pleasant street on which it stood, at the beautifully maintained formal gardens across the way, at the elegant, civilized, courteous Viennese out walking or going about their business. Except for number 22 itself, and the modern cars on the street, everything would have been the same in March of 1938. And yet...impossible to believe...

"My father and I, we stood out there on that sidewalk for two days with a thousand other Jews, all the way down the block, because there was a rumor we could get exit visas, but they wouldn't let us in. A few, yes, but not us. The next day we were in the Spanish Riding School, and four days after that we were in the trains on our way to Lublin."

"The Spanish Riding School?" I said.

"That was where they put us to wait," he said,

still gazing at the plain building. He spoke quietly, in the same unemotional way that Stetten had told me his story. "Many people in Vienna were upset when they heard; they protested to the authorities."

"Well, at least I suppose that shows—"

"They were afraid that we would dirty the place. Which we did, all of those people cooped up in there." He smiled. "It's human nature, I don't blame them anymore."

I said nothing. I would blame them, I thought.

The dog, sensing that he was wanted, came to his master and gazed lustrously up into his eyes. Nussbaum crouched to take him in his arms. "Ah, Wittgenstein, things are better now, it's nothing for you to worry about."

"But to live *here*," I said thickly, "right across the street..."

"And why not?" he said mildly. "It's wonderful. Every day I look out that window, I see beautiful gardens. I look out this window I see there's nothing there anymore at number Twenty-two. Eichmann's dead and gone, the bastard, with his boots, and his armband, and his Heil Hitlers. But me, I'm still right here, here I am."

"That's a good way of looking at things," I said, smiling. Jakob Nussbaum had a lot of good ways of looking at things.

"Besides, I got restaurants in the neighborhood, a Big Billa supermarket two blocks away, a bus right outside the door that goes straight downtown— Excuse me a minute."

The door buzzer had sounded. Still cradling Wittgenstein, he went to open it. I don't know what sense it was that tingled at the back of my neck and made me turn around, but when I did it was to see a hulking figure taking up almost the entire width of the doorway. I felt my insides twist even before I consciously recognized him.

Janko Golubov, the Hammer. Simeon's murderer.

"Don't let him in!" I yelled, but it was too late. Golubov, dressed in what appeared to be the same ill-fitting dark suit and ruler-thin tie he'd worn in Simeon's shop, wrenched the door from Nussbaum's hand and shoved it closed behind him.

The old man stepped back, shocked and trembling. "*Was...was wünschen Sie? Wer—*"

Golubov swatted him irritably, almost carelessly, across the chest with his heavy forearm. Nussbaum gasped and went staggering back, collapsing in a loose heap against the wall, like a puppet that had had its strings cut. Wittgenstein, yapping with outrage, popped out of his arms and charged, nipping at Golubov's ankles. A kick—a shake of one thick leg, really—caught the dog under the belly, lifting him into the air and sending him twisting and yipping across the length of the room and into the *Kabinett,* the closetlike little half room built into the older Viennese apartments for reasons no one has figured out. I heard the small body smack into the wall and slide to the floor. Then nothing.

"*Mein Gott,*" Nussbaum whispered weakly from the floor. I breathed a sigh. At least he was alive.

Through it all, from the moment he'd come in, Golubov had never taken his eyes off me. The astounded look in them couldn't have been clearer: *YOU again!* I knew just what he meant, too.

I snatched up the coffee press and heaved it at him, missing his head by a foot and splattering the white wall with coffee-grounds muck. Then, almost before he'd finished ducking, I followed it with a heavy, square-cut glass ashtray, flinging it like a discus and catching him in the hollow between his neck and shoulder, which must have hurt like hell—but had no visible effect beyond a brief grimace that showed those snaggly, yellow-brown teeth again, and the gap in front. Kicking the ashtray aside, he came slowly toward me, his hands held out from his sides, palms up. He wiggled his fingers encouragingly: *Come on, tovarich,* let's mix it up.

Like hell, I thought. The guy looked more like King Kong than ever. I backed away and moved sideways along the wall, searching desperately for anything else that I could throw at him, while he kept coming. When I ended up, inevitably, in a corner, he moved with a quick lunge to close in and cut me off, then stood there, rocking from one foot to the other. I felt like a matador watching the bull slowly flick its tail back and forth while it considered which part of him would be the most fun to gore.

He shook his wrist. There was a click, and a double-edged knife with a thin, six-inch blade jumped open in his hand. He tossed it lightly from one hand to the other and back again, daring me with rounded eyes and pursed mouth to make a grab for it.

It's funny, I wasn't feeling any more brave or confident than I'd been when I'd faced him in Simeon's shop—my knees were shaking every bit as much, my heart thumping just as wildly. What I was, was *madder*. This repulsive bastard had beaten Simeon to death and pounded me to agonized jelly. Well, that was enough; I wasn't about to let him do it to me again, that's all. Or to Nussbaum either.

I knew he was expecting me to snatch at the knife, because his eyes were on my hands. So I kicked him, aiming for his crotch and swinging my leg as hard as I could, which was taking a terrific chance, because if I missed him I was going to do a half somersault and wind up flat on my back. But I didn't miss him.

I didn't exactly hit him either. At least not in the crotch. I was heading there, but Golubov, despite that UPS-truck physique, was a man of quick reflexes, as befitted his trade. One hand darted down to block my foot. But being a person whose mental reflexes ran somewhat behind his physical ones, the hand he chose was the one holding the knife. My foot caught him in the wrist, squarely and hard, and the knife went flying. When his head instinctively turned to follow it, I started swinging my fists, leaning my body into the blows, hitting him first in the temple and bringing a satisfying grunt, and then, as he turned back to me, in the mouth, splitting his lip and cutting my knuckles on those wolfish teeth.

It pained him, I could see that, but it sure didn't daze him. Hard as I'd hit him, his head, solidly mounted on that gorilla neck, hadn't moved; no give at all. He pressed his hand to his mouth, stared at the blood on his fingers, and then, with a low growl, at me. Now *he* was mad, which didn't make me feel any better about things overall.

Behind him and off to the side there was a startling, shattering crash, and there stood Nussbaum, at the window, apparently having just tossed something through it—the square-cut ashtray, I think.

"*Polizei! Polizei!*" he was screaming at the top of his thin, quavery voice. "*Hilfe! Hilfe!*"

Golubov turned away from me and rushed toward him. My God, I thought, he's going to throw him out the window. I took off after him, using the overstuffed sofa as a sort of launching pad, a trampoline, to fling myself into the air, arms outstretched, for all the world like a middle linebacker going after the quarterback on Monday Night Football.

I hit him solidly, too, God knows how, a fraction of a second before he got his hands on the shrinking Nussbaum, and the two of us went reeling across the room, tumbling over each other on the floor. I was faster than Golubov in jumping up—no doubt because I was more scared than he was—and managed to leap back a couple of steps into the kitchen before he was able to get his hands on me. While he got furiously to his feet, I looked around for something to use to keep him off. Pots, ladles—why did I always seem to be defending myself against this monster with kitchen utensils?

There was a scuffling noise on the kitchen floor, a maniacal yapping, and here came the redoubtable Wittgenstein, conscious once again and scuttling straight for Golubov's ankles. As the Russian drew back one foot for a kick, an energized Nussbaum suddenly burst into the kitchen behind him. Using both hands and almost leaving the floor with the effort, he brought a heavy frying pan ringingly down on the Russian's head.

You may recall that, back in Boston, I, too, had hit him with a frying pan, to no avail. But that had been an aluminum dime-store model with a cheap, nonstick coating. This was the genuine item, a solid, black, cast-iron job that was half an inch thick and as big around as a dinner plate. The Hammer frowned, as if puzzled by the strange ringing in his ears, and dropped like a felled ox, going straight down as his legs gave way, so that his knees hit the floor with a thud. There he remained for a moment, erect and perfectly still, seemingly listening. Then his eyes lost their focus and rolled back, and over he went with a crash, like an ex-dictator's statue being pulled down with ropes.

Wittgenstein, under the impression that it

was he who had brought this colossus down, gave a triumphant, deep-throated bark and trotted off a few steps to stand beside his master, keeping an alert eye on Golubov in case he was needed again.

"Benjamin?" Nussbaum said weakly. "Would you mind putting this pan on the counter for me? I don't have the strength anymore."

When I took it from his rigid hands, I almost dropped it myself. The thing must have weighed five pounds.

"Well, all I can say," I said with a smile, "is that you sure had it when it counted."

I could hear reassuring sounds out in the hall, the heavy footsteps of several people taking the stairs two at a time. Here came the *Polizei*.

All the same, I hung on to the frying pan until they got there.

CHAPTER 31

The rest of the day and most of the evening were spent at police headquarters, mostly sitting around, but also talking to Pirchl, who seemed possessed of a conviction that I had some idea what the hell was going on. And so the same questions kept coming, over and over. Why did Janko Golubov and/or his friends keep showing up wherever I happened to be? Why all the murders? The mafia, whatever else they were, was not capricious; they didn't go around killing people for no reason at all. Why were they following me around, what were they trying to accomplish? And so on, for six hours, except for a twenty-minute break for bratwurst, ham sandwiches, pastries, and coffee that was delivered to the station at eight o'clock.

All I could do was shake my head and say I wish I knew, which didn't improve his mood or mine either. And, as might have been expected, the police were getting no help from the Hammer, who'd had nothing to say since being taken into custody. When Pirchl finally finished with me at 9:45 P.M., I was bored, tired, and terminally grubby, but hugging to myself the considerable consolation of knowing that the Hammer was not only safely locked up but nursing a sore head and a split lip as well.

When we finally finished, Alois offered to drive me to the Hotel Imperial. For a while we drove quietly along Franz-Josefs-Kai, Alois chewing on the stem of an unlit pipe. It had rained earlier, but now the air was still, and the Kai gleamed under the street lamps, almost empty of traffic.

"How's Mr. Nussbaum doing?" I asked.

"Fine. A little shaky, that's all. Don't worry about him, we'll be keeping an eye on him. The dog had a couple of cracked ribs, though."

"I feel for him. Brave little guy. So's Nussbaum, for that matter." I shook my head. "How the hell *did* Janko know Nussbaum was going to be talking to me? How do they *always* know? Have you gotten anything out of him at all?"

"As of yet, no, but let me ask you something: You made your appointment with Nussbaum from Altaussee, right? Was it by telephone?"

"Yes."

He glanced at me as we pulled up to a red light. Alongside us the Danube Canal flowed, black and glinting, with a murk hanging over it. "From your hotel room, I suppose?"

"Yes. You think my telephone was tapped?"

"I see the thought's occurred to you."

"Sure it has, but, Alois, I just don't get it. Following me from one country to another, bugging my room...What have they been doing, watching my every move since I got here? That's crazy."

"Why, how hard would it have been? We're dealing with professionals, and you weren't making any special attempts to cover your tracks, were you? That is, excepting your speedy departure from Budapest."

"No, why would I?"

"Exactly." He shifted inexpertly into first, and with a jerk we started up again.

"But what could they possibly hope to get from following me around?" My voice was getting shrill. I shoved it down a notch. "What do *I* know?"

"I've been giving that some thought, and it occurs to me that they might think you're hot on the trail of *all* the paintings, the whole Stetten collection, maybe the whole Lost Truck–load; that the people you're talking to might lead *them* to the pictures."

"Then why the hell do they keep bumping

them off?" I stared gloomily out the window. The rain was beginning to mist down again. "Anyway, what trail? I haven't gotten anywhere at all. All this chasing around," I said bitterly, "and what have I accomplished? Nothing, not one goddamned thing, do you realize that? Aside from getting a bunch of people killed."

Alois pulled the car up to the curb on a side street next to the hotel, turned off the engine, and lit up his pipe. I shifted a little farther away and rolled down the window.

"Don't be so hard on yourself," he said kindly. "We now have Golubov, thanks to you."

"Thanks to Nussbaum and Wittgenstein."

"No, Ben, thanks to you. And Golubov's involvement here raises some extremely interesting questions. We believe that, until now, he's been used primarily in England and the United States because he speaks the language."

"Barely."

"Enough to do what he needs to do, which is get himself through customs on the way in and on the way out. He doesn't need to be a conversationalist. But now, here he is, attempting to kill someone in Vienna. As far as we know, it's the first time he's been used here. You see the implication?"

"Uh...no."

"Certainly you do. It implies an association between the Chetverk people and Klaus Loitzl."

I shook my head. "I'm afraid—"

"The Chetverk family is the Moscow gang that Golubov works for—I keep mentioning this to you, you should start paying attention—and Klaus Loitzl is the local mafia—"

"Right, I remember. The Viennese John Gotti."

"Correct. And now we find Golubov working in Loitzl's territory. This is significant because these groups take their jurisdictional privileges very, very seriously and such things don't happen without prior agreement. So, whatever it is that's going on with these paintings of yours, it must involve not only the Russian mafia but our more modest local version as well."

"I see." I was starting to fall asleep.

"I'm not sure you do. If I can help it, Janko Golubov is going to be the first crack in Loitzl's armor, our opening wedge. And with your deposition and Mr. Nussbaum's readiness to help, I think our Janko's going to find himself, in the interest of self-preservation, with sound reasons to cooperate."

He jabbed the stem of the pipe at me. "I tell you, Ben, this is going to be a body blow to the mafia's power here in Austria. I feel it in my bones."

"Well, I'm glad to hear that," I said, and the truth is that I was. I mean, how could anybody not be pleased about striking a body blow against the mafia in Austria or anyplace else? But more than that, I was only now fully taking in the fact that I had finally come face to face with the brute who had murdered

Simeon and—with a little help from a seventy-seven-year-old man, a valiant miniature Schnauzer, and a frying pan—had actually landed him in police custody. And whenever Vienna was through with him, it would be Boston's turn. That was extremely pleasant to think about.

My eyes felt sandy. I massaged them with my fingertips. "I think I'd better get to bed before I fall over. Thanks for everything, Alois."

"You'll come back if we want you as a witness?"

"Absolutely. With pleasure."

"I'll look forward to it. Oh, and Ben? You should know that Pirchl's taken the liberty of having his people examine your room for eavesdropping equipment."

I threw him a glance as I got out of the car. "You can tell him I appreciate the service, but it might have been nice if he'd asked me first."

"I agree, but that's not the way Pirchl works. He prefers to operate on the need-to-know principle."

"Right, and why would I have to know? Anyhow, I can assume my room's bug-free?"

"So it would appear. All the same, if I were you I'd use a public telephone for my calls. Just to be on the safe side."

I POURED MYSELF A fizzing glass of Mix-it Sodawasser from the refrigerator, turned off most of the lights, took off my shoes, propped up the pillows, and flopped down on the bed with every intention of making my mind a restful, pre-sleep blank, but it refused to cooperate, jumping from question to question, puzzlement to puzzlement. It wasn't until ten minutes later, when I'd given up trying to make sense of things and was standing under a hot shower trying to shampoo the police-station grunge out of my hair, that a few things began slipping into place. For a full minute, maybe more, I stood there motionless, afraid even to rub the shampoo out of my eyes for fear of jogging the fragile train of thought that had produced them.

It was thinking about Janko that had done it. I'd been going over the scene in the apartment in my mind and remembering the expression of astonishment on his face when he'd seen me. If they had really been following me around from country to country and knew where I was all the time—a theory that I was coming to believe in—what was Janko so surprised about? And how had he come to choose the worst time of all, the very moment that I was right there in the apartment with Nussbaum, to pay his visit? As Alois had surmised, I'd made the arrangement with the old man on the telephone, the day before, from Altaussee. If the wiretappers of whom Alois was so certain had really been at work, why hadn't Janko gotten to Nussbaum long before I arrived?

At which point it came to me. Alois *was* right.

My room in Altaussee *had* been bugged, and probably every other hotel room I'd been in. The mafia snoops had been on the job, all right, and they'd listened in as I'd made an appointment with Nussbaum from the Seevilla for two days hence.

But I never did keep that appointment, because when Alex had left I'd canceled the daylong drive to Vienna. So I'd called Nussbaum the very next day—today—to reset our meeting time to two-thirty this afternoon—only *that* call was placed from a post office pay phone a couple of blocks from the Vienna police station, so no one was listening in. That meant, as far as the mafia people were concerned, that they were sending Janko out to do his work in plenty of time, a full day before I was going to be seeing Nussbaum. No wonder he'd been surprised.

I was too worn out to take it any further, so I toweled off and slipped gratefully into bed; I'd talk to Alois first thing in the morning. It was only when I turned off the lights that I noticed the message indicator blinking. The first person I thought of, with a little surge of hope, was Alex, but that was impossible; she had no idea of where I was staying. I looked at it for a while longer, wondering sleepily if it was safe to pick up the phone, until I realized that if this room *was* bugged, whatever was on the machine had already been overheard anyway.

That made me chuckle, which made me realize that I was too slaphappy to deal with whatever it was anyway. I'd take care of it in the morning.

BUT THE TELEPHONE HAD other ideas, dragging me complaining out of what I thought was a profound slumber, although a glance at the clock radio showed that it was only 11:02. I'd been asleep for less than ten minutes, but that didn't make me any more kindly disposed to whoever it was.

"Hallo," I growled, then went on grumbling to myself in case whoever was calling thought I was being friendly, "Christ, can't they even let—"

"Ben, it's Alex."

"Alex?" I sat up, wide awake. "Alex, Alex, I'm glad you called. It was my fault, I don't know why—"

"No, my fault, my fault. I'm so glad I got you, I feel awful. I'm not like that, Ben, that's not the way I am. I can't believe I was so—"

"Where are you? How did you know I was here?" I stood up, leaning my forehead against the wall, eyes closed. Something deep in my chest that had been taut, and cold, and brittle suddenly relaxed, as if warm blood had begun to flow to it again.

"I'm in Vienna, too, and I knew that this was where you stayed last time, so I figured you'd be here again and I've been calling your room for hours. I was beginning to get worried. Didn't you get my messages?"

"Sorry, I came in and collapsed. If I'd known they were from you..."

"It's all right, what matters is that I got you. I owe you an explanation."

"No, you don't owe me anything. We just got our wavelengths crossed. It happens in the best of families."

"No, there's more than that. My—"

"Look, I'm just glad you called, that's all."

"No, let me finish. You know my mother was Austrian. Well, she was born in Vienna, in 1930. She managed to get out with her parents and her sister when she was a child, but her uncles and aunts, and some of her cousins, stayed behind. My great-uncle Menachem was a rabbi. He was seventy-two years old in 1938. On the day the Nazis came to power, a crowd of people—civilians, fellow Viennese—made him get down on his knees and wash the public toilets with his bare hands, wearing his yarmulke and tallis."

"Alex—"

"He died in the camps. So did all the rest of them. Not one of them lived through it, not one. We have some of their pictures at home. You should see them, they all look so, so..." Her voice trembled and broke, and she took a long, quivery breath. "I've stayed away from Austria all my life, but I thought maybe I could handle it now after all this time, especially with you there, but I kept looking at everybody—even nice old Mrs. Obermayr at the pension—and wondering, Were you one of them? It's funny, because everybody's been so polite and nice, but I guess it was just too much for me. And then, talking to that, that...monster in Altaussee and thinking, Here he is after so many years, calmly picking away at his perfect little fish, while my Uncle Menachem has been—"

"Alex, I'm sorry. God, I wish you'd told me this before. I'd never have let you come with me."

"No, I'm glad I came. I feel better now. Maybe I just had to get it off my chest—only I'm sorry you had to be the one to bear the brunt."

I sank with a sigh into an armchair near the bed. "Thanks for calling, Alex. That's a load off my mind. I was feeling pretty rotten myself."

"We're friends again?"

"You better believe it. Hey, where are you, exactly?"

"At this moment? Downstairs here at the Imperial. I'm on a house phone. I tried to keep an eye on the lobby, but I guess I missed you when you came in."

"A house phone? Look, why don't you come on up? We can order a drink, or a snack, or something."

"That sounds good, but it's late, and to tell the truth, I haven't even made my own room arrangements yet."

"You don't have a hotel?"

"No, I kept thinking you'd be in any minute. I just left my bags in the cloakroom here. It was stupid of me. I just hope I can find something this late."

As I don't believe I have to tell you, swiftness on the uptake is probably not my forte, but that doesn't mean I don't once in a while recognize opportunity when it clobbers me between the eyes.

"All the more reason to come up and have something fortifying," I said offhandedly, or so I hoped. "It's busy season and it might take us a while to find you a room, but at least we can do it in comfort. And if worst comes to worst, there's always the sofa."

There was a fractional hesitation. "All right, thanks."

In the three minutes it took her to get there I was a blur, flinging my shoes and a few other oddments of clothing that were lying around into the closet and slamming the door on them, getting into shirt and slacks, tidying up the bed a little, glugging some mouthwash, and running a comb through my hair. I still wasn't sure of what I wanted to happen, but I was more willing than I'd been in Altaussee to let nature take its course.

It didn't take long. When I first opened the door to her, she looked anxious, even a little worn, but then this lovely, warm, melting look came into those luminous green eyes, and I turned to butter.

"Alex..."

We each moved forward at the same time, and then she was bundled in my arms with my hand holding her head against my shoulder.

We stood there like that in the doorway for a long time, pressed so close that I couldn't tell which of us was trembling, or maybe we both were. When we finally kissed, it was gentle and almost chaste, and that lasted a long time, too. Then we were inside the room, and we kissed again, not so gentle or chaste this time. From then on it was only a question of time.

Later we lay forehead to forehead and knee to knee, and I watched her eyelids slowly, tremblingly drift closed, then open halfway—accompanied by the faintest, dreamiest of smiles—and then close again and stay closed. Her fingers lay, relaxed and curled, on the pillow next to my lips. My hand was on the smooth skin of her waist, caught by the wrist between her arm and her side.

With my own eyes starting to close, I whispered to myself what I hadn't dared to say aloud before, for fear of tempting the fates. The corner had been turned. The gods were with me again.

"Thank you, gods."

CHAPTER 32

I woke up in the morning barely having moved. Alex, now six inches away and buried up to her nose under the comforter, was watching me. As soon as I opened my eyes, she burst out into one of those wonderful, explosive little giggles that made her cover her mouth with her hand in a gesture that was already familiar to me, and moving. I wondered what idiot had long ago told her that her mouth was too large or her teeth too big.

"So that's what you look like when you're sleeping. You're so...tousled. You look like Dennis the Menace. Did you know you have a cowlick?" She reached around to the back of my head and tugged.

"Thank you so very much for pointing it out to me," I said, but I was pleased. She looked so honestly happy to see me there across the pillow. And I sure was honestly happy to see her.

"You know, I really didn't think this was going to happen," she said.

I smiled and touched her mouth with a fingertip. "Regrets?"

"Mmm...too early to tell. Let's see what you're going to feed me for breakfast."

"What would you like?"

"A *lot*. I missed dinner, and I never did get that snack you were going to order from room service last night."

"Sorry about that. More pressing exigencies intervened."

She laughed. "That's one way to put it."

"I'll order up something right now," I said, pushing myself up onto one elbow and turning back the comforter. "How does a full English breakfast sound? With all the trimmings?"

But with a hand on my neck she pulled me, unresisting, back down. "In a minute."

SHOWERED AND IN FRESH clothes, seated at the elegant table that had just been rolled in, we plowed into a strapping meal of bacon and eggs, grilled tomatoes and mushrooms, toast, and tea. And just like a real English breakfast it was, with the bacon underdone and the mushrooms overcooked, which didn't stop us from stowing it away with gusto.

While we ate, I brought her up to speed, telling her about Nussbaum, Wittgenstein, and the Hammer. She listened avidly, but the more detail I went into, the paler and more set her face became.

"My God," she murmured, laying down a slice of toast she'd yet to bite into, "he could so easily have...you might have been..."

Seeing her looking at me like that was balm for the soul, honey for the heart. "But he didn't and I wasn't," I said, reaching across the table to touch her cheek. "Thanks to the noble Wittgenstein, here I am, sitting right here, eating this absolutely terrific breakfast with you, which, of all things in the world, is what I'd most like to be doing."

She sighed. "It's wonderful. I can hardly believe it. You actually did what you set out to do. My uncle's killer is behind bars." Her eyes were shining. "It's just amazing. I *told* you you could do it."

I didn't feel quite as satisfied as she was, because, as I saw it, Janko was merely the arrow, not the bow. Oh, he deserved whatever he was going to get, all right, but as far as I was concerned, Simeon's real killer was whoever had ordered him to do it. And he was still walking around free. All the same, I wasn't about to put up an argument; not with her eyes glowing at me like that.

"Yes, you did tell me," I said. "You know, it really was you that got me going on this. That first time we met at Ciao Bella-I came away steaming mad, but it was just what I needed."

She burst out laughing. "I came away mad, too-and absolutely positive that you were nothing but a self-satisfied twit."

"I *was* a twit; I take exception to the 'self-satisfied.'"

She pushed away her plate and poured us both some more tea. "You've changed a lot since then, Ben," she said seriously. "You're like a different person."

"No, I'm the same person."

"No, you're not. You're—I don't know, *engaged*—in a way that you weren't when I first met you. Since you've taken this on, you've become a man with a purpose; maybe that's what's made the difference."

"Maybe it is," I said, thinking that maybe it was.

When the telephone rang, I motioned to her to answer it; it was on an end table beside her.

"Are you sure you want me to? What about your reputation?"

"It'll enhance the hell out of it, go ahead."

"Hello," she said, and listened for a few seconds. "*Ja. Ein Moment, mein Herr.*" She put her hand over the mouthpiece. "Stetten."

"I'll take it on the other phone," I said, getting up. "Go ahead and listen in; it's bound to be interesting."

It was Stetten in full semihysterical mode. "Ben, where have you *been*? I left three messages last night. Why haven't you returned my calls?"

Because this lovely woman showed up and reordered my priorities and I never did get around to checking my messages, that's why. I mimed a kiss to her. "I'm sorry, Albrecht," I said soothingly, "I was going to call you this morning. A lot has happened. First, Nussbaum won't be putting in a claim on your—"

"Listen, I've had a telephone call. They have my pictures-all of them! They—"

"Who has your paintings?"

"—said I'm to rent a vault at the Banque de la Suisse Romande in Zurich, and then come there tomorrow prepared to make an immediate wire transfer of ten million dollars from my bank in Vienna. They'll have them all there to show me, and they're insisting on—"

"Albrecht, slow up, will you, please?"

"-no police involvement whatever. If the police are informed, everything's off. They wanted me to come alone, but how could I? I'm too excited, I hardly know what I'm saying, I—"

"*Wait!*" I shouted into the phone. "Slow down, will you? I don't know what—"

"—need you, I need—What? Did you say something?"

"Yes, I said I don't have any idea what the hell you're talking about. *Who* called you?"

"What? Why, the people who…well, I don't know, really. It was a man named Adler who telephoned. The account that the ten million is to be transferred into if everything is satisfactory is—Just a minute, where did I…? It's a company called Slalom Super Sport. But I think that may be a, what do you call it, a front."

Yes, just maybe, I thought. "This Adler-he said they'll have *all* your pictures there? All seventy-three?"

"Yes, that's right-well, seventy-two; that other Velàzquez is still in Boston. I'm to engage the vault in the Banque de la Suisse Romande, to make ten million dollars available for immediate transfer, and to meet him at the bank at noon tomorrow."

"And you can do that? Have ten million dollars by tomorrow?"

"It won't be easy, but yes. It means everything I own will be in hock; I'll be in debt up to my eyes. But my credit's good, and I have the collateral. Later on, if I must, I can sell off one or two of the paintings. I'll still have the great bulk of them."

"Yes, but—"

"My God, I'm glad I reached you. I was going out of my mind. Now, listen, there's an Austrian Airlines flight from Vienna leaving at nine twenty-five in the morning and arriving at a quarter to eleven. Flight OS-Three. Can you be on it? I'll meet you at the gate in Zurich.

My plane gets there a few minutes earlier."

"I can, yes, but this is crazy, Albrecht. This is the mafia you're talking about. You're going to let these bloody-handed bastards walk away with ten million dollars?"

"I don't care who they are, if they really have my pictures. Don't you understand what I'm saying?"

"But what's the hurry? They've had the things for fifty years, why tomorrow?"

"I don't know and I don't care," he said impatiently. "I don't see that we're in any position to set conditions. And we'll have the entire day, until four o'clock, to look at the pictures."

"*One* day? One *afternoon*? But—"

"If we're satisfied, the money goes to them and the pictures go to me, then and there, out of their vault and into mine. And that's all there is to it." I heard him catch his breath, and then he added softly, "After so many...*many*...years."

"Albrecht, listen to me. Even if you had an army of experts with you, there's no way to authenticate that many paintings in one day. It can't be done."

"Ah, you're forgetting my father's catalogue. I'll bring it; we'll be able to match them detail by detail."

"All right, that's true, but what about the provenances? There sure won't be any time to verify them-assuming they even have provenances. You have to stall for time. If you get those pictures this way, you'll be setting yourself up for legal wrangling for the next twenty years."

"Yes, but at least I'll actually have them. What do I have now?"

"But—"

"Ben, *please*! I don't know the answers to all these questions, but I beg you, my friend-don't argue with me. Help me. You know I can't let a chance like this pass."

Sure he couldn't, who could? In his place I'd probably feel the same way. But I wasn't in his place.

"Albrecht, please, think this through with me." This was the mafia, I stressed again, the men who had murdered the harmless and good Simeon Pawlovsky, and the not-so-harmless-and-good Attila Szarvas, and Zykmund Dulska, and who knew how many other people-all apparently over these very paintings. And we were supposed to reward them for that with ten million dollars and then let them walk away with it? And had he thought about what they might do with that money? Drugs, guns—

"No!" he said agitatedly. "No, I won't listen to any more! The Nazis, the mafia, I don't care who's had them. I don't care who's been killed—No, that's not true, of course I care." I heard him draw a breath to collect himself, and when he continued he was calmer. "But whatever has happened, it's past, Ben, it can't be undone. And so now the question is, Where are these paintings going to be after tomorrow? Safe at last, or still in the hands of these murderers? And if in their hands, what will they do with them now? What will happen to them? Do you want the responsibility?"

Good questions all, and hard to argue with. I was silent.

"Will you help me, Ben?"

I looked at Alex, listening on the other telephone. We exchanged eyebrow shrugs. "Of course, I'll help you," I said, "but it's a lawyer's help you're really going to need to see you through this, Albrecht. Does Leo Schnittke know about this?"

"Yes, I spoke to him last night."

"And what does he say?"

"Exactly what you do-not to touch this with a ten-meter pole."

I laughed, siphoning off some of the tension. "Well, he's a good lawyer, all right. Are you going to be bringing him?"

"I don't know. He wants to be there. Do you think I should?"

"I sure do. And, Albrecht, there's one more thing. About not telling the police-I don't like that. Look, I've been working pretty closely with Feuchtmüller. He's as reliable as they come. Don't you think we—"

"*No!*" he said shrilly. "It's forbidden. Please, Ben, don't jeopardize this. They mean what they say, I can tell. I couldn't stand the idea of losing the paintings again. It would be too...Later, afterwards, yes, we'll go to them, we'll tell them everything, but not now. I'm afraid. Benjamin, *please.*"

"Okay," I said reluctantly, "we'll keep it to ourselves for now."

"That's all I ask. Then I'll see you in Zurich tomorrow?"

"You sure will."

"My dear friend, thank you. You'll never know what this means to me."

"What are you going to do?" Alex asked when we'd hung up.

"Tomorrow? Fly to Zurich."

"And now?"

"Go to the police, what else?"

She smiled. "Good for you."

"But first I need one more cup of tea."

A couple of minutes later, musing over the last of the tea, I said, "Well, at least now we have the answers to the big questions, don't we?"

"What questions?"

"What all this killing has been about. I always thought that there was too much effort being put into just the two Velàzquezes. Now we know: They have them all, the whole load, maybe the entire Lost Truck; that's what Yuri thinks. *That's* what it's about."

"*What* is it about?"

"What I just said. The paintings, the Lost Truck."

"Yes, but what *about* the paintings? Why all the killing? Why is Attila Szarvas dead? Why did they come after Mr. Nussbaum? One of them was lying and the other one was mistaken; neither of them really had any connection to the paintings at all, so what was the point? And what have they been following you around for? And if they were going to offer them back to Stetten for ten million dollars, why didn't they just go ahead and do it a long time ago?"

I drained my cup and looked at her thoughtfully. "Alex," I said at length, "I don't have a clue."

CHAPTER 33

With Alex I went downstairs to the public telephones, then decided to play it even safer by walking a few blocks to the Bristol and using one of their long-distance booths. A few days ago that kind of wariness would have seemed like paranoia. Now it didn't.

"Polizeioberstleutnant Feuchtmüller is away from the office," I was informed in German. "Is there anyone else with whom you would like to speak?"

"No, thank you—Wait, yes. Is Inspector Pirchl in?" This wasn't going to be pleasant, but I didn't know where Alois was, and time, as Dulska had said to me a few murders ago, was of the essence.

"I'll transfer you to his telephone."

"Please be brief" was Pirchl's typically cordial greeting, and I was.

"Tomorrow?" he said acidly. "And you tell me about this *now*?"

"I just finished talking to Stetten myself. Look, I'm trying to do the right thing here"-shades of Dulska—"and I knew you'd want to know about this. I'm willing to help in any way I can."

"Have you informed Feuchtmüller?"

"No, I, uh, thought I ought to call you first."

A white lie, and it did seem to have some marginal effect. "All right, I'd like you to come in now, please. I'll see if I can get hold of Feuchtmüller."

"I'm off to the police station," I told Alex. "Want to come? You'll love Pirchl."

"No, I don't see what use I'd be. I think I'll just see a little of Vienna on my own for a couple of hours. Any recommendations?"

"Sure, are you kidding? The Kunsthistorisches Museum, the Academy of Fine Arts, the Baroque Museum—"

"Thanks, anyway. I think I'll go have a look at the Prater."

"The park with the Ferris wheel? Why?"

"Well, you don't have to say it like that," she said, laughing. "There *are* other things in this world besides art museums. But mainly it's because it's the only place in Vienna that my mother remembers with any affection. She still gets stars in her eyes when she talks about it, so I'd like to see it for myself. When should we meet?"

"I'm not sure how long I'll be, so let's say two o'clock. I'll see you downstairs at the Imperial—unless Pirchl thinks of something to arrest me for."

I WAS READY FOR every conceivable reaction from Pirchl except the one he came up with: indifference.

"There is nothing for us to do," he told me coolly after I'd been through what Stetten had said. "Even assuming that it *is* the Viennese mafia that has made this offer to Count Stetten, what exactly have they done that strikes you as requiring police involvement?"

I was stunned. "What have they—They murdered Dulska right here in Vienna, they killed—"

"I'm aware of whom they've killed. I am speaking now of the transaction that's going to take place tomorrow in Zurich."

"Inspector, I'm telling you about a deal involving hundreds of millions of dollars' worth of contraband art—"

"Yes, and I'm asking you what's illegal about it."

"What's—"

"The answer is nothing." He leaned forward across his desk and reshaped his mouth precisely around the word. "*Nichts.*"

I hate to have to admit it, but he was right. As he cogently pointed out, it was the Nazis who had stolen the paintings in the first place, not the mafia, and who was in a position to say, after all these years, how they had come into the mafia's possession? What the mafia was now doing was no different from what some of the world's leading auction houses had done time and again since the war: "innocently" selling Nazi loot, the known background of which was obscure or nonexistent. And nobody was threatening to put some of the world's leading auction houses in jail.

"Well, yes, you're right about that," I admitted, "but doesn't the fact that they're asking only a tiny percentage of what they're worth on the open market tell you something?"

"Yes, it tells me that something underhanded is probably going on. It doesn't prove it, and even if it did, how does it concern the Vienna police department? You should be talking to the Swiss—not that I would expect you to have any more success with them."

It went on in this vein for another fifteen depressing minutes. Surely he didn't want to see the mafia get ten million dollars to add to their treasury, did he? No, he said, he certainly didn't, and if I would care to tell him the legal grounds on which it could be prevented, he would be delighted to act. Would Count Stetten care to swear out a complaint? No? And even if he would, even then...

So I got no help at all. Alois, who came in not long after I arrived, and sat listening in a corner of Pirchl's office, got up and left after ten minutes without having said anything, but when I was going out through the reception area, a police officer stopped me. Oberstleutnant Feuchtmüller would appreciate seeing me in his office.

When I got to his fusty den-the same books seemed to be in the same piles-he was on the telephone, speaking in German. "Excellent," he growled happily. "We're greatly in your debt. I'll talk to you later today."

He put down the phone with a look on his ruddy face that said he was onto something. "Let me make sure I have this straight, Ben.

If the deal goes through, the paintings will be transferred on the spot from the one vault to the other, yes?"

"That's the way I understand it."

"But there won't be room-or light-enough in a vault for you and Stetten to examine them. They'll have to be brought out somewhere for you to look at."

"I suppose so, yes. What are you thinking?"

"If they *don't* want to bring them out to be examined, do you think you might insist?"

"Sure. There's bound to be a viewing room or something."

"Good. And most important, do you suppose you could arrange to see to it that all seventy-two paintings are out of their vault at the same time? At three o'clock, say?"

"I don't see why not. Are you planning to let me in on what you're hatching anytime soon?"

He settled self-satisfiedly back, lit up one of his stubby pipes, and let out some billows of smoke. My olfactory nerves must have adapted, because the smell didn't seem all that rank; no worse, say, than the lion house at the zoo on a muggy day.

In a Swiss bank, he explained, the chance of seizing anything in a private vault was nil, absolutely out of the question. But if it was merely on bank property-between vaults, in other words—and if the Swiss police were willing to cooperate and a Swiss magistrate could be talked into issuing the necessary warrant, the property-seventy-two Old Masters paintings, to take an example-might be taken into police custody. And Alois had just finished talking to his old friend Captain Offler of the Zurich criminal police to arrange for both cooperation and warrant.

So at three o'clock tomorrow Alois, Captain Offler, and the rest of the Zurich criminal police, if Offler chose to bring them, would appear unannounced at the Banque de la Suisse Romande and take possession of the paintings, and what did I think of that?

"That's great, Alois, but I'm not sure I understand. Pirchl just finished telling me there weren't any grounds."

"I have a different view. Those paintings are stolen Austrian property, *nein*?"

"Well, yeah, sure, they were stolen from Stetten, but that was over fifty years ago, and it wasn't the mafia that did it."

"No matter. They're still stolen Austrian property, and the Swiss are perfectly willing to treat them as such, at least for the moment. These days, you know, they're very inclined to be accommodating in matters concerning the restoration of Nazi loot, especially if it doesn't cost them anything."

"All right, so you confiscate the paintings. But can you make it hold up?"

"Hold up where? Do you expect the mafia to take us to court?"

I smiled. "I guess not, but I'm still not sure I understand. What's the point of seizing the paintings? They belong to Stetten."

"Of *course* they belong to Stetten," he said,

beginning to get a little nettled. "Can't you see the beauty of the plan? One, we prevent the mafia from getting the money. Two, we take the paintings out of their hands. And three, after all is said and done, Stetten gets his property back from us. Good public relations all around, justice is served, and Stetten doesn't have to give away his fortune. Now, tell me, is this a good plan or is this not a good plan?"

"This," I said, "is a really good plan."

Alex THOUGHT SO, TOO. "But how is Stetten going to feel about it?" she asked over iced coffees at a sidewalk café across from the opera house.

"I don't intend to let him in on it. He'll thank me later."

"Can you really arrange to have all those paintings out at one time?" she said. "I mean, without looking suspicious?"

"Sure, I can tell them I need to have them all available for reevaluating against each other."

"What does that mean, 'reevaluating against each other?'"

"Who knows? But they're not going to know either."

"Ben, you won't take any chances, will you?"

"Alex, there's nothing to take chances about, don't worry."

She sighed. "I know, but—"

"I'll be back on the eight-twenty plane, if not before. I'll tell you all about it then. And we can make some plans for the next few days. We don't have to stay in Vienna, you know, if it's bothering you, or even in Austria. How does Lake Maggiore sound?"

"Fine, but I'd like to stay here at least a little while longer. I'm trying to work out my feelings about it. The Prater didn't do the trick; it must be seedier than it was when Mom was a little girl. It's funny, because I'm half Austrian myself, so I shouldn't be so negative about them, but I don't seem to be able to talk myself out of it."

An idea that should have struck me long before this finally did. "I know somebody you should talk to," I said.

A few minutes later I was on a public telephone. "Mr. Nussbaum? It's Ben Revere. Listen, how would you and Wittgenstein like some company on your walk tomorrow? There's someone I'd like you to meet."

CHAPTER 34

The Banque de la Suisse Romande looked just the way you'd want a Swiss bank to look; that is, like a fractionally smaller version of Buckingham Palace, but every bit as stable, solid, and enduring.

Fancier, though. Its three-story lobby, visible through glass doors from Zurich's tony, tree-lined Bahnhofstrasse, was all veined travertine limestone and gold-leaf molding, and at the ends of the white marble steps out front were heavy bronze urns thickly planted with Alpine flowers. At the top of the steps, a uniformed doorman—a doorman, not a security guard—manned the entrance. If Stetten had told me it was another one of his fancy hotels and not a bank at all, I would have had no trouble believing him.

At the foot of the steps, watching us— Stetten, me, and Stetten's lawyer, Leo Schnittke—as we got out of our taxi, was a chesty man of forty in a sharp, double-breasted blue suit, with a horsey, lantern-jawed face and a big, black mustache that drooped down around either side of his mouth all the way to his chin.

"Count Stetten, I think," he said with a long-toothed smile ("a lemon-sucker's smile," my mother would have called it). "My name is Adler." He spoke fluent English with an accent I wasn't sure of. On second look the mustache didn't really droop around his mouth; it had been carefully shaved into that shape.

"Yes, how do you do?" Stetten replied anxiously. "These gentlemen are Mr. Revere— I mean Dr. Revere—and Mr. Schnittke. You did say that it would be all right if—"

"Yes, it's all right." Once we'd shaken hands—except, as usual, for Schnittke, who made do with a perfunctory bob of his head— Adler motioned us toward the bank. "Will you come with me, please?"

We went up the marble steps to the entrance,

where we were bowed in by the doorman, who greeted Adler by name.

"Please wait here," Adler told us. "I'll get the manager."

Inside, the Banque de la Suisse Romande was like any other bank, just swankier. There were people doing business at tellers' windows and at desks, and carved marble benches were situated at intervals along the walls. I suggested we sit down while waiting, but Stetten shook his head.

"I'm too nervous, I can't sit down." He was clutching his father's notes on the paintings with one hand and had the other flat on his chest. "Ach, Ben, I can hardly breathe."

That gave me a start. "Albrecht—"

"No, don't worry, I feel fine," he said with a nervous laugh. "I only mean I'm a little excited this morning. I'm not sure I believe this is happening."

I laughed as well. "That makes two of us."

"That makes three of us," Schnittke said, looking blacker than usual, possibly because one of the guards had told him to put his cigar away, despite Schnittke's reasonable objection that it wasn't lit. "Tell me, Revere, is it really possible to authenticate seventy-two paintings in four hours?"

"Not a chance in the world," I said.

"As I thought," he said with a venomous look at Stetten, who gave him a weak grin.

Again I picked up that trace of an accent that wasn't quite an accent, that reminded me of…what?

Adler came back with two sprucely uniformed guards—white gloves; oiled, flapped holsters; and lustrous Sam Browne belts and shoes—and a soft, pale, anxious man who bowed, clicked his heels together (or did I only imagine it?), and introduced himself to Stetten.

"*Exzellenz,* I am Herr Schönauer, the director of foreign accounts. Everything is at your service. May I say how honored we are to have your account?"

The familiar kowtowing served to steady Stetten. "Very good, Mr. Schönauer," he said regally. "Shall we proceed?"

"Yes, certainly, *Exzellenz.* Perhaps first you would be good enough to sign for your vault?"

Stetten signed a couple of papers and Schönauer handed him a key, bowing yet again (he *did* click his heels), then led the way to an elevator that took us noiselessly to a lower level. Then we went down a succession of carpeted, brightly lit corridors and through several heavy doors that hissed respectfully closed behind us.

"Here is your vault, *Exzellenz,*" Schönauer said, pausing to let us peer through a floor-to-ceiling metal grille, much like the barred door of a prison cell, at what looked a lot like a large but ordinary safe-deposit viewing room in an ordinary bank; that is, an anteroom maybe sixteen feet by sixteen feet, with three walls of deposit boxes and a few stand-up viewing tables. The only difference was that one entire wall consisted of a single, room-high, polished-steel door with two eye-level keyholes a foot apart: Stetten's vault. "Would you care to examine it?"

"That won't be necessary," Stetten said.

Schönauer took up the march again, leading us, single file, past some similar rooms, through another softly hissing door, and to another room like the one we'd just seen.

One of the white-gloved guards used a key to unlock the barred door, then swung it open, bowing us into the anteroom. The other inserted a second key into one of the two keyholes in the door of the vault and stood waiting until Adler produced and inserted a similar key. They both turned their keys at the same time and the door went *f-s-s-t*, popped open a few inches, and stopped. Apparently the dim lights inside worked on a refrigerator-door principle, because they didn't have to be turned on. I tried to peek around the guard's shoulder but couldn't see anything.

"If you would make them comfortable in the viewing room, Mr. Schönauer...?" Adler said.

The manager promptly obeyed, leaving Adler and the two guards at the vault and showing us to a brightly lit room with a small conference table and a few chairs. On the table were two short-legged picture easels.

"You would care for some coffee?" Schönauer asked.

"Yes," Stetten said, "that would be—"

"No, thank you," I said, "we'd better not; not while we're looking at the paintings."

"No, of course not, what was I thinking?" Stetten said. He was really nervous.

When Schönauer had bowed himself out, Stetten licked dry lips and smiled weakly at Schnittke and me. "My friends...I know that you both have some scruples about the...the irregularity of this."

Did I ever, but I saw no reason to raise them. Alois had telephoned first thing in the morning to reassure me that the Swiss warrants had been secured and the plan was a definite go. Less than three hours from now the cavalry would come riding in, banners waving and bugles blaring, to seize all the paintings. My scruples would be moot.

"We've already been through this, Albrecht," Schnittke said. "You've made up your mind, so let's not waste our breath going over it again."

"But you won't do anything to endanger it, will you—either of you? Think of it—"

But at that point Adler came in, sat confidently down at the head of the table, and began rattling off conditions.

"You have until four o'clock. I will have the pictures brought in for your examination, and you may have as much time as you wish with them. If you find them satisfactory, Count Stetten will have his bank wire the ten million dollars to our account. Upon Mr. Schönauer's verification that the transfer has been made, the paintings will be transferred on the spot into Count Stetten's vault and the transaction will have been concluded. Are there any questions?"

"No, none!" Stetten practically shouted, trying to head Schnittke off.

"Yes," Schnittke said. "Mr. Revere says he can't authenticate so many paintings in four hours. We'll need more time."

"That may be so, but it's not the arrangement," Adler said. "You have until four o'clock to decide."

"Well, I think that covers everything," Stetten said. "Shall—"

"Mr. Adler, we need to know who we're dealing with," Schnittke said. "Are you a dealer yourself, here in Zurich? An attorney?"

"That's of no importance," he said coolly. "I'm merely an agent of the current owner, who prefers to remain anonymous."

Schnittke was starting to look like a man who knew his cause was lost, but he gave it another try. "Now, listen here. You know as well as we do that we have to know where these paintings come from. You can't expect—"

"I'm sorry, you get no provenances."

"Then how is Count Stetten going to say he came by them? How can he prove they're really his?"

"Ah—excuse me?" Stetten said, raising a tentative finger. "But, ah, they really *are* mine, you know."

He did have a point there.

"You also get no bills of sale," Adler said. "You get no papers of any sort. What you do get are the paintings. Do you want to see them or not? Your four hours are now three hours and forty-five minutes."

"Oh, in that case I think we'd certainly better—" Stetten began.

But Schnittke hadn't quite given up yet. "And just how the hell is Count Stetten supposed to get them out of the country with no papers?"

The atmosphere was getting dicey. Adler was losing his patience; he'd begun to tap on the table with his fingernails. And I sensed that Schnittke was becoming irritated with me for failing to back him up. And I was getting nervous myself. The questions he was raising were the right ones, the same ones I would have brought up if I hadn't already known that none of it made any difference. What did the terms matter? Whatever they were, they weren't going to be fulfilled. The only important thing was to have those pictures out of the vault by three o'clock, and I was beginning to worry that Schnittke, with his spiky persistence, was going to get the whole deal called off.

"And just how did they get *into* the country with no papers?" Adler snapped. "It's hardly impossible to accomplish, Herr Schnittke. If you don't find the terms satisfactory, perhaps it would be better for all—"

If Stetten could have reached far enough to kick Schnittke under the table, I was sure he would have. As it was, he made do with a look of dumb, imploring despair in my direction: *Ben, have pity on me, don't let him screw things up!*

"Okay, Mr. Adler," I said, "I think we'd better get on with it. We'll do it your way."

That earned a look of mute gratitude from Stetten and one of contempt from Schnittke, who folded his arms and stared pointedly at

410

the wall. But he was beginning to irritate me, too. It wasn't as if we'd come to Zurich under the impression that we were going to be dealing with a legitimate seller, after all. It was the mafia, and how else did he expect them to do business? They held all the cards (or so they thought), and they were the ones calling the shots.

Adler stood up. "Good, we understand each other. Shall I leave you to yourselves now? The guards will bring the pictures in two at a time, except for the larger ones. Simply tell them whenever you wish to see the next pair."

"By the way, there's one thing," I said. "Will you ask them not to return the pictures to the vault? I'd like to have them left out."

Adler's eyes narrowed. "Left out where?"

"Just somewhere where I can look at them again. In the anteroom to the vault would be fine, and when they run out of room there, you can just have them put them in the corridor, propped against the walls."

"Why?"

"So that it's possible to, um, reevaluate them against each other."

"Reevaluate them against each other?"

"Yes, that's right," I said with a flicker of condescension, always a good idea if you don't know what you're talking about. "If the need arises."

I got by with it, too. After a moment's uncertainty he said, "Very well," and snapped his fingers at the two guards, who were waiting in the corridor. "Bring in the first two."

A minute later in they came, one bearing the now-familiar *Condesa de Torrijos,* last seen in Zykmund Dulska's sitting room at the Imperial, the other a stunningly beautiful *Adoration of the Shepherds* by Georges de La Tour, the great Caravaggesque master. Serene to the point of stillness and classically simple, with the marvelous light provided by a single candle shaded by the translucent fingers of a young shepherdess, it was the kind of thing that slowed down your heart rate simply to look at it. Except for the blurry photo in Stetten's father's records, I'd never even seen a reproduction of it before, and all I wanted to do now was sit there for twenty minutes or so and bask in its glow.

Not a chance. A little arithmetic will tell you that examining that many paintings in the time we had gave us about three minutes each, and that didn't provide for the time needed for the guards to carry them back and forth. Two minutes apiece was more like it.

We were, in other words, busy as beavers. At one point I barely managed to choke back a hysterical fit of laughter. I mean, there we were, confronted with rare, great works by Hals, Poussin, Van Dyck, Copley, Chardin, Tintoretto, Gainsborough, Goya, Ruisdael, Reynolds, you name 'em—and we were plowing through them, zip, zip, zip, like kids flipping through the T-shirt racks at Planet Hollywood.

Still, it was enough time for the purpose at hand. And my purpose was exactly the same as Stetten's: to determine if these really were the paintings from his father's collection. We had his scrupulously detailed catalogue, remember, so all it took was a cursory look at each picture and a quick comparison with the details in his list. If they matched, that was it; I checked it off and went on to the next one. *Watteau? Check. Canaletto? Check.* Peculiar work, and exhausting in its own way, but terrifically satisfying, too. Every check mark I made meant another lost masterpiece coming back into the world. This must have been how those old MFA&A officers felt.

Stetten started off strong but quickly wilted, so that I did most of the actual work with the catalogue while he drifted in and out of reveries, remembering some of the pictures and not remembering others. "Ah, the Copley," he would say about a portrait, as if it were a relative he hadn't seen in a long time. "My brother Rolf used to call him the General—no, the Pirate." Or, dreamily, about a Fragonard: "My father promised he would build us such a swing set...but he never did. Or have I forgotten?"

Meanwhile I would be muttering, "Copley, check. Fragonard, check," and making the little marks in the catalogue. Should I have been more worried about forgery or some kind of double-dealing? I didn't think so. The idea that anyone could have faked seventy-two paintings of this quality, used age-appropriate materials, duplicated the frames, and matched every detail—every chip, scrape, marking,

413

and imperfection, back and front—was beyond belief, an impossible task.

Schnittke, with little interest in the pictures as art, wandered in and out, stumping restlessly around the corridor munching an unlit cigar and cowing the guards with sheer force of personality into pretending that they didn't notice. Where Adler was, I didn't know. At about two o'clock I got up to stretch and also to make sure that the paintings were really being left out of the vault. Alois and friends were due in one hour.

Adler had kept his word. Framed pictures now lined the anteroom to Adler's vault as well as either side of the corridor. Some had been left with their painted surfaces facing outward, not a good idea with people clomping around the place. I asked the guards to turn the wrong-facing ones in the corridor the other way to give them a little more protection and went into the anteroom to do the same for the ones there.

Having retilted the last of them carefully against the wall, I straightened up, brushing dust from my hands. As I did a marking on the back, one of the usual assemblage of scribbles, stamps, and symbols, seemed to snag, like a burr, in the surface of my mind. I knelt to look at it again, a stamped, dull-black *ne-1* in Germanic lettering. It was one of the ERR's markings, which almost half of the paintings bore, so that I'd stopped paying attention to them during our hectic examination, but now...

I stood there looking at it, repeating it to myself: *ne-1…ne-1…,* waiting for whatever my brain was trying to tell me to pop, and in a slow, osmotic way, like a photograph emerging in a developing tank, an idea vaguely began to take shape. What was it that Haftmann, the old Nazi registrar, had told me those markings meant? "A crude clerical notation," he'd said with disdain, "something to indicate the source of acquisition." *The source of acquisition.* I turned the painting around to look at its front again. It was the candlelit *Adoration* by Georges de La Tour, the second one we'd looked at today.

The idea gelled, took on firmer outlines. I went back to the conference room, where Stetten, barely noticing me, was dreaming over a Poussin depiction of ruined Roman arches, and got my MFA&A folder, which I'd brought along with me to Zurich. In it were tucked the photographs that I'd taken of the *Conde de Torrijos* in Simeon's shop. Returning to the anteroom, I thumbed through them until I came to a photo of the painting's back. There, under the *ERR,* perfectly clear and unmistakable, was an *ne-2.*

"My God," I said under my breath. I knew, or thought I knew, or was afraid I knew, what those markings meant. Quickly I located its companion portrait, the *Condesa de Torrijos,* the one Dulska had tried to sell Stetten. If I remembered right, it was marked with an *sr-4*—and I now thought I knew what that meant, too. I closed my eyes for a second, took a

415

deep breath and let it out, then turned the picture around again to look at the back. And there it was, my memory hadn't played me false: *sr-4*.

The source of acquisition, Haftmann had said, plain as could be. How much clearer did it have to be made for me? There it had been, staring me in the eye, and I'd been too trusting, or too stuck in a rut, or just too plain dumb to see it.

The *ne's* stood for *Nussbaum, Eberhard,* Jakob Nussbaum's art-dealer uncle. The *sr* stood for *Sussman, Raoul,* Eberhard's competitor-friend, who, like Eberhard Nussbaum, had given paintings to the Paris gallery-owner Paul Cazeau for safeguarding from the Nazis. The numbers—*1, 2, 4*—were inventory numbers for the individual paintings. *A crude clerical notation.*

When I had so assuredly, reasonably convinced Jakob Nussbaum that the painting in Boston that he was claiming was merely a student study of a Velàzquez painting, and not the real thing, I'd been dead wrong. The Boston Velàzquez, the *Conde,* was his uncle's picture, all right. That's what the *ne-2* meant.

And the *Condesa,* the picture Dulska had brought with him to Vienna? That, clearly—well, relatively clearly—had been Raoul Sussman's "other half of the set," the "sister" that went with the *Conde.* There on the back to prove it was the *sr-4*—which also must have meant that the ERR had confiscated at least three other paintings of Sussman's. If it

416

turned out, as well it might, that all these pictures had been taken from Paul Cazeau's Paris cellar, then we'd probably find *sr-1, 2,* and *3* in there, too.

The *ne-1* on the painting by Georges de La Tour had me puzzled until I realized that Nussbaum had told me about that, too... almost. His uncle, he said, had left a second picture with Cazeau, something by a Frenchman whose name was right there on the tip of his tongue: Lebrun? Delacroix? Le Nain?

Try La Tour.

Put together, it all sounded impossibly rococo, but the proof was in those Gothic black letters stamped on the backs. The probability, given the rest of the story, that these particular sets of initials, out of so many possible others, stood for something other than Eberhard Nussbaum and Raoul Sussman—the "sources of acquisition"—was wildly implausible, a billion-to-one chance.

There was only one possible conclusion. Those paintings had been confiscated in 1942 by the Nazis, all right, in Paris, all right— but from Paul Cazeau's basement hiding place under the place Vendôme—and not from the elegant Stetten apartment on avenue Charles-Floquet (if there ever was an elegant Stetten apartment on avenue Charles-Floquet).

From the first, everything Stetten had told me had been a lie. Neither he nor his father had *ever* owned those paintings.

I know it sounds as if I'd been standing there cogitating for half an hour, but it had been only a matter of seconds. Most of it had come to me in the previous few minutes. The *sr-4* had been the final piece of evidence needed to confirm it.

And confirm it it did. Stetten was a liar and a charlatan—maybe worse—trading on the miseries of others, and I was the credulous, self-important "expert" who had spent the last few weeks doing his damnedest to help him perpetrate exactly the kind of injustice I thought I was rectifying. I was furious with myself for having been used and, on top of that, for liking and rooting for him to boot. I felt confused, exploited, triumphant, and righteous, all at the same time. Also, I didn't feel real bright.

"What's the matter?" It was Schnittke, returning from one of his rambles down the corridor.

"Mr. Schnittke, how much do you know about these paintings?"

"Enough to know they're nothing but trouble," he said. "Albrecht is making a hell of a mistake."

"I couldn't agree with you more."

"What?" He peered at me. "I was under the impression you were all for it."

"Why would you think that?"

"Because Albrecht told me..." He let the words hang. We looked at each other.

"Albrecht lied," I said.

He came closer, squat, fat, and pouchy, but an imposing presence all the same. "If you know something about this that I don't, I would say now is the time to tell me."

"These aren't his paintings."

He took the cigar out of his mouth. "Nonsense."

"I'm telling you, they never belonged to him; he's made it all up. Stetten's in it with the mafia; he has to be. The whole thing is a sham. Everything. We've both been set up."

Schnittke glowered at me, his little goatee quivering. "Now, you let me tell you something, young man. I've known and trusted Albrecht von Stetten for more than forty years, since before you were born. Don't you think I'd know if he were capable of doing what you're suggesting? It's ridiculous. Murder, fraud, outrageous lies—"

"Let me show you something," I said. I pointed out the *ne-1* and *sr-4* on the backs and briefly explained.

By the time I finished, a change had come over Schnittke. He looked like death warmed over, with his eyes sunk deeper than ever in their pouches and his purplish lips working. "No, it's impossible. There has to be another explanation for this."

"Can you think of one?"

He'd been glaring at the backs of the paintings, but now he raised his eyes to mine. "No, I can't," he said slowly, and from the way he jammed the cigar stub back in his mouth and clamped down on it I could see his mood had hardened. He didn't appreciate being made a dupe any more than I did.

"I'll get him in here," he said, turning abruptly on his heel and stalking out.

CHAPTER 35

He knows the jig's up, he can sense it, was my first thought when Stetten came in, leaning on his walking stick and looking scared and frail in his neat blue blazer and gray trousers. Well, Schnittke's scowl would have been enough to scare me, too, and I suppose I didn't look any too cordial either. Now, don't start feeling sorry for him, I told myself.

"Is something wrong?" he asked. "Shouldn't we be—"

I pointed sternly to the *sr-4* on the back of the Velàzquez. "What does this stand for, Albrecht?"

He squinted at it. "This?" he said wonderingly. "The *sr-4*? I don't know."

I supposed that much was true. "But I do. It was put on by the Nazis in 1942."

"But— You mean after it was taken from my father? What significance— How could I—"

"It was never taken from your father," I said as Schnittke looked on silently. "Your father never owned it—or any of them. This was all bogus from the beginning—the haggling with Dulska over the price, the 'surprise' telephone call from Adler—"

"I don't understand!" Stetten cried. "How can you say such things? My father's old catalogue—it's right there in the conference room!"

"It isn't your father's catalogue, and it isn't old."

"It isn't...? But you've *seen* it!" He appealed to Schnittke. "He said himself he'd never seen anything so detailed—ask him!" His eyes were watering. "Benjamin, my dear friend—"

"No, I'm not your dear friend. That's all over."

"Benjamin, I'm eighty-one years old, don't...Where else would I get such precise, complete information? You saw for yourself, it's accurate in every detail."

His voice had dissolved into the plaintive old man's quaver that I'd heard a few times before. I couldn't tell how much of it was real and how much was put on, an attempt to wring some sympathy out of us. A day before it would have gotten to me; now it didn't. Well, it did, but I wasn't about to let it gain the upper hand.

"Of course it's accurate in every detail," I said, trying with certainty of speech to make it seem as if I weren't really about to launch a series of guesses, which I was. "Why wouldn't it be? Since you—or rather your pals in the mafia—*had* the paintings all along, all you had to do was take some fuzzy photographs of them and type up the descriptions—not too difficult, since they were right there in front of whoever was doing it. Make the descriptions look old, put them in a broken-down loose-leaf binder—and, presto, there's your 'father's' catalogue, with more detail—more 'proof of ownership'—than anybody, even the real owners, could possibly come up with."

"But—but to what end? To sell them to

myself? If I already *had* them? Ha-ha, why would I go to such lengths?"

Schnittke looked keenly at me. "Yes, why?"

"Okay," I said a little nervously, because I was working this out as I went along and it was the trickiest part, "I think the whole thing was a mafia scheme to get title to the paintings. As long as they were still officially *loot,* the only way they could be sold was through the black market, where they'd bring only a tiny fraction of their real value."

Stetten glanced nervously at Schnittke. "Leo, let me assure you—"

"Shut up," Schnittke said in a tone he wouldn't have used before with Stetten. "You were saying?" he said to me. "'Where they'd bring only a tiny fraction of their real value'...?"

"But if someone like Stetten could somehow be legitimized as the lawful owner," I said, "he could sell them openly later, at full market value, for hundreds of millions of dollars. That's what the posturing and pretending, the fake haggling, was all designed to do—to make it look as if he were getting his own paintings back. A year or two from now they'd be sold at full price, Stetten would be paid whatever they were giving him for being their front man, and three hundred million dollars or so would go straight to the mafia."

"And the ten million dollars he was paying to them?"

"More sham. There never was any ten million dollars." I looked at Stetten. "Albrecht, am I right?"

Stetten, his veined hands tight on the knob of his stick, stared rigidly at the floor and shook his head; he wasn't going to answer. I knew I was right.

"Then why bring you into it?" Schnittke asked me in a queerly tense, quiet tone. "What did they need you for? All you could do was cause them trouble."

"I was a pawn," I said, "the same as you. I'm a known expert, I've worked with the police, I have a clean reputation. They'd be way ahead if he could fox me into supporting his claim, or—even better—personally authenticating it."

Schnittke nodded. "Yes, and so he did," he said with the ghost of a smile. "But in the end you turned the tables, didn't you? Oh, you've caused a *great* deal of trouble."

I stared at him. The tone was so strange, the remark so peculiar...

Oh, jeez, I thought. I think I made a—

Not taking his eyes from me, he stepped back a few paces, placed his hand on the barred door, and called into the corridor, "Adler! You'd better come in here. We have a serious problem."

Have you ever noticed that when your mind is confused and buzzing away in twenty different directions, sometimes you have a kind of heightened perception, becoming aware of odd, totally irrelevant details? So it was then. As I looked at Schnittke's hand on the bars, I noticed something that had gotten by me before. Leo Schnittke's reluctance to shake hands had nothing to with formality or fastidiousness. The reason he kept his right hand in his pocket most of the time was that it was disfigured; where the thumb and forefinger should have been were nothing but two knuckly stubs.

CHAPTER 36

Adler came in unbuttoning his double-breasted suit jacket. Christ, I thought, the guy's going to pull out a gun!

Which he did, not certain of whom he ought to be pointing it at until Schnittke gestured in my direction. The pistol, a compact, shiny, nickel-plated thing that could have passed for a kitschy cigarette lighter came around and leveled on my chest.

"Hey, hey, take it easy now," I said, palms outward in front of me, as if to stop the bullets. "Don't get excited, we can—"

"Shut up. Keep your hands away from your sides and back up against the wall," he said, and looked once more to Schnittke for further instructions.

"*Schutzmann!*" I yelled. *Guard.*

"Shout away," said Schnittke calmly. "The guards are gone. We're all alone."

"Leo, you can't kill him!" an agitated Stetten suddenly cried. "How would you...how would we explain the body?"

"What body? The vault is still open, isn't it? There's plenty of room in there."

"You'll—you'll have to kill me, too," Stetten bravely piped.

Schnittke looked at him the way you'd look at a cockroach in the tuna salad. "That can easily be arranged."

Stetten did what any sensible person would have done. He shut up instantly, shrank into a corner, and became as unnoticeable as possible.

I found my voice again, or something like it. "The police know I'm—I'm here," I stammered. "They—they'll be here in twenty minutes." Talk about a lame ploy. *I* knew it was true, but if I'd been Schnittke I wouldn't have believed a word of it.

"Is that so? Well, that's a risk we'll have to take. Shoot him, Adler."

Adler hesitated. "I—"

"Don't do it!" I croaked. "You don't want to kill anybody! The police really are coming, they know all about this, they know who's here with me, they know everything—"

"Shoot him," Schnittke said again while I was babbling.

"There'll be blood," Adler said. "It might make a mess." He threw a glance at the open vault. "Wouldn't it be better to get him in—"

Maybe it was hearing my blood discussed in terms of its mess-making qualities, but with that glance, and with my heart in my mouth, I went for him. Adler was six feet from me—two steps— but I didn't think he really wanted to shoot me, and I was counting on his hesitating long enough for me to get there. And if not, what did I have to lose?

Anyway, I guessed wrong. He spun back toward me and without a millisecond's hesitation he pulled the trigger. The gun made a flat, popping sound. I didn't know whether he'd hit me or not, but I plowed on into him, head down, and butted him backward into one of the stand-up viewing tables. The rim caught him hard on the edge of the hip—a spot I knew from experience to be excruciatingly sensitive. With a yelp— "*Ai!*"—he flinched and doubled over sideways. The gun flew from his hand and went bumping over the carpeted floor. I saw Schnittke going after it, but an overweight man in his seventies is no match for me, especially when I'm scared out of my wits.

I got to it with three feet to spare and kicked it out of reach while Schnittke tripped over his feet and fell. By a lucky break the gun went skittering out into the corridor and I followed right after it. With Schnittke on his knees, Adler still doubled over, and Stetten covering his head with his hands in the corner, I had time to pull the heavy, barred door closed behind me. It swung slowly, smoothly on its giant hinges, emitting a deep, solid, satisfying *clook* when the lock engaged.

All of us breathing hard, we took a moment to reevaluate the altered situation. From my point of view it had a lot going for it. They were inside, I was outside. They were locked in, I was free. They were weaponless, I had the gun out here with me.

"All right, Revere," Schnittke said, getting heavily to his feet, "you'd better listen to me before you do anything foolish." He came up to the bars; I moved a prudent step back. "There's a lot of money to be made from this; plenty for everybody. It's not to late to—"

"You killed Simeon Pawlovsky," I said.

"—come in with— Who the hell is Simeon Pawlovsky?"

"Just an old pawnbroker," I said. "You wouldn't remember."

"The old Jew in Boston? That wasn't me, that was Shaposhkin."

"Well, I guess you'll just have to do," I said as the door at the end of the corridor swung open. Through it came the cavalry: Polizeioberstleutnant Alois McGuffey Feuchtmüller and three uniformed Swiss cops.

"*Very* nice," said Alois, looking at the paintings lined up along the walls. "Any trouble?"

"Piece of cake," I said. "I've even got them locked up for you."

He shambled up to the bars, looked curiously at the three men on the other side, and did a double take when he saw Schnittke. "Fancy meeting you here, Herr Loitzl."

"Loitzl?" I exclaimed. "His name's not Schnittke?"

Alois shook his head happily. "This is Klaus Loitzl, an old acquaintance of mine."

Schnittke glared at him, and Alois broke into a slow smile. "I must say, you look very much at home in there."

• • •

Tʜᴇʀᴇ ғᴏʟʟᴏᴡᴇᴅ ᴀɴᴏᴛʜᴇʀ ʟᴏɴɢ, wearying afternoon spent at another European police station—I was starting to think of them as my homes away from home—but this one produced tangible results, not so much from my interrogation, or from the closemouthed Schnittke's, as from Stetten's. Trusting more in the ability of the police to protect him from the mafia than in the ability of the mafia to protect him from the police (other than by killing him), he was positively garrulous—"singing like a meadowlark" was the way Alois put it—spilling every bean he was capable of spilling: names, places, and facts, all of great interest to Alois.

Generally speaking, the conclusions I'd reached were on the mark. Stetten was supposed to get title to the paintings so that they could be sold on the world market for the astronomical prices they would command there. His own motive, unsurprisingly, had been money. He was a count, all right, but a poor one, not a rich one. The wealthy family, the cigarette empire—those things were true, but according to him the Stetten properties had been confiscated first by the Nazis, then by the Soviets, and *then* by the Republic of Austria on the grounds that they had been sold to the Nazis for profit (which Stetten denied). According to Alois, the story might well be true. In any event, Stetten had nothing, and he bore a grudge against everyone. For his playacting he was to receive a hundred thousand dollars, which struck me as a pretty paltry payoff, considering the sums involved.

The story about the Nazis calling on his father at dinnertime, and what followed, was true—except that it had happened to other people, a Jewish banking family he knew of. Stetten had lifted it whole hog. The stories about his wartime service and his mother's death in a bombing raid he claimed to be accurate.

And he continued to maintain that he'd had no part in the killings, not even knowing about them until after the fact. All he knew about were the paintings, and there he simply followed the instructions given to him by Schnittke/Loitzl.

I was inclined to believe it. There had been so much puzzlingly inconsistent behavior: sudden changes of mind and mood, switches of direction, self-assurance some of the time, dithering indecision at other times. Now it was understandable. He'd been taking orders, not giving them. His decisions were being made for him. He'd say one thing to me, reacting on the spur of the moment, and would then be reversed by Schnittke, at which point he would have to reverse himself to me. It all made sense.

Even Schnittke-cum-Loitzl made sense once Alois explained it to me. Schnittke was indeed the Viennese mafia chief Klaus Loitzl and not a lawyer at all. He'd known Stetten for five weeks, not forty years. Interestingly, his name wasn't Loitzl either, although he'd been using it for a half century. He was, in fact, a onetime Red Army sergeant named Pavel Ilich Petrochenko, who had been captured in Austria by the Germans in 1945 and turned loose a few days later, when the war ended. There were already stories drifting back from Russia about the horrible treatment being received by soldiers who had been un-Russian enough to let themselves be captured, so he'd decided not to return.

He'd found a place for himself in Vienna, making himself useful to the bureaucrats in the Russian-occupied sector of the city for the next ten years. When the occupation forces left in 1955, he had gone to East Berlin, where he'd begun his rise in the thriving world of the black market. And in 1989, when the Wall came down, he'd returned to Vienna as an established underworld figure, one of the Old Guard. Few people had any idea that he was actually a Russian from—

"Odessa," I said.

Alois looked at me, surprised.

"The accent," I said. "I knew it sounded familiar, but I couldn't place it. He sounded like my Uncle Jascha—from Odessa. Damn, I should have realized something about him was fishy!"

"Oh, I wouldn't say that. The man hardly has an accent at all. I'd say you did rather well."

I shrugged. "I was pretty lucky. By the way, who's Shaposhkin?"

"Dimitri Nikolayevich Shaposhkin, lord of the Chetverk crime family in Moscow. His relationship with Loitzl goes back a long way, maybe even to the war. They were in the same battalion."

"Schnittke—that is, Loitzl—said Shaposhkin was responsible for Simeon Pawlovsky's death."

Alois spread his hands. "It's possible. Janko Golubov is Shaposhkin's boy, not Loitzl's."

Much later, over a midnight meal of cold roast chicken, potato salad, and beer in the noisy, turn-of-the-century ambience of the St. Gotthard Café on Bahnhofstrasse a few doors down from the bank, a contented Alois filled me in on the rest of what they'd been able to piece together about the details of the mafia plan.

"The upshot being," he said, jaw muscles working away on his second chicken leg, "that you were never in any real danger, except inadvertently."

"Great, I wish somebody'd told me that before. I wish somebody'd told Janko."

"Well, that was your fault; you kept interrupting him at his work."

"I know, damn thoughtless of me." I smiled. "But I'm sure glad I did, in Nussbaum's case."

Janko, it seemed, had been sent to kill Jakob Nussbaum for the same reason he'd been sent to kill Attila Szarvas, which had nothing to do with anything either of them could pass on to me. It was simply because they were claimants to the Velàzquez, Stetten's rivals. Whether they were legitimate claimants or not, the mafia had no way of knowing, and therefore they were best "removed" before they queered the plan to get the paintings into Stetten's nominal possession.

Me they had no interest in killing. In fact, they preferred having me around. I was the frosting on the cake. Who better than the famed (I'm stretching a point here) Boston Art Cop to employ his investigative skills in helping the victimized Count Stetten hunt down his stolen patrimony? Did I want to go to St. Petersburg to look into that Turner from the Lost Truck? Sure, great idea. To Altaussee to see what I could learn about the Lost Truck itself? Absolutely, go ahead. With our blessing.

And why not? The mafia people behind Stetten had no interest in the Lost Truck as such, but only in 73 of the 106 paintings. Why 73? There, with Stetten not knowing the answer himself, we could only guess. But guessing wasn't that hard, as I told Alois. Those 73 must have been what was left from the original haul of 106 after it had worked its way from the Russian Army to Russian officialdom to semiofficialdom to organized crime. The other 33— including the Turner in the Hermitage—had in all probability simply peeled away in various directions in the intervening time, a kind of natural attrition that was common where precious contraband was involved.

"That makes sense," Alois agreed.

"Sure it does. And it means that the mafia couldn't care less if I actually traced down any one of those paintings, or all thirty-three.

432

They were only concerned with the ones they had their hands on—the 'collection.'"

"Which, when you come to think of it, is probably why you're still alive."

I laughed. "That and Mr. Nussbaum's trusty frying pan."

CHAPTER 37

So it all turned out pretty well, considering. And after I returned to Boston, things kept on improving.

First, thanks to Christie Valle de Leon's energetic taking-on of Jakob Nussbaum's case, it looked as if the *Conde de Torrijos,* currently in the evidence room at Boston Police headquarters, would soon go to him. Nussbaum would get to live out his life across from Prinz-Eugen-Strasse 22 on his own means. And Wittgenstein would get his liver twice a day— on a gold dinner plate, if he preferred it that way.

Second, the Swiss government, finding themselves in a potential public-relations nightmare over what to do with the seventy- two looted, ownerless paintings that had been in one of their vaults for over a decade, had gratefully taken Christie up on her suggestion (prompted by *my* suggestion, may I add) that they go to CIAT, which would mount an exhibition of them to be called "Plunder Reclaimed." The show would travel to ten cities in Europe and the United States, partly for aesthetic and educational reasons, and partly in the hope that the publicity would help in finding the rightful owners.

As for Simeon, even if no perfect resolution was possible, at least there was partial closure. Janko Golubov, if the Austrians ever let him out of jail, would face murder charges in Boston, although he was bound to be pretty decrepit by then. So would I, but I was looking forward to tottering into the witness box and testifying against him all the same. As for what would happen to Schnittke/Loitzl, that was less certain, but Alois and Pirchl were both working on it, and that was good enough for me. Shaposhkin, unfortunately, was out of their reach.

Stetten, by the way, had continued to cooperate, and it appeared that he would get off lightly, which, on reflection, was okay with me. I'm not one to hold a grudge, and in the end he did do his best to keep me from getting plugged.

The question that had bedeviled us so often and for so long— Why would a mafia courier pawn a five-million-dollar painting for a hundred dollars?—would probably never be answered for sure, but Alois had his theory, based on putting together a lot of bits and pieces: Korolenko, the courier, had been on a mission to deliver that particular painting to a fence or a buyer in the United States. But once safely off the plane in Boston he'd decided to defect, from Russia as well as from the mafia, and try to make it on his own in the

States. At that point the painting was just something he had to get rid of and, not possessing a brain of high order, had shown up with it in his valise at the nearest pawnshop where Russian was spoken. Of course, it had taken the mafia no time to catch up with him.

It was Alois's guess that it was after the debacle in Boston that they'd decided there had to be a better way to get rid of the paintings than by doing it piecemeal at low black-market prices, and had come up with the plan to use Stetten to move the entire lot of them. Quite possibly this was when Schnittke had come into the picture, which would mean that his claim that he'd had nothing to do with Simeon's murder might possibly be true.

Was that really the way it had all happened? There was no way to know for certain, but it made sense and it tied things up about as neatly as such a thing is likely ever to be tied up.

All in all, then, a lot had been accomplished, and by the time CIAT was finished, a lot of old wrongs were going to be righted. Even better from a personal point of view, I would continue to be involved. "Plunder Reclaimed" would need a curator, and since I couldn't imagine anybody better qualified for the job, particularly since it was my idea in the first place, I surprised Christie by accepting the six-month assignment when it was offered. After surprising her, I proceeded to flabbergast her by saying that if there was any possibility of a continuing position with

CIAT for someone with my background, I was raring to go.

Well, Alex had said it back in Vienna; I wasn't the same person.

"I'll say this much for you," Christie said when she got her breath back, "your timing's good. We're going to be losing Dick Benedetti, our consultant on seventeenth- and eighteenth-century European painting. Actually, I would've suggested it before, but it never occurred to me that you'd be—"

"I'll take it," I said.

"Don't be in such a hurry. If the past is any guide, it'd involve spending six or ten days a month here in New York, on the average."

"That's not a problem; I like New York."

"And there isn't much pay to speak of, but as you know it's in one hell of a good cause, and there's plenty of opportunity for travel, and I know you like that, and there's also—"

"Christie, you don't have to talk me into it; I'm the one who's asking. I'll take it, I'll take it."

"Son of a gun, I wouldn't have believed it. Well, Ben, that's just dandy. I'm going to love working with you. I hope you can say the same for me."

"I'm not showing up at six o'clock in the morning, I can tell you that."

"No, there's room for only one crazy person here," she said. "Now let's get back to 'Plunder.' It's going to open in December, which means you really ought to be here full-time for the next couple of months getting it ready. If you want, we can put you up at our visiting-scholar residence, a wonderful old brownstone with its own private garden on East Seventy-seventh, midway between the Frick and the Met. Now I ask you, what could be better than that?"

"Boss, I can't think of a blessed thing."

"THEN IT'S SET?" ALEX asked. "You've definitely landed a job with CIAT?"

"Yes, I have. It's your fault, you know. It was a couple of things you said to me."

"Me? What did I say?"

"You said you believed in people digging in their heels and getting on with their lives and just pulling themselves up by their bootstraps."

"Are you sure I said all that?"

"That's what I heard. And you also said that when I was chasing down those paintings I was a man with a purpose, and that it did me good. Well, you were right on both counts, so if Christie's willing to give me a chance to do more of the same, I figure I'd better take it."

Alex nodded, watching the swan boats, nearing the end of their season, glide across the lagoon. As the Alps had been a few weeks earlier, Boston was enjoying the last of the good weather; the afternoon was crisp and sunny, with just an edge of autumn bite to the air. For lunch we'd gone grazing at the Faneuil Hall stands— clams on the half shell, oyster stew, egg rolls, and a shared quiche—and then walked to the Public Garden, where we'd found a bench near the statue of George Washington on a horse.

"It sounds wonderful," she said. "I'm glad."

"You don't sound glad. Don't you want me to do it?"

"You're fishing."

"Well, maybe, but I want to hear you say it."

"All right, I will. You know what's wrong. We've just gotten started knowing each other— I mean really getting to know each other; Europe was different—and now, bang, you're going to be gone for two months. What are you grinning at?"

"I didn't mean to. I'm happy, that's all. You couldn't have said anything nicer. Look, it'll be the easiest thing in the world to get back up here on weekends. Or you could come down to New York. Maybe we could alternate."

"Alternate? You mean see each other every weekend?"

"Well...yes, why not? Why not holidays, for that matter? Middle of the week, too, conditions permitting— Hey, now you're grinning."

"Sorry, I'm happy, too." She dropped her eyes to the strutting pigeons near our feet and then said very softly, "I like the sound of this, Ben. I'm starting to think maybe my life is taking a real turn for the better."

"*Your* life!" I jumped up and held out my hand. "Come on, let's walk some more; I feel too good to sit still."

We rounded the lagoon, smiled at the "Make

Way for Ducklings" bronzes, and found another bench before we spoke again.

"Ben, this show you're putting on. Do you really have any chance of finding the people they belong to? After all these years?"

"It won't be easy. Most of the original owners are dead, but don't forget about those stamped initials on the backs of some of them. CIAT's already located the one surviving daughter of Raoul Sussman. She's in her fifties, working as a packer at a discount clothing chain in Rennes. Years ago she'd fought with the French government about getting some of her father's property back and lost on every count. Now, thanks to Christie, she's going to get four fabulous paintings. Isn't that great? She'll be able to buy the whole chain if she wants."

"But how many of the pictures have those initials?"

"Twenty-eight. It was a system that apparently was used only in Paris, and not consistently. We're lucky any of them have them."

"So what about the ones without them? What will happen if people don't come forward to claim them?"

"We're not just going to wait for claims to come in, Alex, we're going to be actively hunting for people—which is very different from the way this kind of thing has been handled so far. We're damn well funded, too, and I'm hoping for good results."

"And if any of them are still unclaimed at the end?"

"Then they'll be auctioned, with the proceeds going to Holocaust organizations."

"That's great, absolutely great. What a
job," she said, reaching for my hand. "You must
really be pleased."

The sun was lower now, slanting down and
picking out shining, honey-colored strands in
her hair that I'd never noticed before. Lit by
that golden glow she was magnificent, with her
smooth skin, and wide smile, and strange
gray-green eyes.

"I am pleased," I said.

Pleased and grateful. And luckier than I
deserved to be. I'd come frighteningly close
to never meeting her; I'd told Simeon a lie to
avoid it. It had taken his death to make it
happen. Strange when you thought about it.
In the end, he really had brought us together.

"I have a good idea," I said. "What do you
say to a big dinner at that Russian restaurant
in Brighton?"

"The Kalinka, you mean, the one we were
originally going to meet at?"

I nodded, thinking that inasmuch as I wasn't
the same person, I didn't have an obligation
to own up to the fact that that previous person
had gone out of his way to get out of it.
"Right. You can invite your relatives and
show me off to the family. Friends, too, if you
want. Don't forget Mrs. Kapinsky."

"Mrs. Kapinsky? You'll have to invite her,
I don't think I know her."

"I'll do that, if I can find her. We'll all

stuff ourselves and we'll lift a glass or two to Simeon's memory."

She squeezed my hand. "A sort of Russian wake for Uncle Simeon. I think he'd like that."

"*Da*," I said happily, and then, unable to stay in one place, started us walking again. "Ve itt lawts piroshkis, ve trinkh lawts vwawdka!"